The Unwritten Rules of Magic

The Unwritten Rules of Magic

HARPER ROSS

ST. MARTIN'S
PRESS
NEW YORK

First published in the United States by St. Martin's Press,
an imprint of St. Martin's Publishing Group

EU Representative: Macmillan Publishers Ireland Ltd, 1st Floor, The Liffey Trust Centre,
117–126 Sheriff Street Upper, Dublin 1, DO1 YC43

www.stmartins.com

Designed by Steven Seighman

The Library of Congress Cataloging-in-Publication Data is available upon request.

ISBN 978-1-250-39455-2 (hardcover)
ISBN 978-1-250-39456-9 (ebook)

Our books may be purchased in bulk for specialty retail/wholesale, literacy, corporate/premium, educational, and subscription box use. Please contact MacmillanSpecialMarkets@macmillan.com.

First Edition: 2026

10   9   8   7   6   5   4   3   2   1

To Brad, Kayla, and Ford,
for all the magic and meaning you bring into my life

The Unwritten Rules of Magic

One

My father kept his good-luck charm locked in the antique curio cabinet in his office. We never saw him use the old typewriter, but sometimes its carriage return bell rang out after midnight. Whenever asked about that, he blustered. Claimed I'd been dreaming. I didn't dare argue, so whatever he was hiding is now buried with him.

The glossy black 1935 Underwood portable still sits smugly against the cabinet's red velvet back panel. His most treasured possession. Its round-as-a-button glass keys gleam under the lights, tempting me as usual. A siren perched on the shelf, within reach yet frustratingly inaccessible.

If you ever touch this, you'll be banned from my office. Am I clear, Em?

I cower as if he's shouting from the doorway. He isn't, of course, and never will again. My breathing rises and falls unevenly with my vacillating memories.

Our life together ended before the invisible bruises his quicksilver moods inflicted on me could fade. Unlike the heroine in the novels I ghostwrite, I haven't figured out how to heal and feel normal.

If I could've scripted this day, I would have written myself as sobbing this morning on the way to church. And at the service, where I delivered a eulogy to hundreds of friends, acquaintances, and his fans. My cheeks would've been tear-streaked when the urn with half his ashes was buried.

Instead, while others dropped long-stemmed white roses into his grave, I thought about how he would've preferred we plant a noble fir there—or anything solid and lofty that would outlast us all.

Readers would label a main character like me cold and unlikable, populating Goodreads and Amazon with hundreds of *Two stars!* reviews. Rachel Moon, my bestselling boss, would care only if it adversely affected her income, which—let's face it—is all anyone paying a ghostwriter to draft her novels truly cares about.

Yet equating stoicism with a lack of feeling is like believing a portrait reflects the whole of a person.

Despite my dry eyes, our final goodbye had pricked my heart. Not a fatal puncture, but the vital organ will never again beat quite the same. For while Jefferson William Clarke may have been an internationally beloved fantasy author, to me he'd always been Dad.

Once upon a time, he'd even been my hero.

The floor-to-ceiling bookcases in his office enclose me in a time capsule crammed with books, knickknacks, and reader awards. Familiar stacks of articles, research notes, and drawings of his story worlds remain strewn across his desk. Messy, like my father's mind.

"You touched so many," I say as if he were here, trapped in another plane. The image wrings a grin from me, because he'd probably enjoy that fate.

I finger the edges of the pink-marble ashtray in which he snuffed a celebratory cigar whenever he finished a manuscript. Cold and hard, like he could be. Yet even on his bad days, fragments of an exuberant spirit glimmered like stars behind clouds. Nothing about him was simple.

When I raise the ashtray to my nose, a whiff of sweet-and-spicy residue brings childhood memories of our random character dress-up days rushing forward like the tide, coating my eyes in warm salty tears. I set the ashtray down, then caress the massive desk's worn edges as if they were his papery skin.

How often I splayed myself on the floor with a Judy Blume novel while my dad's slender fingers pecked at his keyboard. Sometimes he would seat me in the leather chair by the window while he read draft pages aloud.

His imagination enthralled me. His certitude beguiled.

The man was invincible until he wasn't.

"Of course you're in here." My mother, Dorothy, teeters into the office, crystal lowball tumbler in hand. Legs as thin as arms poke out from beneath a vintage Chanel black sheath dress as she steadies herself against the curio cabinet.

If it was anyone else, I'd worry. But Dorothy being drunk in the afternoon had stopped warranting alarmist reactions by the time I graduated from high school. For now, a single cleansing breath helps me recall the younger mother who invented bookstore treasure hunts.

"Has everyone gone home?" I ask, channeling the family-peacekeeper tone adopted ages ago.

"Finally. I thought the Andersons would never leave." Her vacant gaze traverses the room without a trace of grief. "Look at this clutter."

I kick off my heels, freeing my feet from their three-day sentence.

My daughter, Sadie, appears in the doorway, auburn hair neatly twisted in a tortoiseshell hair clip, showcasing the peekaboo purple streaks normally hidden in the underlayers of her hair. Long and lean like my father was, she's lost all traces of girlishness as she barrels into womanhood entirely too soon. Only her face has retained a cherubic quality.

With one fluid glance, she sizes up her grandmother and pats her shoulder while mouthing "drunk" to me. Her overexposure to Dorothy's behavior is a parenting fail, but she handles the situation with more sympathy than I do.

"Why are you guys hiding in here?" Sadie moves to one of the bookcases and fingers an action figure from my father's Elysian Chronicles series. She played with those as a child, always peppering my dad with new questions about that story world.

"Catching my breath." Three consecutive days of endless polite conversation have depleted me.

"Did you see all the leftovers—all that meat? What a waste. Bad for the environment, too." My burgeoning eco-warrior wrinkles her nose. "We should go vegan."

"Vegan?" Dorothy grimaces.

"The meat industry is a huge contributor to climate change. So are cow farts," Sadie says, making my mother guffaw.

"It's true, Gran." Sadie shrugs. "Look it up."

"Maybe we try pescatarian first and see how that goes," I offer. Although I do love a good burger.

"Count me out," Dorothy mumbles.

"For now, but not forever." Sadie's tender reprimand forgives her grandmother things she'd never let fly with me. My daughter seems to admire Dorothy's snark, a trait she's more recently been testing out herself. "Anyway, can we leave soon?"

"Wait!" Dorothy straightens her spine as if trying to match Sadie's height. "I have an announcement."

Oh boy. I plant my hands on the desk and steel myself. "Go on and shoot."

"I'm selling the house." Dorothy's grin resembles that of a teenager who just spilled the tea on her nemesis.

Agape, I'm replaying her statement while Sadie issues a disappointed groan.

Her attachment to the estate goes back to infancy, when I—then an unwed twenty-two-year-old new mother—moved us home for help while learning to juggle parenthood with my first job. "Why, Gran?"

"Because I don't need all this." Dorothy gestures erratically, ice clinking against the sides of the glass. "Never did."

I prefer something cozier, she'd said before Dad bought this house the summer after I finished fourth grade. He, however, always had some justification for why his decisions were for the best. In that instance, I'd been thrilled by the prospect of life on the Connecticut shore.

"But I love it here," Sadie pleads. "Especially in the summer, with the dock and kayaks. Mom said I could have my graduation party here next summer, too."

Dorothy shuffles toward Sadie, reaching up to pat her cheek. "Sorry, baby."

My dad took such pride in this home. She might as well toss his ashes in a dumpster as sell it so fast. Honestly, if she hated life here so much, she should've left him years ago.

Sadie pouts at her, then at me, as if I've ever been able to control the woman.

"Take a breath," I begin, reading my daughter's frown. "Nothing's going to happen overnight."

"Easy for you to say. Meanwhile, you haven't cried once today." Sadie's brittle dig pierces my skin. Normally she's a sunny girl, but these past few days she's been drifting through rooms like a storm cloud about to burst. I'd chalk it up to my father's death, but the edge to her mood suggests something more. With the funeral events finally behind us, I'll be able to get to the bottom of it. Sadie's nostrils flare before she adds, "It's like you couldn't care less that Papa is gone."

The accusation spreads a bloom of heat across my cheeks. She's wrong, and the fact that my dad never once hurt my daughter leaves me envious of her uncomplicated grief and leaves her unable to fathom my tangled feelings. "Honey, that's not—"

"I'm sorry he got so sick, but he's out of his misery now," Dorothy interrupts. A half beat later, she makes the sign of the cross. "And so are we."

Sadie's posture slumps.

I choke back a bitter laugh, nearing my breaking point. "Don't do this."

"Sell?" The crow's-feet around Dorothy's eyes deepen.

"Bash Dad." Not everyone is meant to be a spouse or a parent. Not everyone's best is even good enough, but whose fault is that?

You don't ask to be born with shortcomings. You don't even know you have them until you butt up against them, and in most cases, that's too late.

My parents' demons had permeated everything, but they had been here for me, if moody and unpredictable. In their way, they had loved me. And despite the imperfect circumstances, they had welcomed Sadie's arrival as if she were the queen of England.

"None of us are perfect." My gaze drops pointedly to the tumbler in Dorothy's hand. "Let's remember the good and let the rest go."

That small mercy is something we'll all pray for on our deathbeds.

Dorothy reaches up to grasp Sadie's chin. "I'll try not to criticize him in front of you."

Sadie's face crumples; her fists hang at her sides.

When I move to comfort my daughter, she backs away. The rejection strikes like a karate chop. God forbid our relationship follows the path mine took with my parents at her age.

"I have homework." She blots her damp face with her palms. "Can we please go home now?"

Dorothy's brows rise comically. Rather than subjecting Sadie to more zingers, I nod. It's been a grueling day. I should've asked my best friend, Mel, to take Sadie home when she left thirty minutes ago.

"Take the car. I'll Uber soon." I smile at Sadie, hoping for one in return.

"Thanks." She turns on her heel and takes off toward the mudroom without another word.

Poof. My not-so-little girl is gone.

"Well, thanks a lot," I say to Dorothy.

She looks at me as if I'm speaking in tongues. "What did I do?"

"You couldn't have *waited* to make that announcement?"

Dorothy's expression fills with childlike sincerity. "I've been waiting for ages."

"We're still at Dad's repast." My throat feels as dry as sun-scorched earth. "Maybe take a minute to process the end of an era before you sell my childhood home."

Oh. Rookie mistake. I suck in my lips to prevent another betrayal of emotion.

"I'd rather not dwell on regrets." Dorothy crosses to his desk and raises their framed wedding photograph for closer inspection.

The picture was taken at their reception on her parents' farm in Vermont. She's leaning against him in the image—both are staring at each other with adoration—her posy bouquet wrapped in powder-blue satin ribbons that fall gracefully against her wedding gown.

"Things between Jefferson and me were faltering for so long. Then we'd have a good day or week and I'd think, *Oh, there's the man I loved.*" She sets the photograph face down on the desk. "But those moments dwindled until he became a black hole, sucking the soul from everything in his orbit—too powerful to escape."

She holds up one hand apologetically.

By the end of his life, Dad had become as inaccessible as his good-luck charm. I glance again at the Underwood, my decision cresting like a sunrise.

Dorothy clearly doesn't want reminders of him, anyway. I may never understand why he coveted it, but as the only other writer in our family, I should have it.

"I'd like a few minutes to myself in here." I stare, unblinking, until she bows her head and backs out of the room.

My equilibrium resets. Then I eye the curio cabinet, feeling along its underbelly for the brass skeleton key. No luck. That would've been too easy.

Hands on my hips, I turn toward the disordered desk.

After rifling through several piles, I check inside the leather-bound humidor before moving to the drawers. The center one contains rulers, pens, Post-it notepads, drawing compasses, paper clips, tape, scissors, a letter opener, and loose change. Everything except the key.

The side drawers are similarly jam-packed except for the top left drawer, which contains two pieces of paper. One is an undated typed page that reads:

I give up. Outsmarted myself, it seems.

I trace the words, noting how the *v* sits slightly higher than other letters on the line.

```
After trying and failing to find the right words
to undo all I've done, I wish now only for a
little peace at the end of this life.
```

The allusion to remorse is out of character. He hadn't offered apologies or attempted amends in decades. Had he tried, we all might've enjoyed a little peace.

Did he intend for us to find this or was it a private confession? A sort of diary? That could explain the secretiveness around his typing.

Beneath that page lies a random undated to-do list written in my father's chicken scratch.

-Call Henry about P No. 8
-Track down Welles heir
-Rectify DES
-Destroy evidence

I scratch my head. "Henry" is probably a reference to his agent, and "P No. 8" the unfinished final Pandemonium book, but who are the Welleses and what is DES, and evidence of what, exactly?

Dorothy and I already knew of his casual betrayals. Who could forget the roof-shaking arguments that rattled the windows after Dad's book and movie junkets or after he got off the train from those Manhattan lunches smelling like perfume? That history suggests evidence of something worse than another dalliance. God, I hope not.

Seconds tick by before I fold the pages and slip them into my skirt pocket. Now isn't the time to tear this room apart looking for those answers, but I do want to find the curio cabinet key.

Drumming my fingers on the desktop, I go back to the cabinet and jiggle its door handle. The ornate lock holds fast. Palms now pressed against the cool glass, a sudden irrational itch to smash it pulses through me. The need is urgent. Personal. Necessary.

Pushing away, I close my eyes to conjure old research for the book in which a heroine used hairpins to pick an old lock.

A letter opener is too wide. Paper clips? I fashion two into the shapes needed to jimmy the lock.

Sinking to my knees to become eye level with the keyhole, I slide the mangled clips inside the lock. Working the wires in unison is a clumsy business. On each attempt, the clips fumble in my fingers, crossing each other. "Oh, come on!"

Sitting back on my heels, I peer inside the dark hole. A useless effort. Two deep breaths later, I make another attempt.

The mechanism clicks! A bolt of energy races through my limbs before I toss the clips in the wastepaper basket. The echo of my dad's reprimand grows more distant as my heart skips ahead.

The entire room feels like it's throbbing with anticipation. I open the glass door, flexing my fingers before pulling the equipment out of the cabinet. It's lighter than anticipated and vibrates as if resting on the hood of a running car.

Pursing my lips, I glance at the undercarriage, seeking some explanation. Nothing there. My father's spirit haunting the old girl?

"Don't worry, Dad. I'll take good care of her." My curiosity about his nefarious to-do list is eclipsed by excitement. Thankfully, Sadie isn't here to witness my habit of talking to myself. She thinks it odd. My father always said it was a sign of a vivid imagination.

I set the typewriter gently on his desk and then scale the rolling book-case ladder to reach the carrying case. Outside, peach-colored light dances across the water. A sign of permission?

After loading my bounty into its case, I carry it and my shoes to the mudroom cubbies to set beside my purse. A quick patter through the kitchen confirms that the caterers already put up the stemware. The envelope I left with their check and tip is gone. Leftovers are stacked neatly in containers in the refrigerator.

An eerie silence is broken only by the low hum of the refrigerator.

Although my dad spent the past six months gazing blankly from his wheelchair, his aura had still permeated the house. Its absence is tangible—a frost settling over the surfaces—making the place feel tomb-like.

Rubbing my arms against the sensation, I cross through the dining room and spacious entry hall to reach the grand salon that spans the width of the stately colonial.

Dorothy lies curled on the gray velvet chaise like a kitten. One arm is flung haplessly aside, and her head has rolled backward, bending her neck at an angle that will surely cause a crick.

How freeing it must be to let go so entirely, safe in the knowledge that someone else will take care of everything.

A burn rises in my esophagus, but I snatch a velvet lumbar pillow from a nearby chair and the cashmere throw from the ottoman.

"Psst," I whisper, angling the pillow behind her head.

She swats at me as if I'm a mosquito, mumbling something unintelligible before shifting her body. Her seasoned dance partner, I follow her movement in perfect sync, wedging the pillow to support her head and draping her with the throw.

The empty crystal tumbler rests on the floor beside the chaise. A quick sniff has me recoiling from the gin's potent pine notes. I figured as much, but hope is a foolish squatter I've never learned to evict.

I glance out the windows framing a shamrock-green lawn that slopes down to the coast of Long Island Sound. My father's remaining ashes rest on the table in front of them in an onyx marble urn too small to contain someone whose life was so large. I cross to it, tracing its plaque with my fingertips.

We moved to Darien from the rural town of Easton after my father signed his first major motion picture deal. Our first day here, my dad had held my hand while we strolled past the cheerful yellow daffodils that border the flagstone patio, across the meticulous harlequin pattern created by the lawn service, and down to the narrow dock that stretches over the water.

"Are you proud of me?" he asked.

His blue eyes always sparkled with a peculiar combination of intelligence, mischief, and ennui, exactly like Robin Williams. That evening, the sun set them ablaze as if the fire in his belly sought release.

I nodded, skipping to keep pace with his long stride. "Yes!"

He grinned before capturing me in a bear hug, always happiest on the receiving end of praise. "This is just the beginning. I'm going to give you everything you could ever want. Do you trust me?"

"I do."

"That's my girl." He swiped my nose with his finger and kissed my head, his approval the only motivation I ever needed.

Now I turn away from the window with a sigh. Heaviness settles in my chest when I imagine how strange it will be—sad, even—after this place is no longer ours.

Where will Dorothy go? She belongs in rehab, but I never win that debate.

I can't think about it all right now. These last years of losing Dad in chunks—from his not recognizing me to not remembering what a toothbrush was for—have sapped my fight.

When Dorothy called to say he'd passed in his sleep, my first reaction was relief for the end of his suffering. Since then, each surfacing memory makes my head feel like it might split open.

The long day weighs on me, tugging at my eyelids. I open the Uber app to summon a ride home. A ten-minute wait—just enough time to deal with my mother.

I return to the sofa to stroke her shoulder. "Hey."

She shrugs me off.

Crouching, I whisper, "Let's get you into bed."

She turns her head, her gaze unfocused. "I'm fine here."

If we were a normal family, I'd insist she come home with me so she wouldn't be alone. But we aren't normal, and every time I try to pretend that we are, it only reopens the empty pockets of need I've worked so hard to stitch shut.

"All right. I'll check on you in the morning."

Dorothy offers no thank-yous. No kiss. And certainly no questions about my grief. Just a wobbly nod and a return to slumber, blissfully unaware of the unsettling notes I discovered.

Lucky her.

I pad through the house to the mudroom to gather my things, including the typewriter. My new possession is the rainbow at the end of a stormy day.

After decades of wonder and yearning, I finally get to play with it. Perhaps it will become my good-luck charm, too.

Two

At home, dusky light filters through the windowpanes. I hang my purse on the hook by the door, then turn on a table lamp in the living room to avoid the glare of overhead lights. The collection of Sadie's best drawings, handmade pottery, and other school projects usually lifts my mood.

With an audible sigh, I roll my shoulders in the stillness of my sanctuary.

I pick Sadie's pashmina off the sofa we've worn out while watching movies and eating enough buttered popcorn to fill a swimming pool, then hang it on the hook next to mine. My dog-eared copy of *The Emotional Lives of Teenagers* is upside down on the floor in front of the end table. No doubt the work of Mopsy, our mischievous white Persian.

After returning the book to the tabletop, I reorganize the throw pillows. Still revved, I consider slipping out to the detached garage turned paint-spatter room to work through these feelings. It usually helps, but now it might be wiser to check on Sadie.

I set the typewriter case in my office beside my desk and toss my father's notes on the desktop. Even dead, he's keeping me guessing.

When I pass the hanging photo of us all with Sadie on her first Christmas morning, Dad's obvious glee leaps out of the frame. This is the version of him I want to hold close.

I rap on Sadie's door. "It's me. You hungry?"

She doesn't open it. "No. Working on my history paper."

"Your teacher will probably give you an extension." I lean against the jamb, staring at the floor.

"This *is* the extension."

Oh.

I wait, hoping for . . . something? X-ray vision, for starters. "Sorry Gran upset you. Do you want to talk about it?"

"Not now. I'm busy, Mom."

I rest my palm against the door as if it were her shoulder or cheek instead of a barrier. "All right. Let me know if you change your mind."

Toddler meltdowns were breezy compared with this behavior. What I'd give for any proof that my parenting choices are sound and that everything will turn out well. Most days feel like waking up in the middle of the Sahara without a compass.

I retreat to the kitchen and grab a blackberry seltzer, a cheese stick, and an apple from the refrigerator, then return to my office, light the grapefruit-scented candle, and turn on a classical music playlist.

Mopsy sidles up to my leg, purring. I pull her to my lap and stroke her thick fur. "I'm not motivated. Any advice?"

This manuscript is only two-thirds complete. Each page has been a struggle. Spending every morning of my father's final months with him—surrounded by evidence of his accomplishments—served as a constant reminder that my talent is marginal by comparison. Not exactly a thought that fosters creative genius.

I nuzzle Mopsy before setting her on the floor. The typewriter case draws my attention. The instant I free the Underwood from its case, Mopsy yowls and bolts from the room.

Alone with my prize, I caress its vintage keys like my dad must've done. If someone noteworthy once owned it, he never said. There's no paperwork or demarcation to suggest that, either.

Removing it from its place of honor was a brazen act of defiance. A naughty thrill whips through me, prompting a cat-downed-the-whole-bottle-of-cream smile.

Might as well give it a test drive.

After taking a sheet of paper from my printer, I thread it through the platen. I'll never know why my dad used this only after we all went to bed, but now it's my turn. What to type . . .

My mind is as blank as the page. Minutes tick by while my hands hover above the keys, pulse heavy. It still seems impossible that he's gone. The empty places inside me feel bigger tonight. Without warning, a tear dribbles down my cheek.

I huff mockingly. What kind of fool hopes to somehow connect with the dead through an old typewriter?

This kind, apparently.

With my chin in one hand, I glance out the window.

Dim landscape lights illuminate the pear tree in the side yard. The flowerbeds surrounding our 1930s craftsman are hidden from my view, but they're always unkempt. Unlike the lush gardens at my parents' home—replete with hydrangea, lilies, peonies, and decorative grasses—my azalea bushes are usually wilted, my lavender limp, my tulips sparse.

Sighing, I turn back to the equipment and type:

```
Dear Dad,

     Can you see me? Hear my thoughts?
```

The keys' satisfying weight and jaunty clatter transform the equipment into a musical instrument.

```
     Maybe you're angry that I stole your
typewriter, or you're shaking your head in pity.
I'm sad, Dad. More than that, I'm sorry you died
without us ever having an overdue heart-to-heart
```

conVersation. All I eVer wanted was your loVe and
attention. I wish I'd found the courage to ask why
things changed.

Look where silence has left me! Stealing this
typewriter as if it will bring closure. That's as
pointless as wishing some miracle would reViVe my
neglected flowerbeds or help me lose fiVe pounds
by Mel's birthday party this weekend.

This is real life, not one of our story worlds.
I don't know how to liVe in it without you at the
center pulling all the strings. Funny, giVen how
much I hated that. See? I'm a mess.

WhereVer you are, and no matter our mistakes, I
hope you'Ve finally found peace.

An impossible wish for a man whose restlessness prevented him from
ever being satisfied with any accomplishment. He'll forever remain a
conundrum.

Loud. Creative. Excitable. No one told a better bedtime story or
received more applause at my elementary school's career day. Grown
women and men, many of whom arrived at his book signings dressed
as one of his venerated characters, would break into tears while taking
his photo. He couldn't resist celebrations—release parties, list-hitting
vacations, movie premieres—where his broad smile greeted folks like a
welcome banner.

Generosity poured out of him, whether it was financially supporting
my mother's parents when medical bills overwhelmed them or setting up
a substantial scholarship fund at his alma mater.

But by the time I turned thirteen, another side of him had emerged.
Foul moods spun out, sudden as tornadoes, turning his blue eyes gray.
Sometimes I overheard him talking to himself behind the closed door of
his office.

This past decade, I twice caught him sitting alone, looking panic-stricken, tugging at his hair. The recollection makes me reach for his to-do list, then open my laptop and search "Welles Darien."

A number of hits from 2009 show up on the screen. Orson Welles's daughter was a guest speaker at our local library, but this note can't be that old. There is a local Wells resident, but no Welles with an *e*. It could be anyone, anywhere. Maybe my mother knows.

I then type "DES" in the browser. The top hits involve a discontinued synthetic estrogen that caused cancer. An improbable match.

An architectural firm goes by those letters, but I'm not aware of any planned renovations. Nothing suggests any evidence he'd need to destroy.

"Ugh. What's this about?" I mutter in the darkened room before slamming the laptop shut and forcing myself to recall something good from my childhood.

Magic Mondays come to mind. He'd create a prompt and then we'd take turns contributing a line to our story. Often I acted out my parts. He fostered my fascination with the fictional worlds in which we could always come together even after he fractured my rose-colored glasses. As I got older, we spent countless hours discussing novels and writing.

Our private story sessions must've been a blow to my mother. She'd been a librarian, after all. A lover of words and Dad's first fan and feedback partner. Being pushed aside—for a child's perspective, no less—must've hurt. I can't remember now if he did that before she started drinking or because of it.

In retrospect, he probably chose me because I never criticized.

Unlike him.

Emerson, if you want a breakout story and memorable protagonists, dig deeper. Otherwise, write sitcoms. At the time, I convinced myself he'd shown a level of respect with that honest criticism of my first novella. Tonight his old words sting.

He's no longer here to weigh in on my work. On Sadie. On anything at all. It's jarring to lose our hero—antihero?—in the middle of our life story.

The Underwood will have to be his proxy. At least it can't hurt my mother or me like he sometimes did.

My stomach gurgles as my nose tingles anew. In no mood to edit, I blow out the candle, then take my uneaten snack back to the refrigerator and head upstairs with my copy of Sonali Dev's *There's Something About Mira*.

Mopsy trails behind me to my claw-footed bathtub. Lavender-scented oil perfumes the silky water, its luxurious heat easing the tension in my muscles. Unfortunately, my stomach roils as I turn the pages.

Setting the book aside, I press my hand to my abdomen to massage the discomfort. It warbles again, a noisy warning seconds before the urge to vomit strikes like a gong reverberating throughout my body.

I cover my mouth, nearly killing myself when scrambling out of the tub and slipping naked on the wet floor. My knee bangs against the penny tiles, pain ricocheting up my leg to my core.

Mopsy darts from the bathroom. I barely make it to the toilet before retching a foul chunky liquid. It's a full-body spasm the likes of which I haven't felt since pregnancy.

As if summoned by that memory, Sadie knocks at my bedroom door before entering. "Mom, are you okay?"

"Don't come in. I'm naked!" I slide behind the toilet in case she ignores my plea, water dripping from my skin and forming a puddle beneath me. I snatch a towel off the nearby rack and drape it over myself.

"What happened?" She sounds close—perhaps just beyond the bathroom door.

My hand shoots forward, palm out like a crossing guard's. "Stomach bug. Don't come in."

"Can I do anything?"

I hug the bowl as another heave worms through me. "Keep Mopsy with you and go back to your room so you don't get sick, too."

"Are you sure you don't need anything?"

It's comforting that, despite her earlier behavior, she cares.

"Yes. These things pass quickly." Thankfully, because enduring this will feel like a nonstop ride on Six Flags's Kingda Ka.

"Call me if it gets worse."

"Okay." I choke back vomit to spare her having to hear another gush. "Please go, honey."

"All right."

I close my eyes in thanks before another spasm grips me and dumps more acidic liquid into the toilet. As night falls, I alternate between hydrating and kneeling on the tile floor. Then the stomach bug goes to work on my bowels.

Curled in a ball, I shiver from sweat-soaked skin, becoming so weak it seems easier to stay in the bathroom than to lug myself in and out of bed.

Three

By dawn, the smallest movements shoot pain across my aching back. My stomach muscles feel as if I did two thousand sit-ups.

I hobble to the shower and turn the temperature to scalding. Pounding water pressure eases some of the tightness in my shoulders, but it's a struggle to remain upright.

After I dry off, sleep calls to me, but there's no time for that luxury. In the other room, Sadie stomps around, getting ready for school.

I load toothpaste onto my toothbrush, desperate to scrub the sour remnants of bile from my teeth. A glimpse in the mirror reveals my newly concave abdomen. Eyeing the scale—that old foe—I gently lay one foot on it and then the other.

One, two, three—look!

Four pounds, twelve ounces less than yesterday. I smirk, the little win helping to offset the discomfort of lingering nausea. After spitting out my toothpaste, I admire my flat abs again.

I roll my neck, wondering where the bug came from. Probably from running myself ragged this past week choosing a casket and Dad's suit, writing the eulogy and the obituary, ordering flowers for the funeral parlor, and dealing with the church. There were also the hundreds of hands I shook at the funeral parlor viewings in the days leading up to yesterday's service. Lots of contact germs. Millions, in fact.

"Mom, are you better?" Sadie calls from outside my bedroom, snapping me from my musing.

"Think so."

"Okay, good. I'm going to school now." Her leaden footfalls reverberate when she gallops down the stairs.

I snatch my robe and chase after her, bare feet cold on the wood floors. "Wait up!"

She pauses, taking her keys off the counter. "What?"

"Eat something for breakfast."

"No time." She aims toward the front door.

No time and also no makeup. No flat-ironed hair. No midriff-baring shirt. I'm not even convinced she showered. She's never been a glamour girl, but this utter lack of concern for her appearance is troubling.

"At least eat a yogurt." I take a container from the refrigerator and peel it open, handing it to her with a spoon.

"I'm running late!" she protests.

"Take five seconds. Breakfast is important." I should probably eat some probiotics, too, but the thought of putting anything in my stomach makes it lurch.

"I hate these plastic cups. Please buy the yogurt in glass containers." She sets her backpack on the counter and inhales the contents in four quick scoopfuls, after which she hurls the spoon across the kitchen and into the sink before tossing the empty cup in recycling. "Satisfied?"

"Yes." Rather than lecture about the silverware free throw, I playfully tickle her side to send her off on a positive note. "Thank you."

She musters a benevolent eye roll before grabbing her backpack and striding toward the front door. "It's your fault if I get in trouble for being late."

Despite sporting tangled wet hair, I follow her onto the porch. "Worth it, baby girl!"

Sadie opens her car door, tossing back, "I'm not a baby anymore."

I miss those days, when she shared everything and I had near total control over her environment. Now I've got my nose pressed to the glass, looking for any way to stay close.

She backs out of the driveway, her silver Jeep hybrid shooting away from me like a bullet. I let myself slump a bit, fending off another gut gurgle.

Turning to duck inside before someone spots me, I stop suddenly, my attention snagged by abundant pink azaleas peeking up from the garden beds. Leaning over the railing, I'm also greeted by cheerful yellow tulips that stand where weeds usually reign.

"What in the . . . ?" I haven't tended the beds in weeks. Knotting my robe sash, I hasten down the porch steps to finger the paper-thin azalea petals. Their faint clove scent proves this isn't a dream. As a backup test, I pinch myself.

Nope. Wide awake.

Confusion clouds my already groggy thoughts. There wasn't time to fertilize last fall, after Dorothy left me in charge of Dad's care.

Even when I've made consistent attempts at gardening, my black thumb never coaxed so many blooms. Just last night I lamented that very thing.

Wait. This is really . . . bizarre.

I sway, feeling slightly disconnected from my body. From reality, even. The tingling along my scalp becomes a ringing in my ears that spreads from head to toe. I shake my limbs to rid myself of apprehension.

There's no *way* my note made this happen. It must be the lack of sleep.

I head indoors, clasping at the lapel of my robe with one hand, my thoughts acting like Jiffy Pop.

In the entry, Mopsy comes up behind me. "It *is* strange, isn't it?" I ask her.

She moves away in silence, of course. Muttering to myself, I start toward the stairs, only to then abruptly shift left and shuffle toward my office.

The office door creaks ominously. Mopsy is at my feet again—fur raised, ears pinned back—before she darts away.

The typewriter remains exactly where I left it, the typewritten page still trapped in the platen, morning sunlight filling the room with an aureate glow. I peel the page free and reread the remark about a garden fairy. *Pfft.* There must be a plausible explanation.

A neighbor—probably Dawn, whose immaculate garden is the envy of the street—could've planted those tulips this week while I was planning my father's funeral. She's always doing things like that for people—baking holiday cookies, leaving cards, remembering birthdays.

That makes sense. Thank God.

When a remnant wave of queasiness rolls through me, I wrap my arms around my waist. I straighten and reread the wish to lose five pounds. Two bizarre coincidences, not just one.

Dread shuts down my brain and makes me even dizzier.

I glare at the typewriter as if it were plotting to drive me over the edge.

It glints, almost like a wink.

When I touch it again, a slight current of energy tingles against my palm. My dad *did* keep it under lock and key. His lucky charm . . .

Adrenaline produces a tang in the back of my mouth.

What if?

I hold my breath, hands shaky, perspiration beading along my hairline. What's happening? I look upward as if my dad's ghost will appear to fill me in. Man, I'm losing my shit.

Outside my window, the Oldhams are packing their car for a vacation. Life is moving on as if nothing unusual has happened.

Probably because nothing has.

Best guess? My father's death has temporarily cracked my brain.

"Jesus, get it together." Scowling, I push away from the desk.

Four

November 20, 1995

I hesitate to write this down for fear of memorializing some form of insanity, and yet, there should be a record in case I've accidentally stumbled onto something both mystifying and life-altering.

The 1930s Underwood typewriter—the one I recently picked up at the estate sale on Sunset Road—might be magical.

That sounds preposterous. Impossible! If someone else confided this, I'd laugh my ass off and send them to a shrink. But two sequential experiences feel too on-the-nose to brush off as happenstance.

First, the day I brought it home, Dorothy hit me up with wanting to go to her parents' place for four days over Thanksgiving. Emerson jumped around the kitchen, always excited to visit the farm in Vermont—the horses, ducks, chickens, and goats.

That farm is anathema to me. Cramped, musty old house. Middle of nowhere. Dirt roads. Her mother's incessant chattiness.

When I suggested we start our own tradition and invite them to come here, Emerson cried. Dorothy knew I'd back down if Em pleaded, which I did.

I retreated to my office, where the typewriter was still sitting out. On a whim, I tested its keys by typing a wish that my in-laws would cancel the holiday plans.

Simple yet vague.

The next morning, Dorothy got a call that her dad had fallen and broken his wrist and his leg. Her mother would be too busy tending to him to also host house company so soon, so the holiday plans were scrapped.

Coincidence?

If not, it's important to note that I never intended for anyone to get hurt. I didn't believe for a second that my typed wish would amount to anything other than a release of frustration.

Still, I can't pretend to be disappointed that we're not spending a week in Shrewsbury.

I did nothing about this for a few days, convincing myself it was an unfortunate fluke. A magic typewriter—too absurd to consider. But then, knowing my agent had just submitted a new proposal to my editor, I decided to test the equipment by typing a wish to receive a seven-figure offer for my next three books.

A mid-six-figure deal was expected, given my increasing sales record and growing popularity. A seven-figure deal would be a stretch, something more than a mere coincidence.

Yesterday, Henry called to inform me of a $1.2 million offer. I almost pissed myself. Not because I don't deserve it, but because that damn typewriter might be a game changer.

Could its power be real? If so, why did the prior owners sell it? Are there limits to what it can do? Is this a dangerous road to travel, or one I'd be a fool to ignore?

I'm unsure how to proceed, yet there's no one to consult.

For one, they'd think I'm losing my mind. Dorothy might fear me and take custody of Em. If I publicize the magic, that could gain too much attention and get out of control. The fucking government might even confiscate it for national security.

No. I'll keep testing it to see what happens. In the meantime, it'll remain my secret.

God forbid Dorothy gets her hands on it. I can imagine her wishes. For starters, we'd be living in Vermont.

Five

A therapist once told me that managing other people's emotions isn't my job. Maybe not, but the self-preservation skill developed in my teens is no less integral to my survival than my hands and eyes. It's why I rarely do anything as callous as leaving my mother to sleep it off on the sofa. This morning's guilty conscience doesn't help my stomach settle while I drive across town to check on her.

Dorothy's first night alone in four decades might've been a shock to her system if she'd been sober. Hopefully her big plan to sell the house was merely the gin talking. Sadie would be relieved.

The lengthy driveway comes into view. I pull in and park beneath the porte cochere, curious about the unfamiliar BMW convertible in the turnaround.

Red—like a warning light.

Although tempted to turn around, I let myself in through the side entrance, ditching my purse in the mudroom.

"Hello!" No one answers, so I follow the voices coming from the front hall.

"This timeless grace puts the contemporary farmhouse trend to shame. You've maintained it beautifully, too." The blond woman flattering our home has paired smart navy slacks with silver sandals. A pearl necklace drapes across her décolletage. Her sleeveless white silk top shows off sculpted arms, making me grateful mine are covered with loose-fitted bell sleeves.

Dorothy starts when she notices me. "Oh, my. You look pale."

"Rough night." I shrug, trying to ignore the blond's bald stare.

"Then you should be at home resting," Dorothy says.

"I came to check in. You were so . . . tired when I left yesterday." Of course Dorothy shows no signs of a hangover. The epitome of high-functioning alcohol abuse: never drunk in public, never throws up, never looks trashy.

Even the day after her husband's funeral, she's decked out in a cham-bray linen-blend shirtwaist dress and flats, her sternum and earlobes bejeweled with a colorful Marco Bicego necklace and earring set. Wait—

I grab her left hand. "Where are your wedding rings?"

She withdraws it, rubbing her ring finger absently. "In my closet."

Already? Not that I expected her to wear them for years like some widows do.

A memory of my dad ridiculing her "little" job as a high school librar-ian arises in her defense. For someone so careful with the written word, he could be careless with his speech. *I didn't mean it* never erases an unkind thought.

Those shared invisible scars keep me from giving up on Dorothy, al-though I'm worn thin from her inability to deal with them soberly.

Swallowing my feelings, I extend my hand to the stranger. "Hi, I'm Emerson. The daughter."

"I'm very sorry for your loss. Your father was a remarkable talent." Her face contorts with the extreme sympathy that B-list actresses portray in Hallmark movies. "Kathryn Voss, with Sotheby's."

"Oh." My gaze darts to my mother, who must've had this woman on standby for months. "You were serious."

"Don't get emotional," Dorothy warns, as if it was necessary to recite that phrase at this point in our lives. Does she not recall yesterday's dry eyes? Then again, she was in her own world, so perhaps she didn't notice.

"Kathryn's here to appraise the house. I'm not listing it today, but this place has always been too big for me."

Too many unpleasant memories as well, although that isn't Kathryn's business.

"It's your house," I say, shrugging, needing to sit because last night has left me a little faint. "Do whatever you want."

My tough words don't blunt the ice-water sting of Dorothy's race to sell the family home nanoseconds after ushering mourners out the door.

"You can pick out anything to keep—artwork, china, whatever. I won't need most of it when I downsize." Dorothy beams as if bestowing this consolation prize makes her mother of the year.

I almost confess to taking the typewriter, but don't. A private rebellion.

She will probably never notice or care. Unless, of course, my father shared an experience like mine with her. I try to imagine that conversation. The idea makes me snort.

"What's so funny?" My mother's impatient gaze narrows.

Oh, hell.

"Nothing. I'll wait on the patio until you two are finished." I then offer Kathryn a respectful bow. "Nice meeting you."

"Same. And don't worry. Your mom is in good hands." She offers a game-show-host wave.

"Great." I gladly back away. Brokers are like high school mean girls. They treat you like gold when they want something (say, your father's autograph or a peek in his office), then ignore you as soon as they get it.

Kathryn will kiss Dorothy's cheek—and her ass—to get a plump six-figure commission. Once the agency contract is signed, she'll use words like *buyer's market* to pressure Dorothy into a quick sale; then she'll fade away and buy an even flashier car.

I push past the leftovers to free a pomegranate-and-orange-flavored San Pellegrino from the Sub-Zero before heading out to the patio.

The blue-and-white-striped awning flaps in the breeze coming off the water. A relentless sun whitewashes the world, its rays twinkling atop the sea from the horizon to the shore. A picture-perfect setting, although I prefer the less dramatic views of Tilley Pond Park from my modest craftsman.

There's much to be said for less drama.

Hiding in the shade, I prop my feet up on the weathered teak coffee table and watch a sailboat cut gracefully across the inlet like a giant swan. It looks peaceful and carefree—two attitudes as unfamiliar to me as Sanskrit. For reasons. Like Dorothy getting herself a broker.

I began thinking of my mother by her given name sometime during college. There wasn't a particular incident or trigger, just my response to the distance her insobriety created.

At thirteen, I'd been unable to fill her empty spaces, so she clogged them with Hendrick's and lime twists.

Unfortunately, her remedy poisoned the mother who'd once packed my lunches with love notes, kissed away my boo-boos, and baked incredible pastries. Watching her falter—missing the mother she'd been before—while also coping with my father's increasingly erratic behavior certainly left its mark.

God, it'd been a relief to go away to college.

Hopefully Sadie won't feel that way. On that note, I text her.

Hope you're having a good day!

After adding a kissy-face emoji, I set the phone down. If only I could be like Mel, who adapts to parenting situations without worrying excessively about outcomes. Sadie's recent moodiness mocks my efforts to make her life perfect.

Dorothy finally appears, an ice-filled tumbler in hand. Ten in the morning. *But it's five o'clock in Greece,* she would argue. Her discerning gaze scans the back of the house. "Kathryn thinks it'll go fast."

"I'm not ready to talk about that." I look away, tugging on my earlobe, recalling the notes from my father's desk drawer. "But I do have some different questions. Does the name Welles mean anything to you? Or DES?"

She tips her head up in thought, her brows slightly furrowed. "No. Why?"

"Yesterday, I came across a to-do list in Dad's office that mentions something about finding the Welles heir and rectifying DES." I narrow my gaze, watching for any sign of recognition.

"Him and his secrets." Her jaw ticks. "Honestly, I half expected some love child to show up at the funeral."

She throws back a good bit of her drink while I gape at a possibility I'd never considered.

Dorothy sighs with a lazy wave of her hand. "It's probably story research and something to do with his royalties and rights. He was always triple-checking that stuff. What does it matter now, anyway?"

"Maybe it doesn't." I don't fully believe that, but she isn't interested, so I'm on my own. As usual. Might as well steer the conversation toward my real agenda. "So, what's your plan?"

"I'm moving to the city." My mother sits on a rocker, a delighted expression curving her mouth.

"Manhattan?" I bolt forward, searching her face for the former farm girl. "That's a bit rash."

"Why? I spent thirty years in this town for you and your father. I'm sixty-eight. Don't make me feel guilty for wanting new experiences while I can still enjoy them."

She's never once mentioned wanting to live in Manhattan. This impulse must be a response to grief, even if her grief is over wasted time.

Whatever the reason, her choosing to leave us during Sadie's last year at home deals a special kind of blow.

"The city is a huge change." It'll be impossible to keep her out of trouble there.

"Exactly what I want. I'll get a three-bedroom place with park views so you and Sadie can come for overnights. We'll see shows, go to museums, try Ethiopian food." She sips her drink, wearing a dreamy expression reminiscent of Meg Ryan in some fish-out-of-water romp that ends with laughter and love.

Of all people, she should know that real life never turns out like those films. This is a disaster in the making.

"We can do all that now."

"Not as easily." Dorothy pats the wooden arm of the sofa where I'm seated as if that will appease me. "Trust me. Everything will be fine."

If by *fine,* she means that I'll be scaling Everest-tall mountains of stress each day, then sure.

"You'll be all alone. Plus, the city can be dangerous. I'm concerned . . ."—I pause, glancing again at the drink in her hand—"that you could get yourself into real trouble."

Dorothy scowls. "Don't start, Emerson."

"Then don't ignore the truth."

Closing her eyes, she mutters, "I don't need another boss. I'll manage fine."

I swallow a spiteful laugh. A major move will take more organization and planning than she has managed in decades. That fact might slow her roll a bit. "Fine."

"Good. Now, would you and Sadie please go through the house soon to pick out whatever keepsakes you want? I'll hire an auctioneer to value and sell the rest."

"The rest? You mean all of it?" A headache begins building behind my eyes.

"I need a clean slate. A do-over, as Sadie might say. Do they still say that?" Her facial features quirk in a way that momentarily makes her look ten years younger.

Current parlance is last on my list of concerns this morning. "Why not rent something first to make sure you like living there? We can put all this in storage and take our time to go through it."

"I don't need more time." She swirls her drink. "I've been thinking about this since your father got diagnosed."

Eight years ago!

I press my fingertips to my temples, desperate for Tylenol and a comfy bed.

She stands and walks to the edge of the patio, gulping down what's left of her gin. "You won't believe me, but I tried my best. Bit by bit, your father hijacked my life, distancing me from who I was. He hated me working. He hated Vermont. He even robbed me of my hobbies, hiring a chef and gardener.

"He couldn't share the spotlight with anyone, not even you. Look at how he applauded your ghostwriting rather than encouraging you to tell your own stories." She turns toward the water.

His initial reaction to *The Fires of the Phoenix Queen*—the young adult fantasy manuscript I tinkered with during Sadie's earliest years—still makes me shiver.

It's a fine first attempt, but the premise is derivative, dearest. Try again.

He's no longer here to pick it apart, but critics and his fans would certainly draw comparisons. Children of superstars rarely match—let alone outshine—their parents' achievements. Only masochists invite that kind of rejection.

Suddenly Dorothy spins back to face me. "He undermined you even as he made you think he supported you. Oh, he was very good at that."

That may be true, but writing romantic suspense for Rachel affords me the privacy my father lost long ago. I'm not a household name, but the work itself and the reader response mean as much to me as to any author. My stories are judged on their own merit rather than being compared to my father's, and they give me an outlet for all the noise in my brain. The most priceless by-product is the community of writer friends with whom I chat on a weekly basis.

Dorothy swirls her icy drink, staring into the glass as if it were a mirror. "He took over everything until I had nothing of my own, not even my own personality. Well, I'm staging a comeback." As if finally catching herself, she presses her lips together. "Sorry. I'll try harder not to criticize."

She's not wholly wrong. Jefferson Clarke did prefer to be the king, queen, and jester of this castle. We both made ourselves a little smaller to give him more space. Now there's room for us to blossom—if we can remember how.

"Listen, before you go live your best life, could you please do one thing for me?" I ask.

"What's that, dear?"

The rare endearment makes me pause. It seems a shame to ruin the moment by raising rehab, but I can't let it go if she's determined to pursue this reckless plan. "If you want a clean slate—a chance for real happiness— please first get sober."

Her expression cools as she eyes me over her glass. "Emerson, I'm not a drunk. Ask anyone."

She hides it well, but Betty, the old housekeeper, or my father's nurse would support my conclusion. "You passed out yesterday."

"It was my husband's funeral."

The husband she's gleefully moving on from. "Let's not pretend that was a onetime deal."

"Stop it." She squints at me, face flushed, her petite frame practically quivering.

Mastery of emotional repression keeps me from also shaking. "If you're going to harp on Dad's faults, at least acknowledge the decades you've spent with Hendrick's instead of with Sadie and me."

"I've always been right here for you girls." Her words crackle like hot tinder. "I really don't need this. You can go home now. I've got plenty to do."

This discussion could've gone better, but it went about as expected. "Please don't clean Dad's office. Let me do that, all right?"

"You have one month. I want to show the house soon because it looks best in summer," she says, gesturing toward the water.

One month to discover the evidence my dad wanted to destroy. One month to get her to stop drinking. One month to say goodbye to this home and our history.

"Now if you'll excuse me, I'm meeting MaryBeth for lunch." She rises.

"Do yourself a favor and take an Uber." I fight the urge to cover my mouth and apologize for the harsh tone.

"Show yourself out." Dorothy's eyes glitter before she strides inside without a backward glance.

My head falls back against the sofa cushion as I shout a strangled yelp at the sky.

These past several days without Dad have been unnerving. The air around me feels charged. Not that Dorothy notices or cares.

Before leaving, I slip through the living room and steal Dad's urn, blood running hot through my veins. Minutes later, the marble box is on the passenger seat as I speed away.

What the hell am I doing?

Don't overthink it. Dissecting jumbled emotions is better reserved for the characters in my stories.

Dorothy's behavior isn't surprising. And like always, she assumes I'll bend to accommodate her whims. I'm sick. Of. It.

It'll take at least a gallon of paint to release all these feelings.

My thoughts circle, making the drive home a blur. When I get inside, I set the urn on a shelf in my office. The typewriter is sitting there as if it's been waiting for my return.

Those earlier wishes come true are probably a weird happenstance, but nothing ventured, nothing gained. If nothing else, typed wishes are a more practical way to release my feelings than paint spatter.

I sit and crack my knuckles before hastily typing.

```
Aside from early help with Sadie, I've not asked
my parents for anything. Now, with my fortieth
birthday mere months away and my father gone, I
deserVe time to grieVe before haVing to deal with
an entirely new set of worries. My early birthday
wish is for something to delay my mother's plan to
sell our family home.
```

I pull the paper from the platen and add it to the ones in the folder with my dad's to-do list. Unfortunately, this little exercise didn't even put a dent in my distress.

Time to do the only thing that consistently helps me relieve it. I head directly to the garage, change into my paint-spattered jumpsuit, and blast Linkin Park's "In the End" while opening a fresh can of green paint.

Six

Sadie didn't want to dine out, so we ordered pizza in for dinner. Lukewarm pizza is as appetizing to me as cold oatmeal, especially with my still-weak stomach. I acquiesced in the hopes of making more headway tonight with her than I did earlier with my mother.

So far the only one doing any talking is Mopsy, who is mewling at Sadie's feet.

"What?" I ask because Sadie keeps glancing at my hair.

She circles a finger toward my head. "There's green paint in your bangs. Are you mad at Gran?"

I touch my hair, feeling the tacky clump. My face heats. "I'm not mad at anyone."

Frustrated, yes. But I worked out my anger.

She rolls her eyes. "If you say so."

A few years ago, she caught me mid-spatter when I forgot to lock the garage door. Her horrified amusement caused me to quit for almost a year. These days, I'm usually more careful about hiding my meltdowns.

In any case, the less said, the better.

I glimpse the dozen white lilies in a vase on the counter from Sadie's father, Doug Becker. A stand-in for his sympathy, because of course he couldn't make time to show up for her.

When I got pregnant, he and I were recent college grads stepping into adulthood, blissfully in love, or so I thought. A baby was my chance to re-create the kind of loving family I'd been yearning for. To be part of something genuine and lasting.

Doug didn't agree. His suggestion that we terminate the pregnancy bulldozed the bedrock of our romance. In hindsight, his indifference shouldn't have surprised me. Life with my parents should have taught me to expect it. Many tears—and pounds—later, I found myself alone. We broke up before Sadie arrived, but it's been impossible to completely forget about Doug when he's visible in her round face, doe eyes, and extra-thick brows.

He now lives in Seattle with his wife, Mandy, and two young sons, Rory and Sam. Meanwhile, I've stuck to casual dating and kept my focus on parenting.

Although I sometimes wonder if things with Doug would've turned out differently had I not accidentally gotten pregnant, I've never questioned my decision to keep Sadie. My heart found its rhythm the day my daughter was born. She's given my life purpose and an infinitely expanding love that eclipses everything.

For seventeen years, it's mostly been the two of us against the world. But she'll be leaving for college in a year. My lungs feel like empty caverns whenever I project ahead. Our last year together cannot be marked by this growing distance. The remnants of last night's bug mingle with anxiety, making my stomach rumble.

"How are you, honey? I mean, about Papa and everything." I push my half-eaten slice of cherry pepper and mushroom pizza away.

"I'm okay." Her face pinches together, sealing up her emotions. She's probably learned that from me. Another parenting fail. She should feel safe to express her grief openly in our home. "He was sick for so long, but it's weird to know I'll never see him again. Like, ever."

When Sadie was small, my dad would get down on his hands and knees to give her horsey-back rides. He taught her to play backgammon and watched children's movies with her while describing the characters' arcs and the morals of the stories.

Seeing them together had been like viewing a film of my early childhood. I never begrudged her his special brand of charm despite how nostalgia left me aching to understand why his relationship with me had changed.

"It's better that he's not staring into space anymore," she says. Before his Alzheimer's diagnosis, Sadie thought he feigned confusion to joke with her. "That was awful to watch."

"It was." My dad's blank stretches always left me heartbroken. When he'd occasionally lashed out toward the end, I'd assumed he'd been afraid of what was happening or angry about it. Now I wonder if he'd been worried about whatever evidence he meant to destroy.

Perhaps Sadie has some insight into his mystery note. "Did Papa ever mention a family named Welles to you?"

She looks up, intrigued. "No. Why?"

"Gran thinks it's nothing, but I found an odd to-do list in his desk. One of the items mentions tracking down some Welles heir."

Dorothy's wisecrack about a love child replays in my mind. If Dad had an illegitimate child, the kid would be a Clarke heir—or simply referred to as *my heir*—so her presumption can't be correct. Thank goodness.

"That's weird." Sadie leans forward, elbows on the table. "What else did it say?"

I withhold the final bullet point rather than stain her image of her grandfather. "Something about his agent and the final Pandemonium book, and something about rectifying DES. Does that ring any bells?"

"DES . . ." She scrunches up her nose, which makes her look like my sweet child of yesteryear. A welcome elixir. "He never mentioned that to me, but those are our initials."

I bunch up a napkin and toss it at her. "We're EHC and SHC."

She shakes her head. "Dorothy, Emerson, and Sadie."

"Clever!" That hadn't occurred to me.

His typed note expressed some regrets about his life choices, but what would he need to rectify with Sadie? When my stomach takes another dip, I dismiss the idea. He'd never once hurt Sadie, so her guess can't be right.

I envision the handwritten note again. "He didn't separate the letters with commas like one would if referencing individuals' initials, so I bet that's just a coincidence."

With an insouciant shrug, she adds, "It probably doesn't matter anymore."

Neither she nor my mother would be so blasé if they'd read *destroy evidence.*

Sadie glances at her phone and responds to a text. The screen's blue light illuminates the purple circles beneath her eyes. Her nails are chewed to their beds.

We're seated inches away from each other, but it feels like a hundred miles. Our new dynamic makes my skin itch, as if pieces of me are peeling away. "Can you please put the phone away during dinner?"

She concedes but only picks at her meal. It takes all my grit to maintain a pleasant expression while my insides buckle under the force of whatever is weakening our bond.

When I can't stand another second of silence, I ask, "Do you want to watch *The Bear*?"

Sadie shakes her head listlessly.

"Are you reading any good books?" I venture.

"Just school stuff." She typically enjoys school, reading, soccer, movies, and eating, all of which makes her nonchalance a point of concern.

"Honey, I don't mean to pry, but—"

"Then don't," she says, hunching forward, knees bouncing restlessly. "Sorry. But I don't want to talk."

At her age, I choked down my feelings because my parents were usually embroiled in their own arguments. Sadie doesn't need to hold back— she *wants* to. That hurts . . . a lot.

"Obviously." I force congealed pizza down my gullet and concentrate on not looking offended. Shifting the focus off her, I revert to the other topics we typically cover at dinner. "What's up with the girls? Did Haley get those Billie Eilish tickets?"

"No. Her dad's company gave the box to clients." Her blank expression surprises me, given how excited she'd been about the possibility.

"Bummer. Maybe next time." I pick a mushroom off my slice and pop it in my mouth. "Is Johnny feeling any better?"

Her boyfriend is funny, respectful, and a serious student and athlete. She'd mentioned he'd skipped the funeral service because he was sick.

Sadie blanches and her legs go still. "We . . . we're on a break."

"Oh!" I instinctively reach across the table for her hand. Her withdrawal strikes like a snakebite.

Silence stretches out. Before she looks away, her eyes glisten with tears, casting a pall over the kitchen.

"Honey, I'm so sorry." She's a part of me, so her pain vibrates deep in my bones. It takes conscious effort to keep my hands in my lap. "What happened?"

"It's personal." Red streaks stripe her cheeks.

The kitchen has become a minefield, yet I charge right into its center. "Well, no wonder you've been a little touchy."

"I'm not touchy—I'm busy. You should know better than anyone that I don't need a guy to be happy. I just need some privacy."

Sadie shoots out of her chair, taking her plate to the dishwasher, avoiding eye contact altogether.

You should know better than anyone. Pushing love away is not what I meant to model when making her my priority. Did she get that wrong, or did I?

"Sadie, I know you're grieving, but I'm not your punching bag."

"Sorry." She stands in the middle of the kitchen and sighs. "Did you pick up a color ink cartridge?"

"What?" I rifle my mental filing cabinet and come up empty.

"Last week I said we needed one for printing part of my AP history project."

My face screws up. "You did?"

"Great. Is Staples even open this late?" She tips her head back and groans. "Can I be excused?"

"Of course." It's more a whisper than a response. I'm never forgetful, but this week has been brimming with major distractions.

Sadie refills her water thermos at the sink, then stops in the archway before leaving the kitchen, her voice gentler. "Mom, I don't want to fight. Just give me some space. I'm seventeen—almost an adult."

It isn't an apology, but the détente soothes my bruised feelings enough for the evening. Teens aren't known for being solicitous, after all. "I'm here if you need anything."

Other than ink cartridges, apparently.

Sadie nods solemnly before taking off on her errand. I wrap the left-over pizza in foil and then lift Mopsy and go to my office. Emotions this close to the surface make it easier to dump them into my characters' interactions.

Forty minutes later, revisions to chapter 19 have taken shape. When I close the laptop, the typewriter case mocks me.

How silly of me to suspect, even for a moment, that my dad's good-luck charm could give me the power to control life. Sillier still to be sad that it can't.

That verdict slowly descends like a hot-air balloon that's run out of gas. It'd been deliciously empowering to write out that plea about delaying my mother's plans.

A wish-granting typewriter would be far superior to a winning lottery ticket. Money alone never brought my family real happiness. But scripting a perfect life for Sadie, my mother, and me?

The things I would do . . .

Patch my daughter and Johnny up. End my mom's drinking. Find a soulmate to share time with after Sadie leaves. Maybe even get the courage to publish my own novel.

The dangerously seductive daydream whispers in my ear like a rogue lover until it feels plausible again.

After all, people around the globe testify to miracle cures that doctors can't explain, survival stories that defy the odds, manifestations via vision boards. Whether by praying to their god or visiting fortune-tellers, many hedge their bets and seek help from something beyond their own power.

However, my youthful prayers were never answered. My mother still drinks too much. My father died before we could mend fences. Even my relationship with Sadie feels on shaky ground.

But oh, what if? Maybe I owe it to us all to explore the possibility— however infinitesimal—that Dad's good-luck charm is in fact just that.

The pull is as visceral as the tumbling sensation of falling in love. It takes a few minutes to snap myself out of the trance.

My stomach twists as if to remind me that, if the magic is real, there is no way to predict how a wish will be fulfilled. That gives me pause.

"There's no rush," I mutter at the typewriter.

I'll sleep on it. If it feels right tomorrow, I'll try another test.

Maybe. Probably.

Unless I wimp out.

Seven

The next morning, I'm in the kitchen rinsing out the Pepto Bismol cup when the phone rings. Dorothy's image fills my phone's screen. She rarely calls, so I answer quickly. "What's up?"

"Emerson, did you know about this trust business?" Her voice is gruff.

I hit BREW on the coffeemaker and speak through a yawn. "You mean Sadie's trust?"

When Sadie and I moved out of my parents' home, my refusal to accept any financial support infuriated my father. In an end-run maneuver "to protect her future," he made Sadie the beneficiary of a sizable trust fund that covers her college and graduate school costs and provides a supplemental income after her twenty-first birthday.

"No, not that. Your father put our *house* in a trust." She slams something. Her fist against a counter? A cupboard door? "I can't sell it without your and Sadie's consent. I swear, that man . . ."

My and Sadie's consent?

I run my hand through my hair, needing caffeine to deal with this development. "That can't be right. Who told you this?"

"When Kathryn was creating the listing for the house, she found a recorded deed of trust instead of the normal kind. It's dated from eight years ago."

"Then you must've agreed to it." The hazards of day drinking, one would presume.

"I didn't! He probably slipped the thing in with our taxes or other paperwork. He was always rushing me through signing wherever there were sticky tabs."

Despite their tattered relationship, she trusted him. Deeds need to be notarized, so if he did slip it past her, he also paid off a notary. That thought adds gravity to my disillusionment.

I hold the phone in place with my chin while I open a tin of Mopsy's food and scoop it into her bowl. "Do you have a copy of the document?"

"Kathryn forwarded it. If your father thinks he can control me from the grave, he's got another think coming. I've called our lawyer."

Terrific, because combat mode is my favorite way to start a new day. Surely there are better explanations for his decision.

"Maybe he thought he was protecting you." It wouldn't have been a stretch for him to envision some other man swindling his wealthy, boozy widow out of his beloved home. I pour myself a large mug of coffee, irked he didn't forewarn me about this. "A trust also protects the property from creditors and legal judgments."

"Why on earth would someone sue me, Emerson?"

The possibility of a drunk-driving accident drifts through my thoughts, although I've never known her to drive under the influence.

"I don't know. I'm just thinking aloud." After adding a teaspoon of raw sugar to my mug, I take it to my office, where his urn awaits me. *What were you thinking, Dad?* "Maybe he thought *he* could get sued. Or maybe there was a tax benefit to putting it in a trust. Or he could've wanted it to stay in the family for Sadie."

That feels plausible.

"Naturally you try to justify his behavior." She sighs heavily. "Even if that's all true, I deserved to be told. I deserved a say. It's humiliating to find out like this."

She's got me there.

I sit at my desk, my attention drawn to the photograph of my dad with a toddler-age Sadie on his shoulders, both smiling, sunlight showcasing the red highlights in their hair. He doesn't look like a man who'd betray his wife, and yet he was a man of contradictions.

"You're right," I admit, putting myself in her shoes and feeling the slam of it. "I'm sorry you're embarrassed."

Restlessly I swivel in my seat. When my gaze falls on the typewriter case, my feet hit the floor like brakes. Whatever my mother is muttering gets drowned out by the memory of yesterday's wish to slow the sale.

Could that have created an eight-year-old public document? Impossible. But so are three specific coincidences in as many days.

Pressing my palms to my cheeks, I close my eyes as if that will tilt the axis of reality back to its normal position.

"Can I count on your cooperation with the sale of the house, then?" Dorothy asks.

I glance at the urn again. Did he do this, or did I?

The idea that my father did it secretly doesn't sit well, which makes me quite the hypocrite. The slimy feeling consumes me, reigniting my stomach rumbles. Still, the trust slows her ability to sell, which is not the worst thing under the circumstances.

With my eyes closed, I say, "Send me a copy of the document and let's see what the parameters are, okay?"

"I can't believe this is happening. You don't even like this house."

"This isn't about me." At least not the way she's assuming.

Besides, I don't dislike the house. I dislike how our family fell apart under its teak-shingled roof.

"That's the law firm calling. I'll talk to you later." She hangs up without another word.

Sipping my coffee, I eye the typewriter case stashed beside my bookcase.

My body is jittery—more from my wishes manifesting than from the caffeine. It's exciting. Empowering. Yet the unexpected twists—the stomach bug, my mother's hurt pride—filter through me like ice water.

"Is this why you kept it locked away?" I ask the urn. It must be, although he called it his lucky charm. That hardly suggests doom.

If this typewriter *is* magical, he must've stashed guidelines somewhere in his office. Those would be helpful prior to another test, but there's no time to search today. The manuscript due to Rachel in fifty-seven days won't write itself.

I turn away from the fantasy . . . for now.

Hours later, I've reread and self-edited several chapters as well as moved forward six hundred words in the story.

A satisfied yawn sends my arms overhead as I arch my back. The bottom of my empty mug is crusty with sugar residue. The sun has shifted position, moving the pattern of shadows around the paneling in my snug office. Mopsy snoozes contentedly in the chair.

Breathing in the much-needed moment of calm and accomplishment, I then click to my inbox to check whether Dorothy has sent me the trust deed. She hasn't, but a different sender's subject line makes my stomach a little sick all over again.

To: Emerson@ecwrites.com
From: rmoon@gmail.com
Re: Deadline Problem

Emerson,

I know we agreed on July 1 as the deadline for the draft, but my editor is having scheduling problems. Can we get it to her by June 1 instead? I'll pay an extra 10%. I don't want to have to push the release date.

Best,
R

I reread the request twice. Twenty-six days? I grab my head and squeeze.

Rachel doesn't get it because she doesn't see storytelling as a way of connecting with others. To her, it's about putting out "product" at regular intervals and tweaking social media algorithms to sell as many books as possible. She manages four romance series simultaneously (the Glass Beach romantic suspense books I write, plus a rom-com, a historical romance, and a paranormal series, all drafted by different writers).

My father had opinions about that, of course.

From my perspective, she spends most of her time studying metadata, putting more creative effort into her social media reels than into her books. I have no idea how she comes up with her premises, but suspect AI factors heavily.

Then again, she sells millions of copies, so who am I to criticize?

The Glass Beach novels are her bestselling books and have the overall highest average Goodreads ratings (4.38, but who's counting?) of all her series. My daily "ratings check" is a tad obsessive, but each five-star review helps quiet my father's quibbles with my style, my themes, my settings.

It's been a good run, but lately Rachel has begun pressuring me to write three books per year instead of two. I can't pump out an additional ninety thousand words each year and maintain the quality of my work. It would also rob me of weekends with my daughter when those are already coming to an end. Rather than reply by email, I call.

"Hello, Emerson," she answers.

"Hey, Rachel. I thought it'd be better to talk than email. As you know, my father's final weeks consumed most of my time recently."

I picture the husk of him slumped in his wheelchair and me easing into his old leather chair to read aloud from my favorites, hoping to penetrate the fog. He stared blankly out the window, as if he couldn't hear or understand me.

The pain of that failure lingers.

I'm haunted, too, by the choice I made throughout adulthood to never confront him with my pain. There's no chance for resolution . . . just grief and endless wondering.

"Emerson? Are you still there?"

I blink.

"Yes, sorry. I've still got all of act three to draft," I add, hoping to negotiate a compromise. A refusal might give her an excuse to replace me. Other writers might happily pump out three books per year for a steady paycheck.

"That's twenty-five to thirty thousand words, give or take," she says. "Treat May like NaNoWriMo and bang them out."

The former National Novel Writing Month? Pass. "Banging out" fifty thousand words in thirty days has never been my process.

"If I do that, the pages will be a vomit draft, making Aisha's job harder."

Aisha, Rachel's editor, is used to getting clean drafts from me. Besides, even if I set a target of twelve hundred words per day, stuff always comes up. Words get cut and tossed. Characters can throw you for a loop when you least expect it, sending you back into the story to make revisions to the chapters and arcs.

Stomach bugs hit when you least expect them.

I side-eye the typewriter case, flirting briefly with the idea of testing it again, this time with a wish for six fresh chapters by morning.

But if that came true, the result wouldn't be my work. I'd be cheating Rachel and readers. Worse, I'd be cheating myself of the joy and pride that comes from working through plot knots and writing the HEA grace notes.

Frankly, I'd rather miss the deadline.

"Look, writing sprints may not be your preference, but this needs to happen. The book's detail page is already up on Amazon with tons of pre-orders. If I miss the October release date, Amazon will delete its preorder sales and bar me from putting up additional preorder titles for an entire year."

Exaggerate much? She could bump the release date by less than thirty days without any penalty. Besides, we were set to meet the release date with my *original* draft deadline. It's Aisha's schedule that's causing this problem, not mine.

"What about hiring a different editor who can get to it on the originally agreed-upon date?" As soon as I ask, I know it won't fly. Rachel rightly prefers series continuity with writers and editors.

"No. You're not the only person juggling real life with work," she says. "I'm paying you extra. All my other writers are already writing three books a year with no bonus."

Ah, the veiled threat. The familiar language my parents used with increasing frequency before my dad got so sick. In any case, I'm not ready to be fired.

Would that be so bad?

Dorothy wouldn't think so. Should I reconsider my pet project, *The Fires of the Phoenix Queen*?

Its research binder is buried in one of the cabinets. The Word doc is saved simply as "Phoenix project." A photoshopped mock cover for that book—Solaire font for the title, a young woman wearing a crown of fire—is in a folder on my desktop.

Once upon a time, I promised to revisit it after my father died. In other words, now.

The mere thought siphons air from my lungs.

Best case, it'd be two years before that book would hit the market. Revising it, querying agents, selling it to a publisher, responding to edits, and so forth. I'd need income in the interim.

Either way, the industry is small, so it would be a mistake to risk burning a professional bridge.

"All right." I give in to her demand. Words typically flow easier the closer I get to the end. It'll be a painful but doable stretch as long as the situations with Dorothy and Sadie don't spin out any further. The trust deed should delay Dorothy's plans long enough to let me focus on this book this month. "I'll make it work."

"Super. I'll pay the additional fee when you turn in the manuscript and will tell Aisha to expect it to be in rougher shape than normal."

"I'd better get to it, then. Have a good day." After we hang up, I glare at the phone. "Heartless robot!"

Of course I'm in this pickle due to my own choices. Not that I regret the time spent with my dad. Whatever his mistakes, he gave me life and shared his love for words. He never backed down from taking big swings.

He never thought anything was beyond his ability. It was impossible not to admire his confidence, even when it overpowered mine.

But now I'll pay for it.

Setting the alarm for a twenty-five-minute sprint, I start the next chapter, pouring my real-life angst into the story conflict, secure in the knowledge that my main character will be wise enough to overcome her hardships and reach for that happy ending by the final chapter.

That's something we can't always count on in real life. No wonder readers seek escape into story worlds.

After two rounds of sprints, I take another break. Progress, sure, but I feel detached from the pages. The main characters and setting aren't bringing me any joy.

I'm distracted. Bored.

That means the readers will be bored. Hardly a confidence-boosting thought.

I click open the *Fires* outline and skim the fifteen-page plot summary and internal arc turning points. It's not half bad. Decent bones. Not nearly as derivative as my dad claimed. He was a master too intent on his vision to leave room for mine.

His fans and the trade reviewers might do the same, or at least draw comparisons with his work. If I race to publish too soon, it could be viewed as a crass attempt to capitalize on his death.

Maybe in a couple of years . . .

First, I'd need an agent.

Few writers snag one with their first manuscript. For most, it's a long slog filled with rejection. Then there are exceptions, like the successful indies who get calls from agents without having to query.

Talk about hitting the lottery. Or the typewriter.

Drumming my fingers nervously, I hesitantly open the case. Mopsy stirs, jumping off the chair and trotting out of the room.

"Chicken," I call after her.

With the typewriter on my desk, I thread another sheet of paper and type:

```
If one of the literary agents I'Ve rubbed elbows
with when accompanying my dad or attending
writing conferences reached out, I'd welcome the
chance to work with them.
```

Smirking to myself, I remove the page.

Talk about grasping!

I stick the page in the folder, only then remembering that if this wish is granted, it will likely come with some twist. Inviting an unexpected shake-up in my professional life might not have been a smart bet.

Then again, every decision contains *some* level of risk. At least with the typewriter, I'm guaranteed the desired result.

Eight

October 6, 2000

Things are getting tricky.

My notes from whenever I use the typewriter have taught me a little about what goes right (the result is always right) and what goes wrong (no matter how specific the request, there is always a surprise—like a good plot, actually—and it is not always pleasant).

Unfortunately, there are major limitations, too.

For starters, my time-travel wish (JFK's assassination) went nowhere. Granted, that was a risky gamble. Even if I could've merely witnessed it rather than played hero, my presence could've created chaos. Plus, the twist might've somehow messed with my getting back.

Other failed wishes:

* I can't cure diseases, like addiction or cancer, or end wars.
* I can't change the weather, make myself invisible, or read minds.
* I can't talk to the dead or learn the truth about God. Does the great spirit block the magic, or is there no great spirit?

Basically, the typewriter hasn't much of an imagination or any gumption. If I invented this machine, it would be gutsier.

Hell, it won't even let me influence other people's emotions, like how I couldn't make Dorothy want to quit her job. That left me no choice but to craft an event that forced her out (a budget cut).

Neither of us grew up with much. Now we have it all. The ultimate American Dream. What's the point if we can't enjoy it together?

She should've been happy being more available for Em's late middle school and high school years, which everyone warns can be rough for girls. Better yet, she could finally travel with me to movie sets and on lengthy book tours, which should've ended her complaints about my work schedule.

Everything should've gotten better for us all. A no-brainer!

But no.

She's bitter. Bored.

All over me, interrupting my workflow and pointing out this or that thing that I forgot—like Emerson's open house the other night. Or harping about some dinner party we threw in June that I don't recall.

Doesn't she understand how many events I attend in a year? No one could remember them all. I'm not like her—organized to the point of having the Dewey Decimal System imprinted in my DNA.

I'm a creative. My thoughts ricochet—always have.

Of course if she learned that I engineered her job loss and prevented her from getting three other positions, she'd see it as a gross betrayal. She might even leave me.

Which brings me to my current dilemma.

Emerson's become such a quiet girl. Less sure of herself. I worry she won't have enough friends . . . just Mel. Mel's a good kid, but what if things change? No daughter of mine should feel like an outsider. That can lead to bad places.

I want her to thrive. The sky is the limit as long as pubescent fucks don't screw with her head.

But I worry about tinkering with Emerson's life when I still can't predict the twists. Look at how it backfired with Dorothy.

For now, I've held off.

Sometimes I wonder if my career would be going as well if I hadn't wished for that first major contract. Then I reason that it can't influence emotions, so reader responses are genuine.

My books—my words—are making that happen on their own. That's my own magic, not something manufactured.

That's what I tell myself. Most nights I'm convinced.

When I'm not, well, that's when I'm vulnerable to bad decisions, like that tryst in the city last month. I can't do that again. Too much trouble for a twenty-minute thrill with some woman whose name I don't remember.

I don't want to lose Dorothy and Emerson, and I don't want to have to rely on the typewriter to keep them close.

But I might, if it comes down to that . . .

Nine

After another set of writing sprints on *Tropic Heat,* I push back from the laptop. The house is blissfully quiet, giving me space to breathe and release tension. Such stillness will probably feel different when Sadie's gone. Lonelier.

If Dorothy has felt that way since I left, it's no wonder she's looking to surround herself with Manhattan's energy.

I check my email. She still hasn't forwarded the trust deed or any other document. Was she mistaken this morning? Or drunk and deluded?

I'm about to go to the kitchen when my phone rings. A Manhattan area code. My parents' law firm? Resting my chin on a fist, I answer. "Hello?"

"Hello. Is this Emerson?" The man's voice sounds vaguely familiar.

Absently, I doodle question marks on my notepad. "It is. Who's calling?"

"This is Henry Albright, your father's agent."

I immediately picture his shaggy silver hair, piercing blue eyes, and ruddy complexion.

"Oh, hello, Henry." We first met when I was twelve and attended one of my father's book signings in New York. I'd been dazzled by the army of fans waiting for his signature. Henry also came to the house a few times, the last being for Tuesday's funeral reception. "What can I do for you?"

"I apologize if my timing is indelicate, but your father's editor wants to capitalize on recent events by updating and reissuing your father's older books, perhaps with bonus content."

My teeth clench in response to hearing my father's life is being reduced to a marketable product.

"I assume the publisher still holds all the rights," I say evenly. Even Dad's early books continue to sell above the threshold where reversion rights would kick in.

"It's a bit complicated because of the multiple book contracts and this idea of bonus content. The estate will need to be involved in some decisions, so your family and executor should be prepared for such discussions."

"All right, but we could use some time to let things settle." Honestly, between Dorothy's fire sale, Sadie's grief, and my accelerated deadline, this is more than I can manage.

"I'm sure there's a little leeway. But I'm also calling about another idea. Your father had been working on the final Pandemonium book a while back, but he . . . couldn't finish."

Ah! The first bullet point on his to-do list. Hopefully he took care of the others.

"I'm aware." On good days, we discussed that world, its characters, his vision for where the story should go, and how the series arc would be best resolved. He even drafted forty thousand words, although I suspect he knew it wasn't his best work.

"I know he shared details with you," Henry says. "He relied on your memory to fill in his blind spots and said you had a fine sense for narrative and character arcs."

A sudden lump forms in my throat, swelling and aching until it makes my voice crack. "I didn't know he talked to you about me."

It would've meant everything to have heard that from my dad, but it's better to hear it from Henry than never at all.

"We had a long career together. I know a lot, including that you're a ghostwriter."

I stroke the base of my neck anxiously, eager to know what else Dad had said about me but too embarrassed to ask. "Yes, for about nine years now."

"That brings me to my idea." He hesitates as if weighing his words. "What would you say about writing the last Pandemonium book? I'd represent the estate, of course, but we'd contract you to write the book. The expectation is that *Pandemonium Resurrected* would sell extremely well. Fans want to know how the series ends, so another seven-figure advance is likely."

"Oh! Well, gee . . ." I cough. In my peripheral vision, I glimpse the typewriter. My wish! Except this isn't at all what I intended with that wish.

My thoughts scatter like windswept leaves until I rake them into order.

No other writer knew my father better, understands what themes mattered to him, or knows how he felt about each of his characters. My familiarity might even fool some readers into thinking he wrote the manuscript—aside from the fact that he's dead.

However, it's one thing to ghostwrite for an author who hires me. Quite another to pretend to be my father—or risk tarnishing his legacy—without his permission.

"I'm not sure he'd like the idea. He was very proprietary about his books and reputation." Not to mention mostly critical of my work.

"True," Henry says. "But he also wanted to finish that series for his fans. And you'd be following his outline, with some tweaks we could discuss."

The incomplete series bothered him greatly. He'd finished the Elysian Chronicles before Sadie was born, but the Pandemonium characters are left perpetually dangling on the cliff.

Now it's me dangling, the artery in my neck erratically pulsating during an interminable silence.

"Listen, you don't need to decide right now," he says. "Talk to your mother and get back to me in a couple weeks. The next step would be to update and polish a detailed synopsis and draft a few chapters to be sure this idea has real legs. If all goes well, you'd be working with people in one of the top imprints. Those contacts might be helpful should you ever strike out on your own."

My dream creeps closer, but going through this test to reach it is like playing Russian roulette with my ego. "I appreciate the opportunity and will give it serious thought."

"Terrific. And again, sorry to propose this so soon after his death, but this is one of those 'strike while the iron is hot' situations."

"Understood. I'll get back to you soon."

"Perfect."

Before we hang up, I can't stop from asking, "Henry, did my dad ever mention a family named Welles or something called DES?"

"Not that I recall. Why?"

"I found some notes in his desk and wondered if they were work-related or personal."

A sigh comes through the line. "Sorry I can't be more help."

"It's probably nothing important, honestly," I say, not at all convinced.

"Well, enjoy your afternoon."

"You too." I hang up, create a contact for his number, then scrub my hands over my face. There's no way to simultaneously continue writing Rachel's series and ghostwrite my father's final book. Giving up the security of the Glass Beach series is a huge risk. It's not my nature to make bold moves, but maybe it's time to start.

I eye the typewriter again with reticence. Another wish granted, and yet another twist. Or is this another logically explained coincidence? He said it himself . . . strike while the iron is hot. Timing alone *could* explain that call.

I push back from my desk and go to the kitchen, thoughts tangled around the recent choices I've made and how they are affecting others. Mopsy pads across the counter. Bringing her little face to mine, I ask, "Should I do it?"

She's such a wise cat, I wish she could answer. After I place her back on the floor, her tail shoots upward, hooking at its tip. I refill her water bowl and then check the refrigerator for myself.

Cold pizza. Not the most appetizing choice this soon after a night spent embracing the toilet.

I opt for a few peanut butter crackers and snatch a lime seltzer. Henry's proposal has me rattled, although Rachel's deadline should be what's got me shaking in my slippers.

A rap on the back door makes me start. When I swing it open, Mel is standing there in a sharp navy pantsuit, swigging water. Pink cherry-tree blossoms scatter in the breeze behind her, heralding a new season like confetti. A celebration thrown for all who slogged through winter snow and April showers.

"Just left the courthouse and thought I'd check on you." Her rough, rich voice can often sound like she's just had the best sex in the world.

"Your timing is perfect." I wave her inside. "I've got a dilemma."

Mel's cornflower-blue eyes light up as she sinks onto a kitchen stool. Her confident glow steadies me—the sister I never had. "Shoot."

"Would my father want me to use his outline to ghostwrite his last Pandemonium book?"

"Could you do that?" She eyes me with a hint of admiration.

"Answer first." I take a moment to munch down a cracker, pushing the plate toward her.

"Boy, that's a tough one. My gut says he might prefer that his work ends with him." She hesitates. "Doesn't his publisher own all the rights?"

I plop onto a stool beside her. "His agent approached me. It would be published by his imprint."

"That's unexpected."

"To say the least." Although it shouldn't be entirely unexpected on my part, given the recent series of typewritten "coincidences."

She tilts her head, eyes narrowing. "We can't know what your father would've wanted, so tell me your hesitation."

Isn't it obvious?

"Who am I to mess with my dad's legacy? Who is Henry, for that matter?" I glance out the kitchen window. "Even when my father got sick, he never once broached this subject despite knowing I would've happily done it if he'd asked."

"Fair points." She pats my hand, sympathy tugging at the corners of her eyes and mouth.

"But he did want to finish the series. Working with Henry and my dad's editor could also help me launch my own career." That feels like a secondary concern—or rather, it should be secondary.

"Also fair points." She taps her pursed lips while deliberating, a habit she's had since grade school. "Your dad was ambitious. He'd probably support your using this opportunity as a stepping stone."

Dad was an opportunist. For all I know, he might've used the typewriter to advance his career.

My breath catches at the thought; then I immediately dismiss it. His books were selling nicely before he owned the typewriter. He was too proud, talented, and self-confident to resort to such tactics. I'm sure of it.

Destroy evidence. No. It couldn't mean that, although such a scandal would obliterate his legacy. Oh, please don't have that be true.

I lean forward, forehead to my palm, staring at the remaining peanut butter cracker as heaviness settles in my chest. "I wish we'd discussed it when he was well enough to make this decision."

The fact that he didn't is an insight that I can't ignore.

"You probably think he didn't ask because he didn't trust you, but maybe he was just too proud to admit that he couldn't do it himself." Mel's take is reasonable. He could never admit that he needed help or had made a mistake. "That said, you could get your own book deal without your dad's connections, so maybe your career goals shouldn't be a factor."

If only it were so easy. "Thanks, but it's extremely difficult to get an agent, and even harder to get a book deal."

She shrugs with an invalidating flick of her wrist. "What if his super-fans troll you or the book doesn't sell as well as the publisher anticipates?

Wouldn't that make it harder for you to sell your own work? Maybe it's better to say no."

This chessboard analysis is making my brain hurt. "Why can't I silence the little part of me that wants to do this?"

"That 'little part' sounds more like a daughter trying to keep her dad's memory alive than an impartial writer assessing an opportunity." Mel takes the last cracker while I digest that nugget of wisdom. "On that note, how are you? The funeral service was moving. And your eulogy was great. You painted all the right colors, carefully shading the ugly parts without being obvious."

Mel bore witness to the "Clarke Family Circus" for the past three decades without ever gossiping. Not about the time we found Dorothy half naked on her bathroom floor, or the time my father slammed the French doors closed so hard a pane shattered, or even when we caught Mrs. Faber sneaking out of the back of the house one afternoon, her hair mussed.

Loyalty like Mel's can't be bought or replaced.

"Thanks. I'm still a little numb, honestly. And tired. Things might be easier if my mother and Sadie weren't acting out." I pull a face.

"How so?"

"Dorothy ditched her wedding ring, is listing the house, and—*dun dun dun*—is moving to Manhattan. She's given me the month to collect sentimental items before an estate sale. As for Sadie, she's grieving my dad and a recent breakup, but she won't talk about that."

"Oh, poor thing. First-love heartache is the worst."

"I guess." Will Barnes, a puckish Austin Butler doppelgänger, was my first love.

We met in sixth grade but didn't start dating until the end of ninth, at which point we were inseparable until his family moved to Chicago fourteen months later. Mel nursed me through my first heartache, but it happened so long ago, thinking of him produces a sweet pain instead of a sharp one.

Mel adds, "But Em, Jesus. 'Dorothy in the City' will be a shit show, not a hit show."

"I know. I can't think about it. I wish I didn't care. I'm so tired of caring." Admitting that aloud makes my still-weak stomach sour with shame.

"No judgment here. Listen, let her enjoy her fantasy. Once reality hits, she'll change her mind."

Dorothy's determined expression yesterday suggests otherwise. "I'm not so sure, but it is what it is. I'd shouldn't have brought it up. Honestly, I could use a break from thinking about my family."

"Then let's talk about something fun. Have you found a plus-one for my party?"

Fat chance. I snicker. "I didn't even go looking."

She tsks. "Figures. I can always set you up—"

"Please don't," I interrupt. "Setups are worse than coming alone."

"You've been *coming alone* for too long," she says in her best Samantha Jones imitation. "Seriously. You need a man."

"My vibrator is more reliable than any man I ever loved," I deadpan, and then we both chuckle.

Truthfully, I'm no good at romantic relationships. My parents set a poor example, and then Doug's rejection sealed my fate. Sadie has been my one true love, and even she's pulling away.

"I'm serious. No setups, Mel. I just want to celebrate our friendship. Are you looking forward to the big four-oh?" I playfully punch her arm.

Since she turned thirty-five, Mel has jokingly aged herself backward with each new birthday, but she hides those ageist insecurities from her husband, Chris. Or so she says. I suspect otherwise. Mel and Chris share the kind of relationship that couldn't exist on half-truths and secrets. In fact, he planned the party, choosing the venue, the invitations, the menu, and the music.

"When have I not loved being the center of attention?" Mel's wry tone says everything she doesn't.

The limelight distorted my father's priorities, so I tend to avoid it. That used to be a badge of pride, but it might also be another poor example for my daughter. Encouraging Sadie to claim her own power is probably meaningless if she's seen me working only from the shadows.

"It'll be fun," I say, although I'll hug the fringes of the crowd while Mel jokes with everyone.

"Sure, but if he'd asked me first, I would've opted for Cabo." Mel titters lightheartedly. "If you change your mind about a blind date, I'll rearrange the seating chart."

"No. I'm not interested in spending the night entertaining a stranger." I may be there all alone, but at least I'll be rocking my red ruched dress.

"Fine." She glances at the time. "Well, we're here for you, whatever you need. Sorry I've got to go. Client meeting in thirty."

"Thanks for stopping by." I have a few errands to run anyway. "See you on Saturday night."

I close the door behind her, grateful to have escaped a setup.

Mel isn't entirely wrong, though. Raising Sadie, tending to my sick father, keeping tabs on Dorothy, and working have been convenient excuses to avoid risking another broken heart.

Sadie's leaving for college in a year, so lonely days and nights are coming my way. I also hate the idea of her rejecting love because of my example.

But Tinder? Hinge? Shoot me.

From what my single writer friends report, men on those apps who are my age want women who are barely out of college. I'm not interested in dating someone twenty years *my* senior, either.

Yet sometimes couples like Mel and Chris make me ache for easy companionship and for sex without self-consciousness or doubt. For a man who sees his future in my eyes.

I laugh at myself, unable to imagine that.

Well, that's not accurate. I can imagine it. In fact, I've imagined it often enough for Rachel's books, I could probably write him into existence.

I could probably write him into existence!

The words collide in my head. I hold my breath as if waiting for something . . . a sign, a decision. A slight tremor surfs down my spine as I hustle back to my office.

If my life were a novel, this would be a turning point. A place where the protagonist's heart moves from fearful toward fearless.

Sadie has heard me say that she needs to be the heroine of her own story a million times. When have I taken my own advice? Never.

Any perfect life story would of course include a healthy romance. Who doesn't love the slow burn of new love?

Mr. Right would be a trustworthy man. Not the capricious type like my dad, whose affections and moods were less reliable than cell phone signals in rural areas. Or the kind that would leave me to deal with the responsibility of a child or would be prone to whims that could hurt Sadie.

I stroke the sides of the typewriter uncertainly.

The last remnant of my tummy bug gurgles and twists through my gut. A reminder that details matter. Vagueness leaves too much open to interpretation. Unlike my other wishes, this one is too significant to dash off without thought.

Pen in hand, I jot notes on paper—traits, so to speak—to minimize an unexpected backfire.

After I've prepared, I type out a description of someone that I could love who would also be capable of making me feel safe and well-loved:

```
Mr. Right will soon cross my path in some pleasant
and unexpected meet-cute. Tall, attractive (in
my opinion), with dimples and a killer smile.
He's kind and patient, yet bold and confident.
Steadfast. Honest. Conversant. Able to be
Vulnerable. He doesn't have a difficult ex-wife or
unpleasant kids. He's happily employed. A curious
man, he loves books and animals, and he's a decent
cook and equal partner. Importantly, he and Sadie
will be able to love and respect each other.
```

Specific yet leaving room for surprises, because no relationship is exciting without a few surprises. He shouldn't be flawless, either. I have many, after all.

I'm smiling at the paragraph and George Clooney–esque image in my head until a moment of panic wraps its hands around my neck. My breath comes in fits.

Who am I to rig fate and manipulate someone without their consent? There's no worse foundation for a relationship. Honestly, this sounds more like something my dad might've tried than anything I would do.

My spine straightens like someone had yanked my corset laces too tight. Had he, in fact?

I grab my face, suspicion drilling straight through my brain.

His moods were problematic, but I never before doubted his intentions. Never questioned whether our relationship was riddled with trickery. Oh, God.

I couldn't forgive him if he manipulated us for decades, yet here I am manipulating my mother and strangers. Am I selfish, delusional, or desperate? All three, obviously. And, once again, a hypocrite.

This last wish spreads like a bloodstain on my conscience. I load the typewriter into its case with a bit more force than necessary before shoving it in the cabinet behind a stack of papers.

My romantic wish list has transformed into a sordid ransom note. I crumple the paper in my palm and throw it in the trash. Two seconds later, I pick it back out and smooth it before putting it in the folder with the others.

Glancing at the clock, I grab my keys and head to run errands before Sadie returns from school.

Please, please, *please,* God, forgive me my typewriter sorcery. I'm not out to hurt anyone. I'm just a grief-stricken single mom with an overactive imagination who could really use a few wins.

Ten

I enter Whole Foods armed with my shopping list for eggplant parmesan. While I race through the aisles, stray items like aluminum foil, napkins, and a box of Cocoa Krispies (a favorite "fortified" dessert) also end up in my cart. As I'm on my way to the checkout line, the display of pretty miniature buttercream cupcakes—Sadie's favorite—beckons.

Pressured for time, I hit the self-service checkout, preoccupied with thoughts about my work in progress. I chuck items into a bag, taking out my frustration with Rachel on the poor vegetables. Henry's offer is both a ticket out of that partnership and an advance that would set me up for a long while. I could give Rachel notice when I turn in *Tropic Heat*.

Immediately, the idea of some other creative's fingers all over my Glass Beach characters wrings a possessive grimace. My dad would probably feel a thousand times worse about handing off his characters to anyone, including me. Maybe especially me. "Would you hate that, Dad?"

The woman beside me makes a face. Guess I said that aloud.

Ducking my head, I push the cart through the door and draw in fresh air as the spring sun fends off the last grip of cool weather. A perfect day to play hooky and hit the beach with a book. If only.

While I'm lost in that daydream and loading my trunk, a man comes up behind me and asks, "Are you finished with that cart?"

His voice—part gravel, part whisper—could double for Clint Eastwood's.

I turn to thank him for taking it off my hands and come face-to-dimples with an eye-catching man. My swallowed surprise tastes as pleasant as gourmet chocolate.

Hello, Mr. Meet-Cute Wish-Come-True.

A flush works its way up my neck as alarms go off in my head. Of course he's caught me gadding about town looking like I've just cleaned the attic. Shielding my eyes with my hand, I squint into the brightness to regard him more closely.

Lean. Straw-colored hair. Arresting amber-colored eyes. A twisted eye-tooth adds a slight quirk to his grin. He's sporting black-rimmed narrow rectangular eyeglasses, something I didn't specify but have always considered sexy. All of that, plus an aura that holds the appeal of a long-lost friend.

I hand off the cart uncertainly, apprehensive of this chance encounter. No way this package comes without a major twist. "It's all yours."

"Great." He grips it with both hands, then pauses. "This might sound weird, but I'm new to town and desperate for a haircut. Any recommendations?"

As pickup lines go, it's a little original—if in fact this is a ploy and not a sincere question. My father liked Vlas's barbershop, but this guy's sporting a Harry Styles–like crop of tousled locks you can achieve only with hair product and a good blowout.

"Lanphier is popular." Never have I pictured myself with a man whose hair takes more effort than mine. Between that and his two-toned loafers, something seems afoot. But what? "Been going since my teens."

"So just a few years, then?" he teases, treating me to another display of dimples. His offhand manner stands in such contrast with his curated style.

"Even less," I joke in return, surprising myself. "Seriously, though, they do a great job."

"Thanks." He steps forward, one hand extended. "I'm Sawyer, by the way. Fresh from California."

That explains his disinhibition—and his hair. We could not be more worlds apart, yet I'm intrigued. "Emerson."

"Nice to meet you, Emerson."

The timbre of his voice makes my stomach slide to my toes. Is this really happening or is it some elaborate prank? Feels like the latter. "Welcome to town, Sawyer."

"Thanks." He rests his elbows on the cart handle, his gaze briefly dipping to my left hand before meeting my eyes. "One last question."

A tingling sensation fans across the back of my scalp. "Shoot."

"Colson Whitehead is speaking at the library late next week. I was planning to go alone, but any chance you'd be up for meeting me there?" He pushes his glasses up the bridge of his nose. "We could grab coffee or dessert after."

He will like books.

That wished-for trait knocks me off-balance.

He's more playful than the type I pictured when creating my list. More energetic. More likely to be the kind of guy who breaks hearts. Nothing about this encounter feels especially prudent.

My instinct screams to decline, yet I answer, "Why not?"

"Awesome. See you there, then."

"Y-yes," I stammer, feeling unsteady.

He narrows his eyes. "You won't stand me up?"

Shoot. "Of course not."

"Then this is my lucky day." Another gracious smile emerges. "See you later, Emerson."

"Looking forward to it." Am I? Our flirtatious encounter has bemused me.

He pushes the cart away, bestowing one last friendly wave before reaching the store's entrance.

The exchange was more like some dream than reality. A fun dream, though. I close the trunk and get behind the wheel, blinking as though it will clear the mental fog. Even if one of us bails, that little encounter will sustain me and my vibrator for at least a month.

On my way to the hardware store, the gas gauge warning light comes on, pulling my attention from the mental list of Sawyer's pros and cons. The Shell station is just ahead, so I steer the car in and hook up to an open pump.

Across the pump island sits a sporty crimson Aston Martin. The striking coupe and its futuristic hubcaps lure me into taking a closer peek.

When my nozzle's handle pops, I turn around in time to see a guy in sunglasses walking toward the sexy car from the station. Tall. Blond. Dark sunglasses. Slightly cocky gait.

Before he catches me ogling, I tuck my chin and reach for my door.

He stops short. "Emerson Clarke, is that you?"

I glance over my shoulder as he removes his sunglasses. It takes two seconds, maybe three, to recognize him this many years later.

"Will?" I'm agape, as if an actual ghost has just appeared.

"In the flesh." His hair is a little thinner, his face has matured, but those eyes are pure Will. Light-struck topaz that's hard to forget.

"My God, it's been a long time," I blurt, breathlessly drowning in a sea of memories.

Twenty-odd years, yet my heart reacts as it always did. Guess it's true that some things never change. Look at him, dapper in his gray pants and charcoal-and-lilac-checkered shirt.

I suck in my stomach and tuck my hair behind my ear, wishing for the second time that I hadn't dashed out in yoga pants. "What are you doing here?"

"Just met with a client up the road." He gestures toward me, smiling. "This is quite a coincidence."

He laughs it off, but I'm not sure it's a coincidence at all.

What if Sawyer was a false flag and Will is my Mr. Right? After all, we were first loves. That's a far more substantial foundation for a lasting connection than sharing salon recommendations with a stranger.

A sudden lightheadedness makes me feel like I'm paddleboarding in rough water. "I can't believe it's really you."

I stop myself from confessing how I thought of him earlier when discussing Sadie's breakup with Mel.

"I take it you still live in town?" he asks, thumbs casually hooked in his pants pockets.

"Sure do. Did you move back recently?" Oh, gosh. Mel won't believe this.

"No. I've lived in Larchmont for the past five years." Westchester County, New York, a quick thirty-minute drive across the border. "Hey, I read about your dad. So sorry."

"Thanks. He'd been sick for a long time, so I was prepared." No matter how many times I repeat a version of this sentiment, it rings only half true.

"He was a character." Will's coy smile speaks to my dad's talent for catching us making out, at which point he would embarrass us with bad jokes, like taking the sword off his office wall and waving it around, pretending to defend my honor. "I'm bummed that there won't ever be another Pandemonium book."

"You and many others." This isn't the time to think about Henry's proposal. Not with Will here, as friendly as he was in our teens.

"I'd love to catch up. Do you have twenty minutes for coffee?" he asks.

I glance down because it feels like my feet have left the ground.

"Unfortunately my daughter will be home soon. She's going through a tough time, so I want to be available." When he doesn't blanch, I glance at his left hand. No ring.

"Maybe another time, then."

Is he being serious or polite? Before I overthink it, I say, "Listen, if you're not busy on Saturday night, would you like to be my plus-one at Mel's birthday party? Dinner, open bar, and plenty of time to catch up."

Something churns behind his eyes before he casually shrugs. "Why not? Let's exchange contact info."

"Really?" My insides effervesce. "I mean, great!"

I give him my number, which he tests on the spot. "There we go."

"I'll text you the details later." I tuck my phone away. "Mel will be shocked to see you."

"I bet," he says, now moving to the driver's side of his car.

"Nice ride."

His cheeks pink up. "A midlife crisis car, but hella fun to drive."

His self-deprecating humor is both familiar and comforting. "See you Saturday."

"Great." He waves before sliding behind the steering wheel and revving his engine.

After he pulls away, I sink onto my front seat, press my palms to my cheeks, and blow out a breath. It takes sixty seconds before my heartbeat slows.

Will Barnes! The typewriter deserves a fat tip.

A glance at the time makes me abandon my plans to hit up Ring's End. Gardening tools can wait another day.

"Who am I kidding, anyway?" Neither of my thumbs has ever been green. One less errand also avoids a potential encounter with yet another contender for Mr. Right.

But really, it must be Will. Why else would I bump into him *today* of all days? And what's more romantic than reunited first loves? As romance tropes go, that's a fan favorite. We don't even have emotional baggage to overcome since our breakup happened only because he moved out of state.

At home, I hum a tune from *West Side Story* while putting away the groceries and setting four pastel-frosted cupcakes on a plate for Sadie. Too soon, the high of my flirtations is swallowed by a nagging discomfort.

It's hard to remain heady about Will and Sawyer while knowing they've been manipulated by whatever mystical force is at play. I splay my hands on the counter, shaking my head. "Listen to yourself—mystical forces."

How does one self-diagnose a minor mental break with reality? After all, schizophrenics believe their hallucinations. In truth, we all believe our perceptions are reality, making any self-assessment of one's sanity rather tricky.

Could five successive wishes come to life be mere serendipity? Perhaps magic is little more than the alchemy of asking for something and then opening one's attention to it. Like the promise in that popular book from a while back that promoted notions of effortlessly harnessing the powers of the universe. Or *Field of Dreams*'s famous line about building it so they would come.

I scrub my hands over my face, picturing my father at his desk during his secret late-night typing sessions.

He must've been doing more than typing a diary, though his wishes remain as enigmatic as he was. Knowing him, I assume he attempted pie-in-the-sky wishes. There's no world peace or cure for cancer, but did he tinker with ideas like AI?

He obviously couldn't reverse his Alzheimer's. Or stop my mom's drinking. He didn't do diddly to make Doug marry me and help raise Sadie. Were my good grades the result of his wish or my effort? Was he behind my decision to stay in Darien, or did I choose it myself?

As the questions pile up, a pit opens in my stomach. My mother and I may have been his puppets for decades. He might deserve credit for the outcomes of decisions and actions I've always believed were my own. Does that make him a monster or merely a father who thought he knew best? Maybe a little of both.

I grip the counter, squeezing my eyes shut as my world slides sideways.

This is madness. After all, we all impose our will on others from time to time. At the end of the day, my life is privileged, thanks in part to him and the choices he made. The typewriter couldn't grant him total mind control over me, so I had some agency in my own life. Right?

I grab the Meyer's Clean Day spray and begin feverishly wiping down the counters and cabinets. My life is what it is. My dad's no longer here to control me, if in fact he ever did. I mop my sweaty brow, reaching for forgiveness. He wasn't evil—just driven by a desire for greatness. Frankly, what storyteller wouldn't want to create his or her ideal life story?

I'm not looking for an unfair advantage, but what's wrong with securing results that *should* come from being a hardworking single parent and good daughter? With stepping in where fate got it wrong and making things right?

There's nothing overtly greedy about desiring a sober mother, a happy daughter, or a worthy lover. The key is not hurting others.

Where might my dad have kept his notes about the Underwood?

Sadie blows in through the back door, making me start. Chin tucked, red-rimmed eyes barely hidden by the hair hanging loosely around her face.

Is Johnny already dating someone else? I set down the spray bottle. "Honey, what's happened?"

"Nothing." Her limp voice and posture suggest otherwise.

A wrong step will crack our truce's thin ice. I should trust in the foundation of our relationship and in the fact that she's typically a great kid. And yet . . . "That's obviously not true."

"I told you, I don't want to talk about this. Let me deal with it my way, please."

Her stone-faced expression reminds me of Doug during our final weeks, when we couldn't agree on anything. Pushing him got me nowhere.

Nudging the cupcakes toward her, I say, "Okay. I'm always here for you, though."

The atmosphere in the kitchen is suffocating. The tear trailing down her cheek feels as if it were my own.

"I know." She pops the entire thing in her mouth before mumbling, "I just want to be alone."

Being alone has never helped me feel better, so I cast out another line, hoping to pull her ashore. "I'm making eggplant parm for dinner."

A fleeting twinkle brightens her eyes. "Yum."

"Want to learn how?"

"Not tonight." She shakes her head, already walking away. Conversation over.

Sadie's distant footfalls are as heavy as my heart.

Withdrawal has been my kryptonite since my adolescence. Sadie's personality shift feels overblown for the circumstances, but maybe I'm too world-weary to remember the throes of teen love.

My text notification pings. It's Will, which is a little freaky given that I'm again thinking of teen heartache. Obviously some invisible energy is at play here, even if I can't explain it.

Such a nice surprise to bump into you. Looking forward to Saturday.

It's easy to imagine falling back into a relationship with him. Not that we're kids anymore. Life has changed me, as it's surely changed him. Giddy feelings aside, we might not fit together as well today as we did twenty years ago, despite my typed wish. If my thirty-nine years have taught me anything, it's to temper my expectations.

A thumbs-up shouldn't appear too eager. I then shoot Mel a quick text asking her to add a plus-one to my RSVP without giving details. Can't wait to see her reaction when he arrives at her party.

I turn the phone over on the counter and break into a brief happy dance, insides fizzing like a shaken can of soda despite all logic. Sawyer's dimples and voice were alluring, but Will makes more sense.

Mopsy mewls at me, so I lift her off the floor, confiding, "I deserve something good. Don't you agree?"

Her tail tucks between her hindquarters, so I set her down.

My bubbly feeling continues until a pitiless inner voice reminds me that everything has a price. That theme, woven through every caution-ary tale ever written, has also echoed throughout my deceptively perfect-looking life.

Only an idiot would not be wary of a stolen treasure's ostensible magic. *Dad, is this what changed you?*

Eleven

Following an early dinner, I drive over to the estate to find out why Dorothy has gone dark on me since her bitter call this morning. She was in high dudgeon, that's for sure.

If she's not buzzed, it'll be tough to hide my guilty conscience about this trust business. Assuming it was me. My dad could've done it, with or without the typewriter.

At this point, how it happened matters less than how we proceed.

Their house comes into view, perched among the hedges like a set diamond, landscape lights reflecting off its windows. Dorothy's probably inside setting things on fire while downing booze. I park the car and sit, chin to chest, heaving a sigh.

There's no avoiding this conversation.

The gravel crunches beneath my feet, its lonely sound drowning out the cicadas. To think there was a time when balmy spring evenings by the sea were full of promise and pleasure.

I let myself in through the side entrance. "Hello!"

No answer.

I check the garage. Dorothy's car is missing. Chances are she's not sober enough at this hour to drive home.

Time to text:

I'm at the house. Where are you? Did you learn anything more about the property trust?

A minute passes without a reply. I tuck the phone in my pocket, then march to my father's office in search of more information about the typewriter and that to-do list.

After turning on the overhead lights, I spin in a circle. Such chaos. One corner of the desk is a pile of things related to the Pandemonium series, reminding me of Henry's proposal. Was that call only this morning? My father's been dead little more than a week, yet everything's already changing so quickly.

All his personal things need to be sorted into piles to be saved or tossed. Organizing this will require more stamina and free time than I have this month, regardless of my mother's demands. Tonight my only mission is to find what he's hidden. He would've concealed it someplace no person— the housekeeper, a guest, or I—would have easily stumbled upon it.

The curio cabinet might have a secret panel. The glass door opens easily now, having remained unsecured since I picked its lock. I feel around the cabinet's edges, pausing periodically to press against the panels to see if there is any release. No luck.

Next, I face the floor-to-ceiling bookcases, which span two walls of the office. The ladder is pushed to the far left, so I climb it and begin my search on a top shelf.

With one ear cocked for Dorothy's approach, I thumb through each book, hoping to find handwritten or typed notes—or even a booklet—containing information about the Underwood or anything related to that to-do list.

Forty-five minutes later, I've sorted through two shelves without discovering anything helpful.

There was a pink love letter from some random woman—a fan, a tryst, it isn't quite clear—hidden in his copy of Philip Roth's *Deception*. He also kept early photographs of himself and my mother in a copy of Charles Frazier's *Cold Mountain*. Why he hid those photos can be added to the many mysteries left to resolve.

Several of my childhood drawings were stuffed at the end of one shelf, too. I hoped that the leather box on the second shelf from the top might contain something helpful, but it housed merely a few crystals, an old ring, and an unfamiliar multicolored macaroni necklace.

Thinking Sadie must've made it for him, I loop it around my neck to show her later.

Nothing revealed relates to the typewriter, the Welles heir, or DES, nor gives me any deeper insight into how my father would feel about me ghostwriting his final novel.

My gaze skims two dozen more shelves and some cabinet drawers. This could take all night. I'm eyeing a new shelf when Dorothy enters the house from the garage.

"Emerson?" she calls.

"In Dad's office," I reply, making my way down the ladder.

She comes into the office—a place she mostly avoided—with chin raised, nose wrinkled as if a skunk passed through. "What are you doing here?"

"Going through Dad's things, like you asked."

Her expression softens when her gaze lands on my neck. "Where on earth did you find that?"

She approaches me, reaching for the necklace before pulling back and placing her hand over her mouth. Her eyes shine like the surface of a moonlit pond.

"In a box on the shelf. Did Sadie make this?" I pull it away from my breastbone to peer at it again.

"No." She touches her jaw, eyes widening. "You did."

"I did?" I grimace.

"Yes. In the old house. You worked on it one afternoon when your father was due to return from his first multicity book tour. We baked a cherry pie for his homecoming. You even dressed up in that pink velvet dress you loved, but he got delayed by a storm in Chicago. When he came home the next day, you gave that to him and started crying while you were describing all we'd planned. He wore it for two weeks straight to make up for missing the party." She shimmies as if she's just emerged from a dream state. "I can't believe he kept it."

My heart aches with longing for the devotion that once defined us. The memento is like a flower in a long-fallow field—proof that something good survived.

Dorothy glances at the messy desk and the books everywhere. "You haven't gotten very far. What's the plan?"

"Not sure. Just getting a sense for everything that's here to group things into piles to save, toss, or donate." It'll be tough to throw his things away, but I've no place to store it all and my mother clearly has no use for any of it. "I also want to talk about a couple of things. I got a call from Dad's agent today."

"What about?" She draws back as if expecting another unpleasant surprise.

I recite the main points of Henry's ghostwriting proposal, as well as my primary concerns. "What do you think?"

"Don't do it," she says immediately.

Her vehemence deals an unexpected blow that sends me falling back against the desk. "You don't think Dad would like that?"

"I don't care what he'd like. This isn't good for *you*. Honestly, Emerson, I thought when he died, you'd finally step out of his shadow. Instead, you're considering stepping into his shoes." She raises her arms overhead, obviously exasperated.

"Forget I asked." I fidget with the letter opener, which reminds me of breaking into the curio cabinet. On a whim, I ask, "Did Dad ever mention anything special about the old typewriter?"

Dorothy's gaze moves to the empty cabinet. "Where'd it go?"

"I took it the other day. Do you care?"

She screws up her face. "Not one bit."

"Dad was so protective of it. You never wondered why?"

"Him and his superstitions. That 'lucky charm' never brought our family any luck," she quips, then bites her lip. "Sorry."

I weigh my words before asking the question I'm afraid to hear answered. "Why'd he give it that nickname?"

She shrugs. "He got his first seven-figure book deal soon after he bought it. Then his first movie deal. It became his talisman from then on. Silly man—like all those sports fans and their ridiculous rituals—giving an inanimate object credit for his success." She folds her arms under her breasts as she glances around his office, her expression hardening. "He certainly never acknowledged my contributions, even though I supported him in the beginning, when his dreams and ambitions were costing us money."

She spits those words out like poison-tipped arrows.

On the surface, they smack of sour grapes, but she had supported him, given him feedback, believed in him. Without her assistance, the piles of rejections might've defeated him before he landed an agent and debut publishing contract. Definitely long before he bought the typewriter that seems like it might've juiced his career.

I meet her gaze. "He should've thanked you more often."

The shock of my affirmation prompts a look of surprise that then quickly fades into self-consciousness. The awkward moment between us is an accord, however slight.

Unfortunately, nothing she's said has given me a clearer idea of whether Dad wrote down any rules.

For the first time since she walked in, I take a good look at her. Dove-gray pantsuit, silver silk shirt, modern pumps. Pearls hang around her neck and dangle from her earlobes. Her hair looks professionally blown out. Her eyes are clear and alert. Fiery, even.

"Where were you, by the way?" I ask.

"Seeing the lawyers about this ridiculous trust, then meeting with Kathryn over dinner. Do you know how humiliating it is to need to ask you and Sadie to let me sell my own home?"

She closes her eyes, fingers splayed in the air like she's trying to stop herself from doing or saying something more. When she opens them again, they're dewy.

Unable to recall the last time she cried, I look away before she reads my shame. My motives for making that wish feel less noble now than when I typed it.

"There's no reason to be humiliated. I'm sure it can be resolved," I hear myself saying, despite my reservations. It's not the sale I object to as much as the move to Manhattan. "Did the lawyers hand you any other surprises?"

"No, but I won't have control of the finances until after the tax return is filed, which is complicated by the intellectual property and all those different publishing contracts and potential movie deals. It's a lot, though. More than five families need."

I nod. "I don't want anything, so feel free to donate everything."

She rolls her eyes and scoffs. "This ongoing stance against your inheritance is ridiculous. You've seen how life can change." She snaps her fingers. "You might get sick or be out of work or have an accident and need years of rehab. Something could happen to Sadie. You never know when money will save your behind, so you're a fool to turn it all away just to prove some point. We know we weren't the best parents. Don't compound our mistakes by making one of your own. Taking an inheritance is not giving us a free pass."

Dorothy turns on her heel and stalks out of the office.

That's the first time she's ever acknowledged any mistakes. I shake off my shock before following her to the kitchen. "Can I have a copy of the documents you got today? I'd like to read them and then explain what's going on to Sadie."

My mother opens her gradient Chanel Hobo bag, pulls out some papers, and slides them across the island. "Knock yourself out. But I'd like to keep things moving, so I need you two to sign off on a broker agreement with Kathryn this week."

I shouldn't balk. Until this morning, I would've assumed she had every right to do whatever she wanted with this house. As she would have if my dad (or I) hadn't interfered.

He had that typewriter for so long. It's hard to conceive of what the hell else he did with it.

The last bullet point on his to-do list suggests dreadful possibilities—

possibly even crimes—changing the landscape of my life and leaving me stranded someplace unfamiliar.

"What's the matter?" Dorothy asks.

"Nothing." I hide my face behind the pages of the trust deed, noting the passages Dorothy highlighted.

Something clinks against the counter, making me look up. My mother's opening a bottle of wine.

She doesn't meet my gaze as she fills her glass with a "country club" pour, which she downs in fifteen seconds before pouring another as if daring me to say something.

I gaze at the bottle and then at her. If it weren't for a twinge of guilt about this trust, a smart-ass remark would pour from my lips. "I'd better get home before Sadie goes to bed."

"Don't forget to bring her over to pick out whatever keepsakes you'd like, because I'm going to start packing up the place."

"Noted." I tap the papers against the counter. "Have a good night."

She raises her glass. "I will."

On my way home, the past and present blur, all of it colored by what my father may or may not have done to us . . . or for us? That power now rests in my control. What future do I want? What do we all deserve, or is that the wrong question? Fairness feels impossible when only one person is making the decisions.

And yet my garden is thriving. My waistline is thinner. My career could take a new turn with Henry. I've met a new handsome man and found an old love. I've possibly even found a way to slow my mother down from taking a dangerous misstep.

Despite some imperfections and a few misgivings, things are looking up. No one's been hurt yet, either—well, except for my mother's pride. As was true with my weight loss, the temporary unpleasant price seems worth paying for her safety.

The sooner I find those rules, the better off we'll all be.

Twelve

After school the next day, Sadie enters the kitchen through the back door; she's wearing old cutoffs and a ratty Burton T-shirt. Her continued departure from the care normally given to her appearance concerns me, but I stuff my opinions down my throat. "How was school?"

"Fine." She tosses the key fob on the counter, grabs an apple from the fruit bowl, and takes a quick bite.

"Can you sit for a minute? There's something important we need to discuss."

She stops chewing, her gaze darting around as if searching for an escape hatch. "What's wrong?"

From the other side of the peninsula, I slide the trust document in front of her while explaining what it says.

Sadie sits on a stool, skimming the agreement without really reading it. When I finish speaking, she eyes me. "Did you know about this?"

"No, why?"

She averts her gaze. "Seems like something you'd suggest."

"What?" My mouth falls open, because that hardly sounded like a compliment.

"Gran's drinking bugs you and you like everything to go 'according to plan,' so I could see you suggesting this to Papa when he got sick."

I look down, half expecting to find a giant hole shot through my torso. What an ugly image of me she's painted. It takes every bit of strength to keep the tears from my eyes. "Well, I didn't."

And yet I did wish for this. I may have even caused it, so perhaps she sees me clearly.

"Why would Papa sneak it in? That's, like, low-key mean." Her brows knit as she confronts a side of my father that she has not previously been forced to acknowledge firsthand.

"He probably didn't want to argue about things like tax benefits or probate or whether you and I should receive some benefit." It's clear from the way she's chewing her lip that Sadie doesn't consider any of those goals a good excuse for deceit. With good reason. "What are you thinking?"

"I hate this—the trust, Gran selling, Papa dying." Her nostrils flare like she's fending off tears.

"It's a lot, I know." And it's been only a few days since the funeral. I stroke her forearm. "But we could use this document to ask Gran to hold off selling until you leave for college."

She absently folds all the corners of the pages into triangles. "That doesn't feel right. It's not our house."

"Technically it is, as beneficiaries of this trust."

She scoffs. "But we didn't buy it."

"Neither did Gran." As soon as that's out of my mouth, I recoil. Dorothy paid for that house in ways that don't show up on a balance sheet.

"You want me to tell Gran no?" Sadie glowers.

I can't ask her to do that to her grandmother, so I shake my head.

"What if we conditioned our approval on her agreeing to go to rehab? That way, when she moves away, she's healthier and stable." Surely Sadie will concede that would be for the best.

She slides off the stool with a told-you-so aspect. "See? There you go, needing to control everything."

My hands find my hips. "It's not about control. I'm trying to protect her."

"Did she ask you to? Not everyone wants to follow your rules for life, Mom, like there's only one right choice about everything."

I snatch the trust document off the counter. "It's easy for *you* not to worry. You never had to put out an oven fire after she passed out while making dinner, or rush her to the ER after she fell down the stairs, or make excuses when she failed to show up at appointments."

"Martyr, much?" Sadie crunches into that apple I now want to smack from her hand.

"Watch the tone," I snap. "I'm not playing the martyr. These are facts."

"If she starts a fire or falls or misses an appointment, she'll deal with it. Everything isn't your job. Or your business." After her last bite, she tosses the core in the trash, looking a bit smug. "Anyway, I'm not making conditions, so you do what you have to."

My chest feels like she's used it as a speed bag. "Your vote is noted."

"Good." She takes her backpack and starts to leave.

"Hold up. Gran wants us to choose some keepsakes." Picking through my parents' belongings so soon after the funeral also makes me feel like a vulture feasting on the carcass of their dead relationship. It will, however, give me another shot at digging around my dad's office. "Let's get that over with now."

This request is less about control than about not wanting to go by myself. Each time I've visited the house this week, my father's death becomes real in a way I manage to deny when I'm not there.

"I'll probably finish before you, so I'll bike over." She strides past me without making eye contact.

I take a couple of minutes to cool down before fishing my keys from my purse. My hands remain locked in a death grip around the steering wheel for the duration of the drive. Sadie is already setting her kickstand by the time I pull into the driveway.

When I catch up to her, she says, "Not to be ungrateful, but most of Gran's stuff is old-fashioned or too fancy."

We both walk toward the side entrance. "There may be a painting or something that down the road would be a nice reminder of your grandparents."

She shrugs and opens the side door for me, lacking the sentimentality I would've expected.

Her earliest years here were relatively halcyon days. It was as if her infancy reminded my parents of being young lovers starting their own family. Dorothy even cut back on drinking for several months.

It had felt like a new beginning for us all, but like my own happy childhood, it didn't last.

When we enter the mudroom, Dorothy is in the kitchen, whistling the opening melody of "Don't Worry, Be Happy."

The notes send me back to the kitchen table in the old Easton house. She was helping me make a papier-mâché Winnie-the-Pooh head for my Halloween costume. She'd already sewn the body of the costume from a honey-colored faux fur fabric, creating an interior pocket for a beach ball to mimic his big belly.

I touch my fingertips together, recalling the gluey fingerprints stippled across the table, the golden paint on my arms, and her whistling Bobby McFerrin's famous tune while patiently guiding me.

The loss—the change from that mother to the one she became by my teens—tramples across my chest. My next breath takes effort.

"Are you going to barf again?" Sadie asks, her face screwing up as if she sipped salted coffee.

I shake my head while the heartache eases. "No, it's just . . . never mind. Let's get this done."

We find Dorothy surrounded by cardboard boxes and packing paper. Amid the dozens of half-open Christopher Peacock cabinets and miles of gleaming white marble, there's also a half-empty bottle of Château d'Yquem Sauternes beside a freshly poured glass.

"Well, hello there." Her movements appear loosened by a couple glasses of fine wine. She's probably been drinking on and off since I left last night.

"What are you wearing, Gran?" Sadie asks, her expression suddenly mirthful.

Good question.

"Jeans." She picks at the threads of her distressed faded Guess ankle jeans from eons ago, which she's paired with a crystal-embellished top. "I forgot how comfortable they are. And they still fit." Her hands rise overhead as if she's thinking *Voilà*.

I can't even wear jeans from ten years ago—well, maybe today, but not last week.

Dorothy's face looks younger without lipstick and mascara. Or maybe it's her expression. She looks free. That should be a welcome transformation, but her gleeful race toward the future this soon after Dad's funeral makes me sizzle like water in a hot skillet.

She tilts her head, gazing at me. "You look angry. What have I done now?"

Sadie shoots me a look that suggests she's expecting me to lecture her gran. I hold my tongue so my daughter doesn't have to play ref the way I used to with my parents.

"Nothing. We came to pick out some keepsakes. Looks like we've arrived just in time." I gesture to the boxes.

She chuckles. "Well, I didn't expect you to want kitchenware. Cooking has never been your thing."

True. I'm adequate at best.

Dorothy had been something of a culinarian until Dad hired personal chefs to relieve her of those obligations. At the time, it sounded like an awesome gift rather than something that robbed her of a favorite pastime.

Had he done it intentionally? The mental accusation blisters. He isn't here to defend himself, and yet I can't honestly acquit him, either. These types of ping-ponging thoughts made it impossible to write more than four pages today, adding to my overall stress.

"Is there anything I can't have, Gran?" Sadie plucks a cookie from the glass jar. Meanwhile, I can't help but envy the pleasant lilt in her voice when speaking with Dorothy.

"Sky's the limit, dear," Dorothy says. "If I were you, I'd focus on the art. I won't need a third of it, and my favorites aren't the important pieces."

"Sadie," I interrupt. "Choose something for sentimentality, not for profit."

"Of course, Mom." Her sardonic moue adds an exclamation point to her earlier opinion of my bossiness.

It shouldn't be this difficult to communicate with the two most significant women in my life. Is it me? "Sorry."

Another shrug, and then Sadie wanders toward the living room.

"What about you?" Dorothy asks as she climbs onto a stool and retrieves gleaming white bakeware. I step toward her, arms raised in case she tips over, then move back and cross my arms as she safely descends to the ground. "Got anything special in mind?"

Dad's hidden secrets would be nice. "No. But you're leaving Dad's office to me, right?"

"As long as you finish it before we show the house."

Show the house. She's presuming we'll sign off on the sale. Moving this fast is a mistake, but my refusal to cooperate will only drive my daughter further away.

"There are a lot of Dad's things to catalogue." Too many, frankly. "Do you want to sell any of those?"

I cringe when picturing someone else coveting his personal things.

Mordantly she raises her left brow before chugging the contents of her wineglass. "People admired his talent, but frankly, I liked him better—I liked us better—before he got so full of himself. Selling his personal things for profit would feel like selling out what's left of my soul."

Following that admission, she focuses intently on wrapping another baking dish in packing paper.

Her display of vulnerability suppresses my instinct to play devil's advocate or defend my father. He wasn't anyone's dream husband, but I need to believe that in his way, he wanted us all to be happy. That good intentions mitigate his less noble actions.

If Dorothy and I were more affectionate, I might hug her now or say something reassuring. I can't do it, though. Not when she still turns to that bottle instead of to me.

"Well, I'll try to think up a storage plan." I drum my hands on the counter.

When I stroll away, she resumes whistling, which pinches my heart anew.

Upstairs I find Sadie fingering items in her old room with little apparent interest. On a shelf above the frilly pink bed sits a series of classic children's books, including a signed first edition of *The Tale of Benjamin Bunny* by Beatrix Potter.

It was my father's when he was young, given to him by his grandfather. My parents read it to me a hundred times, and I often read it to Sadie. Some of my happiest memories involve being cuddled in bed with this book.

I lift it off the shelf, caressing its worn cover, my whole body filling with warmth. "Remember this?"

Sadie nods, appearing unmoved by my nostalgic rapture.

The urge to throw my arms around her and hug her secrets out of her swells. "I'll keep this for when you have a family. I can read it to my grandchild or give it to you to read to him or her."

Projecting ahead to the day when my love for her will multiply sparks an indescribable tenderness that has me biting my lower lip.

Sadie, however, blanches. "Don't save it for me. I'm not bringing kids into a world filled with fires and floods and hate-fueled wars."

"Oh, Sadie." They might be legitimate concerns, but she's left no room for hope or progress or change. Jaded at seventeen. "That makes me sad."

"I'm not the only one who feels this way." She draws herself up, raising her chin just like Dorothy does.

What is it that eventually makes everyone I love shut me out and turn away? "You weren't this grim about life a week ago."

"Things change." She emphasizes her bravado by staring me down.

I mentally count to three before speaking. "I'm sorry you're hurting over Johnny."

A dark cloud crosses her eyes as she gestures around the room, choosing to ignore my remark. "I already have keepsakes from Papa. There's nothing else I want, Mom. I'm going home."

"Sadie . . ."

She stops at the door, turning her face toward me, one brow arched.

Her expression reveals no cracks that I might slip between. "If I see something I think you might appreciate later, I'll take it for you."

"All right."

I hug the book to my chest, wishing it were my little girl. Wishing I could excavate whatever has so changed her outlook on life and throw it out with all these other things none of us wants to keep.

So far I haven't used the typewriter in connection with Sadie, preferring not to corrupt our relationship by going behind her back.

Yet the idea stalks me as I meander the house scoping out various items. Did my father have misgivings about making wishes that affected our family? When my mother left me with sitters while she traveled to his movie sets, was that what he wanted? Is DES my mother, Sadie, and me? Is the equipment related in any way to the Welles heir? Will unanswered questions drive me into an early grave?

Twenty minutes later, I've chosen a vintage Tibetan carpet that will look lovely in our living room, the whimsical limited edition Takashi Murakami print that my father had hung in my playroom, and a René Lalique Ceylan vase I'd always thought beautiful. For Sadie, I selected the small collection of bejeweled Jay Strongwater frames in the living room.

The original Keith Haring untitled work from the mid-eighties tempts me, but my dad bought that for seven figures. I can't bring myself to claim it, even though it's mesmerizing.

After setting everything but the rug in the mudroom, I slip into my dad's office to skim through the files in his desk in search of a journal or other typed notes regarding the Underwood.

There are odd papers—old research notes, articles about his books, computer warranties—but no key or anything related to the typewriter. I swivel the seat around to face the cabinets behind his desk.

When I open the doors, I nearly tumble out of the seat.

A safe?

The evidence!

Thirteen

My pulse is throbbing. This is it! I can barely swallow, my throat is so dry. I blow out a few breaths to slow my heart rate. Dad must've written down the combination somewhere.

I scan the mess. He never made anything easy on me. This could take more time than I have tonight. Maybe this is a sign to stop. The last thing we need is for the safe's contents to turn out like Pandora's box.

For a moment, I consider dropping it. No, I need to know.

The combination knob slips in my shaky fingers. I twirl it again, listening for the tumblers to click. Fruitless. My gaze darts in the direction of the kitchen.

Chewing the inside of my cheek, I seek out Dorothy. An empty wine bottle sits on the kitchen counter. The overhead lights are dimmed; the carefree whistling is silenced. Her posture is slouched. Facing the window overlooking the water, she appears rudderless without Dad's strong current to push against.

"Hey, do you know the combination to the safe in Dad's office?" I feign nonchalance despite the churn of anticipation.

She shakes her head listlessly.

I toss the empty wine bottle in the recycling bin, disinclined toward pleasantries. "Any idea if he wrote it down anywhere?"

"What do you think?" Her caustic tone contradicts how especially frail she looks beside the expansive walnut table in the breakfast room, framed by towering windows.

"There could be important documents in there," I say, tempering my sense of urgency. "We'll need to get a safecracker to open it."

"Spare me more surprises." Dorothy toys with a saltshaker.

Fair enough, given the newly discovered trust document.

"You seem . . . troubled." I cross my arms. "Maybe you should slow all this down a little."

Dorothy narrows her gaze. "Are you planning to stop me, Emerson?"

Generally, I prefer honesty. In this case, the truth is precarious. It takes a moment to find the right response. "I'd feel more comfortable if you hit pause."

"Well, I wouldn't." She sighs heavily. "Did you pick anything to keep?"

Our exhausting push-pull dynamic washes over me like water shaping rock. I relent and then recount my bounty before adding, "I'll wait until you move to pick up the rug in the sitting room."

"Nice choices." Her subdued mood thwarts the attempted smile. "No one wants the Balkan dolls?"

Huh?

"The ones that your father bought you in Croatia."

I know the dolls. What I don't know is why they'd be important enough to keep.

"You played with them for a year straight. Remember that rainy day when you used them like puppets, filming made-up damsel-in-distress plays. We made popcorn and watched the movies after dinner. I wonder where those old tapes went?" She drums her fingers against her lips.

"I don't remember that." I shrug, though the cinematic production seems like something that should stand out among the tapestry of child-hood memories.

"That's the second thing you haven't remembered in twenty-four hours." Her color drains, blue eyes sharpening their focus on me. "Your father wasn't much older than you when he first started forgetting things."

My eyes roll heavenward. "I've forgotten two things from a million years ago. Let's not sound the alarm."

Well, two plus that printer cartridge.

She rests her hand on the glass table. "Maybe you should get tested for that Alzheimer's gene, just in case."

Hard pass. "You're overreacting. I've made up a lot of stories in my life. It's not surprising that I can't remember them all."

Dorothy hugs herself, staring at me for a moment before averting her gaze. "It's depressing . . . all the love and attention you received early in life have all washed away like they never happened."

She's kept her guard up for decades, so it shakes me now to see her walls coming down.

I hesitate, sliding my hands into my pockets. "Is there anything about our life here that you'll miss?"

Although prepared for sarcasm, I win Dorothy's wistful grin.

"The gardens. The view. The sound of your laughter when your friends were around." She raps the table with her knuckle. "Mel's a pip."

"She is." No doubt her moxie helps her in the courtroom.

"You two were all youthful energy and dreams. That's how I knew you'd be okay, despite everything." Dorothy waves a hand around, silently acknowledging the house, the past, and the tension that lived with us like another family member.

Am I okay? It doesn't often feel that way. Determined. Steady. But okay? The paint-spatter habit suggests not.

"The best was when you and Sadie lived here." Dorothy's face glows while basking in that memory. "Well, except for the colic months . . . those were hell."

"Those *were* hell." We both laugh, riding the crest of a sentimental tide.

It hits me, then. The energy in the house is lighter without Dad. Could our family be different now? Better, even, without the help of any lucky charms?

Guilt's icy grip numbs me from the inside out. I wince, having reached my capacity for soul-searching today. "Well, if you don't need anything, I have a deadline."

Her features scrunch together. "What did you decide about Henry's proposal?"

"Nothing yet."

She leans against the wall, eyeing me. "Will you ever write your own stories?"

Not this again. I narrow my gaze. "Why do you care?"

Her eyes cloud as she stares over my shoulder, one hand under her chin. Seconds later, she sighs and lets her hand fall to her side. "I don't want you giving up your dreams as easily as I did."

That confession temporarily renders me speechless.

"I haven't given up anything." I flush, because that isn't entirely true. "Publishing is fickle. I'm lucky to have a steady gig that pays the bills."

Her withering stare pierces my cover. We both know that despite my contempt for it, I've got a financial safety net.

Still, it's easier to babble than to give in. "Dad got sick. Sadie was energetic. There was a lot happening. Plus, I like the world and characters of my series. Ghostwriting has made me a stronger writer and Rachel gives me decent autonomy, so in a sense, these are my stories."

Dorothy shakes her head. "No, Emerson. Lie to me. Lie to the world, even. But don't lie to yourself. Every year you give up on your dreams will eventually catch up to you, and I promise you won't like it. Sadie will leave and start her own life soon. What will you have that's yours then?"

I draw back from her mirror, as if we are anything alike.

My next thought isn't kind or honest, but it will shut her down. "Whatever you think of my choices, at least I'm there for Sadie instead of drinking away my regrets."

She tips her chin up, holding my gaze. "You certainly inherited your father's taste for easy targets."

In the ensuing pause, I shrink by half my size.

"I'm going to lie down. Tell Sadie I'm setting aside the Picasso for her."

She moves away from the window, balancing herself with a hand grazing the wall.

"The signed lithograph?" *The Little Artist.* Probably worth fifty grand or more. "That's too much for a kid."

"She won't be a kid forever." With that warning—or threat—Dorothy moves past me, touching my shoulder briefly before leaving me in the kitchen.

Rooted in place, I mentally replay our conversation. Revisit her moods. Her words and behavior. As is true with Sadie, there's more going on than she's sharing. Maybe more than she's admitting to herself.

Should I follow Sadie's advice? Walk out the door and let Dorothy go to Manhattan to live her life. Rid myself of the obligation to check on her regularly or to beg her to try sobriety.

Let Dad's death kill whatever scraps of family remain.

For a moment, it sounds freeing.

Then reality closes in.

She's not perfect, but she's my mother, and she's been hurting for a long time. Abandoning her wouldn't make me happier. Dorothy is inching toward seventy, which also means we're running out of time to heal our relationship.

The tiresome narrative makes me hang my head as I slip out the side door into the shadows of the evening.

Once at home, I place the new items in my office. It looks like Sadie cleaned Mopsy's litter box. That's a win. I sift through the pile of mail on the kitchen counter and then carry the clean towels on the steps up to the linen closet.

Upstairs, I knock on Sadie's bedroom door as I open it. Our gazes lock, revealing our mutual surprise. Not only has she rearranged her furniture, but she's also sitting cross-legged amid piles of clothes on the floor while Mopsy lounges atop her bed.

"What's all this?" I ask.

She continues sorting things, averting her gaze. "I'm donating it."

Hundreds—no, thousands—of dollars' worth of garments lie around her, including a relatively new J.Crew sweater. I point at the navy cashmere cardigan. "That's practically new."

"Other people need these things more than I do." She folds a pair of faded Free People jeans.

Maybe so, but still. "Look, the impulse is generous, but you can't give away more than you keep."

"Why not? I haven't earned any of this. Why do I deserve so much?" Her voice catches ever so slightly. Is this purge prompted by guilt about sharing in the estate sale proceeds? Or has something else happened since she came home that makes her feel unworthy?

Her laptop sits open on her desk, facing away from me. Kids live entirely separate lives online, complete with fake names and multiple accounts. Did Johnny post something nasty or betray her confidence? Or worse, share a compromising photo? Could they be arrested for that?

"Honey . . ." I bite my lip, trying to reconcile these possibilities with the girl who picked out the blush-peach paint on the walls and still sleeps with stuffed animals. "Whatever's going on with you, I seriously doubt emptying your closet is the answer."

"Fine." Her resignation makes my heart sink more than if she'd put up a fight. "I'll put some things back in the keepers pile, okay?"

Shut out again. It's been only a week of this tension, yet I swear I'm getting an ulcer. Keeping my cool is all I can cling to. "I want to go through your donation pile before you take it anywhere."

She takes a deep breath, her expression a mask of indifference. No doubt she's thinking this is me being bossy again, but damn it, I paid for all those things.

"By the way, I saved you the collection of dainty jeweled frames from the living room. I know they're not your style now, but you might like them later. We could put some old photos of you with your grandparents in them."

"Okay." She nods without enthusiasm.

Hoping for more of her attention, I add, "Gran is giving you the Picasso lithograph."

Her head jerks up, brown eyes flickering with surprise. "Why?"

"Because you're special to her." And to me. Can't she feel my yearning to connect?

Sadie stacks a couple of shirts, her facial expression contorting as she shakes her head. "No kid has a Picasso, Mom. Maybe you keep it."

I can't disagree, but someday—a decade from now—she'll have a valuable piece of art to remind her of two people who loved her unconditionally. That stirs unexpected gratitude toward Dorothy. "I'll keep it until you can afford to insure it."

"All right." She grabs her phone from her pocket. "I'll text Gran a thank-you."

"A call would be nicer." That's not bossy. It's simply teaching good manners.

"Okay." When I don't immediately leave her room, she bugs her eyes to dismiss me.

"Sadie, I know you're upset about Johnny and Papa, so I've given you some leeway this week, but this attitude isn't how we treat each other."

"I'm sorry, okay? But you're so clingy. Please stop micromanaging me. I can manage my life my way." She rolls her eyes as if her tone wasn't disrespectful enough.

I touch my nose as if it could be bleeding. More surprising, however, is the second attack I don't see coming—that of a long-forgotten memory.

Dorothy was in the kitchen eating something, wineglass on the counter, when I ran past, upset because my father had torn apart my AP lit essay on *Atonement*.

Within minutes, she came into my room uninvited. I was curled around a pillow, facing away from her, when she sat at the edge of my bed and laid a hand on my hip. "Em, what happened?"

"Nothing," I mumbled, wishing with every fiber of my being that she'd leave me alone.

"Your father isn't used to evaluating high school book reports. His expectations aren't a fair estimate of what someone your age could write. Why don't you let me have a look?"

I whirled around on her, cheeks hot with embarrassment from being caught teary. "You think I can't write a good essay?"

She remained calm. "No. I'm certain it's very good. What I'm saying is that your father's not capable of offering appropriate feedback."

Her audacity to think herself more qualified made me scoff. "But *you* can?"

Her neck flushed as she pulled back, shoulders tensing. "I worked with kids in the library all the time."

"I'm not a kid, and besides, you've been drinking, so thanks but no thanks."

My mother didn't flinch, but her eyes shuttered against the hurricane force of my rejection.

Now my stomach turns queasy again, but not from any stomach bug.

Dorothy is right. I do share my dad's penchant for lashing out at the wrong people when cornered. And maybe my daughter does, too.

My mother's earlier warnings tap along my spine like bony fingers.

I could remind Sadie that not everyone has a parent who consistently showers them with love and attention. Unfortunately, that *would* smack of martyrdom. "Fine. I'll leave you be. Sandwiches for dinner. I'm not up to cooking." I close her door behind me, then thud down the stairs, heavy with hurt and regret.

In my office, I fish out the typewriter. Like before, it emits an unnerving quiver.

Dorothy said Dad acquired it before his first big contract. His ego wouldn't have given up control over his author voice, but it seems likely that he crafted wishes about achievement and recognition. Movie deals. Big advances. Hitting lists.

If that's true, most of what I've believed about the connection between his talent and his success is a lie. Every criticism he waged about my work might be unworthy of the weight I've given it. Every comparison between us might be an utter waste of my time.

I grab my face and groan, tempted to duck out to the garage.

My father deserves the benefit of the doubt. After all, I sat in his office while he scribbled hundreds of edits across thousands of printed pages. Saw him drag himself from city to city to connect with fans. It can't all have been a mirage.

Either way, I've no room to judge him now, having used this power to finesse things from my weight to meeting Mr. Right. If questioned about Henry's proposal, I'd shrink like a suspect in a police station interview room.

I wrap my arms around my waist and hang my head, trying to clear the thickness in my throat. Will I wear this shame forever, always looking over my shoulder, fearing exposure? Could this guilt be what dysregulated my father's moods? That alone should make me cautious.

After hiding the typewriter, I go to the kitchen to fix myself a grilled cheese.

Dorothy taught me to cook my favorite comfort meal when I was seven. Unlike my friends' Day-Glo orange sandwiches, we used Gruyère and provolone on sourdough, with a smear of dark mustard and lots of butter.

While I'm browning the bread, Dorothy's hurt expression revisits me like a bad dream. Nothing erases it. Not the comfort food. Not wiping down the refrigerator. Not reorganizing the Tupperware drawer. Not even having Mopsy purr in my lap while I stroke her fur. "I'm losing my way."

Tonight wasn't the first time that I've berated Dorothy. It was, however, the first time she's called me on it.

She's taken those hits for decades without fighting back. I wince upon the realization that my venom is one of the things she washes away with alcohol.

Releasing Mopsy, I bend forward to grab my knees. Memories of weaponizing past disappointments and justifying them as self-defense make my stomach burn. I've spent a lifetime viewing our family through only my lens, making assumptions about my parents' motives and thoughts. I never asked, though. I simply reacted to a reality created in my own head.

Hell. I'm not nearly as noble a daughter or person as I thought. As I would like to be. Now what?

Apologies have never been our family's thing, but I can give her what she asked for.

My thumb hovers over my mother's phone number, but I don't trust myself to speak. Instead, I text:

I'm sorry for being spiteful when you were encouraging me to believe in myself. Also, thank you for choosing something meaningful for Sadie to keep, and for letting me pick some things for myself. It will be strange not to call it home, but I understand why you want to move on. I'll reach out to Kathryn this week to sign off on the listing agreement. XO

The *X* and *O* feel more honest than an "I love you," three words we haven't exchanged in years. Not with her or my father. Once he got diagnosed, he became preoccupied with his illness, killing any hope of us ever getting back what we'd lost.

My head hurts now, so I rummage for some aspirin. An hour passes without any reply to my text. She could stay angry all evening, but I hope her silence is because she's fallen asleep.

I shouldn't leave things between us unsaid, especially not when I'd hate for Sadie to ever give up on me.

The first step toward mending fences should be easy enough. The time has come to stop referring to my mother as Dorothy.

Fourteen

On cranky days, I'd call myself bland. Nothing particularly sexy (no kitten eyes or pouty lips) or unflattering (like acne scars). Medium height and weight, moderately toned. A bookish girl next door with pale skin, chestnut hair, and curious green-hazel eyes.

Daring typically suits me about as well as a bikini—the idea is enticing, but the reality is mostly embarrassing. Tonight, however, the garnet-red dress flatters my coloring and accentuates my curves, making me feel like a solid eight on a scale of ten.

I spritz Jo Malone on my cleavage, snickering. "You girls haven't seen this much exposure in a decade."

Embracing the new look is difficult when my inner voice keeps shouting that I'm trying too hard. With a last tuck of stray hair, I hit the bathroom light, grab my purse off the bed, and stroll down the hall, stopping to knock on Sadie's door.

"Come in," she says.

It's Saturday evening, yet my teen is huddled on her bed with a book, tucked in with two of her favorite childhood stuffed lovies, Bibi and Mango. A hint of cinnamon spice tea wafts through the room while Mopsy lies curled at the foot of the mattress, sleeping.

It's one thing for a girl to spend a night or two nursing a breakup with cookie dough and a favorite rom-com. It's another to hide out from her friends all weekend. I miss the days when her biggest pain was a skinned knee and her only vexing behavior was the myriad questions she'd ask to delay bedtime.

Sadie's gaze travels from my head to my toes. "You look nice."

Bald astonishment undercuts her compliment.

"Thanks." I tug at the hem of the snug dress I puked up my guts to fit into.

"Where are you going?"

"Mel's birthday party, remember?"

"Oh yeah. You're dressed like you have a date." When I don't laugh off the remark, her gaze sharpens. "Wait—do you?"

Heat curls in my stomach. "I ran into my high school boyfriend the other day and asked him to the party."

Her brows gather with suspicion. "Why didn't you tell me?"

As if we've been so chummy lately. "I've had other priorities this week. Besides, it's no big deal. Just old friends catching up." I fidget with my bracelet, suddenly empathetic with Sadie's reluctance to discuss her love life before she's ready.

She sits forward, the pitch of her voice even more incredulous than when she complimented my outfit. "Do you even know anything about him anymore?"

"That's the point of getting reacquainted. It'll be fun."

"Or awkward." Sadie screws up her face. "What if he's a gold digger or, like, a perv?"

My mouth falls open. "I'm sure he's neither."

"Have you at least googled him?" Exasperation billows around her like smoke.

"No." Has he googled me? Not that there would be much to find. I'm more lurker than content provider. Still, a film of perspiration now threatens to ruin my makeup.

"What's his name?" Sadie demands as if she were the parent in the room. I'll take her concern as a win.

"Will Barnes."

She types the name into her phone. "I'll text you later if I find anything weird. Tell Aunt Mel I said happy birthday."

"I will." Before leaving her alone, I feel the edges of her mood for a soft spot to pry open. "What are you up to tonight?"

Sadie holds up her book—another in Sarah J. Maas's Crescent City series, similar in spirit to my *Fires* manuscript.

"It's a gorgeous evening. You should go eat with friends. Or see a movie. Or at least read on the porch." Each suggestion lands like a lead ball, or so it would seem given her impatient glare.

"Maybe." She directs her gaze back to the page, sending me on my way.

"I'll be home by midnight."

"Don't rush. I'm fine." She turns the page.

I step around the bags of clothes she intends to donate and then kiss the top of her head. "Love you. See you later."

"Bye." She barely looks up.

I close her door and hustle to my car, confident she won't learn something dreadful about Will. The typewriter might throw curveballs, but Mr. Right's criteria should preclude him from being a jerk.

Ten minutes later, the valet at Woodway Country Club takes my keys. At the same time, Will texts to say he's caught in traffic and will be fifteen minutes late.

The cocktail hour is in the Noroton Room, with its expansive mahogany bar, massive stone fireplace, and view of the club's ninth hole. Waiters circulate with trays of bacon-wrapped scallops and champagne flutes while the fifteen or so punctual guests sway along to the jazz combo's rendition of "Take Five."

Mel—a social butterfly—is expecting eighty people. Her boys are seven and nine, so she's still in the thick of things with this community, school, and sports.

Meanwhile, watching my parents navigate friendships taught me to be reticent in any group littered with social climbers. I rarely visit the club, nor do I work out at Club Pilates. My multiple writing commitments preclude much volunteering at the school—plus my kid is roughly a decade older than those of my peers.

Mel smiles when she sees me, then waves me over. Her silver sequins scratch my arms when we hug. I then give Chris a quick kiss on the cheek.

"You look great, Em," he says, winking. "If you'll excuse me, I need to check with the waitstaff about something." He slips away, leaving us alone.

"Ooh la la. Is that new?" I gesture to the emerald pendant around Mel's neck. Her dress is snug and deeply cut, drawing the eye to the jewelry.

"He spoils me." She fingers it fondly. "Meanwhile, you look amazing in that dress."

"Thanks." I don't confess to the pukefest. Mel is the last person who'd believe in the Underwood's powers and the first who'd call a psychiatrist. "Big change from jammy pants and a Springsteen concert tee."

"If only we weren't dying to whip off our Spanx," she jokes, letting loose a sigh. "Now that I'm forty, they'll be a wardrobe staple."

Hardly. The only thick thing on her entire body is her curtain of blond hair.

"Happy birthday." I grab her hand. "I know you said no gifts, but I cleared a weekend in early August with your assistant and Chris and rented us a cottage in Bar Harbor. We can hike in Acadia and be among the country's first to catch the sunrise, ushering in many more trips around the sun. Love you, friend."

"That sounds amazing." She hugs me again and then looks around. "Hey, I thought you were bringing a date?"

"He's caught in traffic but should be here soon."

She pins me with her litigator stare. "Who is he?"

"It's more fun to keep you guessing." Anticipation breathes fresh life into my heart.

"Well, well, this ought to be interesting." She raises her glass, then spies my empty hands. "Go get a drink. There's a special birthday cocktail—a lavender lemon-drop martini with a sugar rim. Delish."

"I'll be back." I make my way to the bar.

While I wait for the bartender's attention, Gina Yates, whose eldest daughter Haley is friends with Sadie, sidles up to me. She's never been shy about sharing her opinions on parenting, the schools, or any other thing. In other words, she's someone whose radar it's wise to fly under. "Hi, Gina. How have you been?"

"Good, good." She tilts her head, her shrewd gaze sharpening as she takes me in. "You look wonderful."

The string of shocked compliments is giving me a complex.

"So do you," I reply. Gina's wispy blond hair, ruffled pastel dress, and pale pink lipstick are deceptively soft and welcoming.

"I'm sorry about your father. You're too young to lose a parent." She surprises me by squeezing my wrist firmly.

"Thank you." No need to elaborate. She's known about my father's illness for some time. "How's Haley?"

"Eager for summer." Gina sips her cocktail while I finally order mine. "Haley says Sadie's been in a funk since the funeral."

Even her friends are talking? I recover myself before she detects my concern. "She's been sullen. Part of that is grief over my dad, but I think it might also have to do with Johnny breaking up with her."

Gina shakes her head while swallowing another sip. "She broke up with him."

I flush, my thoughts scattering like loose change. "I didn't realize. She's being rather stoic at home."

"Haley told me. The girls were stunned. Apparently, Johnny is, too. Sadie won't give anyone a reason for her change of heart." Gina stares at me as if trying to read my thoughts.

Sadie wouldn't be depressed about breaking up with Johnny unless she felt forced into that decision because he hurt her.

"Emerson, are you all right?" Gina snaps her fingers in front of my face.

"Sorry. Yes, just concerned." My stomach is sour. If Sadie's hiding something from everyone, it's got to be pretty bad. "Listen, I hope Haley and the others don't make Sadie's breakup the lead subject of school gossip."

"Of course not. Haley only told me because she was feeling shut out. I told her to be patient and let Sadie mourn her grandfather."

"Thanks." My assessment of Gina softens. Meanwhile, I can't let my daughter's friendships fall apart just because she's as stubborn as my father. "Hey, is Haley free tomorrow? Maybe I'll pull together a get-together as a little pick-me-up for everyone."

"She's babysitting for our neighbors in the afternoon but should be free by four."

"Perfect." My stomach settles a bit upon making a plan. "Please ask her to text the gang about coming over at five. Whoever can make it. It'd be great if they could keep it a surprise from Sadie, too. I'll take care of the rest."

Gina's husband, Denny, calls to her, so she excuses herself, leaving me alone with my thoughts.

The crowd has already doubled in size since I arrived. I'm a world-class introvert, so parties hover near the top of my list of least favorite things. Making small talk with acquaintances is harder than learning a new language.

Will arrives at the exact moment I'm thinking how glad I'll be when he shows up, proving it's kismet. He's striking, dressed in charcoal slacks and a black shirt paired with a black linen blazer. A full-body flutter erupts, exactly like it used to whenever he showed up at a school dance.

He's scanning the crowd, so I raise my arm to wave. When he catches sight of me, he smiles and begins cutting through the crowd.

"You look gorgeous." He kisses my cheek. "All grown up."

A delicious tingle traces along my spine, tempting me to touch the spot where his lips met my skin. "Thanks. Same to you."

"Sorry about the delay. Ninety-five was a nightmare." His look of frustration is familiar to anyone who lives along the interstate corridor.

"Grab a drink," I say, raising my voice to compete with the band.

"Don't mind if I do." He steps up to the bar and flags a bartender. Sadie hasn't texted, so she mustn't have found anything "cringy" to report.

Will leans over the bar to receive his beverage and leave a tip. I use that time to scan the room for Mel's sparkler of a dress.

"So, where's Mel?" Will sips his whiskey.

"Possibly freshening up." Now what? Suddenly my tongue feels ten sizes too large for my mouth.

Sadie is right. All he and I have in common is a brief part of the past. Tonight could be more grueling than a blind date.

Following an awkward silence, I say, "Well, Will, catch me up on the past twenty years."

"Hmm." He scratches behind his ear, an old habit that butts in like a long-lost friend. "The short bio. Went to the U-M, fell in love with an ambitious woman, moved to New York for her consulting job, worked for an art gallery until I landed at Christie's. Divorced four years ago but share a son, Duncan, who's twelve. Currently hurtling through middle age wondering if my hair is disappearing to the same place all the missing socks go." He laughs unselfconsciously, which makes my heart swell. "Now you."

"Okay. Went to Wesleyan. Worked as a technical writer for a decade and now as a ghostwriter for a bestselling author. Never married, but have a daughter, Sadie, who's seventeen and the true love of my life." He might judge me for having never married. Instantly Mel's voice storms my thoughts, screaming, *Cut the patriarchal bullshit!*

"If my son is anything like me and my brothers, I'm dreading his teen years," Will says.

Memories of the Barnes brothers make me chuckle. They would sit on each other and pass gas, pants each other in front of friends, and steal their parents' liquor. One got caught driving without a license. Another hosted a house party during which someone broke a window. And even Will let his hormones drag him out of bed late at night to meet me down on our dock.

"They say our kids come back around in their twenties." I hold up crossed fingers because things are moving in the wrong direction at home. "Sorry about your divorce."

"It's toughest on Duncan. He lives with me and sees his mom on the weekends she's in town. He's a great kid. I hope I don't screw him up." He rocks back on his feet, swirling the ice in his glass.

A parent who cares about being a good one usually is. Shared parenting worries are as good a place as any to start reconnecting.

"You could never." A swell of fondness moves me as I picture Will making pancakes for himself and his son, sitting down to talk about school or sports or whatever boys and fathers discuss. "He's lucky to have your good humor to guide him."

"Always kind." He squeezes my hand briefly. "It's wild being here, seeing you after all this time."

"Same." I flex my hand, missing his. "It's the perfect pick-me-up."

He frowns sympathetically. "Again, so sorry about your dad."

"Thanks." There's not much more I can say, honestly. My father's history comes with a truckload of musty emotions that shouldn't be aired at a party. Especially not while I'm so confused about my family.

"And your mom?" He samples his whiskey. "Will she stay in that house?"

The unexpected question catches me out.

"She could not be in a bigger hurry to downsize. She's even talking about moving to Manhattan, although I hope that idea fizzles." I glance away to let that worry pass.

"Some people need a big change to get through an emotional transition."

"Some people, yes, but you knew my parents. My mother isn't suffering from a broken heart. If anything, she's feeling freer than ever." I drop my gaze to my glass, wishing I'd said less.

Will dips his head to get my attention. "That must be hard, even if you aren't surprised."

Sadie's suspicions were totally unfounded. He's a good guy, but our conversation still makes me uncomfortably warm. "It is."

"You'll miss that house, though. Great property. Better artwork, if memory serves." He glances into his glass before sipping from it again. "Will she sell any of it?"

"Most of it, actually. She's already looking for an appraiser."

He bows like a Shakespearean actor, rolling his wrist a few times. "At your service, my lady. Christie's does everything from estate appraisal to selling, including safeguarding your anonymity, if that's a concern."

His expectant demeanor gives off used-car salesman vibes.

"Oh, wow." My momentary distaste evaporates when I realize this would give us a reason to interact in the coming weeks. "Of course. Yes. What a lucky break that I ran into you."

He nods happily. "Indeed."

Out of nowhere, a hand slaps Will's shoulder from behind and Mel calls out, "Marco!"

Will turns around, answering, "Polo!" before they both burst into laughter and hug.

I stand aside, missing the joke.

Mel asks, "What's with the look?"

"What's with the weird greeting?" I shrug.

Will and she both pull a face before she says, "Naked Marco Polo, duh."

I scoff. "What?"

"You're kidding, right?" She pushes at my shoulder before exchanging a glance with Will. "My parents were away; you two came over."

"With my cousin Damien from Greenwich—remember? He was older than us and could drive," Will adds.

"When it got dark, we skinny-dipped and played Marco Polo. That was my first look at a guy's . . . ya know." Mel winks.

There's only a vague tickle where a memory should be. My mother's concerns about my genetics surface, but I cover with a lie. "Oh yeah, I remember."

"I'll never forget it," Will teases.

Mel's suspicious stare lingers a moment before she turns her attention to Will. "Will Barnes in the flesh. I can't believe my eyes."

"Happy birthday, Mel." He busses her cheek. "You haven't changed a bit."

She raises her arms and shimmies. "Still a girl who loves a good time . . . well, once in a blue moon, anyway. Most of the time I'm in a courtroom or being a mom."

We all sip from our glasses as we fumble for something clever or poignant to say.

"How did you two reconnect?" Mel asks.

"Gassing up while running errands. Three minutes either way and we would've missed each other." I grin, knowing the odds on that timing are so long it had to be the typewriter.

"I'd just finished meeting with a client about some artwork," Will adds. "I live in Larchmont, though."

"Well, I'll have to introduce you to my husband Chris. He's around here somewhere." Mel glances around.

Will's phone rings. He checks the screen and answers, "Hey, Susie, what's up?"

Is Susie his ex?

I stand a little straighter, pretending not to notice the way Mel is eyeing me like she wants the scoop in the middle of the party.

"All right. I'll be there in thirty minutes—forty-five tops." He stuffs his phone in his jacket pocket, then makes a face. "That was my babysitter. Duncan just threw up and he's running a low temperature. Susie can't risk getting sick because she has a big tennis tournament next week."

"Poor baby. I hope it passes quickly." Please don't let this illness be collateral damage from my wish. Then it occurs to me that Will might have a friend on standby to extract him from this date.

"I'm sure it will. Sorry the timing sucks," he says, grimacing. "I feel terrible for ducking out so soon. Rain check?"

Okay. Overthinking, as usual. This wasn't a blind date, so there was no need for him to concoct a plan B.

"Kids first. We can catch up any time." If I'm being honest, it'll be more relaxing to celebrate with Mel when I'm not feeling self-conscious around Will.

"Still a doll," he says, leaning in to give me a quick hug. That endearment always felt like a compliment in high school, but tonight it sounds slightly patronizing. "Let's follow up on the estate stuff."

"Of course." I squeeze his hand before he goes. "Drive safely."

"Bye, Will," Mel says before she drains her glass.

He salutes us both and then weaves through the crowd.

Mel is wearing a funny grin ogling Will's butt as he walks away. "Will was so immature, I can't believe he's someone's dad. Guess he grew up."

"Immature?" That's not how I remember him. Then again, it's possible I glossed over any shortcomings because it'd felt wonderful to have someone's undivided attention.

"Uh, yeah." She emphasizes that by bugging her eyes. "I never understood why you moped over him for three whole months."

"We'd just started having sex. It seemed like the end of the world when he left." That much I do remember.

She pauses. "Not to be indelicate, but could that be why Sadie's so blue?"

Closing my eyes doesn't alleviate the pang of discomfort. "I've considered that, but it doesn't explain why she broke up with Johnny."

"Maybe he pressured her?" All the teasing light in Mel's eyes vanishes, replaced by the world-weary gaze of a criminal defense lawyer.

I clench my cocktail glass. "Honestly, he doesn't seem the type."

Mel tilts her head. "There's no such thing as a type, Em."

The truth of that fact settles like toxic dust, making me itch. "It's only been a week. She's not crying all the time or hurting herself, just being stoic."

"Gee, wonder where she learned that?"

The little jab hits me harder than she imagines. "I'm keeping a close eye."

"I'm here for you guys. You know that." Mel puts an arm around me, which makes me feel less alone.

"Thanks."

She sighs. "Sorry Will left early. Hope you charged your vibrator."

We laugh again. "Actually, it's fine. I'll see him soon enough."

My confidence is due almost entirely to the typewriter. I'm already mentally skipping ahead to the next time we get together and rediscover each other on a more personal basis. Naked Marco Polo could be a very different game at this age.

Why don't I remember that, though?

"What's wrong?" Mel asks.

"Nothing. Just thinking about my dad," I say, which isn't entirely untrue.

Fifteen

The next afternoon, Sadie is sitting at the kitchen counter with Mopsy and a glass of chocolate milk when I come through the back door carrying two large veggie pizzas.

"What's all this?" She drains her glass, eyeing the pizza boxes.

"Surprise!" I singsong, wishing she were still in her room avoiding me until everything was organized. I set the pizzas down to turn on the oven while glancing at the kitchen clock: 4:40 PM. Twenty minutes to reheat these. "I thought you could use some laughs with your friends. They'll be here any minute."

"What?" She jumps off the stool, cheeks red as apples. Mopsy senses an oncoming storm and scoots out of the kitchen. "Why?"

"Last night Mrs. Yates told me Haley felt a little boxed out. You've spent all weekend alone, so I thought a little get-together might lift everyone's spirits." I maintain my calm as if I'm not facing a firing squad.

She wraps her ponytail around her wrist while her expression tightens with distress. "I can't believe you invited my friends over without asking me first."

"That's generally how a surprise works." For most of her life, I've arranged playdates and parties, so the idea didn't feel strange at the time.

My bad, apparently. "There's ice cream in the freezer and a fresh pitcher of sun tea in the fridge."

Turning away from her glower, I open the lids of the boxes and slide each pizza into the oven.

"Unbelievable, Mom." She smacks her palm against the counter. "What if I don't want to have to smile and pretend to be happy with my friends right now?"

"It's too late to cancel." I grip my waist as if my fingertips were holding me together. "Your friends don't understand why you're avoiding them, and neither do I."

"So you force me to do what you want instead of letting me decide for myself what I need?" A bitter tone conflicts with her panicked expression. "Who's coming?"

"Haley, Prisha, and Sarah. Maybe Colette." I raise my arms at my sides apologetically. "I'm sorry. I was trying to do something nice, Sadie. I'm worried about you. Aren't you even a little concerned about your friends' hurt feelings?"

Sadie closes her eyes and draws a deep breath. "Papa just died and Johnny and I broke up. They should understand my need to be alone has nothing to do with them."

The doorbell rings, interrupting us.

"Just great." She fakes a broad grin. "Now I get to do this for the next two hours. So fun!"

Maybe it was presumptuous to go behind her back, but her overreaction is obnoxious. "I said I'm sorry, but please make the best of it for your friends' sake."

She marches out of the kitchen to answer the door. The other girls' voices reach me before they enter the kitchen.

"Hey, Ms. Clarke!" Haley resembles her mother, with loose blond waves and delicate features. "My mom said you looked amazing last night."

"Aw, thanks, honey." The reminder of everyone's shock and awe does me in. "Well, pizzas are warming in the oven. Make yourselves at home. I'll be in my office working if you need anything."

Sadie is standing behind them glaring at me. I slip away and hide in my office, hopeful that, when her friends leave, she'll admit she feels better.

With my deadline flashing like a railroad crossing signal, I close my door and open the laptop to make myself focus on *Tropic Heat*.

I go over the last two pages to reorient myself in the story, but a few lines of dialogue later and my thoughts are already wandering to Henry's proposal.

Old notes regarding my dad's outline for the eighth Pandemonium book are saved on my computer. I click on them and reread, which reminds me of an ongoing debate with Dad about a plot twist. He never came up with anything shocking that didn't also conflict with something in a prior book. It was one of the reasons he struggled to move forward.

Out of curiosity, I then open my old *Fires* manuscript. Thinking about the Hallah Empire and the relationship between Hestia and Kreios revs me up in a way that Rachel's book hasn't lately.

While reading the first chapter, I'm smiling the entire time. Sure, my craft has improved tremendously since I penned this manuscript, but there's potential here. I glance at the photo on my desk. "You dismissed this too quickly."

It'd be easy to get sidetracked for hours, but my current deadline is real. *Fires* must wait until I hit my daily word count.

I switch back to Roman and Laura and the danger stalking them in the dunes of Glass Beach. I left them hijacking a two-man kayak to flee the killer. Now they're trapped in the Alligator River National Wildlife Refuge, with Roman injured.

An hour later, I've written a solid chunk of the new chapter. The rest can wait until I have a good night's sleep and a clear head.

Through my window, I see the girls chatting in the driveway before they hug Sadie and get into Haley's car.

"Thank god." My shoulders relax for the first time in two hours. I push back from my desk to check the kitchen for leftover pizza.

Sadie comes back inside as I'm turning the corner. I raise my shoulders in question. "Was that so awful?"

"That's not the point, Mom. I'm old enough to make my own decisions and you should respect them." She keeps walking toward the stairs.

"Hang on." I wait until she stops and faces me. "I've already apologized for overstepping, but it isn't easy to watch you suffer all week and do nothing. Your silence is making everyone worry."

"Like I keep saying, this isn't about what you or my friends or even Johnny needs or feels. This is about me and what I need."

My heart is lashed over and over as the ties that bind us snap one by one. When she goes to college, will she turn even further away? "As your mother, I'll always be concerned when you're sad, but I will try to give you space."

"Good," she says, then trots upstairs with Mopsy on her trail.

Head hung, I stalk into the kitchen.

The pizza boxes are crushed and put in the trash. The dishes and glasses are in the dishwasher. There's no trace of ice cream drippings on the counter.

Maybe I should trust her to clean up whatever it is she's hiding from me, too.

Sixteen

JEFFERSON'S JOURNAL

October 5, 2009

I fucked up. Big-time.

Broke my 2002 rule against using the typewriter in connection with my family that I instituted after inadvertently shipping Emerson's teen boyfriend out of town.

Back then, her grades were slipping because she'd gotten too distracted by that walking hormone. It galled me that her heart was in it more than his. That cocky kid wasn't worth derailing her GPA and future.

I should've been more careful, though. "A little space" might've caused less upheaval than a major breakup. Subconsciously I must've wanted him gone. But Jesus, I didn't foresee the boxes of tissue it'd take before she got over that guy.

That made me feel shitty. Today, however, is worse.

If only I hadn't sensed that Dorothy was preparing to leave me. Sensed—Ha! She consulted a lawyer.

She says I'm a narcissist. I don't think so. I'm driven, not selfish.

Sure, I have plans and goals, but I've always brought my girls along for the ride. I've given them everything a person could possibly want. What's selfish about that?

Anyway, she'd threatened to leave once before, but her drinking gave me the upper hand in any custody fight, so she stayed.

Our relationship has continually deteriorated since Em first went to college, despite my paying for her parents' nursing home in Vermont. And the marriage counseling we attended for six months to learn to "communicate" better. I'm a writer, for fuck's sake. I know how to communicate!

Her drinking is still a problem, but Dorothy functions all right even when she's not sober. And I like having her around.

She's comfortable and familiar, like a favorite pair of slippers. Sure, I could find fancy new ones if I lost mine, but Dorothy loved me before I was famous. She believed in me when no one else did. She was my first muse.

I don't want a divorce, and not just so she can't take half of everything.

Our marriage is less than ideal, but I won't let her leave me. She's fiery and unerringly honest. She also keeps track of things, which is becoming increasingly important because of my tendency to forget details.

At first I thought Dorothy was giving me a hard time about that, but it's getting harder to write them all off as the hazards of a creative mind and overcommitted schedule.

Anyway, my latest screwup came about because I confronted my wife about her lawyer. Tried everything to get her to call it off, but nothing worked. Not compliments. Not gifts. I swore I'd change. She said I couldn't. She wasn't bluffing, and that scared me.

So I got drunk and broke my own rule, typing a wish for "anything" to keep her from walking out the door.

Yes, manipulative. Yes, hasty and ill-considered. Yes, selfish. Guess maybe I am a narcissist—but my feelings should matter, too.

For two days, nothing happened. I was almost relieved that maybe I'd butted up against yet another limitation.

Then today felled me.

Em just left after announcing that the boyfriend who knocked her up but wouldn't marry her had just dumped her. She swallowed her pride—and that's a big damn swallow—to ask if she could move back in for a while when the baby is born.

Of course she needs our help. She's still a baby herself, starting her first job with no plan for how to support herself and a child. It's killing her to admit that. She's always wanted to prove she doesn't need me—except now she does. For a while, at least.

The defeat in her eyes fills me with rage—toward Doug and toward myself.

I'm not mad about the pregnancy, but my daughter deserved to first find a guy who realized she hung the fucking moon. A guy who'd marry her because he knew he'd never find better. Babies could've come later.

Now she's not only heartbroken by that asshole, she's demoralized, too.

At first I was too furious to see the connection to my lucky charm. But the minute Emerson left the house, Dorothy began making plans to convert a spare bedroom to a nursery. She won't be going anywhere as long as Em and our grandchild are living here.

I got my wish, but at what cost? My daughter's happiness and self-esteem? That's too fucking much.

The damn typewriter. Sure, maybe I could fix this with another wish. Something that gives Em a win—like getting her an agent or something. But I'm afraid to risk causing more trouble for her or, God forbid, the baby.

A baby.

Me, a grandfather.

I hope it's a girl. Adorable and bright-eyed, just like my Em.

I swear I'll be devoted. I'll make up for this screwup by giving Em and her baby everything they need. Absolutely everything.

Seventeen

Most people bemoan Mondays, but Tuesdays are my least favorite day. Monday is a blank page on which to create a perfect week of daily exercise, healthy eating, and high productivity. By Tuesday—or rather Tuesday afternoons—my grand plans typically fall apart.

My downfall can be triggered because I've fallen behind on a story and can't squeeze in exercise, or I need a boost (aka chocolate) to keep writing, or I'm mentally blocked from revising the shitty words written on Monday. Sometimes all three.

Today I've hit the Oreos. More than two, less than a sleeve. Even Mopsy raised her head off the chair at one point as if she were thinking, *For the love of God, stop!*

There was also the hour spent experimenting with a draft of the first chapter of *Pandemonium Resurrected,* the would-be final Pandemonium book.

The story and characters came naturally, but mimicking my dad's writing voice was a challenge. It may not be possible to sustain for six hundred pages. Then there are my personal preferences—subjective editorial choices—that differ from his original vision for this story.

These misgivings weigh heavily on my conscience and make me queasy. I swivel toward the urn.

"Mel's right. I'm being emotional." I tenderly run my fingers along the urn's edges. "I wish you hadn't gotten sick. I wish . . ."

So many things. Tapping my fingers isn't helping me decide anything. Meanwhile, *Tropic Heat* is due in three weeks. I open that document, but then my email pings.

Will!

My heart skips like a young girl holding a balloon.

To: Emerson@ecwrites.com
From: wbarnes@christies.com
Re: Appraisal

Emerson,

Thanks for circling back. Your mother undoubtedly owns many heritage pieces that we'd be honored to appraise and help you sell. I'd be happy to meet with you both this week. Does Thursday at 11 AM suit?

I've attached the FAQ about the process. There are no fees associated with the preliminary visit and estimate. I can explain more about how things work when we meet.

Sincerely,
Will

Such formality. If he'd asked me to review a manuscript he wrote, I would've responded in a tone that matched the fact that, once upon a time, we saw each other naked.

The stiff-arm has me on the defensive. Again. That conditioning is hardwired at this age. My former therapist's advice pushes through the noise in my head. *Perhaps a starting place for change is to stop second-guessing other people's intentions.*

Will's work emails might be monitored. He may even have thought my inquiry was equally impersonal. It still would've been nice if he'd offered to discuss this over coffee. Something—anything—considering he offered a rain check.

What if Will isn't Mr. Right?

He'd been luminous in those dark teenage nights, but perhaps I misread his glimmer for something more substantial. His reappearance now could be nothing more than a sign to stop looking backward if I want to move forward.

A second reading of his email gleans nothing between the lines.

"Stop acting Sadie's age," I mutter, clicking out of email and calling my mother to check her schedule.

"Hello," she answers.

Three o'clock and no slurring. Heartening.

"Mom, I found an appraiser to handle the estate sale."

"Who?"

"I ran into Will Barnes, of all people. He works for Christie's and can meet us at the house late Thursday morning. Does that work for you?"

"The high school boyfriend?" Her voice lilts upward, suggesting she, too, has fond memories of him. "That's quite a coincidence."

"Mmm-hmm." Maybe. Maybe not.

Unless coincidence is a concept someone conceived to explain magic in terms that others could comprehend. Mel thinks the energy we put out brings about the things we want or need. I'm a skeptic because none of the energy I put into healing my family ever helped.

"He was a charmer." My mother's lilting tone plucks a minor chord in my chest. "Is he married?"

"Divorced. One son. Living in Larchmont." Our brief date left me with more questions than answers. "Anyway, can I confirm?"

"Thursday works. But, Emerson, the safecracker comes tomorrow at nine. I don't want to be here for that. Can you meet her?"

"Yes." My knees begin bouncing. Info about the Underwood must be stowed in there. "You really won't stay?"

"No." My mother grunts. Relief whooshes through me until she adds, "Unless there's something imperative, Jefferson can take his locked-up secrets to his grave."

Her voice hardens the way it used to whenever he'd been unfaithful.

She's probably speculating about a surprise birth certificate. With Dad, anything's possible. *Destroy evidence.* That reminder dampens my eagerness to open the safe.

The clink of ice against crystal chimes through the phone line. Gin before dinner. I shake my head.

"Another neighbor dropped off a lasagna today. Do you and Sadie want to come over for dinner?" Her voice is embroidered with affection.

If she hadn't started drinking, it would've been a tempting offer.

"I'm under the gun with my deadline." Not a lie, but not the whole truth. I doodle on a Post-it pad. "Sorry. Maybe another time."

"Sure." Her cooled tone sinks into my skin like teeth. She's probably sitting at the kitchen island, lights off, every sound echoing in the vast canyons of space.

Loneliness drives people to the bottle.

No. That's the sneaky way hope slips inside, yet our history reminds me my company has never once stopped her from drinking.

I grab my forehead with my free hand, shoulders slouching under the weight of her disappointment and my omnipresent guilt. "I'll be there tomorrow morning."

"Thank you."

After hanging up, I stare blankly, second-guessing myself.

When I was in high school, short stories about our family dramas filled my diaries. The twist in each was a happily ever after, unlike our real life. Now that could change. Once I learn the typewriter's rules, I can craft a real-life epic redemption story for us all.

Contrary to Sadie's accusations, this isn't about a need for control. My wishes are about making my family healthier and happier. Who could disagree that my mother's drinking is bad for her or that a sullen teen keeping secrets isn't safe? Yes, these changes would alleviate my worry, but they'd benefit each of them more by making their lives more joyful. That's not selfishness.

After turning off the office lights, I go to the kitchen to refill my water glass, then open the refrigerator. Its contents are sparse—half a bag of lettuce, two kinds of cheese, some apples and berries, deli turkey Sadie won't eat, eggs, milk, yogurt, and syrup.

If I'd accepted my mother's invitation, we could be eating lasagna.

I close the door as if that might shut out the internal voice nagging me. The one that whispers there might be more honorable ways to fix our family without resorting to typed pages.

Eighteen

The locksmith's van is already in my parents' driveway ten minutes ahead of the scheduled appointment. I park beside it, grab the empty gym bag off the passenger seat, and exit my car at the same time the locksmith climbs out of her van.

This morning's stiff air is heavily perfumed with the sulfuric aroma of Long Island Sound. Summer is coming. Our last one here. Pausing, I take in the lush grounds while the pang passes through my chest.

"Good morning. Sorry to keep you waiting." I shake hands with the squatty woman dressed in black pants and a white pullover emblazoned with her company's logo.

"No problem. I'm Dot." Her sleek silver hair is pulled into a short ponytail. She's carrying a tool kit cross-body style. Bright blue eyes that look like they can see through anything or anyone gaze at the thick dentil moldings and the classic black shutters embellishing the house. "Wow. This is gorgeous."

"Thank you. It's a lovely home, but my mother is ready to downsize." I gesture toward the cardinal-red door. "Let's go in."

"Sure."

When we enter the house, I shiver in the air-conditioning. Dot pulls paper footies over her work boots while I kick my shoes off by the front door. "The safe is in my father's office."

She swirls her hand in the air. "Lead the way."

We wander through the entry and the back hallway, my pulse pounding. I stumble along the way, catching myself against the doorjamb. There are stacks of empty cardboard boxes beside the old leather chair. My mother must've put them here for me to fill with his personal items.

Every day we erase my dad a little more. I hug myself as if doing so will also somehow hold on to my better memories.

"Ahem." Dot reminds me that she's waiting.

"Sorry." I open the cabinet doors to reveal the safe, thinking of my mother's worst fears. "I'm a little anxious about what we'll find."

Dot chuckles and waves her hand. "More often than not they're empty."

"Really?"

"Yeah. Even when they're full, it's usually with papers like a will, car titles, birth certificates—stuff people like to protect from fires. Now and then there's some jewelry or cash, but don't get your hopes up."

"I won't." Those aren't the things that would excite me anyway.

God willing, there'll be a manual for the Underwood. Or a certificate of origin. Anything that could help me understand it and my father better.

Perhaps there will also be information about the Welles heir or DES. I pray it's nothing that would force me to choose between doing what's right and protecting his legacy. Until recently, my integrity was unshakable. Now it feels like grief has compromised my moral compass. I don't need another test when the lucky charm already provides a lifetime's worth of moral ambiguity.

I kneel beside my gym bag and look in the cabinet. Dot joins me on the floor, setting out some kind of drill.

"What's that?" I ask.

"A borescope. If I can't listen and feel for the right combination, this helps me drill into the right part of the safe to dismantle the lock. Hopefully it won't be necessary."

"I'll be quiet." I scoot away to give her enough space to get comfortable and focus.

Safecracking could be an interesting career for a heroine in a book.

My thoughts unfurl, making up a character backstory as different from my privileged suburban one as possible. Only daughter in a family of boys. Grew up in the wilds of Maine with three German shepherds. Eschews convention and designer labels, except for her penchant for fine champagne and silk lingerie. Her great-grandfather was a bank robber who died in a shootout outside of Boston.

It seems like no time passes before Dot has opened the safe.

"That was fast." My breath quickens in anticipation. "Makes the safe seem kind of useless."

She opens the door a crack before stuffing her tools back into her bag and pushing herself off the floor with a small grunt. "Most home safes can be opened pretty quickly with a crowbar or a drill. It takes time to learn to feel the combination, but anyone can do it."

"Interesting."

"It's a living," Dot teases, seeming nothing like the character I just invented. "Anyhow, it's your safe to open. I keep my hands clean so I can't be accused of palming something."

"That's happened?"

She nods. "People get weird and convince themselves that something was in there that wasn't."

"That must be unnerving." I pull the cash out of my back pocket and hand it to her, glad I'll be alone when opening the safe. "Thanks so much. Let me see you to the door."

We walk through the house in silence again, with me mentally projecting ahead to how my father's handbook will help me craft artful wishes without twists.

"You have a good summer," Dot says when we finally part ways.

After waving goodbye, I seal myself inside the house, my stomach suddenly a tangle of bees. I pace the hallway, rubbing my abdomen, slowing my breath.

Each time I rifle through my dad's private things, I risk discovering something that'll destroy my belief in his basic goodness. That would be a loss worse than his death.

My mother might have the right idea. I could toss the contents directly into a trash bag. And yet there could be something amazing, like a draft of an unpublished manuscript.

Despite my earlier zeal, I'm unprepared for this moment. For the truth. For how the contents might blow my family apart for good. The path back to his office feels like my own kind of Green Mile.

I kneel in front of the safe, placing my hand on the handle. My heart is beating so hard, I can practically hear it. With a determined huff, I pull the door open.

Empty!

Stars blind me before they shatter along with my hope for answers. I reach inside, placing my palm against the cold metal. This can't be right. I stick my head inside the box in disbelief before falling back onto my butt. "Damn it!"

Why keep an empty safe locked? Why keep an empty safe?

Unless he cleared it out after his diagnosis . . .

Destroy evidence.

The weight of possibilities keeps me pinned there despite the whoosh of relief that comes with realizing there'll be no need for damage control.

My questions about him and the typewriter remain unanswered. All that's clear is that he never wanted us near it.

With a sharp inhale, I look upward. The butterfly effect of any wish, let alone decades of them, is staggering. Incriminating, too. Unforgivable, maybe. This could be the first time in ages that my mom and I have free will. That alone could change everything for the better.

He should've gotten rid of the good-luck charm along with whatever he removed from the safe. Leaving it behind without providing us warnings or instructions was beyond reckless.

A surge of energy propels me off the floor to tear his office apart, shelf by shelf, hunting for answers.

Two hours later, I've flipped through every single book. Some are scattered on the floor, others tossed in boxes. I'm sweating and flustered, having found nothing about the typewriter or Welles or DES. Not even the curio cabinet key. That can't have simply vanished. It must be here somewhere.

"It looks like a tornado whipped through here." My mother's voice startles me. She's wearing yoga pants and a loose top, with her hair held back by a headband. One fist is on her hip; her other hand holds a water bottle that probably contains gin.

Flushed, I tuck my own hair behind my ears. "I didn't hear you come in."

"I walked to the beach and back with MaryBeth." She eyes me more carefully, then pulls back as if steeling herself. "You look upset. What did you find?"

I shake my head. "The safe was empty."

"Empty?" She sniggers with some humor. "Doesn't that just figure."

Tears well, but I can't share the reason behind my disappointment, so I blink them into submission. "I . . . I'm sorting through his things to decide what to keep or discard. Are you sure you don't want any of the awards or leather-bound books?"

"I'm sure."

My arms remain stiffly at my side. Overwhelmed, overwrought, overtired—all the overs frothing inside. "Mom, for better or worse, this all was a big part of your life, too. You helped make this possible. Don't any of these reminders mean anything to you?"

"Nothing in here was about me or us." Her voice sharpens as she gestures around the office. "This was all *his*. He stopped inviting me in here a long time ago, so I have no desire to preserve it now that he's gone."

My front-row seat to the drama of onetime lovers breaking each other sits at the heart of my trust issues. There's no way to change that ending now that he'd dead. I drop my chin, depleted and not wholly unsympathetic. I might share her disdain if Dad had boxed me out of here, too.

"All right. I'll come back to finish this later. My deadline got pushed up. I'm falling further behind every day."

She lifts one brow. "Have you made a decision about Henry's offer?"

"Not yet." I hug myself. "Can't decide which choice I'll regret less."

Her expression softens, but her gaze is unsettling. "My darling Emerson, forget regrets. Make the decision that is best for you."

With a shrug, I admit, "I don't see the difference."

"Maybe that's my fault." My mother's posture sags. "You grew up watching me lose myself to so much indecision. Please find your way back faster than I did." She glances out the window before drawing herself up again and walking away.

The tears I've been holding back begin to roll down my cheeks in thick trails. Nothing is going according to my plans—not my career, not my relationship with Sadie, not getting closer to the truth about my father. I'm so tired. So damn tired.

I wipe my face and stare at the mess I've made, not at all certain it will ever be put in order.

Nineteen

Leaving home without answers—what a perfect metaphor for my life these past two weeks. A lost place between what was and what could've been. All the might-haves and should-haves eating away at me. What I'd give to feel another hug or see my dad's mischievous wink or hear one last *I love you.*

When Kurt Cobain died, Frances Bean's loss seemed unimaginable, but I'd figured she would have his videos and songs to get to know him. In that way, he would live forever.

My father can also be reanimated through the interviews, podcasts, and lectures floating around the internet. At home, I stride straight to my office, open my laptop, and bring up YouTube, typing my dad's name in the search bar.

"Which one, Dad? Which one?" I scroll through the various clips that populate the screen.

The 2010 interview with David Letterman was one of his favorites. He'd reached the pinnacle of his career, riffing with Letterman with his full charm offensive.

I hit PLAY and there he is, bearing the confidence of a man who couldn't lose.

The sound of his voice delivers a chop to my throat. I should've prepared myself better to hear that deep timbre from healthier days.

With my eyes closed, I'm a child again, listening to his Kris Kringle belly laugh.

Before the limo arrived that day to take us to the city for the taping, my dad came into the kitchen dressed in black from head to toe except for a harlequin-patterned gold-and-fuchsia vest.

"Jefferson, what on earth? Take that off and try a nice tie," Mom said.

He tucked his thumbs inside the vest by his armpits. "I want to be memorable."

"Not that way, you don't." Her left brow arched comically.

He looked at Sadie, who'd been only one. "You like it, don't you, sweet pea?"

"Yay!" She grinned up at him broadly.

Sitting in that audience, I felt pride while he discussed the HBO series, unaware that his accomplishments might've been influenced by a secret weapon.

Hot tears burn as I continue watching him on-screen so alive and chuffed. "Was it all a lie? Why? You were a great writer *before* your lucky charm."

I bite my lip, hopeful that someday his on-air persona won't appear calculated. That the not knowing exactly how or why he manipulated us will stop haunting me. But in this moment my questions and disappointments fester like cold sores.

Today the man on the screen looks and sounds like an impostor. By the end of his life, loose skin hung on his bones like a dress on a hanger, with him hunched, expressionless, in a wheelchair. Cloudy eyes obscured his once-quizzical gaze. Drool dripped from his mouth instead of witticisms.

He was neither as magnificent nor as blithe as I once believed. Still, I miss the promise of him and the way he made anything seem possible.

There's no chance now to fix what broke. Or to talk about books. Or to prove myself his equal. Just a blank space where regrets and questions keep piling up like the books stacked in his office.

I blow my nose and toss the tissue aside just before Sadie walks into my office carrying Mopsy.

"Oh!" She stops short upon catching me teary. "What happened?"

I dab the inner corners of my eyes. "I'm watching Papa on YouTube."

Her brows rise an inch. "You do that?"

"First time. Last time, maybe." I forcefully close the laptop I should've been using to work on *Tropic Heat*. "It was harder than expected."

Sadie sits in my reading chair, keeping Mopsy on her lap.

"What made you do it?" The shift in her demeanor—from accusatory to inquisitive—feels like dawn breaking over the sea.

I shrug, pushing away thoughts of the empty safe and the half-packed boxes in his office. "Maybe I hoped it would help me process my feelings and decide what to do with all his things."

Sadie nuzzles Mopsy before looking up, her gaze thoughtful. "There's no point in storing his stuff in a million boxes."

I wince. "I hope you'll be a little more sentimental about my things."

"Don't say that." She knocks on the wooden side table. "All I mean is it'd be better to do something like donate his things to a library. Give money to create a Jefferson William Clarke Reading Room or whatever. He'd like that better."

He certainly would. For the first time all day, I relax. "That's a great idea."

"Thanks." She continues to stroke the cat while twisting her mouth from side to side, as if debating saying more.

Sometimes she looks so much like a young woman, I have trouble recalling the little girl who adored and trusted me absolutely.

We sit in silence a moment, her seeming to be working up to something.

She's looking at Mopsy's face when she says, "Speaking of dads, I'd like to spend an extra two weeks with mine this summer."

The request winds me. Is this a punishment for the pizza party? "You want to spend all of August in Seattle?"

"Yes." She gazes at me through hooded eyes, her arms falling still. "You said you'd consider it."

"When?" I tug at my earlobe, certain we never discussed this.

"Last year, after my summer visit. I complained about not having enough time in Seattle, and you said we could talk about it."

There is a giant blank spot where that conversation should be. Troubling, particularly since it wasn't that long ago. It's also something I would've discussed with Doug.

As disturbing as that all is, it's not as bad as the fact that she wants to leave me for an entire month. "Why is this so important now?"

"Next summer I'll be too busy getting ready to go to college. Then the following few summers will be about internships. This summer Dad and I can visit some West Coast schools." When she pauses, I die a little thinking of her attending college more than two thousand miles away. "It's the last time I can ever spend four weeks with him and my brothers. I'm always leaving just when things start to gel. I want to know them better."

Nothing I did to give her a normal family life could ever make up for Doug's sporadic presence. Prior to his diagnosis, my dad served as her stand-in father figure. His death could be fueling some of her desire to overcome Doug's arm's-length parenting.

It's greedy to deny her more time with him when I've had her for ninety-five percent of her life. The irony isn't lost on me, though. She's just like me, seeking a bigger place in a distant father's life.

She may also want a break from her "bossy, controlling" mother. Her eagerness to bolt from this house feels like a damning statement about my parenting. My love.

A suffocating sadness makes my voice squeak when I ask, "And your dad is okay with it?"

"Of course." She's always quick to defend Doug.

I inhale through my nose, telling myself this isn't about me. Sadie needs something that I'm unable to provide. Loving her means supporting her needs even when it hurts. A lengthy vacation could help her get over Johnny. Developing stronger ties to her siblings will bring more love into her life.

A brother or a sister would be a great comfort to me, with my father gone and my mother pushing her haphazard "comeback" agenda.

"I'll miss you, but it's fine with me if your father agrees." As the words fall from my mouth, the false sentiment chafes. A whole month will be the longest we've ever been apart. Today's ups and downs swamp me in defeat.

"Thanks." Her first genuine smile since the funeral splits her face. She sets Mopsy on the cushion and stands, pressing her palm to her abdomen.

"Is there something else?"

She tugs at her ponytail. "No."

Her expression says otherwise.

"Okay." Waiting for her to open up is wearing on me, but I can't afford another argument. "I should probably get back to work."

"All right." She turns to leave, then stops. "For dinner, can we pick up chili paneer and dal soup from Coromandel?"

"Sure."

As soon as she's gone, I whirl around and retrieve the typewriter.

Mopsy leaps off the chair and zooms out of the office before it hits my desk. My daughter's continued withdrawal has me typing before thinking.

```
I wish Sadie would trust me enough to be honest
about whatever she's still hiding.
```

When the return bell rings, ill ease brushes against me like invisible fingers. I should've given the phrasing more thought, although what harm could come from asking for trust? That conceit dissolves the instant I acknowledge that emotional manipulation undermines the very trust I'm seeking.

My fingers remain on the keys. Can I take it back? My dad's lament about *trying and failing to find the right words to undo all I've done* suggests not. Even if it were possible, deep down I want the truth more than I fear the cost. "Please don't let this be a huge mistake."

Not every wish has had a negative twist. Consider the garden and Will. Perhaps the motive makes the difference. Something like a superficial wish to be thinner extracts a side dish of pain, whereas a heartfelt wish for companionship doesn't. Surely worry for a child's welfare is the purest of motives.

I return the typewriter to its hidden spot in the cabinet. So far my wishes have manifested quickly. While I wait for this one to happen, I'll touch base with Doug about Sadie's plans.

It's possible I blocked out that conversation last summer so I wouldn't have to face it. These memory issues are adding up, though. With my mom. With Mel and Will. Now with Sadie.

The potential genetic predisposition penetrates my thoughts like slivers of glass.

Sadie is too young to lose me like we lost my dad. My mother wouldn't cope well, either. It's ironic that losing my mind might make her get sober to support Sadie through her grief.

Eyes closed, I let the chill sweep over my scalp.

If my father hadn't resisted testing sooner, early intervention might've slowed the illness's progression. Fear probably kept him from seeking answers sooner, just like it bears down on me now.

I thumb through my phone contacts for my father's neurologist, Dr. Rosenthal, and leave a message.

When I hang up, the room comes alive—all crisp sounds and menacing shadows. The potential ticking clock on my sanity renews my sense of urgency for fixing my family's problems. The ethical conflicts baked into using the typewriter might feel inconsequential if I'm diagnosed with that disease.

"As long as my intentions are pure, it's okay." Tomorrow, I'll search my dad's bedroom closet after Will leaves the house.

The phone rings. It's Dr. Rosenthal's office.

"Hello." My heart feels too large in my chest.

"This is Fiona from Dr. Rosenthal's office returning your call."

"Yes, hi. Thanks for the quick response. Dr. Rosenthal treated my father, who died recently with early-onset Alzheimer's. I've been experiencing some memory issues of my own lately. It's probably from stress, but given my father's history, it might be prudent to take a genetic test."

"First you'd need a consultation."

I nod blankly. "How soon can we schedule that? I'm a little nervous, obviously, and would like to address this as soon as possible."

"Hm." The receptionist clicks away at a keyboard. "I could squeeze you in on the twenty-seventh at eleven o'clock."

"Perfect." I give her my full name, birth date, and insurance information while adding the appointment to my calendar. "Thank you."

After ending the call, I sit back, benumbed.

What if I need to squeeze forty future years into ten? I can't stand the idea of missing out on Sadie's wedding or my future grandkids or seeing my bucket-list countries. Will Sadie remember me only as a bossy mom? Who will help her navigate her career, her love life, her own health issues?

Oh, no! What if she's inherited the gene?

My lungs burn.

"Stop projecting!" I squeeze my head in my hands.

God, if you exist, let my missing memories be nothing more than stress-induced forgetfulness, and please let this be the one prayer you finally answer.

Twenty

After banging out a thousand words in my pj's early this morning, I dressed myself in grown-up clothes. A floral sundress, tan linen jumpsuit, and black miniskirt lay abandoned on my bed. Rejects in my quest to strike the perfect balance of casual chic to impress Will without giving the impression that I'm trying too hard.

The winning combo: powder-blue wide-leg linen pants, a ruffled white top, and gladiator sandals. An intentionally messy bun and gold hoop earrings polish the look. If things with Will go as anticipated, I'll have to let Sawyer down easy tonight at the library event.

I arrive at the estate fifteen minutes before Will is due. Sunrays bathe the house in a honeyed spotlight. The idyllic scene almost tricks me into thinking that life can be perfect without any wishes. Almost.

While checking my makeup in the rearview mirror, I tuck loose strands of hair behind my ear before getting out of the car. The side entrance is unlocked.

"Hotel California" emanates from the kitchen, as does the smell of burnt toast. I frown and walk into the kitchen, stopping suddenly as if teetering on the edge of a cliff.

Dirty plates and a half-full tray of lasagna overflow the sink. Blackened toast surrounded by crumbs lies on the counter beside the near-empty pitcher of mimosas marooned on the island.

My mother sits by the window in her robe, hair uncombed, eyes bloodshot. Her lazy yawn suggests she's been up all night.

Unbelievable. A glance at the clock has me breaking into a cold sweat.

"Mom!" I swipe the pitcher off the counter and dump its contents down the drain before shutting off the Bose speaker. While scraping congealed cheese from dishes and briskly loading them into the dishwasher, I say, "Get dressed. Will is on his way."

"Who?" She looks at me dully.

"Will Barnes is coming to appraise the stuff you want to sell. Remember?" My voice reaches a high soprano range.

If it were anyone but Will, I'd happily reschedule the appointment and slow everything down. I don't want to have wasted his time, nor do I relish his seeing her this way.

Her face scrunches up before it erupts into a boozy, coy expression. "Oh, the cute boyfriend."

"Ex-boyfriend, current Christie's specialist." I move around the island and tug at her arm. "Come on. You need a quick shower."

She shrugs me off. "I'm not finished eating."

My patience unravels like a poorly knit stitch.

"Mom, please. Hurry!" I snatch the plate so Will won't walk in on us arguing. "We'll take this upstairs for after you shower. I'll keep Will occupied for ten minutes while you pull yourself together."

"You're such a worrywart." She pats my cheek a touch too hard, as if she doesn't cause my worrying. "Who cares how I look? My husband just died. I'm entitled to a few eccentricities."

We both know she's no grieving widow, and I'm in no mood for games. "You might not care about embarrassing yourself, but I do."

"Not everything is about you, dear," she mutters. I absorb the burn of her sarcasm and stare her down. She snickers. "La-di-da. How *do* you put up with me?"

How, indeed?

I nudge her along and up the stairs. After helping her into the bathroom, I scramble to her closet. Cream-colored flared crop pants and a pink cashmere tunic catch my eye, so I lay them on her bed before racing downstairs to rummage the refrigerator.

Within four minutes, I've got coffee brewing, replaced mimosas with lemon water, rinsed some grapes, and quarter-sectioned two cinnamon muffins.

I'm setting things on the island when the doorbell rings.

"He's here." Twenty-some years rewind, sending me back to tenth grade, eager to impress the boy with the easy laugh and kind eyes. Trotting through the entry, I blot my hairline before swinging the front door and grinning. "Hi, Will."

We greet each other with a hug. My eyes close during the embrace. When we ease apart, I study his face. Cheerful smile lines fan out around his eyes.

Will breaks eye contact first, showing no reaction to me or my outfit. His unsentimental gaze wanders the entry, pausing to admire the Ben Fluno painting in the entry.

"Your father was a great collector," he says. "Better than I remembered."

"He was eclectic." His preference for mixing antique furniture and modern art matched his equally unpredictable disposition. "Unfortunately, he kept accumulating items without purging anything."

"Not to worry. I'm experienced with large estates and will help your mom make decisions about what to sell. Is she here?" Will peers over my shoulder, appearing eager for her arrival rather than hopeful to steal a few moments alone.

He's here like in the old days, and yet nothing feels the same. My mood dips until I remind myself to trust in the typewriter.

"She's getting dressed." I gesture toward the kitchen, wading through the choppy confluence of the past mingling with the present. "Come have some coffee while we wait."

Will follows me. If he's checking me out, I hope he likes the view.

"Cream? Sugar?" I pour coffee into a porcelain cup.

"Black, thanks." He pops two grapes in his mouth.

I pass him the coffee, watching for a sign. "How's your son?"

Will taps the side of his cup; then his brows rise with understanding. "Oh yes . . . the fever. He's better, thanks."

Rather than ask me about the party or suggest plans for the rain check he promised, he strolls to the windows to admire the view. "We had some fun out there, didn't we?"

His eyes reflect the mischief of adolescence.

"We did." I nod, recalling kayak races across the inlet, his always winning. And the fumbling with each other's clothes by the shore at night.

"Do you still kayak?" Perhaps he's also remembering those things.

"Not as often as I'd like." I stop short of asking him to join me for an early morning paddle. It's his turn to make a move, after all.

Will glances at his watch. I, however, am not currently experiencing time like normal, with the past overlapping the present.

He sets his empty cup on the island and folds his arms across his chest. "Mind if I walk around a bit to get a sense of what's here?"

"Oh . . ." I cover my disappointment with a gesture toward the entry. "Sure."

His exploration is quickly interrupted by my mother's grand entrance, which makes me gape in horrified silence.

She ditched the outfit I selected in favor of a peacock-blue satin wrap top, black heels, and thick charcoal liner rimming her eyelids. Twin streaks of rouge and a slash of cherry-red lipstick call to mind the Joker.

The only thing that could make this more mortifying is if she were naked.

Will blinks rapidly, his professional composure faltering.

She swans in, arms overhead, voice too emphatic. "Will Barnes! My word, you haven't changed a bit. Let me take a better look."

She grabs him by the shoulders.

To his credit, he plays along and gives her a half kiss on the cheek before politely removing her hands from his person. "Mrs. Clarke, I'm so sorry for your loss. Mr. Clarke was such a legend."

"Yes, well, you would remember him that way." She flits her right hand around haplessly. "For someone with such a roar, he left this world with a whimper. It's better now."

"Mother!" I stamp my foot reflexively, careful not to look at Will.

"What?" She flings her arms outward, palms turned up. "He suffered for years, Emerson. He never wanted to live that way."

Despite her innocent expression, that's not what she had insinuated.

Will's brows shoot upward before he turns his face away. Involving him in our family's affairs might be a mistake. Now this image will replace any fond impressions he might have harbored.

I grip my mother's elbow. "Can we talk in private?"

"Let's not waste Will's time." She shakes free. "He's here as a favor."

Will defuses the tension with honeyed schmoozing. "Not a favor, although I'm excited to work with you. Will you be selling artwork, furniture, both?"

"Yes." My mother pats Will's chest, her hand lingering there a moment too long.

Shame is too weak a word for what's prompting this hot flash. It's taking every ounce of poise I have to keep me from screaming and running off to hide.

"When I move to New York, I'll redecorate in *my* style. No more antiques. I want comfortable things." She pins Will with a saucy stare. "There are a few pieces of art I'll keep, but everything else can go."

"Rugs, too?" Will asks, maintaining a professional demeanor despite her clumsy flirtations.

"Most." She casts a glance my way. "Emerson wants one, and there are two others I'll keep."

Will opens his leather backpack and pulls out an iPad. "Let's do a walk-through while I make a list and explain a bit about how the process works. Sound good?"

"Lovely." My mother threads her scrawny arm through Will's.

If he's uncomfortable, he's not squirming. In fact, his conduct gives off strong broker vibes.

Could winning this account be why he accepted my invitation to Mel's party? Wow. I flatten my palm against my belly as that helping of humble pie turns my stomach.

While they chatter about acquisition dates and costs, authentication, and more, I trail behind them in silence, letting my romantic fantasies dwindle.

It's possible that the fact I declined last night's dinner invitation set this nightmare in motion. My mother's exaggerated cackle is like a spike through my brain. This outrageous behavior is exactly what will make her an easy mark for users and thieves in Manhattan. I can't protect her from here, especially not with a compromised memory.

Life keeps shifting beneath my feet, making my problems feel too big to carry myself. It's surreal to be here discussing the sale of most of my parents' possessions only two weeks after my father's death.

Vases, paintings, chairs, and chests I glossed over hundreds of times suddenly resonate with meaning. The Maui trip when Dad bought the John Koga *Spirit Tree* sculpture. The nineteenth-century carved walnut Gothic Revival settee Dad shipped from our visit to Germany because it looked like a throne from one of his books. The first edition copy of *Sense and Sensibility* Dad bought for my mom on her fiftieth birthday.

It's one of the few times she'd been visibly moved by his grand gestures. I suspect it was the fact that he'd remembered her favorite novel as much as that he'd taken the time to track down a rare copy. If he'd prioritized her feelings more often, she might not resemble Tammy Faye Bakker today.

All this time I've blamed my father's personality changes on my mother's drinking, but maybe it was the other way around. I wished to be alone. Outside. Anywhere where I could shout at the sky without being seen or heard.

"A de Kooning. Wow!" Will stops to admire it rather than to appraise it. "I love his story. This is *Orestes*. It was part of a show on the cusp of his breakout that originally didn't win much acclaim. Look at the tightness—stop and twist—gritty."

Mom eyes it askance, nose wrinkled as if the canvas gives off an odor. "Jefferson loved it. It's how he saw the world, I think. Dark. Dangerous. A bit off, but occasionally a little funny."

She leans back slightly, as if to steer clear of it, while her shrewd insight about my dad circles me like smoke.

"Excellent summary." Will grins, making a note on his iPad. "De Kooning did play with darkness and humor, replicating our consciousness. He ultimately abandoned this style, calling it the door he went out through."

"His 'door' is my nightmare. This can go." She sighs loudly to emphasize the point, then clasps her hands at her chest. "Excuse me. I'll be right back."

She takes off toward the living room, probably to the bar cart.

I bite my tongue, literally. Whatever fairy tales I made up about how this afternoon might play out, my only goal now is to get through this appraisal quickly and then separate my mother from Will.

"You okay?" he asks.

"Sorry about her drinking. God, this move is a disaster in the making."

"Looks like she's gotten worse." He steps backward, the iPad held to his chest like a shield. His remote manner mirrors his valuing the objects in the room above the people involved.

I try another tack, a final test of my storybook idea of us. "A little different from your big happy family."

"Eh. A bigger family multiplies the problems and disagreements. But yeah, we don't have any major issues—not yet, anyway." He looks at his shoes as if searching for something, then adds, "At least you won't need to argue with siblings about how to deal with your mom."

"Silver lining," I tease without much enthusiasm.

He gestures around at the grandeur. "She's got plenty of resources if she decides to get help. You're better off focusing on yourself and your daughter."

A lifetime of self-composure keeps me civil in the face of his bleak indifference. "Thanks."

There's no trace of the sweet boy of my memories. That kid wouldn't be dismissive of my concerns or my mother's obvious decline. He'd be curious about me and sensitive to my grief.

Will's beautiful transparent eyes are devoid of any tenderness when he says, "Any time."

My mother waltzes back into the room, tumbler in hand. "Where were we?"

"The de Kooning," Will reminds her, back to business without skipping a beat.

"The nightmare. Yes, it goes. But that piece will stay." She points at a painting by an unacclaimed local artist.

The romantic pink, blue, and white abstract is one-twentieth of the de Kooning's value, perfectly illustrating the difference between my parents' tastes.

She values art by how it makes her feel. My father valued it by its reputation.

Despite our many differences, my mother and I are aligned this way. I understand Tolstoy's importance, but I'd rather read Tolkien. My relationship with my mother might improve if I focus on our similarities.

Two hours later, Will has taken dozens of photographs and pages of notes. "Let's talk timetable. There are factors to consider—tax planning and such—when making decisions about what to sell.

"There's also the matter of Mr. Clarke's celebrity. Some in your shoes prefer private anonymous sales, others a public auction of key pieces to trade on the fame. If you want us to manage everything—all the art, furniture, rugs, and so on—it's a more complicated process that involves a team of analysts and lawyers who plan the disposal to maximize profit and minimize taxes."

"Let's not protract the situation," my mother says. "I want to be out of here by August."

"We can't rush the valuation and planning process, but we could collect and store the pieces while that is all worked out," he says, clearly angling to lock her down.

"Mom, we should talk to the executor before making any decisions," I interrupt.

Will glances at me as if he'd forgotten I was here. "We'd work with your executor, of course. Remember, though, it's important to hire experts. Many outfits that claim to be in estate sales are glorified tag sale operators. Christie's will properly value and place things like the de Kooning or the rare 'Jupe' Johnstone & Jeanes 1840s dining table at auction or through private sale."

"Send me the details. I want to move quickly," my mother says.

A conceited grin suggests Will has won what he came for, which clearly had nothing to do with me.

His rejection eats at me like an infection, but I refuse to show my disappointment. If only he hadn't made me feel used at a time when I needed to matter. When it would've helped to know that our life here had more than pecuniary value.

"Understood." Will explains the next steps—the collection and transportation of the auction pieces, the photographs and catalogue they'll make, and Christie's fees.

"Em, what about your dad's office?" Will turns in that direction expectantly.

"There's no significant artwork in there." My blunt, cool tone causes him and my mother to blink.

Still, he presses. "Fans might love items like his desk and chair, or early draft manuscripts with handwritten notes. How would you feel about putting those up at auction? Surely there's a rabid collector's market."

I'm shaking my head, my resistance instinctive. "My daughter wants to donate his things to a library collection."

Will taps his iPad against his thigh, resigned. "Nice idea if you aren't interested in the money."

I'm not at all interested in the money, his opinion of my decision, or him.

"As I said, my father's personal items are not for sale." Each word pulls my heart up into my throat. His belongings are all we have left of him now.

"Listen, kids. I'm getting a headache." My mother rubs her temple.

"I'll see Will out while you find some aspirin," I say, thrilled to end this meeting.

My mother strokes Will's biceps. "Lovely to see you again."

"I'll be in touch soon with details and timetables," he replies smoothly.

"Thank you, dear. Enjoy your afternoon." My mother sweeps up the staircase while I lead Will out the door.

Despite my disappointment in him, I'm compelled to apologize for my mother. "Sorry today was a bit extra."

"Please. We deal with a lot of difficult clients. That was a cakewalk, Em." As he slides into the driver's seat, I'm grateful to have quickly seen through his false charms.

He doesn't meet the criteria of my Mr. Right wish list. That leaves Sawyer, who also may be a letdown. It might be a relief to call the Underwood's powers into question. That wouldn't erase my less noble intentions, but it would absolve me of responsibility for the outcomes of my wishes. "Drive safely."

All my muscles relax after he pulls away. I turn around and go directly to my father's office.

I take twenty minutes to note the items a library might prefer, like the drawings segregated during my last round of snooping.

Leafing through his life's work reveals a little character trait here, another there. His thoughts and values—the grand and the unflattering— are littered throughout his work product. Like me, he displayed love and courage on the page much more consistently than he did in his life.

I stow everything related to the last Pandemonium book in one box for my personal use while weighing Henry's proposal.

Why *didn't* I raise the idea when my dad and I could have worked on it together?

The immediate answer is blunt: I couldn't handle his rejection.

Another round of snooping reveals nothing new about the typewriter. One might begin to doubt he ever used it, except he didn't dub it his good-luck charm for no reason.

When I turn off the light, I'm struck again by the silence—the emptiness—of the house. My mother claims to love her freedom, but a life with no anchor is bound to go adrift.

I tiptoe upstairs and peek into her room. She's fully dressed, lying on top of the bed wearing a silk sleep mask. Utterly vulnerable. It would be reckless—heartless, even—to ignore my instincts about this move out of frustration or exhaustion.

My gaze moves to my father's closet. I walk inside, touching his clothes, my chest aching. His cologne sits on a tray with three sets of cuff links. I spritz my wrist and inhale the scent. Tears collect quickly, but I sniffle and beat them back. Now isn't the time to search his drawers for answers. Besides, Rachel's pages won't write themselves. I need to get back to work.

As I drive home, Will's horrified expression plays on repeat. My mother's drinking will likely increase in New York, where she'll be lonelier. Strangers won't be as careful or patient with her behavior as Will was this morning. If only I could scrub his shocked expression from my brain.

She needs to get sober, particularly if I have early Alzheimer's. Every attempt to persuade her to enter rehab has failed, but that was before I had the typewriter. Perhaps I'll succeed where my father failed.

At home, I use a fresh sheet of paper to type:

```
I've lost one parent without getting closure and
might now be losing my memory. I'm begging the
universe for help with getting my mother to attend
an alcohol intervention program so that we can
build a better family life together.
```

My pulse isn't nearly as erratic as it has been after previous wishes. Come to think of it, Sadie hasn't yet confided more about Johnny. The other wishes manifested rather quickly. Is there some limitation against using it to engender trust?

More guesswork. I sigh and slump in my seat, staring into space. In the quiet, I recall a day shortly before Sadie was born, when I'd stopped by the house to drop off some personal items.

Mom had gaily showed me ruffled pink infant clothes and the plush toys she'd purchased for the nursery. Dad remained unusually quiet, his chin resting on his fist, his gaze intently following our every move and expression.

At the time, I assumed they'd been fighting before my arrival or that he regretted my circumstances. In hindsight, he might've been watching for a particular result from one of his wishes.

Did it turn out how he planned? I close my eyes and shiver at the possibilities of what is versus what might've been. It casts a pall on tonight's "date" with Sawyer. At least I didn't manipulate Sawyer's feelings. I asked only to meet someone who met certain criteria. Does that make it better? Less conniving?

Probably not.

Given the pains I've taken to be different from my parents, it's a blow to admit that I'm turning into them.

I could change course. Toss the typewriter in the trash. I don't remember the last time I heard my dad typing in his office, but it had to have been several years ago. Back before his mind became too riddled with holes to keep track of much.

He had to have known the danger of leaving this behind for us to find. The fact that he didn't could mean he had a plan he never got around to finishing. Or he wanted one of us to eventually discover its power.

I skim my fingers over its keys. "Did you leave this for us, Dad?"

And if so, why?

Twenty-One

JEFFERSON'S JOURNAL

August 15, 2013

Emerson and Sadie are moving out this week to a house so small it barely qualifies as a cottage. It's only three miles from here, but I'm losing my girls. Dorothy may follow suit, for all I know.

Not even sixty, yet everything feels stale. Stiff.

Years ago, I'd wake up to watch the sun rise over the water, and it felt like fire in my veins. I couldn't stop touching Dorothy. My hands, my mind—they were always reaching for something, someone. The characters in my head, the audience at my feet, my wife in my arms. Where'd it all go?

Now there's little laughter or joy. If it weren't for Sadie, I wouldn't remember the last time I felt true amazement.

What the hell has happened?

How is it possible to have more than everything I ever wanted yet feel gutted and left with my skin hanging here, pretending to be me.

Who stole my life? Someone did. Or some thing.

For two nights I've toyed with making the closing on the cottage fall through, but that would merely stall the inevitable. I can't jail my daughter and granddaughter here. Even I know that's taking things too far.

But Sadie is the only thing that still brings a glimmer to my eye, however fleeting.

It's coming at a terrible time, too. This fucking book I'm struggling to finish.

Henry's breathing down my neck for books seven and eight, but my mind keeps slipping. Slipping. Slipping. I'm slipping. How can I write when I don't feel like myself? What if my next book destroys my reputation?

Losing my place. Losing everything. It's all so bitterly ironic.

Even Dorothy is different. We're no longer arguing all the time. You'd think that would be a good thing, but it's like she's gone blank. Her indifference is worse than the fights or the drinking. Yesterday I came up behind her when she was reading and touched her shoulder. She flinched. Flinched!

I broke down and typed a wish to undo all the wishes that hurt my girls. The list is long—embarrassingly so. If it ever got out—I shudder to think. But it's been four weeks since that redemption wish, and so far nothing has changed. It mustn't be possible. Another lesson learned too late.

I'm scared. Scared of being left alone with these wild, suffocating, chaotic thoughts. There's no peace. No answers. Just the same dark cycle.

What comes next?

Twenty-Two

On my way to the library, I notice the clouds rolling in off the sound, their watery shades of gray bleeding into the sunset's vivid magenta. A stunning if temporary distraction. I sigh and hit speed dial to call my mother for the fourth time this afternoon. No answer. No return phone call. No early sign from the universe about turning my rehab wish into reality.

Will's tense expression when my mom hugged him resurfaces, making me grimace. It nags at me that I even care about his reaction, considering his sole concern was winning his sales pitch. He hasn't even sent me a thank-you text.

He probably got a big kick out of my clumsy invitation to Mel's party. Oh, that red dress! Chills break out across my arms when I imagine him looking for ways to avoid seduction despite knowing it would've been a fait accompli.

File this under "we get what we deserve." Only someone stupid or desperate would've eagerly jumped at him that way. For god's sake, he never once looked me up since moving to Larchmont. That Mr. Right wish list blinded me.

Sitting at the stoplight, I feel the temptation to ditch Sawyer yank hard.

My heart sounds like it's thumping between my ears. When the light turns green, I hesitate until a honk from behind makes me depress the gas pedal.

At least Sawyer isn't using me to get something for himself. He knows nothing about me other than the little I shared in the parking lot. Worst case, Colson Whitehead's discussion will be inspiring. It could even help me decide what to do about Henry's proposal.

The library parking lot is nearly at capacity, which is expected for a National Book Award and Pulitzer Prize–winning guest author. I find a spot along the rear wrought-iron fence, a spring chill chasing me as I trot across the parking lot.

My father's global popularity wasn't accompanied by serious critical acclaim. For years, he brainstormed "big" story ideas in hopes of ticking that box. Sadly, those premises became less coherent each year. If he sought the typewriter's help, it didn't work.

More murky limitations to ponder.

And perhaps it's also time for a new goal. A National Book Award would be a delicious offset of my father's criticisms.

Pointless musing for a ghostwriter.

When I open the lobby door, the earthy scent of thousands of old books sparks a bout of wistful nostalgia, like time itself is pressed between the pages. Some of my happiest childhood memories involve the weekly library visits with my mom. Now look at us.

Sawyer waves from his spot near the welcome desk.

A hank of hair flops across his forehead like an awning shading amber eyes that shimmer with good humor. Ivory jeans, crisp blue shirt, and lilac linen jacket might look a bit dandy on another, but he wears the California-chic vibe like a second skin.

The best accessory? His generous smile, which is as earnest as a young child's. "You made it."

His obvious pleasure elicits a shy smile.

"Of course." I accept a friendly one-armed hug. "I've been looking forward to it."

The lie slips out so easily, it mustn't be entirely untrue.

"Same." Sawyer glances at his chronograph watch, an accessory rarely spotted since cell phones became a human appendage. "It starts in ten minutes. Let's find seats. Hopefully there are still two together."

"Lead the way." I gesture toward the theater-style community room, a pleasant hum thrumming in my chest.

The auditorium is near capacity. The jabber of quiet conversation hums throughout the room. Sawyer spies two empties near the back, close to the aisle.

"What do you think of the haircut?" he jokes after we're situated, flamboyantly gesturing with one hand while cocking his head to await judgment.

I chuckle, tension evaporating like mist in the sun. "Looks great. Did you like Lanphier?"

"Loved it. Thanks." He leans back, shifting his hips forward on the seat and crossing his ankles, taking up space like someone entirely comfortable in his own skin. "Any other recommendations for the newcomer?"

"Hmm. I can share recs for doctors, a dentist, and the best cocktails in town."

"Sounds good, except for the cocktail. I don't drink." He's keenly watching for my reaction.

Recovery? I hope not. One alcoholic at a time is the limit of what I can manage. "I don't often, either."

"Then how you know the best local bar must be some story." Mirthful eyes sparkle as he taps his lips with his index finger.

His behavior is the human equivalent of a golden Lab's. Who doesn't love a Lab? They're extremely loyal, too. A key criterion for someone with my hang-ups.

"My best friend drags me out every few weeks for drinks." Girl time with Mel usually entails champagne cocktails, hearty laughs, and high heels.

He loosely interlocks his fingers, bringing his hands to his lap. "What do you enjoy doing for fun?"

"Fun?" I mock myself, scratching my head while screwing up my face. "I'm a single parent of a teenage daughter, so my weekends are about high school sports, shopping, laundry, and chick flicks." When he doesn't balk at that list, I add, "I'd also been managing my father's care until he passed two weeks ago. Fun hasn't been on my calendar lately."

He gently takes my hand while intently looking at me. His Eastwood-esque voice deepens with sympathy as he says, "I'm sorry for your loss. So recent, too."

Sawyer's compassion might be a throwaway moment for others, but the ground beneath me heaves. I breathe through the swell of emotion his touch unleashed before letting go of his hand.

"Thanks. Life's been a lot lately." And could become much more complicated if I've inherited my father's illness.

Sawyer gently elbows me, his gaze soft. "I think we were fated to meet."

"How so?" I cough from guilty surprise, my face heating like a sun lamp.

"Sounds like you could use some pampering and relaxation, and I excel at both." He gestures toward the stage, where a staff member is checking the microphones. "Even nights like this—discussing stories that reflect the human experience—remind us we aren't alone. It's comforting."

I nod, still stuck on the idea of being pampered—by him or anyone.

I'm considering this when my phone buzzes. "I need to check in case it's my daughter."

"Of course." He waves his hand.

When I don't recognize the number, I stuff the phone in my purse. "Spam."

"So annoying, right?"

My eyes bulge. "Yes."

The phone rings again almost immediately. Same unknown caller.

Defiantly, I press BLOCK, then decide to learn more about his life. "You must miss California and whatever friends or family you left behind."

"My parents are in L.A.—Brentwood—and my sister lives in Hermosa Beach. But I went to NYU and have friends all over—Boston, Chicago,

New York, Miami. I got my MBA at Berkeley and worked in San Francisco until recently. Haven't been in Connecticut long enough to miss California yet, but I do not miss the traffic."

"Manhattan traffic isn't as bad?" I tease.

"I work in Greenwich."

Home to many hedge funds and private equity groups. He's obviously smart and ambitious. Ambition can be problematic if, like my father, the ego drives one's decisions. But Sawyer seems to strike a balance between work and play.

"That explains your decision to live in the burbs."

"I love green space and the shore." He pulls a face, adding, "Of course, your beaches aren't exactly what I'm used to."

"Definitely not." I snicker. Long Island Sound's brackish water is no substitute for Pacific blue.

The spirited light in his eyes reminds me of my father. "Ever live anyplace else?" he asks.

Doug and I talked about getting jobs in Boston, but then I got pregnant. Once we broke up, the familiar—if slightly rotted—roots of home offered stability. I'm thinking this might make me sound cowardly when my phone buzzes again.

I mumble "sorry" while checking. This time it's Sadie.

A librarian is escorting Colson Whitehead down to the stage, so I whisper, "Hey, honey, the event is about to start. Everything okay?"

Her earsplitting response is as swift as it is shocking. "Gran's been arrested!"

Twenty-Three

"What?" I exclaim, drawing the attention of those around us. Sawyer leans forward, trying to catch my gaze.

"She tried to call. Why didn't you answer?" Sadie's accusation sets me back.

"She didn't call." Oh! Those spam calls. My vision flickers like someone turned on a strobe light. "What happened?"

Sawyer's brows draw together in concern. I close my eyes to focus on Sadie's voice.

"DUI. She hit a tree, but no one got hurt," Sadie says. I reflexively hunch forward as that image fills my mind. "She needs a ride home from the station."

My daughter's frightened voice provokes a fury that overwhelms my concern for my mother.

"I'm leaving now. I'll be home later." I drop my phone in my purse, chin trembling, eyes burning like hot coals while the librarian begins her welcoming remarks.

Sawyer touches my arm, all traces of the happy-go-lucky man wiped away. "Are you all right?"

I shake my head, thinking back on my mother's behavior this morning.

That shirt. The makeup. I shouldn't have left her alone so often since the funeral.

"I'm so sorry, but I've got to go. My mother . . . well . . ." Mortification makes it hard to push the words out. "She's been arrested. DUI."

Empathy softens all his features. "Oh, man. I'm so sorry."

The woman beside Sawyer gives us a pinched look. I shrink from her, but Sawyer calmly eyes her as if telepathically saying, *Give us a moment.*

I cover my face, wishing that made me invisible.

"You're too shaken to drive. Let me take you." Sawyer leans forward as if to stand.

His kindness presses against me, soft yet relentless, loosening something I'm not ready to release. I'm tempted to accept his help, but we barely know each other. He shouldn't have to miss this event.

"Thank you, but I'm fine. Besides, the police station is literally behind the library." I hook a thumb in its direction.

"Good to know," he jokes to break the tension before leaning close enough that the citrus notes of his cologne stir a desire to be held. "But I insist on escorting you when you're this upset."

Colson's speaking now, prompting the woman beside me to pointedly shush us.

My reluctance to leave is shocking considering how, thirty minutes ago, I would've paid the devil for a way out of this date.

"I hate to make you miss this."

"I won't enjoy it now, anyway." He gestures with his hands to scoot us along. We make our way out of the row, apologizing as we wedge past the people sitting along the aisle.

When we get outside, he says, "My dad's a heavy drinker and his brother's a mean-ass drunk. That's why I don't tempt fate . . . or hangovers." He laughs at himself.

Candor ticks an important box, which doesn't say much for me and my secrets. The wind kicks up, so I wrap my jacket more tightly around me.

"My mother's drinking problem spans decades, but it's getting worse.

I knew she tied one on this morning and should've checked on her before coming out."

Sawyer walks beside me, hands clasped behind his back. Twilight shrouds us in shadow. "It's easy to feel responsible for the people we love—like we can save them—but in my experience, life doesn't really work that way. Until she decides to help herself, the best you can offer is compassionate support."

The truth makes me stop and grab my face again, my reserve dissolving from my lack of compassion.

Sawyer gently rubs my back until I regain my composure.

"Sorry." I'm on fire with shame. "This has got to be your worst first date ever."

"Clearly, you haven't dated much." He grins. "Trust me, this isn't even close to the worst."

Miraculously, he gets me to snigger.

He is lovely, but given his family history, he doesn't need someone with my baggage. There's also the fact that I manipulated the "fate" of our first meeting. And if my neurological exam goes badly, that's a third strike.

Sawyer deserves someone whole and healthy, two things I haven't been in decades. It would be easier to walk away if he weren't so chivalrous.

We approach the modest brick police station. Thank goodness this happened here, because no Manhattan station would be this inactive. Then again, my mother wouldn't be driving in Manhattan.

At least no one got hurt.

Outside the station, ominous green globe lights thwart any sense of calm Sawyer has instilled. I lumber up the steps to the glass double doors and enter the lobby in front of a display case of historical memorabilia.

The spotless room's gray flooring, brown brick walls, and low acoustic tile ceiling make it feel like a coffin.

"There." Sawyer points to an orange call buzzer located outside the main window.

When I press it, a female officer appears within seconds. "Can I help you?"

"Hello," I say, my voice quavering as if I'm the one in trouble. "I'm here to pick up my mother, Dorothy Clarke. She was arrested for driving under the influence."

"Hang on." She lumbers to the back of the room and disappears through a side door. When she returns, she's carrying paperwork. "The bond is five hundred dollars. You need to post ten percent."

"Of course." I open my purse and rifle my wallet for fifty dollars, which I pass through the window.

She stamps some papers, then prints out a receipt and slides it beneath the glass partition. "Someone will bring up your mother soon."

"Thank you." I turn to Sawyer. "I appreciate your help, but you don't need to wait with me."

"How about if I stay until they bring your mom out? We don't have to talk. I'll just sit with you."

Such good manners. How can I say no?

"All right." We take a seat on the wooden bench. My knees bounce while I text Sadie to let her know everything will be fine. "Do you think jail is a possibility?"

He wrinkles his nose, shaking his head. "Fines, probably."

"Public notice in the local paper, definitely." I groan. She'll hate that. As do I.

A band of pain cinches my chest. I grip the edge of the bench seat until my fingers ache. My parents have been so careless—with each other, with me, with their own lives. I would never put Sadie in this position.

"Has your mom's drinking gotten worse since your dad died?" Sawyer asks. "You don't have to answer if that's too personal."

"Apparently, but not for the reason you think. They had a difficult relationship, and he had Alzheimer's, so he was gone long before he died. But I do think it's rocked her in ways she didn't expect. He was a force of nature—good and bad."

"Sounds like a character," Sawyer says kindly.

"Yes." I decide to tell the truth. "My dad is Jefferson Clarke."

"As in the author?" Sawyer's eyes brighten. "I love his books!"

"Thanks." Whatever my father's faults, anyone who can bring that much joy to others has good in them. That's worth remembering. "He loved writing them."

"Wow." He shakes his head. "I was addicted to the Elysian Chronicles in high school and college. I think the set is still on the shelf in my parents' house."

I try to picture his childhood bedroom—part surfer dude, part bookworm. I bet he was organized and neat, even as a teen, chilling on his bed reading while listening to bands like the Arctic Monkeys.

"Sorry. I didn't mean to go all fanboy." He mocks himself. "Anyway, when things settle, your mom might embrace this next phase and want to get sober."

"A girl can dream." I sigh, doubtful that anything could sway her at this point.

When the door beside the main window opens, I look up. A young male officer escorts my mother into the lobby.

I gasp at the sight of her swollen, bruised face. Her hair is matted to her head and mascara smudges surround her eyes. She's carrying a plastic bag containing her purse and phone and jewelry.

Sawyer doesn't blanch or show any sign of distaste. He simply takes my hand to help me stand. "Would you like me to stay?"

"No, thank you. My mom will be embarrassed," I fib, already disgraced enough for us both. "Again, sorry about tonight."

"Don't give it a thought. I'll be in touch." He winks and then greets my mother with a slight bow of the head. "I hope you're feeling better soon, Mrs. Clarke."

When she raises her chin and casts a defiant glare my way, my mouth falls open. The audacity!

Sawyer gives me one last consoling look before turning to go. When he exits the station house, I find myself wishing . . . well, that our night had ended differently.

The officer with my mom says, "Good evening."

I check his name tag.

"Hello, Officer Constantine. Sorry about this." I turn to my mother, stuffing all my prickly feelings into the darker chambers of my heart. "Mom, how badly are you hurt?"

She plays mute, so Officer Constantine says, "The EMTs checked her out, but she refused to go to the hospital."

"Were they worried about a concussion?" I rub at the tightness building in my chest.

"Yes. Maybe cracked ribs, too. She's petite, and airbags can pack a wallop."

"My ribs are fine." She holds her arms wide open and takes exaggerated breaths. "No pain."

Unless alcohol is masking it.

"Mom, have a seat for a minute, please." I steer her safely toward the bench. She rests her head against the wall, refusing to meet my gaze, so I turn to the officer. "Could you walk me through what happened? My daughter said she hit a tree."

He rubs the space between his eyes before explaining that my mother drove off the road, plowed down a mailbox post, and crashed into a tree. The homeowners called the police.

By the time the cops and ambulance arrived, she was already out of the car. Although a little dazed, she declined a trip to the emergency room.

The officers performed three mandated field sobriety tests, each of which she failed. Per protocol, they brought her to the station and gave her the option of taking a chemical test after explaining the consequences of refusal.

He adds, "She didn't want an automatic six-month license suspension, so she took the test and blew a point one-four, which is of course almost double the legal limit. Given her numbers, I was surprised she wasn't more incoherent, but maybe the accident sobered her up."

Or she's developed a high tolerance through years of experience.

"So what's next?" The evidence sounds irrefutable. "Is it too late for a lawyer?"

"There'll be a court date within two weeks. She'll need a lawyer for that and the DMV hearing, and to deal with the property damage." He points at the paperwork. "The address of the property owners is in the paperwork."

Long Neck Point Road. Her street. I think it might be the McKinseys' place. More shame to choke down. I scrub my face. "DMV hearing?"

"We're required to forward a form to the DMV in DUI cases. Your mom's license will be suspended for forty-five days. After that, she'll need an ignition interlock device for another three months."

The weight of carrying her has grown so heavy, I'm barely able to stand. I've no siblings—only Mel to lean on, and she has her own family to care for.

Officer Constantine crosses his arms and tips his head, looking like a man who is about to throw me a pity party. "Listen, some first-time defendants get the charges dropped by agreeing to go into the IDIP program."

I'm half listening now, my thoughts busy grappling with these charges and legal proceedings. "What's that?"

"An alcohol program monitored by the state. Her lawyer can raise this with the court."

When my mother doesn't bark a refusal, I glance over my shoulder. She's slumped on the bench, eyes closed, slightly snoring.

Good. Better than her complaining or refusing. Wiping her record clean is one incentive, but getting my mother into an alcohol program is what I've wanted most for years. The perverse windfall feels this good only because no one got badly hurt. If I had been alone, I would have broken into a jig.

What a lucky break. Damn lucky.

Or . . . no, not luck.

I feel faint remembering the hasty wish typed after this morning's debacle with Will. I'd been so angry. Fed up. Desperate.

Everything but careful.

I did this. My mother could've died or killed someone else. How reckless of me. Selfish, selfish, selfish. I flatten a hand across my stomach, then reach for the officer to steady myself.

Officer Constantine holds my forearm when my knees buckle. "You okay?"

I'm on the verge of throwing up, tugging at the shirt now sticking to my back. "I'm sorry. I just . . . stress."

He walks me toward the empty spot on the bench. "Have a seat. I'll get you some water."

"Thank you." Sitting beside my sleeping mother, I hold my head in my hands, grateful Sawyer left before this revelation struck.

Sadie is right about my control issues. They have made me as addicted to using that typewriter as my mother is to alcohol. Tears clog my nasal passages. My skin feels too taut, but there's no escaping this body or my shame. I glance at my mother, my chin wobbly.

"Ms. Clarke, you look pale." Officer Constantine hands me a paper cup of water. "Drink this."

"Thank you." The cool liquid helps douse the fire inside. "It's the shock, I think."

"Better?" he asks as I finish gulping it down.

I nod. Recovering myself, I toss the empty cup in the trash and then jiggle my mother's arm. "Mom, we need to check you for a concussion."

"No." She runs her hands through her hair, tucking it behind her ears as if becoming less disheveled solves everything. "Take me home."

Officer Constantine steps forward, thrusting a business card at me. "I forgot to mention, Grant's Auto Body towed her car. You should reach out to them to arrange having it fixed."

I slap my forehead. "I forgot about her car."

He wrinkles his nose. "Front end took a beating."

My fault. I'll call the neighbors tomorrow, but gossip has likely already started to make its way throughout our community. I mentally construct the local byline: *Jefferson Clarke's distraught widow drunkenly plows through residential neighborhood.*

Another flush of heat rises from my torso to my scalp.

"Thank you for all your help, Officer." I fold the papers and put them in my purse, then take my mother's arm. "Come on, Mom. Let's go."

Twenty-Four

Moving as if my limbs are filled with sand, I clumsily navigate my mother toward the library parking lot. *My fault, my fault, my fault.* That indictment turns my skull into a prison.

Maneuvering my mother past the end of the fence, I link arms with her to prevent her from stumbling.

"Where are we going?" The silent treatment ends.

"Here." I unlock the car remotely. "I was at an author event when Sadie called."

She balances herself by placing a hand on the trunk, her head bobbling. The lamppost light illuminates her purple raccoon eyes.

Squinting, she asks, "Who's the mystery man?"

A full-body wince seizes every muscle. What must Sawyer think after this fiasco wrecked our date? And yet his tenderness slipped inside and opened my heart, exposing long-buried vulnerability.

Every expectation for this day has been upended—by Will, Sawyer, and my mother. If my father is watching us now, he's shaking his head, thinking to himself, *By God, you girls really can't manage without me.*

"Emerson," she says when I don't answer.

"Honestly, Mom, that's the last thing we should focus on tonight," I deflect, helping her onto the seat and closing her door.

My body quakes while I move around the car. As bad as this is, it could've been so much worse. For her. For some unsuspecting bystander.

I didn't pour her drinks or hand her the keys, but she might not have been behind the wheel if not for my typed wish. A shock of pain reverberates up my arm after I slam my hand against the trunk. Hardly enough punishment.

What's next? My pores leach sweat. I can't catch my breath. God, I can't breathe. The wave of remorse carries my insecurities and fear in its undertow.

Bending forward with my hands on my thighs, I suck cool air in and out. Think, Em. Or stop thinking, for that matter. Behind me, people start streaming out of the library, snapping me out of my self-pity party.

Slipping behind the wheel, I turn the engine over and drive toward Stamford Hospital. My mother leans her head against the window, her bruises as dark as a night sky. Bony arms hang limp at her sides.

Neither of us speaks during the ride. Outside, the houses and streetlights blur together and fade into the night. Helplessness—loneliness—builds with each mile.

When Stamford Hospital comes into view, my mother emerges from her stupor and purses her lips. "I don't need a doctor, Emerson."

"Humor me." Thankfully, the emergency room parking lot is half empty. "You could have a brain bleed or hairline fracture."

"You're being ridiculous," she mutters, unbuckling her seat belt.

Before she opens the door, I grip her arm. Strained vocal cords roughen my voice. "You're lucky you hit a mailbox instead of a person. You could've killed somebody, so maybe cooperate and be grateful that I care enough to insist a doctor check you out."

She freezes as if I'd dumped a bucket of Gatorade on her head. As the shock wears off, she stares at my hand until I release her arm. We exit the car, enduring another exercise in silent forbearance.

Following check-in, we take two seats in the waiting room, repelling each other like magnets' similar poles.

Across the room, a curly-haired toddler with flaming red cheeks who's dressed in blue-bunny footies coughs and cries and crawls all over his young mother while she murmurs to him in Spanish.

My mother was that gentle and patient once. People would've thought I was a lucky little girl. I was for a while. Lucky and loved. Our connection melted slowly, like a snowman in the winter sun. I've played a role in that—particularly today—but this night has been decades in the making, with me taking cover from her choices.

My mom squeezes my hand. Startled, I recoil before meeting her misty gaze.

"I'm sorry." Her voice is so small, it's clear her apology extends beyond her arrest.

Words stick in my throat, entwined with the confession about the typewriter that I cannot offer. Nodding an acknowledgment, I squeeze her hand in solidarity. "Me too."

We divert our attention to the television, although neither of us is invested in the reality dating show.

Every minute feels like an hour. When they finally take her back for imaging, I text Sadie with an update. Next I text Mel, never more thankful that she became a defense attorney.

Help! My mother got a DUI. Can you stop by my house tomorrow to explain our options? I'm specifically interested in the alcohol intervention program called IDIP. Can't talk now, though.

Within five minutes, she texts back.

OMG, I'm so sorry. Is she okay?

I reply:

She hit a tree but appears fine. At the ER now just to be sure. No other parties involved.

A few minutes pass before I get another notification.

Glad to hear that. I'll be there at 8:30 AM. Email me a copy of the police report tonight.

I say a mental prayer of thanks and then text:

Big thanks! I'll send scanned copies shortly. XO

I dash to my car to scan the police report with my phone app, then return to the waiting room and scroll my email for the first time in hours.

Naturally, there's one from Rachel, because more pressure is exactly what I need.

To: Emerson@ecwrites.com
From: rmoon@gmail.com
Re: Status Report and New Outline

Emerson,

Checking in to see how you're coming with *Tropic Heat*. Also, I've attached a few paragraphs outlining the next book in the series. We should set a time to brainstorm and flesh that out a bit. It will be due on November 15.

Best,
R

I lean forward and hug my thighs while the floor falls away. There's no way to brainstorm the next book while playing catch-up on the current manuscript and facing the legalities of my mother's arrest.

Quit. The thought raps on my brain like an unexpected visitor.

Equally unexpected is my instinctual resistance. Glass Beach may technically be Rachel's series, but my heart and soul are woven through every page. The fans are "ours," even if they don't know me. The thought of letting someone else finish the series makes me bristle.

My reaction mimics my father's probable resistance to anyone writing his characters in his world, even if the story would be based on his outline. That weighs heavily against accepting Henry's offer.

Tonight isn't the time for big decisions, so I reply:

Rachel,

I'm in the middle of a family emergency right now that will require my attention for a few weeks. I'm making every effort to finish the current manuscript per the accelerated schedule, but I can't brainstorm new ideas until I have a better handle on this crisis. Thank you for your understanding.

Em

My legs jiggle. A kind person would express concern, but Rachel has never struck me as someone who'd take well to pushback.

I tuck the phone in my pocket and glance around the room. The mother and toddler are gone, replaced by six other sick or injured people. Our feet scuff as we shift around in the vinyl seats trying to get comfortable.

The familiar if unpleasant antiseptic smell reminds me of my dad's various checkups and tests. That hits especially hard considering I, too, may end up spending too much time here in a decade or so. My eyes close to shut out those thoughts.

With the exception of the twenty minutes spent with Sawyer, today has been a spectacular catastrophe. His easygoing grin and disarming directness streamed like rain through the cracks in my dry, splintered heart. I'm thirsty for more, but if he has any sense, he's grateful we forgot to exchange numbers. I don't even know his last name.

A nurse signals for me to follow her back to where my mother is asleep on a gurney waiting for a doctor to discuss her test results. She's hooked up to a heart monitor and an IV for rehydration.

The clock reads nine-twelve. When I blink, my eyes feel dry and chalky.

I shift in my seat, text Sadie the latest, play a little Scrabble, all while listening to beeping call buttons and other patients' moaning.

The staff shuffle around, stopping occasionally to chat with each other or share a joke. Laughter seems out of place when surrounded by so much suffering. I suppose compartmentalizing is how we all move forward in the face of uncertainty and pain and loss. Why is that so much harder for me than for most?

A young woman enters the room and introduces herself as the PA. "Aside from a mild concussion, your mother's okay. The scans show no fractures or bleeding."

"That's a relief." Sadly, the news doesn't negate my mother's legal issues.

Her grogginess makes it unclear how much of the conversation is even registering as the PA explains the paperwork. "The doctor will stop by to answer any questions you might have. Then a nurse will be in to unhook the IV so you can go home."

By the time the doctor appears and they discharge my mother, it's past ten o'clock.

After we return to my car, my mother reclines her seat. "Take me home, please. I'm exhausted."

"Come to my house tonight, just to be safe. I'll take you home tomorrow." I put the car in reverse, yawning and heavy-limbed.

"Emerson, I want my own bed."

"I'd like to keep an eye on you tonight without disrupting Sadie."

"I don't want her to see me like this," she says quietly.

"Neither do I," I reply. "But she knows about the accident and the arrest. Those bruises will take more than a week to fade, so there's no hiding from her. Besides, Mel will be over first thing tomorrow to discuss the charges."

My mother hangs her head with a whimper. "I'm embarrassed."

I reach across the car to stroke her forearm, her shame made more painful to bear because of my own. "She's like family, and she's seen way worse."

By the time we get home, we both look as if we've pulled consecutive all-nighters.

Sadie bursts through the front door, rubbing her arms to ward off the night air's bite while we clamber out of my car.

"Oh my gosh, Gran! That looks so painful. Are you okay?" She wraps my mother in the hug I never offered.

I ache, standing on the outside, yearning for that same connection. We're a mess: me with my typewriter, Sadie and her secrets, my mother's addiction. Things have to change.

My mother gingerly kisses Sadie's head. "It's not as bad as it looks."

"Don't lie, Gran. I had a concussion freshman year from the New Canaan match. It hurt like a mother—" She pauses, catching herself. "It hurt a lot."

My mother nods, but my stomach drops as the ground turns soft beneath my feet. Sadie had a concussion? Surely I should remember that.

"What's the matter, Mom?" Sadie's brows draw together.

"Nothing." I rub my forehead as if that will reanimate my faltering memory. Nada. It's terrifying. Was I so consumed with my father's mental decline that I never noticed my own?

Hold it together. Don't scare Sadie.

"What took you guys so long?" Sadie asks.

"Red tape. Understaffing. Who knows?" I nudge them along the walkway to get us out of the cold and into bed, although a good night's sleep feels like a pipe dream.

"Everything was fine, like I said." My mother's chin rises.

Everything except for a mild concussion, a court date, and a suspended license.

Not that I utter a word. Anything that smacks of judgment will hardly improve things between Sadie and me.

The porch steps creak beneath our weight as we help my mother climb them. She winces with each step, pain beginning to bleed through now that the alcohol has worn off.

After we're safely inside, I say, "Sadie, please get Gran some water while I make up the guest room."

Thankfully, my mother is gracious about this sleepover in front of Sadie.

I trot upstairs to make up the bed with fresh sheets, still trying to refill the blank space where memories of Sadie's concussion should be. My head feels like I'm the one who crashed into a tree. Splashing my face with cold water doesn't help.

Armed with one of my nightgowns, two fresh towels, a new toothbrush, and two Advil, I go to the guest room and make up the daybed before returning to the kitchen. Mopsy brushes against my mother's leg while she drinks a cranberry-lime seltzer.

"Let's get some rest so we're sharp for our appointment," I say, desperate for a few moments to myself.

"What appointment?" Sadie asks.

"Mel is coming to discuss Gran's charges in the morning. You have school, so off to bed as well."

My mother tosses the empty can in the recycling bin and then gives Sadie another kiss on the forehead. "Good night, darling girl."

"Good night, Gran."

"Do you need help?" I ask my mother.

"I'm not an invalid." She moves away, her posture as erect as any dignitary's. When she reaches the doorway, she glances over her shoulder and locks gazes with me. "Thank you, Emerson."

There have been many times I've wished for her gratitude. Tonight it's unearned, given that her present situation arose from my manipulative impulses. If anything, I should be apologizing to her. "Don't mention it."

After she's gone, Sadie eyes me. "You look mad."

"Shaken, not mad." It might be a relief to confess, but it's too much to put on a teen, especially at this hour. I default to other truths that have me worried. "It's hard to know if this is her first time driving drunk or simply the first time she got caught. Will there be a next time? Plus, these legal headaches are coming at the worst time, with my accelerated deadline. I'm just really tired."

Sadie drops her chin and picks at her nails. "People make mistakes, Mom. Can't you just forgive her instead of being so disappointed?"

My defenses rise faster than a quick-drawn pistol, but her demeanor suggests she's speaking to more than my mother's transgression. My response may determine whether she ever shares her problems with me.

"I forgive her, honey, but I want her to stop hurting herself. If she'd talk to me instead of brushing off my concerns, we could find answers together." As subtext goes, that wasn't subtle.

"Maybe she figures it's too late to change anything, including your opinion."

How can my daughter think me so callous when my entire life has been a steady diet of forgive and move on? "Sadie, I've never given up on anyone I love."

"You judge them, though."

I swallow thickly. "I've never judged you."

"Not yet." Her solemn gaze breaks something inside. My heart, sure, but my entire sense of us is also rocked.

Of all my traits she could've inherited, she pulled the chronic-overthinker gene, rendering useless everything I did to provide stability and comfort to free her of that burden.

"Not ever," I promise.

Her dubious expression persists. "Guess I'll go to bed."

"Good night." I hug her long and hard, as if somehow that will wash away my sins.

After she leaves, I exhale, body quivering. Not even an hour of flinging paint around would do the job tonight.

Instead, I check the cupboards for alcohol, collecting half bottles of gin, vodka, and whiskey. I take them to my car and lock them in the trunk so my sleep isn't disrupted by worry about my mother sneaking booze in the wee hours.

On my way back inside, the flowerbeds taunt me. Reminders of those first wishes that sent me down this dangerous path.

I drop to my knees, muscles spastic. The bulbs sway in the breeze. How did we get here?

That typewriter. My dad's secretiveness. All the dysfunction and drama trace back to when he became someone I barely recognized long before he was diagnosed. Years' worth of questions gone without answers, making me dizzy with anger.

I reach out to finger the waxy petals only to then crush the flower in my palm. I pluck its stem, and then another, and another. My fingers dig into the cold earth to rip the roots from the hard ground while I mutter to myself.

I need a fresh start. A do-over. Something—anything—to fix what's so broken in me. Some new method of coping with life's disappointments and uncertainty that doesn't push my daughter away. She's all that is good and beautiful in my life. It breaks me to think I might become the reason she walks away.

When the last tulip falls from my hand, I sit back on my heels, swiping snot and tears with the back of my forearm. Stalks and petals lie scattered around me like the body parts of a butchered murder victim. My heart aches so much it barely beats.

All the lights in my house are dark. I glance around to see if any neighbors witnessed my breakdown. Hopefully not. Crawling around, I gather the broken stems and buds, then throw them in the trash can and look heavenward for help.

Quietly I enter the kitchen, where I scrub at my hands and nails in hot water until they're raw.

Mopsy follows me from the kitchen into my office. I lock the door and lift her off the floor. Sinking onto my chair, I run my fingers through her thick white fur. "You know I never wanted to hurt anyone, right?"

I cuddle her closer to my chest, but even she can't help me feel better tonight.

When she jumps to the floor, I open the folder containing my wishes. The most recent sits on top of the pile.

```
I'm begging the universe for help with getting my
mother to attend an alcohol intervention program.
```

If not for this note, my mother might be safely at home. I might've enjoyed dessert with Sawyer instead of Diet Pepsi in the ER. Except I probably wouldn't have met Sawyer without the Underwood. And this arrest could lead to my mother's sobriety—a significant silver lining. Despite everything I've ever believed, perhaps there are shades of gray around right and wrong.

This must be how drugs work. The object of addiction somehow also feels like the only solution. My mother battles this push-pull every day. Alcohol is her escape, just as mine is attempting to magically create a more perfect life.

Funny thing is, I'm no happier or less worried today than I was before stealing Dad's typewriter.

Mopsy pads to the door and lies down, as if she wants to be as far away from me thinking about those wishes as possible. I rip the typed pages into strips and toss them in the trash.

The contentious lucky charm remains stowed in my cabinet. I could destroy it, but demolishing his beloved keepsake feels as wrong as using it again would. Unless, of course, it's "the evidence" he meant to destroy.

The fact that he didn't suggests he found a way to minimize the risks. If only I could, too . . .

One glance at my dirty knees reminds me not to consider it.

I back away from the cabinet, keeping my eyes on its doors as if they might fling open and suck me inside.

"Let's go to bed, Mopsy." When I reach the office door, I shut off the lights.

It can't hurt anyone else as long as it remains hidden.

Twenty-Five

A blue jay soars from the dogwood tree outside my kitchen window, headed for greener pastures. Lucky bird. It's 8:05 AM. I yawn while measuring out coffee grounds. Twenty-five minutes until Mel arrives. Thankfully, Sadie has already left for school.

Overhead, the floorboards creak beneath my mother's footsteps. Impressive, considering she had a fifty-fifty chance of feeling too sick to get out of bed.

It's been at least twelve hours since her last drink. According to Google, the earliest symptoms of withdrawal—dry mouth, headache, nausea—should be hitting her now. More concerning is that a cold-turkey withdrawal can be life-threatening. She's likely to fight my ideas about how we should approach this week, which means I, too, will soon have a headache.

I check my email on the phone. Rachel hasn't said anything about my pushback beyond a short *Good luck. Will be in touch soon.* What does that mean? It doesn't sound like she's rescheduling the brainstorming session.

Mercifully, the coffeemaker beeps. I pour out a cup, indulging myself with a full teaspoon of sugar. Steam tickles my nose while the coffee's comforting aroma goes to work on my muscles. Fairly sure my surviving the next hour is dependent upon caffeine. It may also require Oreos.

My mother descends the stairs slowly, her injuries slowing her pace.

When she rounds the corner to the kitchen, I shrink at the sight of her swollen face.

Borrowed pink cotton loungewear drapes a bit over her shoulders. She's rolled the hem of the pants, but it'll do until we bring some of her clothes here. That is, if she agrees to my plan.

She sits beside the glass of water and ibuprofen I've already placed on the counter. I pass her a cup of coffee along with the legal engagement letter Mel emailed late last night.

"Thank you." She practically lunges at the painkillers.

"Would you like toast or eggs?"

"God, no." She sticks out her tongue. "I feel sick."

As expected, although there are no obvious signs of perspiration, dizziness, or shakiness. Worse symptoms would include a racing heart, disorientation, seizures, and delirium.

The safest course of action would be to check into a facility for the first week of detox, but that suggestion can wait until Mel arrives. Otherwise, it's likely to devolve into an argument.

We enjoy a few sips of coffee in silence, me eyeing her while she closes her eyes. There are other things to discuss, and now is as good a time as any. "Mom, can we talk about some stuff before Mel gets here?"

Elbows on the peninsula, she's holding her head with one hand. "I'm not up for a big discussion."

"Me neither, but it's time-sensitive."

She blows out a breath. "I know it was selfish to drive yesterday. I do. I don't know why I did it. I really don't."

The typewriter, probably, but that's not what I want to discuss. Sadie's opinion about me has me choosing my words carefully. "It's fair to say you haven't been happy for a long time. Dad . . . he changed a lot over the years. He wasn't always kind or predictable, even before he got sick."

Her gaze remains downcast, as if her coffee mug were the most interesting thing in the room. I hesitate to press, but this feels like a once-in-a-blue-moon opportunity to force a turning point.

"My point is, you might not be mourning him in the traditional sense, but you've been more erratic since he died. The haste to sell the house. A move to Manhattan. Yesterday's behavior with Will and the arrest." When I pause, she hits me with a *what's your point?* expression. "It seems like this isn't the time for you to spend so much time alone. Would you consider moving in here—temporarily?"

"I don't need a babysitter." She shakes her head. "I'm fine, Emerson."

"I beg to differ." I gesture to her bruises. "Besides, you can't drive for a while. If you're here, Sadie and I can chauffeur you around."

"Three of us here? We'll suffocate each other, especially with you watching my every move." She rubs her temples.

There will be challenges, but I owe her this much considering my role in our situation. "You used to prefer cozy spaces. Plus, you'll get to spend more time with Sadie before she goes to college in a year."

The world momentarily disintegrates beneath my feet. I'm not prepared for an empty nest, especially if my working memory is set to prematurely expire. That's an overwhelming stressor I can't think about this morning.

My mother eyes me skeptically, remaining silent.

"While you think on it, I have another question." I pour myself more coffee, stalling. "It's personal, so you don't have to answer."

She rolls her hand in that get-on-with-it way.

Here goes nothing. "The other week you said Dad made it impossible to leave, but he didn't lock you in the house. Why didn't you divorce him?"

With her hands clasped under her chin, she stares through me like she's debating with herself. "I tried, twice. The first time, you were fifteen. He threatened to exaggerate my drinking to sue for full custody. He always got everything he ever wanted, so he might've won. But he swore he'd change, so I stayed."

Dad's threat is no shock, but her decision to stay in an unhappy marriage for me despite my attitude toward her during high school sure is. I mask my surprise behind a neutral expression, hoping to learn more. "What about the second time?"

"After you graduated from college, I met with a lawyer. Your dad confronted me, but this time he couldn't hold custody over my head. I was halfway out the door when you asked to move back for help with Sadie." She sighs sheepishly while I try to make sense of my father's desperate attempts to stay married when he so often treated her with indifference. "It felt like a sign."

"Gosh, I'm not sure how to feel about that." Guilty. Stunned. Grateful?

She rallied during Sadie's infancy, providing me with both support and experience. If they had divorced, that first year with Sadie would have been infinitely harder.

It dawns on me that my father may have orchestrated this the same way I inadvertently engineered last night's accident. If my relationship with Doug got sacrificed to satisfy his desire to stop the divorce, did he consider Sadie's fatherless childhood acceptable collateral damage?

Of course I haven't proof of his intervention. Only suspicions. Those, however, are bitter enough to produce tears.

"Don't cry, dear," my mother says, misreading my dewy eyes. "I don't regret that decision. Sadie was our little miracle. I treasure those days as much as when you were born. Your dad could be a bastard, but he loved little kids. Sadie brought out his best. Remember how good things were for a while? He could be the most magnanimous, funny person. Those moods always gave me hope." She shudders as if coming out of a dream.

My family's past takes on completely different colors, knocking me off-balance.

Met by my silence, my mother smooths a hand over the counter. "I don't know. Maybe I was always a stupid woman."

"Or optimistic." Romantic, even, in a regrettable way. My age-old misperceptions make her something of a stranger now.

"Same thing, sometimes." She smiles wanly. "By the time you moved out, I was in my mid-fifties and figured better the devil I know. We'd learned to live around each other by then."

She glances at her ring finger, rubbing it where the wedding band used to sit. "It's sad. When we met, he was full of life. Full of promise and big dreams. I wanted to take the ride with him, too blinded to notice the high cost of admission."

The doorbell interrupts us, which is a welcome diversion, because I'm too raw to respond.

With my coffee in hand, I say, "Let's set up in the dining room. Grab a pen from the junk drawer to sign that letter so this is official and everything stays confidential."

My mother slides off the stool while I greet Mel.

"Good morning." Mel looks sharp in a red belted pantsuit. All business. Exactly what we need after that conversation.

"Thank you so much for coming on short notice." I hug her, holding my half-empty mug to the side. "I really appreciate it."

"Oh, don't be silly." Mel's head tilts as if the weight of my family history has rushed to one side of her brain. "Of course I'm here for you two."

Thank goodness.

"Come on in." I wave her inside. "Can I get you some coffee?"

"No thanks. Is your mother here yet?"

"Yes." I gesture toward the dining room. "Her car is in the shop."

Placing that call is on today's to-do list, pushing *Tropic Heat* farther down the page. I should probably feel worse about that fact, but Rachel's recent attitude makes it easier for me to deprioritize her demands.

My mother rises slightly, extending her cheek for a cordial kiss hello. "Mel, you look fabulous. Most people today dress so casually for work."

You'd think she was lunching at the country club instead of discussing her criminal court date. Then again, concealing emotions is another way she and I are more alike than I ever realized.

"Wish I could return the compliment, Dorothy. That all looks painful." She circles her finger around my mother's face. "Are you feeling up to this?"

My mother waves off Mel's concern, sliding the signed engagement letter across the table. "I'm fine. There's no need for us all to make a big deal out of nothing."

Mel and I exchange a look as she sets out her tablet and takes a seat, moving the letter aside. "It's not nothing. I'm glad you're all right, but I read the police report. Property damage, car damage, and a blood-alcohol level nearly twice the legal limit. A judge is likely to take this matter rather seriously even though no one else was involved. That part was pure luck."

My mother looks down, tapping her fingers against her cup.

"Thank goodness, too, or you'd be looking at felony charges," Mel adds firmly.

That loaded f-word makes my mother blanch, proving Mel's directness had its intended effect.

I remain silent, letting Mel be the one to convince my mother to acquiesce. She walks us through the process—the court hearing, the potential fines and, in some cases, jail time, even for first-time offenses.

My mother blots her damp forehead. It's hard to determine how much she's processing when she's obviously in discomfort. Her skin is growing pale beneath the bruising—a warning of intensifying withdrawal symptoms.

"May I be frank?" Mel asks.

"Always." My mother folds her hands on the table, shoulders squared as if Mel is the judge about to hand down a sentence.

Mel sighs, setting her iPad aside and leaning forward. "I think you should view this as an opportunity."

Amen.

"How so?" Mom asks.

"It's a chance to reassess your relationship with alcohol before something worse happens."

My mother would light into me had I made that remark. Good manners keep her in check with Mel. Only her brittle tone hints at her mood. "Reassess?"

"In my experience, half of DUI offenders struggle with heavy drinking, defined as fourteen drinks per week." Mel lets my mom do her own math.

My guess? She's double that amount.

Mel continues, "Connecticut offers a diversionary program to first-time offenders called Impaired Driving Intervention Program, or IDIP. Basically, we can ask the judge to enroll you in an alcohol program. If you complete it successfully, the charges get dropped. No DUI conviction on your record. Plus, you'll exit the program with a better handle on your drinking. It's a win-win."

My mother crosses her arms on the table. "Wouldn't it be better to fight the charges?"

"On its face, the cops followed procedure, so there's no obvious basis to exclude any evidence. They've got the alcohol test results, the failed field sobriety tests, the property damage and eyewitness testimony." Mel shrugs. "I'm not a magician. Maybe if you'd been pulled over before you damaged someone's personal property, we could've gotten it kicked. But there's a third party involved who may raise a stink. In my honest opinion, you're looking at fines and a misdemeanor, maybe community service."

My mom drums her fingers on the table, her gaze directed over our shoulders into some middle distance.

Mel leans forward, her expression more concerned doctor than lawyer. "Dorothy, we're basically family. Your drinking affects everything from your health and safety to your relationships. Now it's even threatening others' lives. After all you've been through with Jefferson's Alzheimer's, give yourself the gift of this help. Start this next phase in better mental and physical health."

Sudden streaks of red climb my mother's neck and cheeks. "You two are ganging up on me. Maybe I should hire an impartial lawyer."

"This is impartial advice," Mel says, although I suspect she's trying to help me as much as defend my mother.

Guilt might shut me up if I wasn't desperate for change. I rest my hand on Mel's forearm while looking at my mother.

"When I was little, you were happy. A librarian who loved to read. A mom who made elaborate birthday cakes. Who whisked me off to the farm in Vermont for a few weeks every summer, both of us up to our elbows in muck. There was so much passion in your face. So much laughter." Tears wash over my words, which spill out in a hushed tone. "I'd give anything for Sadie to know that woman before it's too late."

Mel hands me a paper napkin to wipe my sniffles.

My mother sits frozen as an ice sculpture, staring over Mel's shoulder at the wall. Her sweat-coated forehead is the only outward sign of distress.

"Dorothy, I work for you, so no matter what we think, you get to decide," Mel says. "If you want to plead not guilty, I'll do my best."

Clever move. Giving my mother a chance to save face might make all the difference.

"That said," Mel continues, "I believe the IDIP is the best scenario legally and for your family."

"This incident will be in the paper, won't it?" my mother asks, stalling.

Mel nods. All arrests are reported weekly in our local online newspaper, which everybody reads, mostly for gossip about the police blotter and the real estate transactions.

"I don't want to sit in class with a bunch of convicts." Quite a judgment considering that her actions make her one, too. Everyone becomes a hypocrite eventually.

Mel nods in sympathy. "We could ask for a special accommodation, given your family's notoriety. Silver Hill in New Canaan has an intensive outpatient DBT program for substance abuse. Three mornings a week for ten weeks. It's known for its discretion. I could ask the judge to allow that option to fulfill the IDIP requirements."

It sounds more rigorous than what the state would require, not that I need Mel to confirm my suspicion. The entire room feels like it's holding our collective breath.

"Sounds like I don't have much choice," my mother concedes.

Mel raises her hands, sporting a "you got me" face. "This is the smart choice. The criminal record will go away, your insurance rates should remain stable, and best of all, you'll get a new lease on life."

My mother's nostrils flare. She's got to be furious—with us, with herself, with the fact that her drinking caught up to her in such a public way. "Fine."

"Great." Mel slides her iPad and stylus back in her briefcase before standing. "I'll start the paperwork to get this approved at the hearing. In the meantime, I'll call Silver Hill to make sure they can provide what you need."

I interrupt. "Can I add something? Last night I read up on the detox process. It can be fatal in some cases."

"Honestly, Emerson." My mother grips the table's edge, her face warping into a scowl. "You act like I'm a drunk in the street."

She was last night. "You drink daily, are in your late sixties, and weigh one hundred pounds, tops. Those are all risk factors. I'm not a nurse. I don't know how to deal with seizures. Maybe we should consider a supervised detox at Silver Hill."

"You just invited me to move in here, and now you're shipping me off to rehab." Her eyes flash like lightning.

"I'm not 'shipping you off.' I'm asking you to take five days to make sure you survive withdrawal before you move in."

"It's a good idea," Mel says. "It'd also spare Sadie from witnessing some frightening side effects."

My mother grabs her face to hide from us. "You girls have all the answers, but I won't be railroaded. I don't want to go to a hospital."

"Mom. Please."

My mother glances at me. "I'll hire a private nurse like we did for your dad. Maybe Sadie can stay with a friend for a few days."

Mel interjects, apparently sensing a compromise. "We'd be happy to keep Sadie."

This isn't my first choice, although pushing other options may be counterproductive. "What if we can't find someone to start today?"

"Everything can be had for the right price," my mother huffs.

"That's asking a lot of Mel and Sadie, Mom." Not to mention that my deadline will be harder to meet if I'm playing hostess to the nurses who rotate through our house.

"You've bullied me into this IDIP, but I'm drawing a line." She tips that nose of hers upward.

Living through her withdrawal may be my karmic payback for having had some hand in causing the accident. It'll be unpleasant, but at least she'll be monitored by a professional. "Fine. I'll let Sadie know and make some calls."

"I'll tell Chris to expect Sadie this evening." Mel nods. "I've got to get to the office. If you have any questions, let me know."

"Thank you." My mother stands to kiss Mel's cheek.

"I'll be in touch," she says.

I show Mel out, giving my mother a few moments to compose herself. At the top of the porch steps, I grab my friend for another hug. "Thank you so much. I pray this fiasco twists into a gift."

"I think it might." Mel pats my back and rocks us side to side before easing away. "I'll let you know once I confirm everything with Silver Hill."

"Fingers crossed." I hold up both sets. "And hey, sorry to interfere with your family's weekend. Maybe after the first couple of nights, things will settle down enough for Sadie to come home."

"Don't worry about it." Mel stops on the first step. "Wow, these tulips are amazing. Did you finally hire a gardener?"

I assume she's joking until I glance down. Dozens of perfect yellow tulips greet me like soldiers standing at attention, leaving me slack-jawed. How are they back? Ablaze with panic, I snap my mouth shut and choke back surprise. Once I recover myself, I say, "Fertilizer."

Of the typed-wish variety.

"Nice job." She waves, then gets into her car and pulls away.

If she only knew. This is no joke, though. More like a warning. A reminder of my father's lament about being unable to undo all he'd done. To judge by these flowers, there really isn't any way to undo what's been typed. Jesus, that's terrifying.

What does it mean for me and my wishes? Will the sale of the house be indefinitely delayed? Will I take to puking any time I gain weight or keep being asked to write my father's final book? What about my mother's autonomy?

I stumble down the steps and finger some petals. It's incredible. Totally real, despite last night's meltdown. Was that a dream?

I jog to the garbage can, removing the lid to check for the remnants of my breakdown. There's nothing there. But I'm sure I did it. I washed my hands afterward, didn't I?

This permanence is sickening. No wonder my dad's remorseful plea begged for a little peace of mind. I tremble, having doomed myself to forever question the ripple effect of my wishes.

My pulse lapses into an asynchronous rhythm. What the hell got into me, playing around with my life—other people's lives? My mother may come out here searching for me, so I head inside, cycling through my wishes, looking for booby traps. Worse than the guilt and the fear is the knowing, deep deep down, that despite the cost, I'm grateful for the ultimate outcome of my last wish.

The outpatient program isn't perfect, but it's happening. It's finally happening. If it works, it gives my mother back her life. It also gives me back my mother, so I can't fully regret it.

Clearly I need a detox program for magic addicts. This is it. I am done with the Underwood. I swear it.

Inside the house, the dining room is empty. Mopsy must be hiding, which she does whenever there's tension. My mom isn't in the kitchen, either, so I go upstairs to the guest room, where I find her by the bed snapping her purse shut.

"Is there alcohol in there?" I point at her purse. The cravings must be hitting hard. I should've checked that handbag for small bottles while she was sleeping.

"No." She clutches it to her chest. "I don't have to put up with this. I'd like to go home now."

"You agreed to stay here with a nurse." I cross my arms, bracing for an argument.

"Not if you're going to treat me like a prisoner." She points her finger at me. A preview of the moodiness ahead. "I don't answer to you."

"I'm asking you only to be considerate of my feelings."

My mother thrusts her purse forward, opening it to show me that there's no booze stowed there. The room temperature plunges to an arctic climate.

"Now, I need to go home to get some personal things and my own clothes." She tugs at the too-big top for emphasis. "Will the warden allow it?"

"I'll come help you pack." It's not like I have a deadline or anything.

She plants a palm on her forehead. "Emerson, I can't be watched all the time. That's what your father did. I don't want to live that way anymore."

Her high pitch reverberates with desperation.

"This isn't forever." I soften my stance but not my position. Not when her house is loaded with all her favorite drinks. "You're my mother. I'd like things between us to be better. Wouldn't you?"

She backs herself against the dresser. "You act like this friction is entirely my fault. Like you haven't pushed me away. But you rejected me first, Emerson. You always took your father's side."

"That's not true," I answer.

She's fighting tears. "Now who's not being honest?"

Her lens, like Sadie's, captures me at an unflattering angle.

I think back, trying to peel away the filters and be honest with myself. Really honest. It's neither easy nor comfortable to question my own beliefs. Especially when I'm now seeing some of my father's less gracious attributes in myself.

"Maybe that's true. Dad made life fun. He ignored limitations. Despite his moods, he was a dreamer who made me believe anything was possible." I sigh. "Maybe I blamed you for making Dad unhappy with your criticisms and drinking, which wasn't entirely fair because it let him off the hook for his faults." Had I known about the Underwood, I might've blamed his moods on that obsession instead of my mother. "But, Mom, when you drank, that felt like rejection. Like that mattered more to you than I did. So, yeah, I withdrew."

The confession sits between us for a long moment. It's awkward standing there saying nothing, so I roll my shoulders and add, "We can't change how we got here, so we either hold a grudge or start over."

I lean against the doorjamb, entirely depleted and heavy with dread. This is it. It's either the end of us or a new beginning.

My mother regards me in silence, lowering her purse. "Then I guess we start over."

Twenty-Six

June 12, 2018

I don't want to write this entry because, once I put ink to paper, it will feel real in a way it hasn't yet. And I don't want it to be true.

I'm losing—hell, have lost—the ability to write my stories. It's humiliating. I've created entire worlds with words my whole life. Now they slip from me like dreams, leaving me clawing through fog. Words I can't find. Plotlines that dissolve like sugar in tea. Even this journal can be a challenge.

I tried keeping a detailed to-do list to move myself forward, but there are the days I forget about my list or forget to cross off items.

One word that's always with me is regret. Regrets! So many regrets.

Dorothy's complaints and examples of my memory lapses had often seemed piddling, and the bigger ones, well . . . I figured they were normal with age. But I couldn't keep fooling myself.

I finally saw a neurologist, hoping for some pills or shots or surgery. Anything! After a series of tests, today Dr. Rosenthal told me that I'm in the early stages of Alzheimer's.

At sixty-four.

That news makes a man take stock of his life. In my case, that's no comfort.

Take my career. How much credit can I take? Sure, there's a bit of luck in any writer's journey. And things were going well before I bought that typewriter. But I tipped the scales with those early wishes.

Facing the end of my life as something of a fraud is almost worse than this illness, but at least it's one memory I'll be happy to lose.

But my girls—I don't want to forget them. And I don't want them seeing me as feeble.

What will Dorothy do when I'm gone? I'm pretty sure her anger toward me keeps her alive.

I wish I'd never bought that Underwood. At least I will eventually forget how it felt to bend the world to my whim. Maybe then I'll have some peace.

But here's the kicker, as they say. It may sound paranoid, but I think the damned typewriter caused my memory problems.

How's that for poetic justice? My fucking good-luck charm might be a curse.

Before the appointment with Dr. Rosenthal, I leafed through my old notebooks to make a list of examples so the doc had accurate information. Turns out a lot of the "forgetting" occurred after I typed a wish.

I know. Sounds ludicrous. This whole damn thing is, but that doesn't make it a lie.

I wonder if the prior owner had memory issues. So many decades have passed, it may be impossible to track down that family.

My old journal shows I picked up the typewriter on Sunset Road circa November 1995. A tag sale. Not much to go on.

Learning the truth about whether the equipment caused this won't change it, but I need to know if I did this to myself.

If so, I should get rid of the thing before my girls get their hands on it.

That's an item for the to-do list I can't afford to forget.

Twenty-Seven

Last night's sleep was interrupted a dozen times by my mother's groans, restless thrashing, and vomiting. With each occurrence, I fumbled down the hallway to take her temperature and feel her pulse. The only thing that got me out of bed this morning was the promise of this hot shower.

After five minutes, I lower the temperature to spike my energy with an icy spray before wrapping myself in a fluffy towel. The nurse will be here shortly, thank goodness, or I'd never get through today's long to-do list.

Before brushing my teeth, I slip into a robe. Seconds later, a soft moan drifts down the hall. I spit out my toothpaste, pull my wet hair into a twist, and wring out a cold washcloth before trotting to the guest room.

Mopsy remains at the foot of the bed, where she's been camped all night. My mother's sheets are damp, as if she, too, has just showered. Matted hair, face etched with pain. Her pores emit the sour odor of leached toxins.

I kneel beside her to wipe her forehead and neck. In her fever dream state, she left a fresh deposit in the bucket by the bed. Pushing it aside, I breathe through my mouth while reaching for the still-full water bottle on the nightstand.

"You need to stay hydrated to ease some of the symptoms, Mom." I bring the bottle top to her lips.

"Just let me die," she whines dramatically, although there's little doubt that she's already in hell.

"Come on. Drink a little." I pry the bottle top through her pursed lips.

Half the water dribbles down her chin. Her rapid pulse beats against the fingers I've wrapped around her wrist, causing my own heart rate to take off. She's limp. Frail. Pitiful, with so little fight in her. What I'd give for her haughtiness to return for five minutes.

She manages a few swallows before pushing the bottle away. "Enough."

During the roughly thirty-six hours since the accident, she's called me colonel (not in a complimentary way), bossy, unreasonable, and cruel. She's pleaded for sips of wine or gin, throwing pillows and weak punches whenever I refused. In the middle of the night, her hands began trembling.

The indignity is reminiscent of my father's unforgiving end. Please, God, let this exorcism yield a better result.

Could the typewriter ensure that? Maybe . . . but I'm too afraid to risk breaking my vow. The arrest and car crash weren't in the realm of my intentions when wishing her into rehab. The Underwood might kill her to "stop the pain."

My mother writhes in bed, craving the poison that has infected her. Her body continues to fight a healthy change rather than embrace it. In that way, it's not all that different from mental trauma. Familiar discomfort can seem safer than the unknown, keeping us pinned in our misery.

It's 8:01.

"Where is the nurse?" I mutter to myself, on the verge of weeping.

My mother shivers, so I add another blanket to her pile. Her agony intensifies my guilt. My penance is wiping her sweat, helping her to the bathroom, cleaning up vomit. It doesn't feel like enough, but confessing is out of the question.

When the doorbell rings, my body goes limp with relief.

"I'll be right back." I lay my hand on the blankets.

She doesn't care. Her face remains pinched with discomfort.

Removing the trash can to the hall, I then jog downstairs to welcome Nala, the nurse from Home Detox Agency.

According to yesterday's email, Nala has ten years' experience with the company and twenty years' experience in ER care.

Her smile is outlined by full, berry-stained lips, which complement her dark skin and eyes. She's carrying a hefty bag of medication and whatever devices she'll use to keep my mother alive.

"Welcome, Nala." I extend my hand. "I'm Emerson, Dorothy's daughter."

"Good morning." Her firm grip matches her outward confidence. "You look tired."

I laugh, flummoxed by her candor, then wave her inside. "I'm so glad you're here."

She's built like an apple on toothpicks, yet she enters the house with swagger. "Where's the patient?"

"Upstairs in bed." I scrub my hands over my face, my cold shower failing to keep me alert. "It's been hard to keep her hydrated. She's thrown up three times. She's sweaty and a little shaky. Her pulse feels rapid, but otherwise she's hanging in there."

"Show me to her so I can make my own assessment." She rubs the tip of her nose like it tickles.

"Of course. This way." I lead her to the guest room, where I crack open the windows to let in some fresh air. "Mom, this is Nala. She'll be one of the nurses taking care of you these next few days."

Twenty-four-hour care for five days should get us through the danger zone.

My mother grunts, her body coiling into a ball. Abandoning all good manners, she neither says hello nor opens her eyes. Nala appears unperturbed as she sets her bag on the small desk.

I cross my arms, feeling helpless. "Should I show you around—like the bathroom in the hall, or the kitchen, or whatever else you need to know?"

"I'm good." Nala shakes her head while unzipping her bag.

"I'm happy to help, whatever you need."

She waves me off. "I know you're worried, but it's gonna be okay. Trust me. I've got it from here."

I inhale my first deep breath in twenty-four hours, tempted to fall at her feet in thanks. "All right. I have to run some errands but should be back in a few hours."

At which point I'll park myself in my office and play catch-up on *Tropic Heat* after taking yesterday off.

On my way out of the guest room, I turn around. "Can I at least bring you coffee or water or something to eat?"

"No, thank you." Nala glances over her shoulder. "I brought my own lunch for later."

With a half shrug, I relent. "Make yourself at home. My cell number should be in the paperwork, but I'll leave it on the kitchen counter, too." I hesitate. "You'll call me if there's any trouble?"

Nala points at me. "I see you're a worrier, but you can leave that to me now. We'll be just fine, won't we, Miss Dorothy?"

She retrieves an iPad and a blood pressure cuff from the bag and sets them on the desk.

"Thank you." It's past time to take Nala's fourth not-so-subtle hint to heart and leave. "Mom, I hope the worst is almost past."

Closing the door to give them privacy, I then empty and rinse the bucket before setting it outside the guest-room door. After pulling on jeans and a T-shirt, I pad downstairs. My stomach turns when I pass by my office.

It's not just the pressure to finish *Tropic Heat*. Rachel sent a calendar invitation to brainstorm the new book for the day after the manuscript is due. Our power imbalance has begun to chafe like a too-small shoe.

I do have a choice. Henry's still awaiting my response. This ongoing waffling could cost me that opportunity and my current job. The truth is that the one story that keeps invading my thoughts lately is *Fires*. But it's too uncertain. So much editing is needed. Given everything going on with my family, I don't think this is the time to invest in myself or that project.

Tropic Heat has to be my focus today. But first I've been commanded by Kathryn to remove personal items from my parents' home prior to the impending broker open house this week. On my way over there, I swing by Mel's to check on Sadie.

Mel opens the door decked out in a plum-colored yoga outfit. Her face is freshly scrubbed, blue eyes brimming with the vigor of stress-free sleep. "Oh, hey. I was on my way to a class."

I grimace. "Sorry to show up without calling. I came to check on Sadie."

"Come in, come in." She grabs my arm and drags me over the threshold. "Tell me what's happening."

Mel's habitually untidy house is one of the pleasant constants in my life, and not only because it always smells like freshly baked bread. Stepping inside is as comforting as snuggling under a blanket in front of a fire. "The nurse is with her now."

"You look like you've been through the wringer." Mel narrows her gaze, pinning me with the "spill it" look she perfected in high school. "How rough was last night?"

"Lots of vomit but no major crisis. She's suffering, though. It's not pretty. I'm trying to focus on the future, when things should be better." If anyone understands what this detox could mean for my family, it's Mel.

"Good." She releases my arm, taking the scrunchie off her wrist and looping her hair into a high ponytail. "I know it sucks, but really, this is for the best. I mean, when you think about it, this arrest might've saved her life."

That's what I tell myself whenever guilt bares its teeth and chews at my conscience. But my secret doesn't allow me to fool myself for long.

As if reading my mind, Mel says, "Em, I know you struggle when life messes with your plans, but try to have faith." She squeezes me tightly. I collapse against her, holding back tears. She pats my back, letting me borrow her strength for an extra minute longer than normal. "We'll get her into Silver Hill's program, the charges will be removed, and by autumn, she'll be sober."

Her words have the effect of the hands of a masseuse, easing the tension from my muscles. Confidence in happy endings is a gift she takes for granted. I've never needed to believe her more than right now.

Not only because of my mother's crisis, but also because of the upcoming neurological exam. My stomach turns any time I imagine slowly forgetting my entire life. I want to tell Mel about my appointment, but can't. Not now. Not here. Not when I've got so much on my mind.

But the possibility circles like a stealth bomber that will shatter me and everyone who cares for me. I get woozy thinking of how that diagnosis could cause my mom to relapse and create uncertainty for Sadie. The last thing my daughter needs is more grief. She's also way too young to lose her mother.

I draw myself up before Mel notices my mood. "I owe you for watching Sadie."

"Don't even!" Mel rolls her eyes, holding up her hand like a stop sign. "I love having another lady in the house. Is there anything else you need?"

"No, thanks." I shake my head. "You're doing plenty."

"All right. I think Sadie's in the family room. I'll catch up later. Stay strong!" She grabs the yoga mat by the door to the garage. Just before she leaves, she winks. "Oh, and don't think you're off the hook about Will. I want the four-one-one when the time is right."

That won't be half as juicy as she hopes. Hell, my life keeps changing so quickly, she doesn't even know about Sawyer.

I wander through the kitchen to the great room, where Sadie is reading on the overstuffed velvet sectional. Grant and Kevin are seated around the enormous coffee table, building an intricate Lego model. They barely glance up when I enter the room.

Sadie sets her book down, brows high but pinched. "Mom?"

"Hi, honey. Hey, guys!" I stride across the room, high-fiving the boys, then bend over to give my daughter a hug. She smells like sunshine and coconut, but dark half-moons underscore her eyes. "How are you?"

"Fine." Except she's not smiling.

"Sorry I was too busy with Gran last night to check in. Did you have a good day at school yesterday?"

"Not really." She pales and leans over to zip open the backpack tucked on the floor, retrieving a piece of paper and a pen. "You need to sign this."

She hands me the items.

"What is it?" I assume it's a permission slip until the word *detention* makes the entire floor feel as if it tilted thirty degrees.

I flatten a hand on the cushion to steady myself. The parenting books warn against overreacting, but that's a challenge, especially when I'm blindsided. "What happened?"

Sadie worries her lip. "I skipped some classes."

My shoulders slump. Who is this impostor and what has she done with my child? I jerk my head toward the kitchen to move this conversation away from Mel's boys. Sadie follows me with the enthusiasm of a witch being dragged to a stake.

"I don't understand, Sadie." My daughter normally frets over a B, yet the only thing she appears to care about now is getting this conversation over with as quickly as possible. "Why? Where did you go?"

The sharpness in my voice makes her wince.

She hesitates before answering. "Weed Beach. I was having a bad morning, but I felt better after cleaning up all the litter."

I mentally count to three to avoid a bigger argument. She's been handed a lot lately, and my mom's arrest and accident haven't helped. "Sadie, you can't run away from your responsibilities just because you're upset."

"I know, Mom. I just . . . I needed some space." She crosses her arms, acting bold despite the quaver in her voice. "Cutting class isn't the end of the world. I'm sorry, okay? It was one time."

I hold her gaze while thinking. It has been a shitty couple of weeks, and I doubt she'll do this again. My support may help more than a lecture about something she already knows is wrong would. The school-imposed consequence should do the heavy lifting, so I sign my name at the top of the paper and hand it back to her.

"Will this affect your captaincy for next year? Will this go on your transcript? Under the circumstances, maybe the principal might show some compassion."

Sadie shakes her head. "I don't deserve special treatment."

I would call myself, but after the pizza party debacle, I'm hesitant. "This could affect your college applications. After all your hard work, you could at least ask."

She looks at me through half-lidded eyes. "Or maybe it becomes an essay topic."

Sarcasm, the refuge of the belligerent.

"Oh, Sadie." I want to shake sense into her, my own desperation tearing at my restraint. "This all feels driven by more than a breakup or our family situations. Did Johnny do something to hurt you—did he pressure you?"

"No!" Her immediate response is both a relief and a puzzle.

She and I have discussed how victims of sexual assault often hide it due to misplaced feelings of shame or guilt. Those conversations were meant to make her feel safe coming to me if that happened. Of course, hypotheticals can't always prepare someone for a visceral experience.

"We've always been able to talk things through. I don't know what's changed." I touch her cheek with my thumb. "I promise to keep whatever you say between us, but let me help."

Clenching her jaw, she closes her eyes like she did when she was two and thought that made her disappear. The longer she withdraws from me, the larger her secret looms.

"I already told you everything." She opens her eyes. "It's done. I'll deal with the consequences. I'm sorry I'm not perfect like you, but can we let this go?"

That sass needles me. "Antagonizing me is the wrong move. Besides, I never claimed to be perfect."

"You've told me a million times how you never rebelled in high school because Gran and Papa had enough problems."

She's got me there. Some version of that history has been repeated more than once, although never to suggest the idea that I was perfect.

"Sadie, I'm not happy about the detention, but I'm not overly worried about it, either. I *am* worried about *you*. Something is bothering you. Something so big you think you can't share it with me. I know it's hard, but talking about problems can make them feel smaller."

"If you want to help, let me deal with my stuff my own way. Please, Mom. Please." Her voice cracks, sounding as brittle as the surface of a thinly frozen lake.

I waver, considering the worst-case outcome of each choice, which is impossible because I don't even know what she's running from. "If things get worse, you're going to have to talk to me . . . or a counselor."

She doesn't answer. Composed, like me, which makes me regret my role modeling. As Mel has teased more than once, resorting to a paint-spatter room isn't a typical coping mechanism.

Deflated, I switch gears. "Everything else all right here? Anything you need from home?"

She shakes her head. "How's Gran?"

"Not too bad." I withhold the unpleasant details. "Less self-conscious with you out of the house, so thank you for cooperating."

"I read that she could seize or have a heart attack." Her nostrils flare—a sign that her composure is slipping.

"Try not to worry." I rub her arm reassuringly. "The nurse is with her now. We should focus on what comes next, like how to support her sobriety."

Sadie casts a quick glance over her shoulder at the boys to see if they're listening, but they're so absorbed in their project, we could dance in our undies without attracting their attention. "You don't think she can do it."

The challenge in her tone clicks into place like a pistol's hammer.

I wish I did, but fewer than twenty percent of alcoholics make it an entire year without relapsing. Forty percent backslide before the end of the second year.

My mother's commitment to beating those odds isn't something I'd bet my life on. "I hope she can."

"But you don't trust her." Sadie bows her head, clearly discouraged.

The accusation makes me bristle, as if my mistrust is unfounded. "Trust has to be earned, Sadie."

She cocks a brow. "How can it if you won't give second chances?"

The nerve of her lobbing that complaint when I didn't even ground her for cutting classes.

If she's thinking of Doug, I didn't send him across the country. He chose to run as far as possible, just like he chose to start a whole new family. His original wish to abort her is why I'll never fully trust him with her heart—not that she knows that history.

"Stop attacking me. I haven't done anything wrong," I say.

The lie burns. After all, I set this whole situation in motion with that typewriter. I've even used it to try to manipulate Sadie into talking to me. Perhaps I should be thankful that wish didn't work. Otherwise my obsession might've cost me the most important person in my life.

"Mom, you always expect the worst from people. Then if you're right, you hold it against them," she says.

My head explodes with an army battalion's supply of defenses, including an encyclopedic volume of incidents when my father or my mother or Doug let me down.

I mentally count to twenty.

As the ashes of my outrage settle, the truth shines beneath them like a new penny. Sadie's right. I do prepare for the worst, but that's because disappointment is easier to bear when you're expecting it. Not because I'm a shrew.

"Whatever you think, I still hope for the best, Sadie, especially for you. But it's hard to hand out second chances to people who never change."

"Gran's trying now." She crosses her arms.

"She had no choice." Hardly the same as wanting to change.

"That's not true. She could've gone home. She could've kept drinking, even after the DUI. She's choosing to try. Isn't that enough?" she pleads.

Sensing subtext in her question, I recalibrate my response.

"Maybe it is." I expect the clouds in Sadie's eyes to clear, but her gaze remains muddled. "All this talk about second chances . . . is Johnny pressing you for one?"

Sadie sighs in exasperation. "No, Mom. It's not about him. This is about our family."

"All right." This visit is making things worse. Time to cut my losses and go pack up my parents' things. "You seem like you've got all you need here, but call me if something comes up."

"I will."

Seeking a friendlier tone, I ask, "Are you on babysitting duty?"

"Sort of, but it's fine. I'm reading *Fourth Wing.*"

My dad would be pleased by her enjoyment of fantasy novels. It makes me ache to think of all the things he'll miss—her graduation, her college years, her marriage, and potentially his great-grandkids. That could be my fate, too.

A prickly sensation snakes along my spine. I look away so she can't detect my alarm.

"Listen to Mel, okay?" Grabbing Sadie into a hug, I smooth a hand over her hair, wondering how many more years I'll get to share with her. "She enjoys your company."

"It's relaxing here. Better than listening to you and Gran bicker."

I take a breath. *She's a scared kid,* I repeat to myself a few times before responding. "We're not bickering, but the next few days will be very unpleasant."

Sadie takes measure of me. "Tell Gran I'm proud of her."

A parting shot, putting me in my place. She strides back to the sofa and opens her book.

Before I leave, I ask, "What are you and the girls up to tonight?"

"There's a party at Bobby Tanner's, but I'm not going."

"You can't avoid Johnny for the rest of high school. It'd be a shame to keep missing out on all the fun."

She eyes me evenly. "I know what I'm doing."

"Fine." It doesn't look that way to me, but this isn't a conversation to continue in front of Mel's sons, even if they aren't particularly interested. "I'll call you later."

"Bye."

I say goodbye to Mel's boys before leaving the house in defeat.

Sadie sees my stability as controlling and begrudging. Is her perception of me the fun-house mirror one or is mine?

Because that's not who I am—not in my heart, anyway.

And if my time with her gets cut short, it's certainly not how I want to be remembered.

Twenty-Eight

After loading my parents' framed photographs into boxes, I snoop through my dad's bedroom closet. The faint scent of the cedar notes in his cologne practically brings him back to life then and there. His pronounced chin. His twinkling blue irises. The booming laugh of yesteryear. I close my eyes to imprint the images for a few seconds.

His closet is organized in order of color—white to black. I sweep my hand across the sleeves of the Robert Graham shirts, whose bold colors and patterns made them his favorites. His shoes are neatly stacked on their shelves, untouched for years in favor of the old leather slippers that now lie abandoned on the floor.

Inside each built-in drawer, I push aside underwear and socks, T-shirts and shorts, searching for a manual or notes of any kind. The sum total of my booty comes down to random receipts, a wallet, a tin of Altoids, and a few lint brushes. Diddly about the typewriter.

I thumb through the wallet. Driver's license. Credit cards. A business card for Michael Welles of Welles Engineering. *The Welles heir.*

Blood rushes from my head, pooling heavily in my feet. I flick the card a few times with my finger. Dare I? Stomach aflutter, I call the number, chewing on my thumbnail while the phone rings.

A man answers. "Michael Welles."

"Oh, hi," I stammer, wholly unprepared. I tug at my collar. "This is Emerson Clarke. I found your business card in my late father's personal things and wondered if there were any unfinished business dealings our estate administrator should know about. Did Jefferson Clarke engage your firm for any projects?"

"The author?" he asks. "No, but he came by several years ago asking about my dad's old typewriter. Apparently he bought it at the tag sale my mom had after my father died."

Several years ago. Finally, a time frame for that list. Right around the time of his diagnosis, perhaps.

"Interesting." The unexpected connection between Welles and the typewriter heightens my senses. Does he know something about its magic? "Do you recall what he wanted to know?"

I hold my breath, my limbs sparking with nervous energy.

"He thought it might've belonged to someone important during World War II. I don't remember who, though."

With a single dissatisfying whoosh, my chest deflates. My father wasn't into World War II. That story must've been a cover. I scratch my forehead. "I'm guessing there weren't any old records."

"No. My father picked it out of someone's garbage in Manhattan during the sixties." He coughs, sounding old and tired.

"I see." Such careless disposal suggests the original owners never experienced its magical properties. Is it possible that only my family has? Was my dad looking for confirmation or, like me, useful rules? "Did my father say anything else?"

"Just polite small talk."

Damn. Another dead end.

It shouldn't feel this disappointing, truthfully. Even if Mr. Welles knows about the magic, he wouldn't wax on about it to a stranger. "Well, thank you for your time, Mr. Welles. Have a nice day."

"You too. And sorry for your loss."

"Thank you." I hang up, shaking my hands restlessly.

At least the mysterious Welles heir isn't a blood relative or blackmailer. Hooray for small favors.

If the evidence my dad meant to destroy is the Underwood, he didn't remember to take care of it. At this point, I've got more pressing matters to address, not the least of which is getting Sadie back on track. Cutting class. Detention, for god's sake.

I pack my mother a small bag with some jewelry, perfume, and scarves for when she's feeling human, then take it and the boxes of personal items downstairs.

While I'm making a final sweep of the house, my Facebook messenger notification pings. Sawyer's name—his full name, Sawyer Rhodes—and image appear in my DMs:

Emerson,

After leaving the police station, I realized that we never exchanged numbers. Luckily, social media helped me find you. I waited a couple days to give you time to settle. Hopefully this note comes across like a concerned friend instead of a stalker. ☺

I trust your mother is recovering from her injuries and that the legalities aren't too complicated. If you need an ear or shoulder, I'm available.

In other news <cue drumroll>, the main reason I've stalked you (yes, I confess) is that I'd like a second chance at a first date. I realize we barely know each other, yet this feels like something worth exploring. If you aren't interested (maybe you hate my new haircut), I will respect that and your privacy, but I hope that's not the case.

Sawyer

I press the phone to my breastbone. A sudden desire to hug something makes me shimmy with delight.

The feeling lasts a delicious ten seconds before reality closes in.

If my romantic relationships couldn't last when I was young and hopeful, what chance is there now? Sawyer has no idea I'm teetering on the edge of a nervous breakdown. Or that our meeting was orchestrated by magic. And how selfish would it be to encourage his attention when I might be losing my memory?

My thumbs hover over the keyboard as a little voice whispers, *Maybe you're looking at this wrong.*

A month from now I could get good news from Dr. Rosenthal. My mother might get sober. Sawyer could bring something good into my and Sadie's lives when we most need it.

If these past few weeks have proven anything, it's that I don't understand much about creating true happiness. What I *do* know is that I'm tired of living in fear.

Sawyer,

As stalkers go, you're far more polite than my father's ever were. Thanks for your concern. My mother is undergoing detox while waiting for her hearing, and she's enrolling in an outpatient treatment program. The road ahead won't be smooth, but perhaps we've reached that turning point you predicted.

She'll be staying with me for a good part of the summer. With her, my teen (who's nursing her first broken heart), and a fast-approaching deadline on my book (did I mention I'm a ghost-writer?), I'm rather exhausted.

I consider mentioning my upcoming appointment with Dr. Rosenthal, but it feels premature. If I get diagnosed, I'll tell him.

I'm hardly the least complicated woman in town, so I won't be offended if you rescind your offer. If, however, you like a challenge, I would love a second first date after I get my feet firmly beneath me again.

P.S. My cell is 203-555-4321.

My heart is beating as hard as if I were in a Zumba class. I hit SEND.

Look at me, putting myself out there for rejection. It feels a bit like drowning, but at least I'm trying to swim.

Floating on newfound courage, I go to my dad's office to segregate more personal items that might be of interest to a library: his editor's notes to his very first manuscript, a notebook filled with character sketches for the Pandemonium series, roughly drawn story-world maps and landmarks.

The marble ashtray and his favorite coffee cup, a 1990s pottery mug with the Galdur family crest from the Elysian Chronicles etched on it by a fan, should also be part of the exhibit.

If we donate the desk, all the items can be laid out for viewing. Of course, the exhibit will showcase a neatly ordered desk . . . unless I take a picture of what it really looks like and ask it be set up as such. Either way, Sadie and I will have a place to revisit my dad's things when we're feeling nostalgic.

Eyeing the empty curio cabinet, I consider donating it and the type-writer. That would remove the temptation to keep using the Underwood, but it could also quickly turn dangerous if it was to fall into the wrong hands.

After composing an email proposal to our local library, I tuck my phone away.

Glancing around at the half-emptied office, I feel similarly plundered. Grief wrings me out differently each time it strikes, squeezing my heart this way and that. I'd give anything to make one final good memory with my father.

"You were one of a kind, Dad. I miss . . . the old days."

I watch for a sign: a flicker of light, wind at the window, anything at all. The stillness is physically painful, the way misery cinches your lungs when you've lost something valuable.

Sitting in his chair, I take in his former writing view. As he got older, he would stare across the water, his cheeks slack. He'd jolt when I touched his elbow, then dissemble when asked what he'd been thinking. People think they know him through his books, but his real life's story had too many redacted pages to paint a complete picture.

Nobody will remember my name in a hundred years, but I'm determined that my daughter will understand my heart and unequivocally know she was loved. That will be my legacy, however long our time together lasts.

To do that, I need to first make peace with the fact that my father's secrets will remain buried with him. No more trying to prove myself worthy of the glimmer in his eye. Or aiming to be his equal in talent.

When my mental fog clears, I'm sure it's time to turn down Henry's proposal. The concession doesn't hit as hard as expected. Enlightenment? Exhaustion? Or simply an acknowledgment that no one should write my father's final story. It was his, and his only, to tell.

I can satisfy his fans' curiosity with a lengthy essay summarizing how he'd planned to tie up the series.

Decision made, I text Henry a polite note declining his offer and advising that the estate will not approve of another ghostwriter taking up the project.

After stuffing my phone in my back pocket, I stack the cardboard boxes of personal items in the corner of the garage and then load my mother's satchel into my back seat.

The coming weeks will require me to keep an even keel while Sadie and my mother pull themselves together. I've also got to finish Rachel's book in record speed.

I sit behind the steering wheel, studying the mansion that brokers will label a dream home.

So many memories. Good ones, like the abundant Christmas lights festooning the trees and Dad's beloved Fourth of July lobster boils. And less pleasant ones, like coming home from school to discover that my mom had fled to Vermont for a few days after one of their fights. Or walking in on my dad crying in his closet, then backing away in silence out of fear of what he might confess.

It's a beautiful home, but it was not a safe place—emotionally—for me.

A couple of weeks ago, I balked at my mother's impulse to sell it immediately, but now I'm glad of it.

Our family lost its way in these vast rooms and hallways. It's time for us to begin again somewhere without all the ghosts.

Twenty-Nine

My mother endured five brutal days and nights punctuated by shaking, crying jags, rage, and self-loathing. There were also bouts of profuse sweat, violent puking, and two ugly, emotional meltdowns.

But she didn't seize. Her heart remained strong.

My heart, however, feels as bruised as her face from the continual beating myself up about the wish that produced this situation. We've finally enjoyed a few quiet days without nurses, but my mother has mostly kept to herself.

When she comes downstairs dressed for her hearing, she's blown out her hair and put on earrings. Her navy Armani pantsuit, cream silk blouse, slingbacks, and pearl necklace paint a picture of propriety and grace.

Aside from weight loss she could hardly afford, the convincing costume hides the fact that the glue binding her newly sober insides is not yet dry.

"All set?" I sling my purse over my shoulder.

"I told you I can take an Uber." She checks her reflection in the mirror, hopefully seeing someone different from the woman who left Will dumbstruck on the day that changed everything. "You have that deadline."

The daily chaos here and visits with Sadie so she didn't feel abandoned stalled my progress on *Tropic Heat*. I've outlined four scenes to reach THE

END, but meeting the deadline at this point is a toss-up. Having turned down Henry's proposal, I wouldn't risk Rachel's wrath if my mother didn't need my support today.

Sadie moved back in yesterday evening, as withdrawn as ever. We bickered because she'd turned off her Find My Friends feature all afternoon. She barely looked at me this morning when she left for school. She did, however, wish her gran good luck.

"I want to be there for you, Mom." I can't remember the last time I genuinely felt that way, but the fact that it's true feels like a win.

She eyes me, one hand on her hip. "I won't stop at a bar on my way home, if that's your concern."

I reel back, having not given that a thought. "That's not why I'm coming. You don't have to face this alone. Besides, the judge should see that your family supports you. Now, let's not be late for court."

My mother walks in front of me, waiting while I lock the door. "Did I hear moaning in the bathroom last night or was that a flashback nightmare?"

"Sadie's stomach hurt," I say. "She felt a little warm last night, but no fever this morning."

She probably contracted a bug from one of Mel's boys last week. Younger kids bring home every conceivable germ.

"Mmm." My mother dons Jackie O–style sunglasses before following me to my car. It's the first time she's left the house since her arrest. "I'm sorry to put her through this. I know you want to protect her from my behavior."

The acknowledgment floods my heart with hope even though we're only at the beginning of this journey.

"She's proud to see you coming through this stronger." I start the ignition, contemplating my daughter's apparent inability to bounce back from her breakup.

I jump off that bullet train of worry so I don't lose focus on my mother. "How are you feeling?"

"About the hearing?" Mom asks.

At the red light, I give her a quick glance. "Well, sure, but I meant in general."

She rolls her neck from side to side and fidgets with her purse strap. "I trust Mel."

"I do, too." After passing through the green light, I add, "For what it's worth, you look amazing."

Her mouth curves slightly. "It feels good to wear something other than pajamas."

"And mentally? Physically?" Her cravings must be at least as strong as the itch I had to rig this hearing. As for my mother's triggers, I've cleared the house of any temptation. "Do you need anything?

"Nala said chewing gum helps some people curb their cravings." She stares through the window, a touch of pink climbing her neck. "Maybe I should try."

"I have some in my purse." I nudge it with my elbow, grateful that she's being honest about the struggle. "I'll pick up more this afternoon. Let me know what flavor you like."

"I don't suppose they sell lime," she says dryly, alluding to her beloved gin and tonics.

Too soon, Mom. "How about something fresh, like spearmint or wintergreen?"

"It doesn't matter." The fatalistic tone whispers a warning.

I reach across the center console and squeeze her forearm. "I know this is hard, but I'm proud of you."

She looks out the window, hiding from my compliment, perhaps too unfamiliar with one to accept it as genuine.

We pull up to the Stamford courthouse, an imposing brick monolith. A criminal hearing is another first for us, although that's nothing to brag about.

Mel is waiting on the front steps in front of its two-story glass lobby, dressed in a smart black dress. When we come to a stop at the main entrance, my mother licks her lips, clutching her purse to her chest as if it were a security blanket.

I pat her thigh. "I'll meet you inside."

She picks her way up the stairs to Mel while I go to the parking garage. So many cars. So many people battling each other or their own demons. Everyone else's obstacles should make me feel less alone, but they don't. It just makes me sadder to think about how often we all complicate our lives with poor choices.

By the time I make my way inside the courthouse, the judge is in session.

Mel prepared us that my mother's would be one of multiple hearings on Judge Reyes's morning docket. I slip in quietly and take a seat in the back row.

Other anxious people are seated around me, squeezing hands, sniffling with worry, casting wary gazes at the judge.

He's an attractive man with shorn salt-and-pepper hair and world-weary eyes who probably views my mother as an overprivileged, overly entitled woman who doesn't deserve a break.

That's not entirely untrue. She had the resources to create an exceptional life. If only my father hadn't made that impossible—not that I can raise the specter of black magic in her defense.

Whatever her past mistakes, she's trying now. I hope that counts for something with the judge.

When my mother's case is called, Mel informs the court of the plea bargain and the prosecutor's support for the IDIP, adding details about her recent detox. Judge Reyes gives nothing away. If anything, he looks slightly perturbed while Mel asks him to approve the Silver Hill arrangement. The prosecutor does not object.

The judge's stern expression causes my stomach to clench. My mother's chin remains slightly elevated, her cheeks flush with emotion. Doesn't he understand that the added stress could hurt her recovery?

Judge Reyes looks down from the bench. "Mrs. Clarke, driving under the influence is a serious business that can have catastrophic consequences."

My mother bows her head. "Yes, Your Honor. I know."

He rustles some papers in his fingers, his stern frown casting doubt upon the outcome. Perspiration breaks out all over my body until he looks up again. "I'll approve the plea, but . . ."—he wags a finger at my mother—"if you miss a single session, we will revisit this arrangement."

"Thank you, Your Honor." My mother sets her palms on the table as if balancing herself.

"Next case." Judge Reyes is handed another file by a clerk.

I slouch with relief, while my mother murmurs something to Mel before they leave the defendant's table.

As they exit the courtroom, I join them. "I almost peed my pants."

Mel pats my shoulder. "He's serious but fair. I knew we'd be okay."

"Thank you. You're the best," I say.

"Don't forget it," Mel teases before turning to my mother. "Dorothy, remember to get sign-offs every session and send the forms to me. The program will be over before you know it. By September, you'll have your life back."

"Thank you, Mel." She puts her sunglasses back on, whether to hide from the sun or from our intent gazes is unclear. "I'll do my best not to have wasted your time."

"Will the McKinseys file a claim for the property damage or are you settling privately?" Mel asks.

Their old-growth oak tree held its own against the Mercedes, but the mailbox, wooden fence, and boxwoods weren't as hardy.

"They're filing a claim."

While the McKinseys and my parents were never social friends, they have been acquaintances for well more than a decade. They even came to my father's funeral reception, though now I suspect that was motivated more by morbid curiosity than sympathy. They've been cordial if not neighborly, preferring to do things by the book.

"Your insurance company will negotiate with theirs, but if you have questions, don't hesitate to call me." Mel rubs my mother's biceps.

"Thank you, but we've taken enough of your time. I'm sure we can manage." My mother smiles thinly, standing as still as someone trying to avoid a bee's sting.

"Well, I've got to get back to work. I'll check in later." Mel waves before striding toward the parking garage.

My mother's shoulders slump, all pretenses dropped. "I'm exhausted, Emerson. I'd like to rest."

I've got an appointment at the library to discuss a potential exhibit in an hour. With the nurses gone, no one is at home to keep her from hitting the Darien Liquor Shop, a thought she planted in my head with her earlier remark.

"Let's not waste your great outfit. Join me for lunch and then come to the library to discuss arrangements for the donation." I make a "pretty please" face.

She snaps impatiently, "You promised you wouldn't be a jailer. I just want to change into something comfortable and relax."

My fear won't go down without a fight. "You've been cooped up all week. Wouldn't you enjoy lobster mac and cheese at Ten Twenty Post?"

"Emerson, I'm not ready to see people." Her nostrils flare, and then she looks at her shoes, hints of yellow bruising still darkening the tops of her cheeks. "It's too fresh. I don't want to make awkward small talk or overhear whispers."

My heart cracks open. I've been so focused on getting through this hearing, it didn't occur to me that she'd have an entirely different set of concerns.

"All right." I'll have to trust her eventually. "I'll take you home."

As we speed along I-95, I consider how the typewriter lured me into its web with the promise of eliminating my anxiety.

Dating involves risk, unless you can write the perfect man into existence. Teens worry their parents, unless they are transparent about their troubles. An alcoholic parent is a constant source of stress, unless you can magically force her into rehab.

It's time to start facing possibilities rather than fighting them.

Without my continued interference, my mother may very well drink again or find a worse vice. If I publish my own work, it could be roundly rejected. Sadie may move across the country someday. Sawyer might let me down.

But honestly, none of that will matter much if I lose my memory. Unfortunately, the possibility I fear the most is the only one I'm certain can't be fixed by the Underwood.

Thirty

"I love your vision and am confident we can make this happen," Julie, the library's director, says as we rise from our seats. "I'll be in touch with more details once the preliminary plans are approved."

"Wonderful. We do have a bit of a situation with my mother selling the house. Would it be possible for you to pick up the items and store them in advance of setting up the exhibit?" My stomach rumbles with hunger.

"I'll reach out to the facilities manager and see what we can arrange."

"Terrific. I'll make myself available at your convenience." I shake her hand. "Thanks again. My father would be proud."

"Thank *you*. I'm thrilled by the chance to house this exclusive collection."

I exit her office, making a brief stop at the café for a blueberry muffin before leaving the library. The other week I was here was with Sawyer. Before that, I was out with Will. A week earlier, my father was still alive. Even if I could control life, there is no stopping change.

On my way to my car, I recall helping my mother pick her way across this parking lot. The shame is still sharp, even though it seems like it happened longer ago. The only thing that hasn't been in overdrive since the funeral is my progress on *Tropic Heat*.

I bite into the muffin just before my phone rings. After that misstep with the police calls, I answer this unknown caller. "Hello?"

"Emerson? It's Sawyer."

As if I wouldn't recognize his sexy rasp. A sharp burst of pleasure causes me to choke on the muffin.

"Oh, hi." I cough into my hand. "Sorry. How are you?"

"Better than you, it sounds."

"I'm fine." Fine? Try elated.

"Good. I hope it's okay that I called. I know you're busy."

I lick my lips. "Of course it's okay, although I *was* thinking maybe you'd come to your senses."

"Good sense is overrated."

The mental image of his lopsided grin prompts one of my own. "I missed that memo."

He chuckles. "Seriously, though, how are things?"

I provide a brief rundown of my mother's sentence and her cravings. There's no reason to share my daughter's detention and let this phase she's going through influence his opinions.

"Sounds like your mom is already doing better than my dad and uncle ever did. I know you're busy, but remember, a little self-care will go a long way, too."

Maybe so, but it's hard to carve out "me time" when every mental and physical resource is dedicated to keeping things on track. One wrong move and my mother could falter. "That'd be easier if I knew I was doing all the right things."

"What's that mean?"

I pull the phone from my ear and stare at it, frowning. "Giving my mother the best support, not saying anything triggering, not making her uncomfortable."

"No, I mean, why the focus on certainty?"

"Because . . ." Isn't it obvious? "Then I'd know everything will turn out okay."

He hums before saying, "Well, let me know if you figure out how to get guarantees. In the meantime, maybe you'll feel better if you simply believe *you'll* be okay no matter how things turn out."

Sounds like Californian nonsense. "You don't know that."

"Sure I do. Just look at you. Single mom. Child of an alcoholic. Grieving your dad. All that, yet there you are, jumping in and handling this situation. You're strong. Besides, there's rarely one right path or outcome. As long as you can pivot and adapt, you'll be okay."

I stop outside my car, one arm resting on the roof.

"Emerson?"

"Sorry. Still here. Guess I can't argue with that."

"Good, 'cause I don't like to argue." He chuckles. "Now that we've dispensed with the therapy, let's move on to my big news. First, are you the jealous type?"

"That depends."

"Well, I must confess. I've fallen for a gorgeous boxer from a shelter in Norwalk who I'm adopting on Friday. Any chance you can join me for a quick lunch and the pickup?"

"Wow. That's a huge commitment."

"Lunch?" he quips.

"No." I chuckle. "A pet."

"Ohhh." He drawls the word out. "If you haven't already noticed, I act on impulse. Like I did with you."

I raise my brows, not that he can see me. "You may end up regretting that."

"Doubtful."

His flirtatious tone rolls through me, tickling every nerve ending. I'd forgotten how overwhelmingly delicious desire feels. "Well, I can't spare any time this week because of my deadline, but as soon as I turn in the book, I'll call. What's the dog's name?"

"Ruby. Not my first choice, but it'll grow on me."

"That's a cute name."

"I'll be sure to tell her," he deadpans. "I work from home on Fridays, so when you come up for air, we'll make a plan."

"I look forward to it." More than he knows.

"And remember, you got this."

"Thanks." For a few seconds, I believe him. Or at least I want to. "Have fun with Ruby."

"I will. Bye."

I hang up and notice a voicemail I hadn't seen earlier. The high school attendance office. Sadie skipped another afternoon class yesterday, so she's getting another detention and a three-day parking pass suspension.

I text her to ask what the hell is going on. She replies:

I didn't sleep well thinking about Gran's trial and her selling the house, so I went over to the dock to think.

Without thinking, I type back:

Your behavior makes me think I should get your father involved.

Her reply is swift:

PLEASE DON'T!!!! I swear it won't happen again. Please, Mom.

I worry my lip, deliberating.

We'll talk after school.

Can't even ground her because she's already avoiding friends. I'll have to think up extra chores.

I open the car door and toss my purse inside before collapsing onto the driver's seat. For every victory, I'm hit with another loss. No wonder it's hard to focus on *Tropic Heat,* let alone make time for self-care.

Sawyer may be capable of effortlessly fielding curveballs, but I've spent a lifetime building walls to avoid them. Even if I'm stronger than I believe, I've no idea how to escape my self-made prison.

Thirty-One

My mother's second week of therapy has her feeling vulnerable to the point of brittleness. Interestingly, her presence here has blunted the edges of Sadie's moods, but my daughter continues to hold me at arm's length. I've been more or less locked in my office trying to finish *Tropic Heat* on time. Tomorrow's neurology appointment is making it impossible to focus. I reread the last paragraph four times now.

Pushing back from my desk, I sneak outside to steal a peaceful moment for myself. Our porch swing offers the perfect vantage point of Tilley Park Pond across the street. Watery afternoon light glints off its mirrored surface until a raft of ducks cuts a V-shaped wake across the water. I sip my mint tea and close my eyes.

In the distance, the diesel train to New Haven rumbles into the station as a muffled announcement of its next stop sounds over the speakers. Two doors down, the Wilson kids' laughter peals through the air—their unbridled joy recharging my soul.

The sense of calm is cut short when my phone rings.

"Hey, Mel. What's up?" Please don't tell me there's a problem with my mother's compliance.

"Checking in to make sure you and your mother aren't killing each other."

I snicker. "Nope. Just some scrapes on our soles from all the eggshells."

Physically, my mother is past the worst of her physical transition to sobriety, but the mental game has just begun. She's been chewing gum by the fistful. I gave up chocolate last week in solidarity. The timing wasn't great, given my deadline, but my cravings give me empathy for hers.

Mel sighs heavily. "Well, you should know that the McKinseys aren't being discreet about the accident."

There goes my last scrap of tranquility. "How so?"

"Chris and I ran into the Castillos at the club. Maria let it drop that Beth McKinsey was bitching to her book club about the restorative work on their yard and how 'extremely wasted' your mother was. I don't know who else she's talking to, but I didn't want you to be blindsided."

I hug my knees to my chest and rest my chin, fantasizing about typing a paragraph that plagues the McKinseys' gardens with an aphid infestation. Not that I've touched the Underwood since the accident, but the desire hums quietly in the background.

"I'd warn my mom if I weren't worried it'd trigger a relapse. She's sticking close to home, so she might not hear anything." Even without the typewriter, I'm still making choices for others.

Mel clucks her tongue. "I'm sure it'll die down soon."

"I'll ask MaryBeth to keep an ear out." I roll my shoulders to break up the tension knitting through them. Sawyer thinks that I can handle any fallout. I'm unconvinced, particularly because we might all get thrown a huge curveball after my doctor appointment tomorrow. "Thanks for the heads-up."

"Of course." She pauses. "Before you hang up, what's up with Will?"

I grimace, still haunted by his expression when my mother groped him.

"Crashed and burned." My face warms. It's humiliating to think I'd been excited to reconnect with someone who could not have been less interested. "Pretty sure he agreed to come to your party only because he wanted my mom as a client."

"Asshole!"

Her salty reaction soothes my hurt feelings. "I just wish our brief reunion hadn't killed my good memories. Seems my first love was a mirage."

"Screw him, Em. When you're ready, the right guy will show up."

I almost mention Sawyer, but don't want to jinx it. If Dr. Rosenthal gives me an all clear, then I'll let myself get invested. "Maybe."

"I'll swing by late this week to offer moral support."

"My mom always enjoys your verve." I shoo an insect away.

"Well, she's got great taste," Mel jokes. "Talk later."

I hang up, preparing to return to work, when a red convertible BMW comes to a screeching halt in front of my house.

Kathryn exits her car and marches past the picket fence, waving pages overhead, eyes glowing like she's swallowed sunshine. Her heels click against the porch steps, punctuating her excited pronouncements.

"Most successful screened-client showing of my career. Of course, several qualified buyers were merely lookie-loos. One couple thought your mom's arrest might be leverage to lowball! But there were a few serious, excited buyers, so we've got a decision to make."

So quickly? I'd lobbied to delay the showing, concerned that added stress could threaten my mother's recovery. She's still learning to regulate her emotions without the numbing aid of alcohol. Some mornings she's teary from poor sleep. Other times she snaps at me, like last Friday, when I was six minutes late picking her up from therapy.

"This is unexpected." I swing my legs around to plant my feet on the ground. "But please don't mention the gossip about my mom's arrest. She's still vulnerable."

Kathryn winks. "Gotcha."

Things are bad when I'm forced to rely on a broker's discretion. "I'm still not convinced this is the best time for my mother to make big decisions."

In a firm tone, she replies, "She strikes me as a decisive woman."

Impulsive is more accurate. It leads to the same place, albeit with more chaos.

Kathryn wouldn't bring us bullshit offers, so there won't be a legal basis to block the sale under the trust agreement. Not that I would, despite my misgivings.

I open the door and wave Kathryn inside. "Have a seat in the dining room. Would you like something to drink?"

"Water would be great, thanks." Kathryn beelines for the table, spreading the papers out in a neat row before taking her seat.

I call up to my mother from the base of the steps, then go to the kitchen to fill a pitcher.

Sadie is at the sink eating fresh raspberries. "Who's here?"

"The real estate broker." I set out a tray and a few glasses, then seize an opportunity to treat my daughter like an adult. "You should join us, since you have a say in what happens with the house."

She stops midbite. "I don't . . . I mean, won't that upset Gran?"

I shrug. "Maybe, but you should be informed, even if you defer to her in the end."

She makes an uncertain face but grabs her bowl and follows me to the dining room, where Kathryn is already seated.

I introduce Sadie to Kathryn, who then pours herself a glass of water and takes a sip, her cherry-red lipstick staining the rim of her glass.

My mother comes down—trailed by Mopsy—dressed in pink slacks and a crisp white blouse. Her eyes get clearer every day. Even her skin looks healthier. Of course her mood is low. From what I've read, depression is common after withdrawal. Her lips part when she sees Kathryn, but she quickly recovers herself.

"Hello, Kathryn." My mother pulls out the seat across from her. Mopsy purrs at her feet. "I'm surprised to see you. Weren't the showings just this afternoon?"

"Yes. An unmitigated success. It's a gorgeous home with unbeatable views, so I expected a lot of interest. But its celebrity status put it over. The. Top." She emphasizes this with jazz hands, then leans forward conspiratorially. "I overheard several prospective buyers confiding about how cool it would be to buy Jefferson Clarke's home."

There's little doubt that she intended that as a compliment, but referring to it as Jefferson Clarke's home erases the rest of us from its history—as if our lives were entirely subjugated by his. While there may be some truth in that, it certainly isn't flattering. My mother's flattened mouth suggests that she felt a similar hit.

"I was telling your daughter that we got multiple offers. Very exciting." Kathryn taps the bottoms of the papers.

My mother folds her hands on the table like a schoolkid. She's been so eager to sell the house, I would expect a more animated expression. "Well, which is the best?"

"Depends on your preference, really. There are two offers over asking. One is all cash, the other is fifty grand more but comes with traditional contingencies, like a ninety-day window to sell their house." Kathryn slides both offers across the table to my mother. "Is the extra money worth the risk of the deal falling through if those contingencies fail?"

Sadie sits on the chair, hugging her knees, her gaze bouncing between my mother and me. I hold my tongue, yielding control over this meeting to my mother.

"And the third?" My mother pointedly stares at the other pages, then lifts Mopsy onto her lap and strokes her fur.

Kathryn shrugs. "This offer is also cash, but only at asking. I'm obligated to present it, although I don't expect you to take it. The buyer did include a personal appeal. She's a single mother with three kids and a generous divorce settlement." While sliding a handwritten letter across the table, she adds, sotto voce, "Her husband left her for a much younger woman."

My mother's self-possession splinters, her gaze sharpening as she reaches for the letter.

Kathryn dished out that unnecessary rumor with a little too much glee. No doubt she'll be equally indiscreet about my family in future conversations.

My mom reads the page-long handwritten note. When she finishes, she sets it aside and glances out the window toward Tilley Pond, stroking Mopsy while thinking.

Kathryn shoots me a questioning glance, as if I could ever read my mother's mind. I suspect, however, she feels simpatico with the divorcée's unexpected and salacious circumstances.

Two or more minutes pass before my mom turns to Kathryn. "I'll sell it to the single mom."

"But it's the lowest offer, Dorothy. By a hundred thousand dollars." Kathryn's arched brows signal her dismay.

My mother deploys the withering glare she gave my father whenever he was being obnoxious. "That woman and her kids need a fresh start more than I need that money. If the house brings them joy at a time of painful upheaval, that's something I feel good about."

Sadie nods at her gran, wearing the expression of a proud parent.

Kathryn turns to me. "If I recall correctly, you and your daughter have a vote."

I'm flabbergasted that she'd embarrass my mother with that reminder. Mom, however, slides the letter over to me. I skim it mostly to keep from snapping at Kathryn.

The heartfelt note hasn't a single reference to my father's legacy. Aanya Joshi mentions her middle school son's interest in crew and fishing. She recounts growing up on the water in Michigan. She compliments the chef's kitchen and extensive gardens.

I envision her children staring at those kayaks and daydreaming about picnics and playdates and sea views from their bedrooms. For a moment, I'm young again, standing at the dock with my father, brimming with anticipation.

The house never was our fairy-tale castle, but that doesn't mean it won't become theirs.

I pass the letter to Sadie. "It's a good decision, Mom."

Kathryn's perturbed expression gives me some self-satisfaction. Perhaps that's unkind, but my distaste for brokers has only intensified since Will played me.

Sadie passes the letter back to my mother. "I agree."

"I'll let everyone know." Kathryn's mouth turns downward, but she

accepts the decision without further badgering. The difference in her commission will be roughly equivalent to the cost of her designer cross-body
bag. Few would disagree that a family's well-being is more important than
another purse. "How soon can you vacate?"

"We're waiting on a date from Christie's to pick up most of the things.
I can store the rest while I'm still living here," my mother says, looking to
me for an update.

Coordinating the auction completely slipped my mind amid everything that's happened since we last saw Will.

He sent follow-up information, but between the hearing, chauffeuring
my mom to therapy, and my deadline, his email dropped to the bottom of
my to-do list. Spite might also play a role. I'm only human.

"I'll reach out to Will to schedule something," I reply.

Kathryn opens her phone, presumably checking her own calendar.
"Why don't we propose a July thirty-first closing? That gives you roughly
two months to settle things on your end and gives the buyers a few weeks
to settle in before school starts."

"Perfect." My mother's gaze reflects a level of personal satisfaction
that's been absent for decades.

I catch myself staring, my heart opening itself to hope again, although
this time that doesn't feel as futile.

Kathryn asks, "Should I start a search for your new home? Inventory
is low, but I have a lovely renovated colonial on Peach Hill Road. Three
thousand square feet—a substantial downsize, but still roomy. Flat yard
with a new outdoor living space and small saltwater pool."

I bite my lip, waiting to learn if my mother still wants to leave the area.

"I'm thinking of moving to Manhattan," my mother says with slightly
less conviction than in the past. No matter how she dresses it up, she's still
choosing to surround herself with strangers rather than spend more time
with my daughter and me, and that stings.

"Really, Gran?" Sadie's disappointment drags her mouth and shoulders
downward.

My mother averts her gaze, frowning in thought. She turns to Kathryn, rising to signal an end to the discussion. "I'll let you know if I change my mind."

She'll expect my unwavering support of either decision when she finishes treatment, but Manhattan still feels like a mistake. After the initial excitement of decorating a new place, meeting a few neighbors, and enjoying new restaurants, she'll be sitting in an empty apartment in a city with thousands of temptations.

Kathryn gathers the papers. "Well, ladies, this has been a pleasure. I'll reach out to the other broker about contracts and escrow funds, so I'll be in touch soon."

"Thank you for everything." My mother puts Mopsy on the floor and then extends her hand. "I appreciate your expediency."

"You're welcome." Kathryn's smile does a credible job of masking her disappointment about the commission.

I walk her to the door, waving goodbye as she speeds off like a red wasp. When I return to the dining room, my mother and Sadie are hugging.

"Thank you for supporting my decision, even if it's dumb," my mom says to me.

"It was a generous and compassionate choice," I reply.

Sadie appears pleasantly surprised by my compliment—a tiny win in my battle to reset our relationship.

"I didn't mean to sound cavalier about money, but it seemed selfish to take the highest bid just to add to my pile." My mother cracks her knuckles. "Your father still gets nice royalty checks."

Astounding, given that he hasn't had a new release in almost seven years.

"Those will probably increase after they reissue older titles with bonus material," I say.

"Even dead he lives on. We had our problems, but he loved his work. Surprised himself with how well that all turned out." My mother's gaze is tinted with some admiration for the "self-made" creative genius.

A month ago, I would've agreed. Now I'm convinced he plotted that success, page by typed page. That might be more forgivable if he hadn't used his stature to validate his criticisms instead of offering encouragement.

A wave of resentment washes my heart in a toxic red tide.

I can't share these feelings without threatening my mom's sobriety and robbing Sadie of her fond memories. So I suffer in silence.

"I need to find something productive to fill my time." Mom scrubs her hands over her face. "I can't sit around all day thinking about regrets when my go-to way to forget is . . ."

She needn't say another word.

"What about part-time work at a local library?" I ask.

"Yeah, Gran. Mom said you used to love that job." Sadie's looking at her grandmother as if trying to picture her working.

"With today's emphasis on digital information, I'd be a dinosaur." She points at herself while pulling a face. "I *am* a dinosaur."

She's getting older, but so are many librarians.

"You're not a dinosaur, but yeah, everything's digital now," Sadie says.

I sigh. "How about a bookstore?"

"Maybe." My mother fidgets with her hair, her collar, her belt, like she doesn't know what to do with her hands if she's not drinking.

It'll be months before either of us makes it through a day without worrying about whether she'll relapse. "Is this the right time to take on the stress of a new job?"

My mother crosses her arms. "Being productive would decrease my stress levels."

I turn my palms up. "All right, but first, why not focus on tying things up with the McKinseys and finding a storage situation for the furniture you want to keep."

"Fine. Please schedule up a pickup with Will." She cocks her head, sizing me up. "By the way, whatever happened with that other guy—the date?"

"Wait, what?" Sadie whips her head around.

"I'll reach out to Will today," I say to my mother. "As for the other guy—" My heart squeezes while I force myself to remember the reason not to get ahead of myself. "We've spoken recently, but he's not a priority given everything else going on."

"What other guy, Mom?" Sadie demands, as if she hasn't been keeping secrets, too.

"Someone from the library event the night of Gran's arrest, but it's not anything yet. I'll tell you more if things evolve into something . . . real."

My mom interjects, "Don't put your life on hold because of me."

"I'm not, I just—" The weight of my impending neurology appointment cuts off my words. If I have the gene, then Sadie might, too. The thought of handing her that news makes my eyes mist over. My voice croaks when I say, "I'm not ready yet."

"You're almost forty, dear. I suggest you get a move on." My mother shrugs and then walks away, Mopsy in tow.

"It's because of me, isn't it?" Sadie asks glumly.

I swallow, thinking she's somehow read my mind. "What's because of you?"

"You're alone because of me. If you hadn't had to raise me, maybe you'd be married like Dad." Sadie holds herself still, a storm rising in her gaze.

My mouth falls open at that horrible thought. "You couldn't be more wrong. I'm *not* alone *because* of you, honey. I've never once had even a second of regret about that decision, either. Not ever!"

Judging by how her face crinkles up like she might cry, my words weren't persuasive.

I grab her into a hug and hope, for both our sakes, that my appointment with Dr. Rosenthal doesn't devastate us all.

Thirty-Two

"Having a first-degree relative with early-onset Alzheimer's increases your risk compared with those who don't. But I sense your father's recent passing is lending exaggerated significance to your isolated memory lapses." Dr. Rosenthal sits on his swivel stool, long legs crossed, clipboard on his knee. His poise contrasts with my jitters. "Your MMSE test is perfect."

"That doesn't mean something isn't starting to happen in my brain. My father waited too long to get answers. I'd rather take the genetic test and prepare."

Would I, though? The implications of bad news shoots acid up my esophagus. I never appreciated my good health until recently. Never felt an urgency to travel or learn to play the guitar or even to savor—truly relish—the good things in my life. Now all I think about is what I might miss.

He clicks his pen's retractable plunge a few times. "I hear you, but you need to understand that the results are complex to interpret. Most of those genes are also affected by lifestyle habits, like exercise or smoking, and other factors, so the results aren't cut-and-dry. For example, having two APOE e4s greatly increases your risk, but it's still not a guarantee that you'll get the illness. Yet if you get that result, you'll live the rest of your life anxiously making choices based on something that might never happen."

"But aren't there some genes that do cause Alzheimer's?" I rub the back of my neck to loosen the stiffness accompanying my shameless pleading.

"APP, PSENs 1 and 2 do appear to cause the illness, but they're *rare* genetic mutations. We don't even know if your father carried them." He sighs as impatiently as a mother dealing with a relentless child.

I crack my knuckles, growing equally impatient with his stonewalling. "Well then, if I don't have those, I'll breathe a sigh of relief. But if I do, then I can take action, like entering new clinical trials."

Dr. Rosenthal's pinched expression makes clear his distaste for Dr. Google. "You're glossing over privacy concerns and other problems that go hand in hand with these tests. Either way, we must first do a comprehensive neurological exam." He cocks an eyebrow in a paternalistic manner.

Perhaps a female doctor would take my concerns more seriously. "You seem annoyed by my proactive approach, but I have a daughter to consider."

He sets the clipboard aside and folds his hands in his lap. "I'm not annoyed, and I apologize for coming across that way. I'm trying to assuage your concerns and lower your stress. Typically, this disease starts with short-term memory losses and cognitive issues, not with forgetting childhood memories or chores like what you've described. Stress, grief, and lack of sleep are most likely what's affecting your memory these days."

That alleviates some of my concern, but not all. "Wondering is more stressful to me than knowing."

Despite the impasse, I hold his gaze.

"Understood," he says. "You'll need to meet with a counselor before any genetic testing. He or she will walk you through the pros and cons and also advise you and your loved ones on strategies to cope with any unwelcome results."

There's not a coping strategy in the world that will make me feel better if I get bad news. "I'll do that."

"All right, then. Let's do a comprehensive neuro workup. Then I'll give you the name of a genetic counselor. After you meet with her, we'll take next steps."

I smile weakly. "Thank you."

Is this good news, though? It's hard to relax when the ramifications for Sadie sit in my periphery like a tornado on the horizon. This all makes whatever she's been hiding from me seem incredibly unimportant.

It's been a trying few weeks and now a new wrinkle might further complicate our lives. Am I strong enough to endure?

On second thought, Dr. Rosenthal's insistence on meeting with a genetic counselor might not be a waste of time.

I leave the doctor's office knowing the preliminary results of his neurological exam confirmed his opinions about my condition.

He reemphasized how rare the troublesome gene mutations are and cautioned me not to spend the upcoming weeks dwelling on remote possibilities. On the off chance that I am a carrier, he also mentioned promising new treatments, referencing an ultrasound therapy that breaks up the plaque on the brain and retards the symptoms.

His confidence has me walking out the door on sturdier footing. The genetic counselor isn't available until July. Until then, I must focus my mental energy elsewhere. A good first step would be to stop settling for mere survival and start aiming to thrive.

This afternoon, I should be able to dive back into Rachel's book with a clear head—pun intended. I need three thousand words today to have a prayer of meeting the deadline.

When I enter my house, a sweet almond scent hangs heavily in the air. My mouth waters as old memories of sampling my mother's pumpkin cheesecake, apple brandy tarts, orange chiffon cakes, and pineapple galettes arise. On special occasions, she'd make a raspberry crème fraîche tart with lavender honey.

I'm nearly giddy for Sadie to get a taste of my mom's particular love language. After hanging my purse on the hook, I defer work and head toward the kitchen, stopping short to eavesdrop.

"What are these?" Sadie asks.

"Pignoli cookies," my mother replies. "The flavor profile is better suited to autumn, but the soft, dense texture is a comfort thing. Try one."

Seconds pass before Sadie says, "They're really good. Who taught you to bake?"

"My mother." My mom's voice sounds rich with love and longing.

She and Grammy spent hours in the old farmhouse kitchen, with its banged-up wide-plank floors and 1930s porcelain sink.

I can still picture Grammy's flour-spattered apron, gray hairs poking out of her bun, laugh lines bracketing her eyes, the gap between her front teeth capturing my attention whenever she laughed. I'd "help" them, cracking eggs and fishing out the shells, rolling out scraps and pretending to create my own braided-dough masterpieces.

Our visits to Vermont became more sporadic by the time I hit high school. No one said why. My father never enjoyed the farm, but I suspect my mother also knew she couldn't hide her drinking from her parents.

A tender warmth swaddles my heart as the moment unfolding in the kitchen refills the void of our lost connection.

I'm about to join them when Sadie asks, "Why didn't you teach my mom?"

My wizardry with box brownies has been a joke between us for years. I'd like to see my mother's expression but am more curious about her protracted silence.

"I wasn't the mother I'd planned to be, Sadie. I lost control over one part of my life and let that frustration contaminate the other parts." There's another pause before she asks, "Does that make sense?"

Sadie's silence is its own kind of answer.

The oven door hinge squeaks, followed by the scrape of metal against metal.

My mother says, "If I could go back, I like to think I'd be smarter.

Trust myself more. Trust my parents to help me instead of trying to hide from them. That might've spared us all a lot of hurt and shame."

The living room feels like it's shrinking. The confused little girl inside who went too many years without hugs awakens, sending tremors coursing through my limbs. Now, finally, vindication. It was not ungrateful to feel hurt and neglected and incidental despite my privileged lifestyle. It was the truth, and my mother knows it. Her remorse helps release the burden of old wounds to make room for love and forgiveness and peace.

"Having regrets doesn't always mean that you made the wrong choice, Gran." Sadie's voice is etched with defiance. "If you'd reached out to your parents, they probably would've just felt sad and helpless. If you'd left Papa, you might've ended up in an even worse situation. No one knows. Maybe you should be proud of doing the best you could. You were sparing them. I think that's brave."

It sounds like the person Sadie's trying most to convince with that pep talk is herself. I cover my mouth and lean against the wall. What is my daughter sparing me from knowing?

"Honey, refusing to get help isn't strong," my mother says. "Besides, I doubt your mom feels she was spared anything. Don't use me as an example of bravery, okay?"

My nose tingles with newly formed tears. Sobriety is already bringing the mother I once knew back to life.

"Anyhow, just because Em didn't learn to bake doesn't mean I can't teach you," Mom says, her tone brighter.

"I'm down for that," Sadie says.

Swallowing thickly, I draw a deep breath.

Their bonding session doesn't change the fact that Sadie won't confide in me. We were so close, or at least I thought we were. Did my focus on building us a perfect life make her afraid to show me any imperfection?

If so, I need to fix that somehow. My wish for her confidence is the only one the Underwood hasn't granted. Is there a problem with the intent or wording that makes the difference? Then again, I'm no longer using the Underwood, so maybe I let that puzzler go.

Decision made, I enter the kitchen. "It smells amazing in here. What's cooking?"

Sadie stiffens like a spooked squirrel, while Mopsy pads along the peninsula trolling for crumbs.

"Pignoli cookies." My mother turns to retrieve the last tray from the oven. The sight makes my mouth water for the second time in ten minutes. "Want one?"

"Of course." I kiss my daughter's head when passing behind her. "If this keeps up, we'll all need new pants by September."

Sadie glances at the clock. "Where were you? I thought you were on deadline."

"I am. Just running errands." Not a complete lie. I deflect by grabbing a fresh-from-the-oven treat. "It's nice to come home to this, Mom. Delicious."

She moves to the sink to wash the cookie sheet. "I'm going to teach Sadie."

"Lucky me," I say, finishing the cookie. If this keeps up, the five pounds I lost will be erased by next week, unless my weight-loss wish is permanent. "Sadie, I've been pulling things together for the library exhibit. Would you like to go through Papa's first manuscript to flag editorial notes you think his fans might find most interesting?"

"Really?" Her shocked gaze darts between my mother and me.

My mother's expression remains inscrutable.

"The exhibit was your idea. You should be involved," I say.

For the second time all month, her smile appears genuine. I take a second cookie because even small wins deserve a big celebration.

"Thanks, Mom." Sadie glances at the clock and slides off the counter stool. "I'm meeting my Spanish partner at the library to study for a test. See you later."

I refrain from making a scene by hugging her before she leaves the room. After she's gone, I turn to my mother.

She eyes me askance. "You made her day."

"Finally." I tilt my head. "What about you? You said you need something to do. Why not participate in this curation?"

"No, thank you." Her shuttered expression ends that conversation. "I did give the bookstore idea some thought, but working with the public feels a bit tricky right now, with people gossiping about my mistake."

For all my dire predictions about how she might react to that, she's taking it rather well.

"I'm sorry." The urge to hug her strikes, too, but before I act on it, she folds the dishrag and crosses her arms.

"It's fine. I'm focusing on my to-do list. The estate lawyer sent a list of action items needed for the tax returns. There's also my outpatient home-work." Wearing a self-deprecating smile, she pushes off the counter and heads out of the kitchen. "Like you, I've got deadlines."

"Mom, wait," I say, then hesitate, having not really planned what to say. When she stops at the doorway, I stammer, "I . . . I just want to say that you're doing really great."

Her expression loosens. "Thanks, Em. And you were right. It's been helpful to have you and Sadie around."

This newfound weepiness feels less comfortable than skinny jeans. I blink rapidly to clear my eyes. "Glad to help."

After she leaves, I remain in the kitchen standing sentry over the cookies as if they embody hope's sweetness. Then I remember my deadline.

Thirty-Three

The *Tropic Heat* vomit draft has been completed and submitted. Yes, a couple of days late. Yes, it's nowhere close to my best-ever manuscript. But given the challenges this month, it feels like a miracle. One that occurred without the typewriter's help.

I would celebrate, but within ten minutes of my sending it to Rachel (with an apology for the delay), she replied with an outline for the next book and a four-thirty PM Zoom link to discuss the same.

As if I'm not exhausted from the marathon writing sessions.

I scarf down a quick snack while making some notes on the new outline. The reminder dings at 4:28 PM, so I click on the Zoom link and swallow some seltzer to wash down the apple.

Too soon, Rachel's face takes over my screen.

Here we go. "Hi, Rachel. How are you?"

"Busy, as always." Her inanimate expression doesn't exude good vibes.

"Same here. Again, apologies for missing the deadline. The draft needs work, but after the edits, it will be something we can both be proud of."

"I would hope so."

I wait, anticipating at least one question about my family crisis.

Nada. That's offensive. We've worked together for nearly a decade, yet she probably doesn't remember my daughter's name. At least I know that she's thirty-four, single, childless, and living in Phoenix with her Frenchton, Elektra.

Our little stare-down ends when I blink first. "Anyway, I read your synopsis and have some ideas."

"Super. Let's hear them." She slurps her giant beverage through a straw, her knees drawn up to her chest.

My three-star comment—the highest rank in my note-prioritization system—will require some finesse. "First, what if we reconsider Roman and Laura getting engaged at the beginning of the book? I think it'd be better to push that to the midpoint."

Rachel wrinkles her nose. "I want to start with a hopeful beginning. Fans have been *dying* for these two to move things along."

"Sure, but we should be thoughtful about how to do that without sacrificing story and series momentum. If we open with him shopping for a ring, that's hopeful. Then if we move Laura's secret mission forward—create a reason she must leave without telling him—we foil his big plans and add tension at the same time. Her mission will dovetail, of course, into the real danger—the drug overlord."

"You're basically rewriting my outline." She sounds more annoyed than offended.

"No." Perhaps if I approach this from another angle, she'll relax. "I'm restructuring your ideas to maximize their impact."

"My readers care about sexy times, not a perfect plot. If Laura's off on a secret assignment for the first third of the book, that's less sex on the page."

"But *more* sexual tension." Even readers who enjoy open-door sex scenes adore the delicious burn of anticipation.

"I don't agree."

Fatigue has worn me raw, like a blister about to erupt. "You should. Tension drives pacing, which keeps readers turning the page."

Her eyes narrow. "It's my book. My name. My bestseller creds."

Considering that I've written this series, she shouldn't brag as if she did. I count to five in my head. "That's true."

She may be mollified, but my interest in writing a poorly structured story is less than nil.

Normally, she doesn't push back this much. She must be punishing me for missing the deadline. In a sudden sharp moment of clarity, I no longer give a shit.

"Given our differing opinions, this might be a good time for me to bow out and let you finish the series your way." I hold still even though shock makes me slightly faint.

I've never quit anything. Never knowingly disappointed anyone. Never leapt into the unknown without a plan. My stomach turns as sour as month-old milk. I grip the edge of my desk to brace for her reaction.

"Don't be like that. I value your input, but I should set the direction in my own books." She pulls herself so close to the screen, her pores resemble craters. The off-putting move cements my decision.

Interlacing my fingers in front of me, I say, "You absolutely should. No doubt you can find another ghostwriter who'll write exactly what you want."

Her clenched jaw ticks. "You're being unprofessional. How will I find a replacement who's familiar with the series and characters in time to meet the next deadline? And what about the fans—can you really leave them hanging?"

Guilt is a high hurdle, but I promised myself I wouldn't take time for granted anymore. I've wasted enough of it writing other people's stories. It's time to take a leap of faith.

No more excuses.

"I disagree, Rachel. I'm giving you fair notice. There are plenty of writers who will rearrange their schedules for a lucrative ghostwriting gig. I can even offer a few reliable referrals." Most authors need second jobs to make ends meet. "I'm happy to consult with whomever you choose to bring them up to speed and ensure continuity. Fans will adapt to a new voice."

She huffs, raising her hands in the air. "Fine, rearrange the story however you want."

I shake my head. "This isn't a ploy. Honestly, I've been considering writing my own books since my dad's funeral."

Rachel cocks her head as if I'm trying to pull a fast one. "You can't piggyback off this series or these characters."

"I'll be writing fantasy, not romantic suspense." An exalting sense of freedom builds in my chest. It's torturous to suppress it for her sake.

Her feet hit the floor as her expression hardens. "This is seriously the last thing I expected to deal with today."

"I'm sorry." This obviously wasn't planned or I wouldn't have taken the time to analyze her outline. "It's been a trying month. Life-changing, actually, which has affected my aspirations. It's not personal."

That's mostly true, although her attitude hasn't helped her cause.

"Can I count on you to revise the last manuscript on time once we get the editorial notes?"

"Of course. I'll give it my very best effort." That much is true.

"Well, when those come through, I'll forward them. Guess I better get busy finding a new writer." She sweeps her hair away from her forehead, eyes glazed, mouth pouting.

"I'll email my notes on this outline in case you're curious." A sudden and surprising swell of gratitude softens my attitude. Working on the Glass Beach books sharpened my craft and taught me a lot about the industry, reader expectations, and discipline. I'm a better writer today thanks to this job, and for that, I owe her something. "It's been a privilege to help you build this series. We've had a good run. I wish you the best of luck going forward."

"It's not about luck. You'll see once you're hustling for yourself." Maybe, yet my focus will be on delivering a great story, not on hustling. "The edits should land by late June. You'll have six weeks, like usual."

I nod, making a note. "I'll block out my calendar."

"Well, guess this is pretty much it then." She barely looks at me. I may be the first author to quit on her. "Take care."

She unceremoniously ends the session before I say goodbye.

I push back from my desk, slightly shaken. It wasn't the ideal way to end our partnership, but in the long run this will be best for us both.

Freedom.

The extra breathing room will come in handy when heading into Sadie's senior year.

Having just pissed away an advance, I'll need to live off my share of the money from the sale of my parents' house while I revise and try to sell *Fires of the Phoenix Queen*. Admittedly, relying on that safety net doesn't feel as awful as I expected.

I can do this. I want to do this.

Sadie and my mom are banging around the kitchen, probably making dinner. I take a few minutes to pull out my story files. Research notes and images. Character sketches. World-building maps and explanations.

Some of these notes are fifteen years old. It'll take time to fully refamiliarize myself with the characters and themes. To organize. To update it for current social mores and my own altered perspectives.

Sadie taps on the doorjamb. "Dinner's ready."

"That was fast."

She shrugs, her hip cocked. "We went with a lentil quinoa salad. Gran also made chicken for you two."

"Be there in a sec."

After she closes the door, I feel the need to celebrate. Emboldened, I text Sawyer.

Book is in the can. Are you and Ruby free on Friday?

I tuck the phone in my pocket and go to the kitchen, where my mother and daughter are dishing out dinner.

After we're all seated, I blurt out, "I just quit my job."

"Really?" My mother's shock sends her brows upward.

Sadie's mouth falls open. "Why?"

I fork a tomato and eye my mother. "I've been inspired by your courage, Mom. No more excuses. It's time to take a shot with my own work."

Believing that my father probably cheated his way to the top makes the prospect of future comparisons less intimidating. Any win I earn—however small—will be genuine.

"It's the right decision." My mother reaches out to squeeze my hand.

Our clasped hands feel like a bridge to a better future. "Thanks."

She helped my dad push through rejections. Maybe she can help me, too.

"It'll take a lot of work to revise my old manuscript," I add. "I could use some help."

"Help how?" Sadie asks.

"You could read the old draft and highlight things that are out of touch with your generation," I suggest.

She tucks her chin, uncharacteristically bashful. "After finals, I will."

My mother quietly chews her food.

"Perfect." I then turn to my mother. "Mom, would you help me, too?"

She was instrumental in critiquing his early work, which gained him a solid fan base before he owned that typewriter.

"You want my opinion?" Her hand grips her fork as her eyes cloud with doubt.

It shames me to see it, knowing that my behavior toward her has probably contributed to her low self-esteem. I wait to catch her gaze. "I'm actually quite curious about what you think."

A tenuous grin curves her mouth. "I'd be thrilled to weigh in."

My chin starts to wobble.

"What's wrong?" Sadie sets down her fork, casting a quizzical gaze at us both.

I dab the inner corners of my eyes, embarrassed yet chuckling. "I'm happy."

Sadie's grimace suggests she thinks I've lost my mind.

She can't fathom the unexpected victory of a pleasant family meal with my mother after so many decades without one. It's hard not to fidget.

"Will you use a pen name?" Sadie asks.

"What do you think of Emerson Hale?" I bite my lip, floating the use of my mother's maiden name. It's not just about distancing my brand from my father's. It's about giving my mother a little credit as well. After all, she fostered my early love of fiction just as much as my father did.

Mom flattens a hand on her breastbone. "I love it."

I feel a shift, like a cog falling into place. Peace of mind, finally. It's wonderful—or it would be if it weren't due in part to the typewriter. That makes it still a bit precarious. Unearned. And definitely subject to a twist.

Hopefully our fledgling bond can withstand whatever happens next.

Thirty-Four

My mother paces the estate's entry hall, her patent leather shoes scuffing the wood floor while she nibbles at her perfect French manicure. Her concentric circles are making me dizzy. The prospect of seeing Will again makes *me* uneasy, too. If I had to guess, he might also be dreading the impending pretense.

I would've skipped out on this if my mother hadn't asked me to help ensure that things go smoothly. More likely she wants moral support.

It's 9:40 AM. The movers must've hit traffic coming out of the city. I peek out the sidelight window into a blur of fine mist blanketing the world. Hardly ideal weather for transporting fine art and antiques.

"Mom, would you be able to look over a revised synopsis for *Fires* tonight?" I glance over my shoulder.

She stops suddenly, bringing her hands together in front of her waist. "Of course. How do you feel about it?"

"Nervous." Sharing my own work feels only slightly less terrifying than being held at gunpoint. Despite my shifting perceptions of my father, his opinions are so deeply embedded, it'd take an excavator to remove them. "I made substantial changes in act two and layered another motivation for Hestia."

"I can't wait to dig in." Her tone rings more distant than enthusiastic. She resumes her pacing, which raises some alarm.

"Are you having second thoughts?" I ask. "I'm sure you can keep some things you previously offered to sell."

"It's not that." She stops, rubbing her arms as if fending off a cold breeze. "Being back here—it's harder than I expected."

That's not surprising. Every corner here holds a memory. It can't be easy to say goodbye, no matter how much she wants to escape certain ghosts. Sobriety must make letting go of everything at once especially challenging.

"If you want to Uber back to my house, I'll take care of everything here."

She draws herself up, shaking her head. "I need to learn to deal with hard things. I just want to get it over with."

The crunch of tires on the driveway diverts my attention. Through the window, a moving van and an SUV come into view.

"They're here." Without glancing back, I open the door, donning an overconfident smile to cover my discomfort.

No doubt Will assumes I'm harboring a crush. It'd be satisfying to casually work my upcoming date with Sawyer into conversation. In any case, whatever humiliation I feel today will be worthwhile if my mother can revise Will's last impression of her.

Three brawny uniformed men climb out of the moving van. Drawing myself up, I look toward the SUV. A bespectacled willowy redhead exits the vehicle. I wait, but Will doesn't emerge. That jackass fobbed this off on an underling?

"Wow," I huff.

I fiddle with my shirtsleeves while my toes curl inside my shoes. It's oddly temperate despite the fog.

The redhead crosses the driveway and strolls up the front steps, dressed in a gray skirt and pale pink shirt that perfectly matches her nail polish.

"Ms. Clarke?" She extends one hand as I tear my gaze from her flawless skin.

"Emerson, please." I shake her hand.

"I'm Leslie Fallon from Christie's. Mr. Barnes apologizes for not being here to oversee the collection and transfer of items to our storage facility. Something came up, but he's given me the complete list of items." She pats her iPad.

If something came up, Will could've—should have—told me himself. He hasn't grown into the man I imagined he would. Peeved, I mutter, "Wimp."

"Excuse me?" Ms. Fallon asks, her forehead scrunched up like an accordion.

"Nothing, sorry. Come in out of the weather and meet my mother, Dorothy." I gesture inside and wait for the entire crew to enter before closing the door.

The transport team begins eyeing the surroundings, taking in the scale of the job or perhaps admiring the decor. I turn to introduce my mother, but she's not there.

"She must've stepped away to the restroom," I say.

"We can start without her." Leslie pulls up the work order. "Our team will take exceptional care with the handling of your things, from packing to transport and storage."

"Wonderful." White-glove service is worth whatever it costs because I don't want to be responsible for handling the expensive items.

"On a personal note, I'm a huge fan of your father's. I can't wait until my son is old enough to read the Elysian Chronicles and Pandemonium books. So tragic that there won't be more." Then, as if remembering herself, her cheeks flame with regret. "Sorry. The tragedy is his death, of course."

"It's all right. I understand." I think back to Dad's funeral, before I knew the truth about his good-luck charm. Before I got lured into manipulating the world around me. Before my mother's arrest. A lifetime ago, or a month depending on how you view it.

If my mother hadn't crashed, what else might I have wished for? How far might I have been willing to push in order to structure our lives to suit my needs? Worse is knowing that, under the right circumstances, I could be tempted to use the Underwood again. I shiver, pushing that thought away. "So tell me, how long will this take, and what do you need from me?"

"For starters, we'd like to use the garage as a staging area. Could you open the bays?"

"Of course."

"Perfect." She nods pertly. "Now let's walk through the rooms to confirm my list, then I'll take over from there. We'll work as quickly as possible, but packing the artwork takes time. Someone will need to sign off on everything before we leave."

"I'll open the garage doors and then meet you in the living room." I point to my right before trotting in the opposite direction.

When I return, my mother is still MIA.

A tingle works its way up my neck. I emptied the bar cart and wine refrigerator last week, but there may be a bottle or two stashed elsewhere. "On second thought, let's start upstairs and work our way down."

"As you wish." Leslie follows me up the curved staircase and through the double doors to the primary suite.

Light pours into the generously sized room through several tall windows. Cream and taupe silk-satin bed linen with pops of dusky rose adorn the four-poster bed, which sits atop an elaborate hand-knotted Turkish rug. The romantic decor could grace the cover of *Town & Country* or *Architectural Digest*, but knowing what I do, I see it all as a sham.

Leslie's eyeing her list. "There's a Tracey Emin drawing above the mantel." She lifts her gaze to it and chuffs. "Oh, that's lovely. I wish I could afford it."

"Mmm." I cock my head after something sounds from my mother's closet. "Excuse me a moment."

When I open its door, my mother is sitting on the floor beside an open suitcase.

"What are you doing, Mom?"

She barely glances over her shoulder. "Grabbing a few extra things. A wardrobe refresh . . . for summer."

Tension oozes around her, yet there aren't any bottles in sight. No shot glass. No pungent pine scent permeating the air.

I crouch to her level. "If you're hiding in here to avoid Will, he didn't come. His associate, Leslie, is going through the house with me to confirm the list. Are there any last-minute changes you want to make to that?"

She sits in silence, her shoulders and spine rounded.

My arms and shoulders twitch as if I'm overcaffeinated. If she were anyone else, I'd expect some melancholy, but my mother couldn't wait to divest herself of all reminders of this life. "Mom?"

She lets loose a fatalistic sigh. Without looking at me, she says, "Please, Emerson. I'll come down when I'm ready, but nothing has changed. Everything on the list goes."

Every cell in my body snaps to alert. She's hiding something. I know it.

Beyond the closet door, Leslie clears her throat.

Leaning forward, I murmur, "If you're struggling, please tell me. We can reschedule this."

She looks up, eyes brimming. "Stop managing me. Let me feel what I feel for however long I need to feel it."

Suppressing the urge to shake her, I step back.

For decades she needed me to manage her. To manage my dad's moods. To manage their disagreements. That reflex doesn't disappear after a measly few weeks of her sobriety.

But fine. I'm fresh out of fight. "As you wish."

After closing the closet door behind me and unclenching my jaw, I return to Leslie.

"My mother's going through her clothes, so I'll finish up with you." I gesture with my head for her to follow me to my old room, which feels claustrophobic despite its ample size.

Favorite old photographs are still stuck to a bulletin board: Mel with me on the dock sticking out our neon-blue tongues at the camera, half-eaten freeze pops in hand; Sadie's christening, her beautiful lace gown flowing over my arms; me on my dad's shoulders at the Javits Center during a book con after his debut released; him with his arm around my mother's shoulder, both so young. Fresh. Happy, even. She's gazing at him with unabashed pride.

Their once-loving union deteriorated to an estrangement so fraught that every sentence sounded like a gunshot. Yet my mom wants to steep in the bloody business of their ruined love. To *feel* it.

Should I admire her strength? My go-to is to run from feelings. That's hardly better than numbing them with booze. The reflex keeps me living a sort of half-life. Here but not fully present. Aware but on guard. Invested but one step removed.

"Emerson?" Leslie asks, expecting an answer to a question I didn't hear.

"I'm sorry. What did you ask?"

"Are you certain you want to part with this?" She's hovering near the two-and-a-half-foot-tall restored 1895 coin-operated Swiss railway station automaton music box. It plays multiple tunes while its three dancers twirl behind the glass. Leslie strokes the top. "It's a special piece."

My father gave the hundred-year-old instrument to me on my eleventh birthday, intrigued by its history as train station entertainment for travelers.

My mother felt no enthusiasm for the gift.

"This heirloom isn't a toy, Jefferson. You don't give it to a child," she said. Their quarrels became untenable when they chose petty disagreements as a way of avoiding dealing with the larger problems in their marriage.

"Emerson is a careful girl. She won't break it," he replied, turning to me. "Will you, sweetheart?"

I'd shaken my head, the responsibility for cutting their argument short sapping the joy out of accepting his gift. In fact, they'd both been correct. That's true of most disagreements—seldom is one person entirely right or wrong.

I shrug at Leslie. "I have no place to keep it."

And no need for unpleasant reminders, regardless of how beautiful the instrument.

Forty minutes later, the crew is downstairs, removing paintings from the walls and crating them. Each one leaves behind a faded rectangle—an imprint to prove it existed.

My father's imprint lives on in the panel moldings and ceiling medallions he had installed, and the expanded dock and outdoor fireplace. My mother's fingerprints are all over the gardens. Sadly, I cannot identify a single mark of my own that will endure.

At best, I played a supporting role in this story; at worst, I was a footnote.

I climb the stairs to check on my mother, tapping on the bedroom door before entering. A zipped suitcase sits by the reading chair in one window.

My mother is hunched on the bench at the end of the bed, teary, clutching something in her hand. Her knuckles are white.

"Go away," she says.

"What's wrong?" Crossing the room to kneel in front of her, I try to cradle her face in my hands.

She struggles, jerking her head from side to side. "Please, Emerson. I can't see you right now."

My stomach drops at the first whiff of the familiar odor on her breath. A panicked impulse chokes me.

Detox washed away with a few quick swallows.

Sinking back on my butt, I let my chin fall to my chest. Each heartbeat hurts—for her, for us—while my vision goes dim.

Back at square one. She wasn't ready to feel what she felt after all.

A warning? Or perhaps a lesson.

Recovery is like playing against the house in Vegas—the odds aren't with you.

Slipups will always be a possibility. This one might have been prevented with a few keystrokes. For a second, I question my ban against all wishes. The circular argument—balancing the ethics of asserting one's will against others' free will—is exhausting. It's not so clear-cut, either.

Sometimes we're stuck with only poor options, like the classic thought experiment of whether to sacrifice one person to save ten.

Today the only thing I know to be true is that lasting change will take more than mere wishes.

Clasping her hands in mine, I gently pry her fingers open to reveal an empty airplane-size bottle of gin.

"Mom, look at me." I place my fingers beneath her chin. "It's okay. This is a just a hiccup."

She meets my gaze. "I'm sorry."

I nod. "I know. The important thing now is how you handle this. Call your counselor or sponsor or whomever today. Tomorrow you'll go to group. I'm here to help, however I can."

"I didn't mean to do it. I didn't. I came up to collect myself, then thought I might as well grab some summer things. The bottle rolled to the front of my shorts drawer." She sniffles, then pinches her nose. "It's this house. Being here reminds me of how much time I've wasted. I don't know how I became this person—this nothing of a woman. A weak waste of space."

Each of her self-recriminations reverberates like the drumbeat of my own insecurities. If I can't commit to a bolder approach to living, this could be how I feel about myself in ten or twenty years. "Mom, don't talk that way."

"It's true. I used to be smart. I cared about things. About my job. I had everything a person could want yet shrank from each challenge. I did nothing. And now that's what I am. Nothing."

It's an effort not to shake her. "You're not nothing. You're my mother. Sadie's grandmother. A woman taking charge of your life and making it whatever you want."

She pulls back with a deep, weighted sigh. "I'm almost seventy. It's a little late to make something of myself."

"It's never too late!" I shout, as if volume alone will convince us both that we still have time to live up to our potential. "Let's talk about this later. Wipe your eyes and drink some water, then rest here while they work downstairs."

I look around, suddenly aware of the sheer number of drawers and cabinets. "Are there more bottles in here or in the bathroom?"

"Probably." She's half slumped over on the bench.

"Okay, come on." I stand and grab her hands, helping her rise. We walk to the dressing area's small beverage refrigerator. I unscrew a bottled water and hand it to her, then steer her to her bed. "Finish that and lie down. I'll do a quick search to clear out any liquor."

She sits on the edge of the mattress and glugs down water.

I beeline back to the closet to ransack the drawers and cabinets, finding two small bottles of gin, which I dump in the wastepaper basket, which I then carry to the dressing area and bathroom. Soon the trash can contains four small bottles.

In the main bedroom area, I work quietly, opening drawers and running my hands along the bottoms and edges. This effort yields nothing, for which I'm grateful.

Drawing the blinds to cloak the room in darkness, I stare at my mother as helplessly as a child.

What lies ahead? How will this affect her treatment? Her sentence? Such loud questions. I press my hands to my ears.

When I return to the kitchen, I empty each bottle in the sink before tossing them all in the recycling bin. Guess I won't be sharing my synopsis with my mother tonight.

If I can't control her recovery, at least I can control my story world. I take out my laptop to revise some early chapters of the old manuscript. It's slow going. Every few sentences, one worry or another pops up and distracts me. Two and a half hours later, I've revised one chapter. One!

I sag in my chair, staring at the screen. *Let me feel what I feel for however long I need to feel it.*

While things have improved these past couple of weeks, we're still far from healthy. The truth cuts me in half, leaving me weeping like a child until the whir of a drill punctures the air.

I grab a napkin to dry my face before Leslie catches me out.

My mother needs me to be strong. And diligent. Maybe I should cancel my plans with Sawyer on Friday so that Mom doesn't have an opportunity to drink in private. No, that's not thriving. That's going back into survival mode. I can't spend my future looking over my mother's shoulder or keeping an eye on Sadie.

"Whatever happens, you'll be okay," I mutter to myself. If only repeating Sawyer's mantra made it feel true.

Thirty-Five

In the days following my mother's relapse, we've been living on tenter-hooks. More than once, I've handwritten test versions of a wish for her lifelong sobriety. Haven't found phrasing that can't backfire, though.

Besides, our family needs another secret like it needs to visit wineries in Napa.

Today, however, I'll savor a short break from the stress. MaryBeth made lunch plans with my mother after her therapy, so I can see Sawyer without worry.

I park my car near Waveny House in New Canaan. The massive brick Tudor-style mansion (and childhood home of actor Christopher Lloyd) sits amid nearly four hundred acres of parkland, much of it wooded with wide walking paths. Across the side of one driveway is a small playground. Beyond that are the large fields used for youth sports. At the far outer rim of the acreage sits a fenced-in dog park and a public pool.

During the short walk to its circular driveway, I give myself a pep talk. "It's just a casual date. No pressure. No expectations. No promises."

A brilliant early June sun has coaxed people out of their homes to enjoy the now-public property, which is overrun with parents and children, dog walkers, and runners.

"Hello!" Sawyer calls, approaching from the left. Ruby drags him by the leash, nubby tail wagging while her tongue hangs out. Her black face contrasts with her shiny fawn-and-white coat. She's a beauty.

The sight of them bounding toward me has me grinning.

I wave and wait for them to catch up, letting Ruby sniff me as I bend down to greet her.

"She must smell my cat, Mopsy." I rub her head and scratch behind her ears. "Hey, pretty girl. Aren't you a happy pupper."

She's got a proud stance. Fierce even, despite her playful attitude. A perfect partner for Sawyer.

"We've been excited to see you." Sawyer looks sporty in lightweight navy joggers and a dove-gray long-sleeve tee that hugs his chest and biceps.

I stand, leaning in for a buss on the cheek, then gesture around. "Isn't it gorgeous?"

He waits until we lock gazes. "Stunning."

The compliment sinks beneath my defenses, tempting me to embrace this possibility. To trust that he is who he appears to be. If only the typewriter hadn't arranged our meeting, I could stop searching the sky for that Jimmy Choo to drop on my head.

I nod to my right. "Let's go this way. The outer loop is about one and a half miles, but we can extend that by crisscrossing the inner pathways. There's also a pond and a few gardens on that side of the house."

"Lead the way," he says as we stroll toward the stone and clapboard Carriage Barn, the town's local artist collective. "I'm in no rush."

"Playing hooky?" I tease.

"I started early this morning to free up my afternoon." He slows to let Ruby sniff various plants and trees as we leave the paved road and enter the woods.

The forest bed's loamy scent deepens my sense of well-being. I needed this more than I knew. But now I have to make conversation. With a man I hardly know. And be cute about it.

"What exactly is your work, if you don't mind me asking?" Gosh, that's boring. I'm out of practice.

"Of course not. I'm in venture capital, focused on health care.

Specifically, mental health. We invest in apps and AI that support people—particularly youths—struggling with various disorders."

It's fitting for someone with his outlook to invest in things that help others achieve that balance. "Libraries. Dog adoptions. Mental health apps. Have I met the unicorn Wall Street altruist?"

He laughs, waving a hand in front of his forehead to draw attention to the missing horn. "Sadly, no. We're in it for the money, too, but I prefer promoting products and services that help society."

"Cheers to that." A rush of affection floods my system. "And how's it been going with Ruby?"

"Epic dog. I feel sorry for whoever gave her up. We go out early for long walks. She's obedient and friendly. Good company."

Ruby tugs at the leash, crisscrossing the path, scenting the other dogs that have walked along the lane. Sawyer beams at her as if she were his toddler.

I clasp my hands behind my back, my whole soul grinning. "Sounds perfect."

"Pretty close." He tips his head. "So, congratulations on turning in your book. How many have you written?"

I wince, recalling my last conversation with Rachel as well as that vomit draft I dread having to edit. "Fourteen. All romantic suspense novels."

"Fourteen? I can't imagine writing *one*. Not sure my ego can handle playing you on Words with Friends," he mocks himself before yanking Ruby away from another animal's poo. "Your dad must've been proud that you followed in his footsteps."

"I don't know. He read only one of my books and wasn't effusive with praise." I shrug, then add, "It's not a genre he enjoyed."

A flicker of sorrow dulls Sawyer's pretty eyes, hinting that my nonchalance doesn't fool him. "I'd like to read one."

I swallow thickly.

Millions of readers and strong ratings should boost my confidence, but none of those folks pictured me while reading. The thought of Sawyer making assumptions about me based on what he gleans between the lines unleashes a full-body flutter of nerves, which only intensify when I consider the sex scenes.

"I'm not supposed to let people know whose books I write," I stall.

"I won't tell," he promises.

No way out but through, as they say. "Try Rachel Moon's *White Heat.* But if you tell anyone the truth, I'll have to kill you."

"Your work has given you a taste for blood." He playfully cocks a brow.

I bump shoulders, staring at the ground. "It's taught me how to cover up crimes, too, so consider yourself warned."

"To think you looked so innocent in that parking lot." He eyes me fondly, stopping while Ruby pees on a fern.

He might not feel so charitable if he knew I'd been there fresh off a wish to meet someone exactly like him. I'd consider telling the truth if it wouldn't make me sound like I've lost touch with reality.

"Do you ever think of writing something of your own?" he asks.

"Funny you should ask," I joke. "I actually just quit my ghostwriting gig to work on a passion project that's been on the back burner since my twenties."

"Wow, why so long?"

"Fear," I confess with a grimace. "My dad's success is intimidating, and he wasn't exactly encouraging. But I promised myself I'd do it after he died, so here we are . . ."

I look at my feet, taking several steps in silence.

When I quit, I'd been optimistic about my mother's progress. Now I can't stop projecting how many more relapses there will be. That reminds me of all the other things I don't control—like where Sadie goes to college or securing an agent and publishing deal in a merciless marketplace.

"Did I make you uncomfortable?" Sawyer asks.

"Not at all." I scratch the back of my neck. "I've just got a lot on my mind. My mother took a drink this week. I'm worried about whether she can get back on the wagon and stay there."

He makes a clucking sound. "Sorry. Hope she's not beating herself up too much."

"She's been quiet but sober these past few days. I thought—hoped—she'd at least make it through the treatment program without slipping. I don't know how else to help. It's exhausting watching over her every second."

He nods. "All you can do is be patient and have some faith."

"*Faith* has never been my strong suit."

"It takes practice." His otherwise cheerful expression slips, reminding me that his childhood was far from perfect. "But I think you're selling yourself short. You have some faith, or you wouldn't have quit your job. You wouldn't have moved your mom in with your daughter. You wouldn't have shown up here today, either."

I slow down, having not seen my actions through that lens. He's not wrong, but that doesn't exactly convince me to relax.

"You've survived your family drama much better than I have. How do you stay so open and optimistic?"

"Therapy?" He snickers. "And my sister and I are close. That helps a lot, because my mom is often preoccupied with my dad's messes. And my uncle's. I do what I can for them, but I also make sure to keep building the life I want for myself."

We continue walking beneath the canopy of summer leaves, sunrays filtering through their gaps in wide golden beams.

"See? So healthy. You can't be this perfect, though. Tell me you're hiding *some* skeletons."

He pushes his glasses up the bridge of his nose. "Definitely not perfect. I sometimes let my laundry go for too long. I can be overly competitive at games or in a negotiation. My last girlfriend didn't think I was fun because I don't love big parties and am not a great dancer."

Her loss is my gain because that last set sounds pretty perfect to me. "Last girlfriend, huh? Can I be nosy and ask what happened?"

His dimples make an appearance. "Not much to tell. I've had only two serious adult relationships. One in graduate school that ended when she chose a job in London over me."

"Ouch," I say.

"Clearly a poor decision, right?" he teases, although his gaze still carries a trace of regret. "The other ended about a year ago, when I realized she liked my checkbook more than she liked me. Frankly, I felt stupid for not seeing it sooner."

"Sorry. I know something about being used for money, too." I clench my jaw as Will's face drifts through my thoughts. The commission he'll earn on the sale of my parents' things pisses me off.

Fortunately, Sawyer doesn't ask me to expound.

Still, his honesty nudges me to be frank. "My daughter's father was my worst heartache. Despite the unplanned pregnancy, I thought we could be a happy family. He wasn't ready. Looking back, we probably weren't as well-suited as I'd believed. I suppose I'd been naive."

"Or in love and mature for your age."

"That's kind." A person could get used to his ability to reframe mistakes into something more complimentary. "Honestly, I didn't stick with therapy, so I don't know what a healthy relationship feels like."

My cheeks must be flaming red from that confession.

"If you mean to scare me off, you'll have to try harder," he teases. "To me, a healthy relationship's main requirement is honesty. At thirty-eight, I'm too old to waste time on games. If you can make that promise, I'd like us to get to know each other."

"I can do that." From this point forward, that is. I can't undo how we met. Given that manipulation, I should feel sorrier. Selfishly, as we walk together, all I feel is hope. "You've already got me thinking differently. Like what you said on the phone about needing certainty only in my own resilience."

"I said that?" he teases. "Yeah, sounds like me."

It also sounds like good advice, but like *all* advice, it's easier to give than to follow. It's also something you might not have to fall back on if you have the power to control life's pitfalls altogether.

I decide to test my theory. "For the sake of argument, what if you didn't have to bounce back? What if you could eliminate pain altogether?"

Imagine if my mother remembered her marriage differently. Or if I could undo my dad's criticisms. Or fix Sadie's heartache.

Sawyer tilts his head, appearing intrigued. "Eliminate it how?"

I picture the Underwood. "Pretend you had a magic wand that could change your circumstances and take away pain." When he smirks, I lightly swat his arm. This is serious business. "Humor me. Would you use it?"

"What kind of pain? An injury?" He tugs at the leash to pull Ruby away from a dog passing the other direction.

The passersby nod at us and we return the greeting. Then I answer, "No, more like erasing a bad decision or memory."

He looks upward as if the answer is hiding in the treetops. "I don't think so."

"Why not?"

"Well, what's the point? I mean, do you plan to spend your whole life erasing every bad outcome? Seems like a lot of work."

"No. Only the really bad ones." I cross my arms, although we're still walking the footpath while Ruby continues to explore the fauna.

He frowns. "The ones *you* think are really bad."

"The kind anyone would find painful."

"But no experience is only painful." He glances at me and then, reading what must be my skeptical expression, says, "A high school friend of mine died of cancer before graduation. His final months sucked—seeing him suffer, knowing he knew it was all coming to an end. But he had such dignity. He remained generous, even at the end. So vulnerable and grateful for his friends and family. Going through that experience made me value my life in a way I might not have otherwise. Do I wish he'd lived? Yes. But I don't want to forget that he died. And maybe I might be a different person—a lesser version of myself—had I not grieved that loss at that age."

It feels like a fist has grabbed hold of my heart.

"I'm so sorry that happened." He really is a strong person who thinks deeply about life. Does every situation have a bright side? I can't think of any related to my father's moods and my mother's self-recriminations. "But what about bad experiences that don't have silver linings?"

He shrugs. "They teach us to endure."

That stops me. "I suppose."

When Ruby squats at the edge of the path, Sawyer asks, "If I had a magic wand, you know what I'd use it for right now?"

I point toward the dog's business. "Making that disappear so you don't have to carry it?"

"After that," he jokes, stepping forward with a little green baggie.

"I give up. What would you do?"

"I'd throw it away." He hooks the baggie to the leash and then gestures around the forest. "Look around, Emerson. There's already so much magic in the world. Every day. Every place. Every person. You just have to make a point of noticing it."

He holds my gaze so assuredly. So utterly genuine in his gratitude. His awe.

I take him in, with the trees and sun-dappled path. Ruby jumping ahead, tugging us along. The birds chirping. The sky. The breath in my lungs and all the dreams in my heart. Even the way my heart speeds up when he looks at me.

Maybe he's onto something.

When we resume walking, he takes my hand, intertwining our fingers. My tender bud of a heart opens to his firm, evocative touch like daisies in the sun. It feels completely natural. Fated, indeed.

The connection awakens a jangle of nerves. An overwhelming whorl of emotion stirs in my chest and nearly brings me to tears. The trick will be learning to hold on to these feelings in the face of a crisis.

Thirty-Six

JEFFERSON'S JOURNAL

August 10, 2018

Since my diagnosis, the walls are closing in. I'm aware of it now—that sense of running out of time.

I haven't left this house in weeks. ~~I think~~. No, wait, I did . . . for this—

The typewriter's prior owner wasn't hard to find. Google Maps helped me locate the aging Sunset Road farmhouse where I bought the thing, and then online property records showed the Welleses owned it in 1995. Another quick search turned up Richard Welles's obituary. **NOTE: CHANGE DEED so people can't track us.** Welles died just before that tag sale. Alzheimer's, like I suspected.

His obit says he was an entrepreneurial engineer (?). Owned patents on various small machinery parts. Survived by a wife, three kids, and five grandkids.

Richard never cured himself, but hell if I'm going down without a fight. I'm a wordsmith, for fuck's sake. A master creator. Maybe I can't pull together 100,000 words anymore, but I need only the right 100-word Hail Mary.

Except sometimes the letters swim on the page, twisting into serpents. Or I lose my place . . . like now, going back to reread and remember why I started this entry. Terrible.

I'd try anything, though. An alien abduction that cures me and sends me back. The hand of God showing me some fucking mercy!

But first, I needed to learn more about Richard.

His son Michael now runs his father's company with his own son.

Generations working together—a family legacy. Something to be proud of. Maybe even something worth what it cost Richard. My wishes haven't turned out so well. I'd love to know what he did differently.

Anyway, I took an Uber to Michael's office, pretending to want to authenticate the typewriter's origin. Lied about believing it belonged to Cordell Hull during World War II.

Michael remembered the typewriter. Said his dad picked it out of someone's garbage in Manhattan. Hard to believe someone simply threw it out. The path from there to here—fate? Accident? Curse?

He didn't mention anything about magic. Probably didn't know.

Apparently, Richard got the patents and started his business after he found the typewriter. No shock there.

He said his dad retired early to "write a book," so he spent a lot of time locked in his office typing. Ha! If they only knew.

Michael called his dad a quiet man. It took the family a while to notice how bad his memory had gotten. Safe to say Richard wasn't aware his obsession with the magic portal was slowly stealing his grip on reality.

Now, what to do? Tossing it feels like a mistake.

Even if my fate is sealed, I should try to turn things around for Dorothy, Em, and Sadie. Otherwise, my family life will be one big failure.

My wish to make Dorothy sick when she drank failed. Guess you can't intentionally inflict pain, even for a good cause. The typewriter's inability to factor in intentions is a serious flaw.

Most important, I need to figure this out before I forget what it is I'm trying to do in the first place.

Thirty-Seven

My mother stands beside the flagpole in front of the rambling white clapboard building on Silver Hill Hospital's campus, speaking with a raven-haired younger woman wearing a hot pink jumpsuit and chandelier earrings. I turn down the radio before pulling up to the curb.

Upon seeing me, my mom gestures toward the car as if explaining that she has to leave. The other woman hugs her suddenly before moving toward the parking lot, keys in hand.

"Who was that?" I ask while my mother buckles her seat belt.

"Another inmate," she says drolly. "Anna. She's very . . . intense."

I shift into drive and follow the winding driveway out of the hospital campus. "In what way?"

My mother turns her palms up. "Just, everything she does, she does with ferocity. She speaks in staccato. She leans forward to listen. She lacks any sense of personal space." With a half shrug, she adds, "She means well. She was giving me a pep talk."

I briefly glance at her. "Did something happen in group?"

"I finally confessed my slipup." My mother gazes out the window as if mesmerized by the rock walls and old-growth trees.

The honesty is encouraging. "Are you able to complete the program or do you have to start over?"

She whirls around on me darkly. "My sentence doesn't forbid me from drinking. The state only cares about responsible drinking, which I have always done . . ."—she holds up a hand ahead of my protest—"with the exception of that one night. I agreed to this more drastic program to prove to myself and to you that I don't need alcohol. That doesn't mean that I'll never again enjoy a glass of wine."

It takes all my strength not to close my eyes and drop my chin.

Her defiance—the laying of a foundation for returning to her old ways—feels like a bigger backslide than that mini-bottle she chugged.

Heated breaths fill my lungs, but I don't want to fight. I turn up the radio volume and stare at the road, a headache pulsing along to the drumbeat of an old Fleetwood Mac song about chains.

A tense twelve minutes pass without conversation before I pull into my driveway. "I have to go meet the crew picking up Dad's things for the exhibit."

She slides me a sideways glance. "Thanks for the ride."

"You're welcome." I catch her gaze. For decades, I've refrained from confronting things and being honest about how they affected me. No more. I need to speak my truth. "For what it's worth, it's been nice for Sadie and me to spend time with you sober. I was looking forward to your help with my book, too. If you pick up where you left off once this program ends, it'll be a loss for us all."

My mother's cheeks flush with color, but she offers no reply. Without another word, she exits the car. I throw it in reverse, fighting the urge to peel away.

Logically, I know Sawyer's not wrong. I'll survive whatever happens, but I'm so over survival mode. I don't want to cut her from my life, but I can't spend another decade on this emotional roller coaster. I deserve to find happiness and love and to set boundaries. She has to be the one to fix herself . . . or not.

When I get to my parents' house, I enter through the front door. The entry hall looks naked. I run my hand along the wall, recalling the Fluno painting that hung there.

Three-fourths of the furniture and artwork that made this place home are now locked away in some storage facility waiting for Will's team to evaluate them.

Someday the Keith Haring painting will grace someone else's living room. Another family will carve its Thanksgiving turkey at our dining table. At least Will can't auction off my memories.

Today's pickup shouldn't take nearly as long as the last. I'm eager to get back to work on my book. It's been a while since I've felt entirely invested in fictional characters. I won't let myself get distracted by waiting for my mother to slip up again.

A knock at the door interrupts my musing. I spin around and open it, footsteps echoing in the open space.

"Hello." I glance at the young woman on the stoop and the small moving van in the driveway. "You're here from the library?"

"Yes." She waves a clipboard. "I'm Gillian, the director's assistant. I'm here to oversee the collection of your father's desk, chair, rug, and three boxes of personal items for the exhibit."

"Terrific, Gillian. I'm Emerson, his daughter. I think it'll be easiest to bring the items through the front door rather than tote them through the garage."

"Whatever you prefer is fine." She turns around and waves at the van. Three men emerge and join her on the stoop.

After a brief introduction, I lead the group back to the office, where I identify the items on Gillian's list. I then remove the annotated manuscript Sadie flagged from my gym bag and add it to the pile.

While they work, I sit in the leather chair by the window, unsurprised when the men struggle with the oversize desk.

The plan is to re-create a miniature version of this room. The shared items will lie on his desk, protected from theft and destruction by plexiglass. The written pages and maps and such will be affixed to a wall and similarly protected. I'm sure he'd approve.

Yet the removal of his things brings another wave of angst and unresolved feelings whose weight temporarily pins me in place. He'd always been moody—someone who could be shockingly cruel or tender. The typewriter merely exacerbated those traits. I'll never know all the ways he may have used it to undermine us. Frustrating.

It's possible I'm judging him wrongly or, conversely, not harshly enough. Perhaps it's better that I never found *the evidence.* These imagined slights might fade faster than the truth.

Gillian approaches me as the men grunt and drag the heavy carpet away. "Could you sign here, please? This verifies the permission you've given us to display these items, and that we've taken only what you offered."

"Of course." I skim the documents before signing.

"I can see myself out. I'm sure the director will be in touch about the exhibit. If you have any questions, feel free to call me." She casts a gaze around the bookcases. "Looks like you still have a lot to catalogue."

I nod. "Tough to choose what to keep and what to let go."

She offers an empathetic smile. "Good luck."

After she leaves, I pace the room, glancing at the half-filled boxes and semi-empty shelves. The worlds and characters he created in here will live forever, bringing pleasure to so many. The rest is really just stuff.

I sift through some stacks of old manuscripts that I didn't give to the library, including the last Elysian book. My dad's familiar scribbles decorate its pages. This could make a fun gift for Sawyer someday. I pull it from the pile.

The room looks barren without the desk—Dad's command station. I take a final moment to stand where he normally sat, which is when I notice a square cutout in the wood floor.

I frown, crouching to inspect it more closely. How did I never notice this before?

Glancing back at the distance from the bookcase, I realize it would've been covered by the carpet. There's a small metal latch along one side. I reach for it in slow motion, understanding that the secret compartment might contain the information I've been seeking.

The room's stillness makes it feel like the whole house is holding its breath with me.

When I tug at the latch, the floorboards creak open. There's no light inside the hole, but it's easy to see inside the shallow space stuffed with composition notebooks like the ones he used for research.

Are these ideas for new books? Quite a treasure were I to hire a ghost-writer to release his work posthumously.

A single sheaf of paper falls to the side, a skeleton key taped to its bottom.

My stomach drops.

I trace my dad's shaky, uneven handwriting with my finger.

Don't hate me.

A buzzing makes me lightheaded, but gratefully I'm already kneeling on the floor. The room darkens and starts to spin. My breath falls shallow and my limbs tremble as I reread the three words weighted with regret and warning.

When my peripheral vision returns, I pull the notebooks from their hiding spot. The classic black-and-white covers are each dated with a Sharpie.

The first is from November of 1995, when I was nine and still living in Easton. The last is dated 2018. Twenty-three years. As that sinks in, I recalibrate the potential impact of his scheming.

He must want us to know everything, though his short note hardly encourages me to dive in.

I sit back, using my arms as support, and stare at the ceiling.

These aren't legal documents. We could live the rest of our lives not knowing his private thoughts and secrets. Not second-guessing or being enraged by his decisions. Not wondering what might've been different if he'd never bought the damn typewriter.

Then again, there might be helpful details about the typewriter. Not that I should care. Pretty sure I can't build a normal, happy life through supernatural means.

It might be best to burn these journals.

I would, too, if I didn't think they could finally bring me some closure.

After a shaky breath, I stack the journals on the floor where I've read so many books. With my back against the cabinet, I open the first notebook to its first page. November 20, 1995.

My father's voice narrates the words in my head.

I hesitate to write this entry for fear of memorializing some form of insanity.

As I read the first entry, my body feels as if it's losing its shape. My tongue is thick and dry. My face prickles. He did know. He knew for most of my life and said nothing.

Tears blur my vision, but I keep reading. And reading, and reading, and reading.

As I fall headlong into his increasingly madcap experiences, time collapses.

Thankfully his grandiose wishes went nowhere. Time travel, for god's sake. Those attempts shouldn't surprise me as much as they do. But the carelessness of them—as if my mother's and my lives were little more than addendums to his own—burns.

What didn't work is less interesting than learning what he had wanted when making those wishes. At first blush, he appears to want to make our family lives easier. The familiar justifications make me wince and fill me with shame. The truth is, when you drill deep down into the needs fulfilled rather than any lofty stated intentions, the wishes always served the wish-maker. That might be why there are twists. A sort of slap on the wrist for trying to fool yourself or others.

At various points, Dad's entries fill me with dismay. Other times, my chest aches with sorrow and even empathy. Each revelation illuminates an insecurity—a narcissism—driving his obsession and his reasons for keeping us close. This clears the fog around our history, and if I'm giving him the benefit of the doubt, may be why he didn't destroy them.

He tinkered with his career and my mother's. Even my relationships were collateral damage to his ideas of what was best. The fact that he didn't intend for Doug to leave me when wishing for a way to keep my mother from leaving is hardly soothing. The destruction wrought from that single choice overriding ours has affected Sadie's life to this day.

My outrage is short-lived. After all, I've crossed those same lines with disregard for Sadie's or my mother's feelings.

Shadows shift around the room as I skim through repetitive or self-indulgent passages. His late questioning of his career strikes me.

That cheat—the open question about whether he would've achieved such success without the typewriter—was a punishment all its own.

Then I come to a paragraph that makes me gasp.

I think the damned typewriter caused my memory problems. How's that for poetic justice? My fucking good-luck charm might be a curse.

I speed-read to an entry about Michael Welles. My dad's methodology is hardly scientific, but neither is magic. Upon reflection, I realize that my wishes loosely correlate with the timing of my memory lapses. That supports Dr. Rosenthal's skepticism about my symptoms. Now the question is whether my weeks-long use will lead to the same fate as my father's decades-long obsession.

I blow out a long breath. If I were ever tempted to use the Underwood again, this should stop me.

By the time I finish the final notebook, tears hit the page, smudging words written shortly after his diagnosis:

I woke with a start—a memory, not a dream. A miracle considering my situation. But my first date with Dorothy remains clear.

We saw My Dinner with Andre, a movie that made me squirm with its unerring take on life and goals and death. I didn't want to believe it all so absurd and beyond our control. So pointless in some ways. Dorothy found my consternation humorous, saying, "Life is just life. We're lucky to be a part of it, so soak it up while you can."

I thought her a little simple but sweet.

All these years later, I see that she was right. I got so focused on my vision for the future, I missed out on the present. Missed out on my actual life. Rather fitting, then, that my memories are being stolen.

Seven entries later, I close the journal, numb.

The sun is lowering, cooling the room. Still, it feels as if I have swallowed scalding coffee.

I'm shattered. For him. For my mother. For all the things that might've been different if he'd never bought the damn typewriter.

Yet what's done is done.

Benumbed, I lie back on the wood floor and stare at the ceiling.

Readers love to hate a villain and cheer for the protagonist's heroism. In real life, none of us is all evil or pure goodness. Courage often comes in fits and starts. Deceit sometimes begins with protective intentions. The way we hurt others often stems from how we've been hurt.

All this time, I've told myself I was acting in everyone's interests, but in truth, my unstated goal was mitigating my anxiety. As with him, my fear of the unknown and my need to control the future overwhelm my enjoyment of the present. How much joy have I sacrificed in my quest for equanimity?

Tears fill my eyes, stinging badly. I let them flow, feeling alone and ashamed. Time slides around while my thoughts mire in regret. Then my phone vibrates.

Mom.

I clear my throat to hide my mood. "Hello?"

"Emerson, you need to come home." She sounds rattled.

I blink, having no strength to handle another relapse. "What's happened?"

"Sadie's . . . upset. She's having a panic attack."

A panic attack?

I bolt upright as an icy chill ricochets through my chest and arms. "I'll be right there."

Without thought, I sweep the notebooks into my gym bag and dash to my car. All my laments fall away as one truth crystallizes.

Nothing matters more than Sadie.

Thirty-Eight

I stumble across the driveway toward my house, skin damp, mouth pasty. Dropping the gym bag inside the door, I then take the steps two at a time.

At the top of the staircase, I catch my breath. How am I this unprepared for a situation that has been brewing for weeks? Mopsy bolts through the crack in Sadie's door and yowls a warning before padding down the hallway.

With one hand pressed to my churning stomach, I cross the hallway and enter my daughter's room. Sadie is curled on her bed hiccupping while my mother strokes her hair. Dread numbs me to the point of paralysis.

I draw a deep breath, grasping for balance.

The sound catches my mother's attention. We exchange looks, but she shrugs, shaking her head. She mustn't know anything.

Bending forward to kiss Sadie's head, my mom says, "Your mother is here now. Let her in, honey. She loves you."

She rises off the mattress and crosses the room, touching my shoulder as she passes by, our earlier argument set aside for now. On her way out, she closes the door.

I crack open a window in the stifling room, feeling helpless about how to comfort my child. Words haven't been persuasive lately, so I crawl onto the mattress and spoon her, squeezing my eyes shut.

She sniffles, trembling. She neither pulls me close nor pushes me away. I snuggle her for my own sense of security as much as for hers.

I keep silent, mostly to avoid saying the wrong thing. Her shaky breath is tough to bear. Since my dad's funeral, my ability to detach from emotions and think clearly has weakened. All I can do now is cling to Sawyer's belief system and pray that, no matter what comes next, all will be well.

Two minutes pass in silence before I say, "Honey, no matter what, you're safe. I love you. Whatever you need, I'm here. I swear, you can trust me. I'll do everything I can to help, but I can't do anything if you keep me in the dark. Please talk to me."

"I can't." Her words break over a sob like a wave against rock. She coils herself tighter, hugging her knees to her chin. "You won't look at me the same."

The hairs on the back of my neck rise as my stomach prickles with pain.

Did she get expelled? Did she hurt someone? Does it matter? Whatever her mistakes, she'll always be my most beloved. The fact that she doesn't believe that is my biggest failure.

"Nothing could change how I feel. Nothing." I kiss the back of her head and lay my cheek against her neck. "No one is more important to me. My love for you is infinite."

She's shaking her head, mumbling into her pillow.

I stroke her hair, aching with the need to absolve her shame. "Is this about Johnny? I keep thinking he hurt you."

"No." Her answer is immediate, but continued tears raise doubts. "He didn't do anything. I did! I did, and I can't take it back. I wouldn't even if I could, but still, it wasn't something I ever planned on."

I hold her tighter so she feels less alone. My thoughts churn endlessly, wondering if she betrayed him. "Shh, shh," I whisper against her ear to coax her body into relaxing.

We lie there for what could be ten seconds or ten minutes. If I press her, she may push me away. My stomach is ablaze. "Sadie, keeping this secret isn't helping you. You've been withdrawn. Then the cutting class and detention. Now this panic attack. I'm worried things will get worse if you don't talk to someone. If you're afraid to tell me, how about a therapist?"

She blows her nose, shaking her head. "Therapy won't change anything."

Her body gradually uncurls as her breathing settles.

Hope rises in my chest when she rolls toward me, but as soon as our gazes lock, her face crumples. She reaches for me like a small child, causing me to cry as well.

"Sweetheart, I don't know what to do." My heart aches more than it's ever ached, making my own breath pull up short. I clasp her to my chest, helpless as an infant. Eventually I brush her hair off her face. "You're right, no one can change whatever has happened, but I can help you deal with the fallout. Trust me, baby."

Her chin quivers before she throws herself forward on the bed and shoves her hand beneath the mattress to retrieve a pamphlet. She hands it to me, gaze averted, her breath turning heavy and hard.

The front cover of the Planned Parenthood leaflet reads *Pregnancy Options.*

I take a shaky breath, instantly reliving the overwhelming emotions that my own unplanned pregnancy unleashed at twenty-two. "You're pregnant?"

Stone-faced and ghostly white, Sadie whispers, "Not anymore."

My field of vision narrows. I plant my palm on the mattress to avoid tipping over. My poor baby, making that huge decision at such a young age. She must've been in misery every step of the way.

Sadie bursts into tears. "You think I'm horrible."

"That's not true." I take her hand, knowing how shame leads people to poorer decisions. "I'm just worried that this will change how you see yourself."

Her brows are gathered low. "Don't lie. I know how you feel about this."

"Honey," I plead, "I've barely had a second to feel anything, let alone whatever terrible things you're assuming."

"You know what I mean. You didn't get an abortion, so I know you're disappointed that I'm not as good of a person as you."

As good of a person? I shake my head. "Our situations aren't the same." No two women's situations ever are.

"You were young and unmarried, but you kept me. Maybe that was your first big mistake," she spits out, self-loathing glazing each word.

A flash of heat travels from my feet to the roots of my hair. I grab her face, holding her gaze. "You are *not* a mistake. You're my greatest gift, Sadie. When I got pregnant, your dad and I were graduating from college soon and starting our first jobs. I thought we'd get married. I wasn't in high school fresh off the junior prom."

I grab her into a hug, kissing her head while my own tears fall. "If I'm upset with anyone, it's with myself for not being more attuned—for not being someone you felt safe turning to in a crisis."

"I'm sorry, Mom. I messed up so huge." Snot is running down her face, so I grab tissues and hand them to her, holding her tight a little longer.

"You don't owe me or anyone an apology. Everything will be okay." I hope she's more convinced than I feel, because deep down I know a decision this big is something she will likely revisit throughout her life.

Her lips quiver beneath bloodshot eyes, but she nods her assent.

I stroke her hair, berating myself for not cutting through her defenses sooner. "Can you tell me exactly what happened?"

"My period was late the week hospice said Papa only had days left. I couldn't say anything then. You were already dealing with the nurses and writing his obituary and saying goodbye. I took a pregnancy test the day after he died, but then we had to get through all the funeral stuff. It seemed pointless to tell you. I didn't want a baby, so I broke up with Johnny and took care of it."

Took care of it. Her detached terminology may be a coping tactic. I glance at the pamphlet. "I wish you would've told me—not so I could stop you, but so you weren't also having to hide this on top of feeling everything else."

"You had the funeral and Gran's move and arrest."

"None of that matters more than you." I kiss her again, my heart rate returning to something close to normal. "Did you speak to a counselor at Planned Parenthood?"

Sadie nods. "I went twice. First to talk about all the options. That's the first cut class." Her nostrils flare. Now her behavior makes sense. How did I not put any of this together sooner? "They brought up adoption, but I couldn't imagine being pregnant my senior year just to give it away. And then what? The rest of my life I'd wonder if my kid felt unworthy or empty or something because I didn't keep it, or worry that it ended up with a bad family."

I wipe tears from her cheeks while nodding with empathy. No matter what decision she made, she was bound to have second and third thoughts.

A shaky breath later, she says, "I weighed the options for several days, then went back one afternoon to get the medical abortion pill. They kept me there a couple hours. Then I came home."

That night in the bathroom—the cramps and low-grade fever. The blocked phone tracker.

If anyone should hate themselves, it's me. I've been consumed with the idea of magically manipulating everything instead of staying present for Sadie. I failed my daughter. It should be only me suffering recriminations, not her.

"Sometimes we're stuck with only bad options. It's okay to struggle with what's happened, honey, but you're strong and you'll be okay." I rub her back. "This will teach you things about yourself that should help you the next time you face a tough decision. But from now on, if you're sad or afraid—about this or anything else—please talk to me, okay?"

She nods, blotting another round of tears with her arm.

We hug again. I try to hold on to the moment and embrace the relief of knowing the truth. To have faith in hope for healing. To be grateful for the trust she's finally given me, even if I coaxed it with that typed wish.

When we've caught our breaths, I ask, "You seem a little calmer. Can you tell me what happened today specifically that upset you?"

She picks at the bedspread. "My friends were talking about colleges they want to visit this summer. Haley decided not to apply to UT or Tulane in protest of their state's abortion bans. Then Sarah said she didn't care about that because she wouldn't be dumb enough to get pregnant. I almost lost it right there. I mean, we used protection, but it didn't work. The Planned Parenthood doctor said sometimes condoms tear, so maybe that's what happened. I don't know, but I bolted home before they knew I was upset."

"I'm sorry. People say a lot of ignorant things, especially about this topic. But it won't be the first or last time it comes up in your life, so you need to be prepared."

"I know." She closes her eyes, her cheeks growing red.

I grab her into another hug. Then it hits me that she hasn't mentioned Johnny at all. Gina said he didn't know why Sadie dropped him, but he must've been covering for her. "Did Johnny come with you to the clinic?"

"No!" Her eyes go wide.

"Because . . ."

"He doesn't know."

Now my eyes go round. "You didn't tell him?"

"No, Mom. I told you, I didn't tell anyone."

I try to keep my expression blank, but I'm not sure how to feel about her completely cutting Johnny out of the conversation. "Might that be partly responsible for some of your conflicted feelings?"

"No." She shakes her head confidently. "He doesn't want to be a dad right now any more than I want to be a mom. There's no way he wants to mess up his lacrosse scholarship to Brown. We talked about the what-ifs when we first decided to have sex, so there was no point in both of us feeling like terrible people now. At least he'll never have to feel guilty. Cutting him out is the one good thing I did."

My heart sinks. Those justifications, while rational, sound like so many of my father's journal entries, or even my own excuses for using the type-writer to override someone else's choices.

And yet she didn't hide the truth out of malice. She believed she was sparing him the pain she now feels, so I won't second-guess her.

I will, however, steer us both toward better decisions. "I've done similar things thinking I was protecting others. Lately I've started to question that logic and the fairness of taking away someone else's options. I don't have the answers, but life is hard and there will always be new challenges. It seems easier to carry any burden when you seek support and make choices together. Maybe remember that the next time you're overwhelmed."

"Trust me, Mom. Johnny's better off not feeling like a baby killer." Her features wrinkle as she works to stave off another round of tears.

"You're not a baby killer, Sadie," I say sharply, hating that phrase.

"Lots of people don't agree."

"A fetus is not a baby. You terminated so early, there probably wasn't even a heartbeat."

She rolls her eyes. "You're reaching, Mom."

"No, I'm not." I understand why some people wouldn't make Sadie's choice, but their particular faith and opinions don't make my daughter a murderer. "You know, there's no law that forces people to donate marrow or kidneys or other things to save the lives of actual living people."

"What's that have to do with anything?" She frowns at me.

"Well, does it seem fair to force a woman to use her body to grow a life when no one else could be forced to use their body to save that same life after it's born?"

"Donating organs is risky." She wipes her face and grabs a tissue to blow her nose.

"So is pregnancy. High blood pressure, gestational diabetes, preeclampsia, placental abruption, ectopic pregnancies, and so on. Some of those are life-threatening complications. Look at the cases in Texas, where women are suing the state because of suffering serious pregnancy complications or death due to new bans." I shrug. "I'm not saying there shouldn't be any debate about this. I'm not even against reasonable limitations around late-term abortion. But if it isn't murder not to risk your health to save someone, it isn't murder to terminate a pregnancy before that fetus is viable."

"Maybe that's true." A shadow smile of relief passes over her lips. "Still, I don't want to tell anyone, okay. Not even Gran."

"It's your private business, so I won't say a word. If Gran asks, I'll tell her about the detentions."

She nods, then her body folds in on itself again as she sniffles. "I miss Johnny."

Of course she does. "So call him."

She shakes her head. "I can't date him with this big lie between us. And if I tell him now, you know he'll tell his brother or one of his friends. It would get around, and then all anyone would think when they see me is *That's the girl who got an abortion.*"

It sounds like hyperbole until I consider internet trolling and the bullying that drives teens to suicide.

"That's probably true." I hug her again, chin on her head, thinking about how often people butt into other people's business as if their opinion is the only one that's right. "If I could take your pain away—erase this from your memory—I would in a heartbeat."

As those words leave my mouth, it dawns on me that I might be able to do just that.

Those journals give me new insight into crafting more effective wishes. Despite the risks, the idea has already formed deep roots.

I could bang out a quick wish in which Sadie wakes up with no memory of the pregnancy. No memory of the abortion. No memory of why she broke up with Johnny . . . only the thought that she wants to reconcile.

That'd leave me as the only person to ever know about or suffer over this situation from this day forward.

I could fix this for her.

I could.

"Mom?"

I start, then look at Sadie. "Hmm?"

"What were you thinking?" Her eyes are wide and trusting, which deals a fresh punch to my chest.

I kiss her forehead and stroke her arm. "I'm thinking about how much I love you. How proud I always am. And how there is nothing in the world I wouldn't do to help you heal."

Thirty-Nine

Ten minutes later, Sadie is more composed. "Thanks, Mom. Maybe I should go for a run to work out some of these feelings."

"If you think that will help." Meanwhile, I can barely pick myself up off her bed. I go into the hallway to give her privacy to change. Minutes later, she trots down the stairs and out the front door.

She'll feel a little better tonight, but real peace will take much longer.

My mother pokes her head out of her room. "Is she okay?"

I pinch the bridge of my nose. "She will be."

God, it hurts to talk.

"Are you?"

I scoff, the typewriter's pull reaching a crescendo. "Working on it."

"Can I help?" She stares at me from a safe distance by her door, this morning's tension still hanging between us.

Sadie asked me not to betray her confidence, and I wouldn't risk handing my mother another possible trigger. "She's gotten into a little trouble at school. But don't ask about it, just be there to listen if she comes to you."

"Of course." My mother rubs her chin. "I'll cook dinner so you can settle yourself."

"Thanks." A trip to my garage is definitely in order.

"I could use a distraction, too," she says. "Maybe you could finally send me your synopsis tonight."

"Sure." Although *Fires* is the last thing on my mind.

I jog downstairs and head outside, passing the gym bag with the journals that made me reassess my life.

Everything I learned today should kill the desire to type away Sadie's memory, but the enormity of her anguish feeds oxygen to the flame.

By the time I reach the garage, I'm quaking. After locking the door, I lean against it, grateful for some privacy. The image of Sadie curled in her bed sobbing with self-recrimination keeps repeating. Anguish surfaces as a yelp. I hold my fists at my sides, arms tight and trembling.

My fingers fumble—with the zippers on my overalls, with my hair tie—even while I'm scrolling Spotify to find Nine Inch Nails' "Hurt" to connect to the Bluetooth speaker.

I reach for a gallon of peacock-blue paint and crack it open with a key. The ammonia scent triggers my Pavlovian yearning for release. I grab a wooden stir stick from the coffee tin and swirl it around the paint can several times before pulling it out and thwacking a glob of brilliant teal against the wall to my left, adding to the thick web of paint colors—greens and golds and reds and purples.

How do we go forward from here?

I hunch forward to coat the stick again. Thwack, thwack.

The song's eerie melody and mournful lyrics infiltrate my thoughts, aligning too closely to my conflicting sense of hope and hopelessness. I dab my face against my arm as I sniffle.

Thwack.

Will Sadie heal?

Thwack, thwack, thwack.

Will this scar her for life?

"This isn't helping." I let loose a loud groan before slinging another glob of paint.

Do I force her into therapy or wait and watch for her signals?

Thwack, stir, thwack.

Doug should probably know about this, but I can't tell him, can I?

"Argh!" Thwack, gloop. Paint lands on the floor.

One typed paragraph could make this disappear. She could be restored to a happy-go-lucky girl for the price of one more memory. Just one . . .

Thwack, thwack, thwack, thwack.

Maybe my dad left that typewriter behind because he knew there'd come a wish that would be worth the cost.

Six minutes later, the song has ended. My cheeks are damp. My throat aches. I hang my head heavily, swiping my forearm across my forehead.

Silence. I scrape the paint stirrer and drop it into the tin, then sit on the metal folding chair and stare at the kaleidoscopic wall—a poor man's Jackson Pollock.

A portrait of pain and failure. Of loss and confusion. Of dysregulation.

My blood heats like rocket fuel. I grab the open paint can with a wild groan and empty its contents against the wall in one big splash. Spatter drips onto the floor, its trail resembling a gigantic exclamation mark.

Spent, I let my head fall back as the empty can rolls past my feet. Uncertainty beats on me while I hug myself and cry.

If Sadie returns and finds me out here, she'll never believe that I'm not angry or disappointed. I peel off the overalls, turn off the lights, and race back inside to shower.

Before climbing the stairs, I hide my father's journals in my office. Mopsy lifts her head off the reading chair, where she's probably been asleep all this time.

"You're worse than me in a crisis, and that's nothing to brag about." I drop the gym bag and crouch to the cabinet to free the typewriter.

A sharp snarl sounds at my back before Mopsy leaps off the chair and races from the room.

"Oof." My mother's voice sounds from outside my office, as if she nearly tripped over Mopsy. I close the cabinet door just as she peeks her head into the room.

"Chickpea enchiladas for dinner?"

I stand, lacking much of an appetite. "Sure."

Her gaze runs from my head to the blue paint on my right forearm.

"I'm about to shower." As if that explains everything. My mother nods and steps aside as I pass by.

Was her interruption a warning?

If so, it didn't quiet the impulse.

Forty

I pretend this evening is no different from any other to reassure Sadie she's not loved any less. My mother fills in the gaps in conversation by planning another baking lesson and talking about a Netflix show Sadie previously recommended.

When Sadie finally takes herself upstairs at nine, my mother remains in the living room watching television. She's probably hoping I'll crack and divulge some details about what's happened.

I'm determined not to allow the weight of all my secrets to break me, but anything is possible.

"Emerson, did you send me your updated synopsis?" Mom asks. "I'd like to read it in bed."

"Oh, right." Perfect. The sooner she goes upstairs, the sooner I can sneak into my office. "I'll email it now."

Five minutes later, she checks her iPad. "Got it."

"Thanks for taking a look." My voice sounds half-hearted despite my gratitude.

She scooches forward on the sofa. "I know you're preoccupied, but I'm excited to read this. Not that you need my insight to strengthen the story, of course. But this is fun for me."

Unaccustomed to our cooperative dynamic, I squirm on the cushion. "That's great, Mom. Sorry I can't muster more enthusiasm tonight."

"I understand." She stands, iPad pressed to her abdomen. "If you don't sleep well, I can Uber to therapy in the morning so you can rest."

"I'll be fine." I can't afford to fall apart now.

She stands there a moment longer as if weighing her words, then plants a gentle kiss on my head. "Good night."

After her bedroom door clicks shut, I race to my office and lock the door behind me.

I yank the Tiffany lamp's pull chain before sitting on the floor to retrieve the typewriter. Its shine appears sinister tonight, finally reflecting the hefty cost extracted for each wish.

With my eyes closed, I picture Sadie in bed. Is she asleep or staring at the ceiling, eyes coated with silent tears?

I can't grasp all the implications of her decision. In a post-Dobbs world, she'll never escape reminders. The topic will come up each time a state passes another ban, or voters support a referendum, or another woman endures a horrible outcome because of ambiguous laws.

Who else might Sadie push away now? Will she feel unworthy of love? Will guilt color her decision to ever have children?

I don't have answers, but I could eliminate the questions with a few keystrokes.

If only there were a way to ensure my wish would happen exactly as I imagine. No twist. No collateral damage. And no additional lost memory.

That's no small thing to sacrifice, especially if I lose an important one.

I've always believed myself willing to die for Sadie, but what if the memory that's taken damages our relationship? Can I live with that?

Memories are what give our lives and relationships meaning and context. They are not expendable currency.

My past forged me, just as this moment will reshape Sadie and me. If I bend fate, what form will we take?

There's no one to help me make this decision. Not Mel. Not Sawyer.

Not my mother. I'm on my own, just as Sadie was when she walked into Planned Parenthood.

I stroke the cold typewriter's smooth lines and electrified metal. While touching its glass keys, I turn over my options like a coin between my fingers.

Sawyer's outlook is ideal, but I don't see a silver lining in Sadie's situation. She's strong, but that alone doesn't guarantee she'll come through this thing whole.

Swimming in a sea of misgivings, I crawl over to grab a sheet of paper and feed it through the equipment, fingers shaking. The room temperature drops so fast, I expect to see my breath. Then the air shifts as if something or someone has arrived.

Dad? I squint into the dark corners but see no apparitions. No spectral image hovering. Only the gym bag at my feet. *Dad!*

Digging around for his final journal, I flip to the last paragraph of the last page, written five years ago during a sporadic moment of clarity.

I've spent decades trying to master this typewriter, thinking it would make me happy. In doing so, I missed out on everything I had and forgot things I'd once loved. What an old fool.

My throat tightens upon rereading that passage. Like him, I've been a fool, and not just because I also chased utopia with this magical machine. Fear of loss kept me from loving more fully. Fear of mistakes kept me from pushing my boundaries, from growing. Fear of disappointment made me preoccupied with structure instead of staying open to possibility.

Keeping my emotions on a tight leash didn't make me smarter or stronger, nor did thinking I could outsmart life. All my actions have done is reveal me to be a coward and a fool, just like my dad.

If I use the typewriter to spare Sadie her remorse, she'll lose the chance to look back someday to see how far she's come. Erasing her pain will leave her less prepared when confronting some future obstacle.

Sawyer is right.

Magic is not the way to help my daughter. Neither is wresting control over her life from her.

Sadie must learn to live with her choices, as I must now reconcile mine.

With trembling hands, I close the journal and stuff it back in the bag, then cover my face and cry.

Forty-One

At six-fifteen the next morning, I'm awakened from a fitful sleep by the aroma of freshly baked muffins. Apparently, my mother didn't sleep well either, despite the calmness she exuded last night.

I tug the robe off my bathroom door, fasten the belt around my waist, and pad downstairs.

"Do you want coffee?" I scoot behind her to get the Italian roast from the cupboard.

"No, thanks. I've made tea." The timer dings, so she puts on an oven mitt and pulls a tray of sugar-dusted blueberry muffins from the oven. Moving around me to set it on the stove, she says, "Careful."

The mixing bowl is soaking in the sink along with wisps of lemon peel. Signs of normal family life and love are both jarring and comforting.

I fill the coffeemaker with water. "You got up early."

"Didn't sleep much." She takes her teacup with both hands and sips from it. "I was listening for Sadie."

It's been so long since someone else who loves Sadie has shared my worry. I doubt my mother fathoms what a gift it is.

"Me too." I shovel several tablespoons of coffee into the filter and then hit the ON button.

"You look worn out."

"It's been an emotional twenty-four hours." Kicked off by our argument yesterday morning.

My mother nods. "It's been an emotional month. And I know you're still grieving your dad, too."

Her gentle tone is my undoing. I'd grown so used to our distance, I convinced myself I was doing fine on my own. It's humbling to admit a need for support.

"I kept thinking all night, trying to understand why my relationship with Sadie isn't what I hoped it was." I suck in my lips.

"Why do you say that?" My mother begins to arrange the muffins on a platter. "She turned to you when she was ready. That's all you can hope for."

I can't share what's upsetting Sadie or my handful of magic tricks. It's even a struggle to articulate the dejection and regret mingling in my gut.

"I've dedicated myself to building us a good life, but she's misinterpreted my behavior. Maybe I've miscalculated, too. I mean, she pulled away when she needed me most. I don't know how we got here. I was determined to do better than . . ." I stop myself from finishing the thought, my cheeks flush with heat.

"Better than me." My mother offers a feeble smile.

My gaze drops to my mug. "I didn't say that."

"You didn't have to." She splits a muffin and hands me half. "Sadie's only seventeen. Her perceptions will change in ten years and again in twenty. Every parent makes mistakes, but you've tried your best every day. She knows you love her, and she loves you. You've done a good job. In the long run, she'll be fine."

That's exactly what I need to hear even if it's not entirely true. I swallow the softball-size lump in my throat. "Thanks, Mom."

"You're welcome." She chews a bit of muffin and then licks the sugar off her fingertips. "Emerson, I'm sorry I let my disappointments keep me from being a better mother. And for snapping at you yesterday about my drinking when you've been patient and supportive. Quitting has been harder than I expected. It makes me irritable, but I shouldn't take it out on you."

"I get that." Vulnerability doesn't come naturally, but I want to build on what we've started. "I meant what I said about enjoying these past few weeks."

She runs her hands through her hair, scratching lightly at her scalp. "I hate the idea that I'm not normal—that I can't enjoy a single glass of wine—even though it's probably true."

Awash in gratitude, I set my coffee down and grab her hand. "Thanks, Mom."

"For what?"

"For being honest. And for listening. For all the feelings you've shared." I release her hand.

She's so radiant, I might cry again. Look at me. It's as if I sprung a leak and let loose decades' worth of tears.

"You're welcome," she says. "Maybe if I live long enough, I'll become half the mother you are."

A sweep of affection prompts me to hug my mother for the first time in years. It's a clumsy embrace, but a milestone nonetheless. "It's enough that you care."

She lays one hand on my head and then cradles me like a child.

I allow myself to melt into the embrace, securely exposing my exhaustion, sorrow, fears, and confusion. If only my father and I could've had such a breakthrough, too.

That regret lingers, but this moment is important. With my eyes closed, I allow the silence to hold us in peace.

It doesn't last long. Our new beginning remains fragile because of my secrets. She believes herself to be a weak failure, but she was at the mercy of forces beyond her control. Dad. The journals. The typewriter. My manipulations.

She deserves the truth, but not while Sadie is in earshot.

When we pull apart, my mom fixes herself another cup of tea. "One good thing came out of my sleepless night. It gave me time to read your synopsis."

"Oh?" I'm not ready for this conversation.

"I love the premise. You also surprised me with two terrific twists."
She smiles. Her praise is a pleasant surprise after years of my father's less
enthusiastic commentary. "I have a few suggestions where you might juice
Hestia's agency as the story unfolds. Sometimes she lets other people push
her into decisions rather than acting from a place of confidence."

That feels uncomfortably familiar. "I'll take a look after I've had more
coffee. Thanks."

It's a little moment—maybe a nothing moment for some mothers and
daughters—but I'll tuck the much-needed bit of encouragement into my
heart.

"I'd love to read some chapters when you're ready." She dunks a hunk
of muffin in her tea. "In other news, I have an idea of my own."

"You're writing a book, too?" My lips part.

"Lord, no. I'm thinking of founding a local literacy nonprofit. I'd hire
someone to run it but could volunteer to work with students."

I grin. "It's a perfect fit and a nice way to honor our family's love for
literature."

"Mmm." Her brows rise as she sips more tea.

I take my first bite of the fresh muffin and offer an approving moan.

My pleasure is cut short when Sadie enters the room and slides onto a
stool. She's dressed for school, but her eyes are puffy. "The muffins smell
good."

"They're still warm." I rise to fetch another plate and napkin.

"Thanks, Gran." Sadie keeps her head low.

"You're welcome," my mom says. "If you'll excuse me, I need to get
dressed for therapy. I'm lunching with Anna the Intense after the session
today."

Making new friends and going out in public are huge steps, but I don't
embarrass her by making a fuss.

My mother wraps her arm around Sadie's shoulder. "I hope you have
a better day today."

"Me too," Sadie says without enthusiasm.

I slide the plate and napkin in front of Sadie. "Me three."

After my mother leaves the room, I ask, "Are you up for school? It's okay if you need a mental health day."

I could use one myself.

She looks at me steadily. "I'm okay. Better than yesterday, anyway."

"That's a start." At this juncture, getting her into therapy might be the best way to help her. "Honey, I think you should speak with a therapist this summer. At least a handful of times. A professional can help you work through your conflicted feelings."

"Maybe."

"More than maybe. Honestly, if I'd stuck with it in college, I might've learned to connect with my emotions instead of retreating behind worry. That would've made me a better mom."

"You're a good mom, even if you sometimes need to throw paint around." She makes a silly face.

"Gee, thanks." The sting of embarrassment is eased by her acceptance. "I'm happy to look up therapists or you can do it, but I want you to give it a try."

"All right." She glances over her shoulder as if my mom is lurking. "Let's drop the subject now."

"Sure." I fold her into a quick hug, as much for myself as for her sake. "Love you."

This is what makes a life perfect. The love. The ups and downs. The little and big moments that make up each day.

Projecting ahead to manage the future—thinking my way through life instead of feeling it—has mostly brought me anxiety and disconnect. I need to sit with whatever is happening. To feel the pain and the pleasure so I can be closer to those I love and trust that we will all find our way.

Only then will I be ready to fully live—and tell—my own story.

Forty-Two

I'm revising chapter 3 of *Fires* when Anna the Intense drops my mother off after their lunch.

We have an hour until Sadie gets home from school. It isn't the best time to come clean, but my secrets are keeping me from healing. Hopefully the reveal won't send my mom back to the bottle, but if it does, better now, while she's still in treatment.

I already set the gym bag filled with journals on the coffee table next to the typewriter. The short walk to the living room has me sweating like I'm crossing a high wire.

My mother enters the house looking relaxed as she hangs her purse on a hook. "Oh, hi. Taking a break?"

"Actually I've been waiting for you. There's something we need to talk about." I need to sit down before I faint.

Her gaze moves to the typewriter and gym bag, at which point she waves me off with a hardened expression. "I told you, I don't want to know anything more about your father's shenanigans."

"I know, but it's not that simple." My ears ring as I clumsily land on the sofa. My mouth is too pasty to speak, so I gesture for her to join me.

"Please, Emerson." She covers her eyes as if to make me disappear.

If only she knew how much I'm dreading this, too.

"I need you to listen, Mom." I wait until she drops her hands and looks at me. "It's the only way for us all to recover."

Her chest rises and falls before she seats herself on the cushion farthest from me, clasping her hands in her lap.

I cover my face and inhale before dropping my hands. "This will sound completely implausible, but please keep an open mind."

She nods, her expression turning warily quizzical.

With a hand on my stomach, I begin describing my personal experiences since stealing the typewriter, sharing everything from the garden to Sawyer to the night of her arrest. At the end of my confession, I'm nauseated and slick with sweat. My behavior sounds so much worse than how it felt in the moment.

Contrary to my expectations, my mother doesn't jump up and shout, or throw a pillow at me, or stomp off in a rage.

Instead, she remains as stiff and unexpressive as a corpse. She's either too angry to move or too panicked about my sanity to speak. Either way, I'm not finished, so I show her my father's to-do list and share the highlights from Dad's journals as well as my call to Michael Welles. "After reading the journals, I'm convinced DES is you, Sadie, and me."

By the time I finish my explanation, she's as pale as when she was detoxing. "Mom, are you okay?"

"Oh, honey . . ." She brings one hand to her mouth, her eyes reflecting an uncommon alarm. "This isn't . . . possible. What you've described are coincidences. Strange coincidences, but still just coincidences."

"That's what I thought at first, but it can't be . . . not every time, all those years."

Technically there is no proof of causation, but given the overwhelming circumstantial evidence, how could it be anything else?

"Sometimes when we get an idea in our heads, we look for evidence to prove it. Or we subconsciously take actions that make it happen." She worries her lip, eyebrows furrowed. "But a magic typewriter is just . . . it's a fairy tale. The culmination of your and your father's vivid imaginations run amuck."

"What about those tulips?"

"Maybe you dreamed it or you didn't tear out as many as you thought."

I'm sure I did, even if the remains went missing the next morning. "But Dad's journals. Decades of random 'coincidences' aren't statistically possible." I unzip the gym bag, pulling one out at random. "It's all here. Read them. They prove you weren't weak at all. You were manipulated. Everything from your job loss to not divorcing him—he controlled us with wishes, trying to create some kind of perfect life."

My mother rubs the bridge of her nose with her index finger, letting her shoulders collapse on her exhale. "I know you've been upset and miss-ing him, but this . . ."

"You're not listening. These are full of specifics. He never would've stopped if he hadn't gotten Alzheimer's, which ironically wouldn't have happened if not for the typewriter." I pause as the sad fact rolls through me and lands in my heart.

Her knee bounces as I describe his investigation into the connection between his memory loss and the wishes. "Like my recent memory lapses. That never happened to me before the typewriter."

"Emerson, stop." She stands and looks away, pressing her hands to her ears.

This is too much for her all at once. Another mistake to add to my growing list. "I'm sorry. I know this is a lot, but I had to tell you. I'm so ashamed of myself. Can you forgive me? I haven't used the typewriter since your arrest." When she doesn't respond, I ask, "You believe me, don't you?"

My mother grips her waist, her expression softening but still cloudy. "I believe you believe it. And your father, a fantasy writer who saw magic everywhere. Sure, he believed it. It's . . . it's harder for a pragmatist like me to accept. But let's say it's true. Let's agree that he miraculously found a magic typewriter and you both used it to orchestrate certain circum-stances." She shakes her head as if she can't believe we're having this con-versation. "What difference does it make now? He's dead, and we are where we are."

"It makes all the difference!" I shout, then rein myself in. "If he hadn't taken away your job and hobbies, you probably wouldn't have started drinking. If I hadn't made that wish about rehab, you wouldn't have been arrested. Honestly, your whole life could be better if no one had interfered."

"Stop it." She shakes her head, waving her hands in front of her. "If I've learned anything these past few weeks, it's that I'm responsible for my choices no matter the circumstances. That's true for everyone, including you and Sadie." She sits on the table next to the gym bag so that we're face-to-face. "Magic or not, I chose my reaction to whatever life threw at me. I'm responsible for the consequences. That's it. That's *all* that matters."

I run my hands through my hair. She doesn't understand. "But it wasn't fair. We used an advantage to get what we wanted, and that hurt you."

She raises her hands at her sides. "Everyone does that sometimes. We're human. Your guilt proves you wouldn't intentionally hurt anyone. I know you love me, Emerson. That's what counts. So you don't owe me any apologies, and honestly, making any excuses for my behavior is the last thing I should do."

I'm a little dizzy from this conversation. Uncertain of my logic. Doubting my own experiences.

But if she forgives me because I love her, she might also make peace with my dad if she knows how he loved her, too. "Dad's journals have a lot of entries about you. His love for you. His concerns. He made terrible decisions, but his feelings never wavered. If you don't believe anything else, I hope you believe that much."

"I'm not sure it matters at this point." Her gaze drifts over my shoulder as she appears to travel back in time. "His capacity for love was limited by how he saw us as extensions of himself, like the house and his characters. He charmed us to secure our admiration and validate his worth. That's not a healthy kind of love. And even before the typewriter, he was always thinking about what he wanted to accomplish instead of focusing on what he had. Honestly, I feel sorry for him. At least I've got a chance to fix my mistakes."

I slump onto the cushions, rubbing my temples to push away the weight of a description that could also apply to me. This didn't go as I hoped.

My mother fidgets with her hands and belt.

"Have I made you want a drink?" I ask.

"I always want a drink. It'll be years before that urge fades. But let's drop this topic. I'm not interested in digging up the past. It's behind me, for better or worse." She walks to the coffee table and lifts the gym bag. "We should get rid of these things before they fall into the wrong hands and destroy his legacy. That would be painful to you and Sadie. Let her keep her fond memories of your father. And don't give her reason to worry about your mental state. Being a teen is hard enough."

I made only one wish about Sadie, and we're coping with that fallout without any magic. But a single glance at the glossy typewriter's shiny glass keys conjures my father's mischievous smile.

"We can get rid of the journals, but the typewriter feels like my last connection to Dad." I look away, embarrassed by my nonsensical sentimentality, considering the damage it's done.

"It's not. His books. Your memories. Even the color of your hair. Your dad lives on in you and Sadie. Given what you've described, whether magical or not, that typewriter represents his weaknesses and faults, not his better qualities. Why hold on to those?"

The pulse point in my neck is throbbing, but she makes a good point. "All right. Let's take this to my garage."

For the first time since she came home, there's a glimmer in her eyes. "I've always wanted a peek in there."

I flush. "Mom, do you forgive me for the arrest?"

"If that plea caused my accident, at least it came from concern. It means you care, so what's there to forgive?"

She leans forward to wipe the tear trailing down my cheek. I'm trembling, questioning whether my experiences were real or merely a string of coincidences woven into a story that gave me a feeling of power at a time of upheaval.

"Em, if you take one thing away from all this, please stop trying to control the world. Learn to manage your reactions to what happens, which is the only thing truly within your power."

She sounds so much like Sawyer, it catches me unaware.

"I'll try." I roll my head to loosen my neck and shoulders, then head toward the back door. "Should I cancel my dinner plans with Mel? Maybe I should stick around."

"No. You live your life and let me manage mine." We cross the driveway together with our contraband. While I unlock the door, my phone pings. I check it quickly. A text from Sawyer.

Loving *White Heat*. Let's plan dinner soon to discuss!

I respond with a heart-eyes face and open the door. My mother steps inside and gapes at the spattered walls and floor. "Wow. It's almost pretty, isn't it?"

It's hard to see my outpouring of unpleasant emotions in that light, but maybe it's another of my perspectives that needs to shift.

My mother pulls the oversize black garbage can into the center of the room and begins to shred one of Dad's journals.

Before I lose my nerve, I grab a hammer off the wall and then walk back to the typewriter. I grip the hammer with both hands, standing like a golfer teeing up. But I hesitate, the last fearful part of me clinging to the control it represents.

"You've got this, dear. Let it go." My mother tears into a second journal, treating this as routinely as if we're folding laundry.

With my eyes closed, I land a first blow. A metallic crunch sounds out. I open my eyes. The left side now sports a dent. I raise the hammer again and crush a few keys, yelling a strangled sound with each repeated blow. Eventually I drop the hammer and then raise the typewriter overhead and smash it on the floor.

I stop and wait for the earth to open up and swallow us.

Nothing happens. The world keeps turning. My mother calmly hands me another journal the way she used to hand me a bag of sugar and a measuring cup.

In some way, perhaps we are in the middle of creating a new recipe for our family. A sweeter one.

Time will tell.

Forty-Three

I print the first seven chapters of *Fires* and then go to the kitchen. Sadie is rummaging in the pantry, wearing a turquoise bathing suit and white jean shorts. Her beach tote is on the peninsula. My mother is wiping out the refrigerator—a new "old" habit she's rediscovered.

I set the pages on the counter. "Where are you off to, Sadie?"

"Going to the pool with Haley." Her mood has improved with a few therapy sessions. Hopefully she'll absorb her decision without letting it inhibit her ability to live and love fully in the future. "Do you need me home by any certain time?"

My mother pops her head out of the refrigerator. "I called Kathryn about that house on Peach Hill."

The shocking reversal makes me want to turn a cartwheel. "That's great, Mom."

"Kathryn can get us in at four o'clock." My mother wipes another shelf before restocking it. "If you two want to come . . ."

"Definitely." I send my daughter a questioning glance. "Sadie?"

"Sure. Why not," she says.

"It's not on the water," my mother cautions her. "But it does have a pool."

"I know you're downsizing." Sadie grabs the bag of pretzels. "Before the old house sells, could I invite some friends over one last time—you know, to kayak and paddleboard and stuff?"

The closing is soon. For a decision that once seemed too impulsive, it now feels like it's coming at the right time.

My mother nods. "Certainly."

"Pick a day and I'll pull together a picnic," I offer.

"It can't be Thursday through Sunday because of my Swap Shop hours." Her summer volunteer work at the local government recycling operation for gently used furniture and other items is a perfect fit for her. "I'll talk to my friends and come up with the best day."

"Is that place busy?" my mom asks, closing the refrigerator door and tossing the dishrag in the sink.

Sadie pulls a face. "Not like Starbucks or anything, but people shop there. College students buy cheap tables and stuff. Way better than it all ending up in a landfill."

Landfills—graveyards for junk.

"You know, when we go back to the estate, let's take a handful of Papa's ashes and sprinkle them in the garden outside his office. He loved that view." I hold my breath, awaiting their reaction.

Sadie's eyes mist over. "That's nice, Mom."

My mother simply nods and busies herself with straightening out the silverware drawer.

"And while we're making summer plans, let's sneak in a little vacation before you go to your father's," I tell Sadie.

"We should combine it with a couple of campus tours." Sadie begins counting her fingers to list her preferences. "Wesleyan, Boston College, Northeastern."

I nod, ruffling her hair. "Great schools. Maybe we can borrow Mel's house at the Cape for a few days."

"That sounds fun," my mother says. "Can I tag along?"

"Of course," I say.

Sadie grabs her tote bag to leave, then pauses. "Mom, we're still meeting Sawyer tomorrow at your birthday dinner, right?"

Sawyer and I have taken things slow. Part of me has worried that my typewritten wish doomed us from the start. Lately I've decided my wish wasn't any different from hiring a matchmaker or using a dating app.

Every date since our meet-cute has been honest and sincere, so I feel confident introducing him to my friends and family. "Yes. Mel's family is also coming. It's time you all get to know him."

"It's weird to think of you dating." Sadie wrinkles her nose. "But I mean, it's good, too."

"Thanks." It's also good for her to see me in a healthy relationship. Someday soon I hope she'll take another stab at one herself, whether with Johnny or someone new. "I like him a lot."

"I'll bake a raspberry crème fraîche tart with lavender honey," my mother says, then taps Sadie's shoulder. "You can help me."

"You don't have to go to that much trouble, Mom." Although I would love it.

"I want to. It's a big birthday, and that calls for a big dessert." She holds up a finger. "Speaking of which, I have something to give you beforehand rather than in front of others."

"What's that?" I brim with excitement for a surprise gift.

"Wait here." She scoots out of the kitchen, leaving Sadie and me in suspense. When my mother returns, she hands me a jewelry box. "I thought it appropriate to give you something from your father and me on your fortieth."

"From Dad?" I question her, opening the lid to reveal a simple platinum chain with an emerald-cut diamond pendant that looks to be the exact size and clarity of the engagement ring my mother hasn't worn since Dad's funeral. "Oh, Mom. Is that—"

"It is." She pulls the necklace from the box to fasten it around my neck, then kisses my cheek. "He would have wanted to give you something special to mark the milestone."

I hug her, weepy. Sadie joins in, too.

The necklace is lovely, but my family's healed relationship is the most important gift I could receive.

When we finally ease apart, my mother eyes the printed chapters. "It looks like I've got some pages to read."

I nod. "If you have time. I'm meeting Mel for lunch and have some errands to run."

Mel insisted on lunch today, probably to interrogate me about Sawyer before meeting him tomorrow night.

"Well, I'll be back by three-thirty!" Sadie promises before she heads out.

After she's left the house, my mother says, "Good to see her coming back to herself."

"Mmm." I nod, knowing Sadie is still a work in progress. But aren't we all?

We stand in silence a moment; then she takes the stack of pages off the counter. "I'll see you later. Give Mel a kiss from me."

I grab my purse, slip behind the steering wheel, and check my face in the mirror before putting the car in reverse.

As I turn onto the Post Road to meet Mel, I finger my new necklace. Leave it to my unpredictable, valiant mother to set aside her own feelings and find a touching way to include my father in honoring my birthday.

Dad's journals voiced concerns about how we'd fare without him, but my mother and I have done the work. We've risked rejection and grown a lot these past couple of months, earning our renewed connection regardless of any wish he may have made. Can he see that from wherever he is?

"I wish you were here, Dad. I know what Mom thinks, and maybe some things were just coincidence, but that doesn't mean there isn't also some magic in the world. I wish you could've stopped using the typewriter sooner—wish you'd seen how it was taking you away from us and everything. But I understand the pull. I forgive you. Thank you for the things you did well and the way you always made me believe in magic, even before I stole your lucky charm. I hope I make you proud."

I roll down the window and tilt my head into the fresh summer air. The wind feels good in my hair as I zoom in a better direction.

No map. No good-luck charm. Just me learning to rely on my instincts and roll with the punches. Being present for my life without overthinking it.

Maybe Sawyer and I will build a fantastic life together, or maybe it will end with someone hurt. Maybe my mother will stay in Darien, or maybe she'll move elsewhere. Maybe my daughter will accept her decision, or maybe she'll have lifelong regrets. Maybe I'll publish my novel to acclaim, or maybe it will be roundly rejected.

I have no idea what comes next, and for the first time in decades, I'm ready to savor it all without fear.

Author's Note

One of my favorite parts of writing is the illusion of control—the ability to dictate every word spoken, every choice made, and exactly how each character will react. In stories, everything unfolds the way I want it to, with tidy arcs and satisfying endings—so unlike real life, where uncertainty often leaves us grasping for ways to steady ourselves. That desire for control is what first sparked the idea for this book.

Like my protagonist, I can be guilty of seeking ways to keep anxiety at bay—often through books or writing. Stories have always been a refuge, offering a safe space to explore life's uncertainties without the fear of falling apart. I imagine many of you reading this might feel the same.

Emerson's journey reminded me—both as a writer and a woman—that sometimes the beauty of life is in its imperfections, in the messiness we can't predict or fix.

As I wrote, I found myself reflecting on the ethical questions that arise when we try to bend life to our will. How do we know if we've crossed a line in trying to force a certain outcome we believe is best for someone else—especially someone we love? Is it an act of care or a quiet form of control? The question feels especially complicated as a parent. I know there have been times I've stepped over that line, but I'm learning—slowly, imperfectly—that my job isn't to script my children's lives, but to walk beside them as they write their own.

Thank you for spending time with this story. I hope it leaves you with a little more grace for life's messy middle, and the courage to trust that even when we can't control what's ahead, we're exactly where we're meant to be.

Acknowledgments

Writing a book is a team sport masquerading as a solo endeavor, which leaves me with scores of people to thank. I'll begin with my agent, Jill Marsal. Before writing this story, I pitched you several "solid" ideas (or so I thought at the time). Knowing my personal goals, you batted each aside, urging me to dig deeper for something truly special. Had you greenlit any of my lesser concepts, this book would not exist. Thank you for your sharp understanding of the market, your honesty, and your unwavering belief in my work—even when I wasn't entirely sure I believed in it myself.

That said, it's a long road from concept to execution—a winding road full of plot holes and far too many discarded Post-it notes. I could not have finished this book without a host of author friends who helped me brainstorm, read chapters, and, most importantly, kept me from throwing in the towel when I felt stuck. From the bottom of my heart, thank you Jane Haertel, Regina Kyle, Megan Ryder, Jamie K. Schmidt, Gail Chianese, Sonali Dev, Priscilla Oliveras, Barbara O'Neal, Virginia Kantra, Sally Kilpatrick, Tracy Brogan, Liz Talley, Harmony Prom Dixon, Laura Wiltse Prior, Juliet Howe, and Sarah Babb for your sage advice, savvy eye, and friendship. You each brought something unique to the table—whether it was brilliant feedback, encouragement, or just the perfect meme to remind me to relax. I am truly blessed to have you in my life, and I hope my support has been half as valuable as yours.

To Tiffany Yates Martin, you slogged through my very rough draft with, I imagine, a strong cup of coffee in hand. Thank you for your keen eye and help in shaping my early work into a manuscript worthy of consideration.

Publishing is a fickle and subjective industry, so I couldn't be more thrilled to have found an editor who not only loved my story but also had a laser-sharp vision for how to make it shine. Christina Lopez, I am so excited—and lucky as hell—to be on this adventure with you. Thank you and St. Martin's Press for publishing this book. I'm eternally grateful for your collaborative spirit and your passion for this story and its characters. We did it! I hope you're as proud of this book as I am.

On that note, I also owe a huge debt to other St. Martin's Press team members who helped polish this story and launch it into the world, including Ginny Perrin, Gail Friedman, Lizz Blaise, Sophia Lauriello, Kejana Ayala, Althea Mignone, and Brant Janeway. And thank you to Ervin Serrano for creating such a perfect cover for this book.

I'd also like to thank authors not already noted above who offered their time and generous praise in connection with this novel. In no particular order, I'm so appreciative of Patti Callahan Henry, Barbara Davis, Heather Webber, Melissa Wiesner, Robyn Carr, and Ali Brady for lending their names to help launch this title. I hope to return the favor someday!

Outside of the publishing industry, I consulted a few experts who deserve a shout-out. First, Officer Constantine Bouzakis, formerly of the Darien Police Department: Thank you for taking time from your day to walk me through your police station and the DUI arrest procedure with such thoroughness and patience. Any errors in translating those facts into fiction are entirely mine (and let's hope nobody notices). Similarly, thank you to attorney Mark Sherman for graciously walking me through the DUI process from a defense attorney's perspective. Again, any liberties I've taken are on me, but your expertise was invaluable. I will respect the privacy of two people who spoke with me about their experience with abortion, but I honor them and their choice, and thank them for helping me shape Sadie's responses.

To my husband, children, mother, brother, and closest nonwriter friends: You keep me sane and keep me going. You make me want to be the best version of myself—and to write stories that, at the very least, celebrate the values we all share. I hope I've made you proud with this one. It's finally time to celebrate.

Lastly, to each reader who chose to spend time with this story, thank you so much for giving me a chance. I hope this made you laugh a little and maybe ache a little (in the best way). Mostly, I hope you walk away from this story committed to staying present in your life while also knowing that you can handle whatever life throws at you. Be fearless!

About the Author

Kate Kahut

Harper Ross has enjoyed a lifelong love affair with the dramatic story worlds in books and movies. After leaving her legal practice to raise her kids, she discovered her own creative side and began writing novels that explore friendship, family, and forgiveness. Because she also appreciates the magic in everyday life—from the spark of attraction to those serendipitous moments we all experience—you'll find a dash of that in her work, too. When she's not at the keyboard, she's likely to be singing badly in her car, dancing in her kitchen, or walking her adorable dog, Mo. She's also a lucky wife and mother to a very patient and supportive family.